STILLED VOICES

Alex Walters

ALSO BY ALEX WALTERS:

STILLED VOICES

CHAPTER ONE

They always came in the small hours, in the deepest, darkest part of the night. He slept well, mostly, but on those nights he would wake, disturbed by their presence.

The whispers. The whisperers.

The voices he could barely hear, but which filled every space in the room. Beneath the bed, in the windows, echoing down the long-unused chimney into the fireplace. The voices that had woken him, and that would remain with him till daybreak.

If the voices had been there every night, it would have been unbearable. But they came only occasionally, perhaps once every few weeks. There had been times, early on, when he'd thought they had finally ceased, when the gap had increased to a month, two months, sometimes even three. He had thought that, finally, he was free of whatever condition or curse this might be. But then, for no evident reason, they'd returned, as overwhelming and insistent as ever.

He could barely recall when this had begun. He had no clear recollection of the first time it had occurred. All he knew was that there had once been a time, a decade or more before, when it had not been part of his life. Now it seemed it always would be.

He had never worked out what made them come. What prompted them to begin their insistent whispering. There was no warning, no obvious trigger. They just came. Sometimes he thought the occurrences were becoming more frequent. At other times, he thought they might be diminishing. The truth was he had no idea. There was no pattern, no sequence.

In some respects, that was the most disturbing part. He was accustomed to recognising patterns, to identifying relationships and connections. It was what he did. Taking a range of apparently unconnected data and phenomena and translating it into meaning. Drawing the lines on the chart to explain why this alignment of stars and planets informed that sequence of human events. Explaining why the coincidence of your birth at some random point determined the person you were and the life you could expect to lead.

He ought to be able to make sense of this. He should be capable of finding some correlation that would explain why this was happening and what it might be telling him about himself, or his life, or his future.

For all his efforts, he could find nothing. Just temporal white noise. As far as he could tell, the whisperers came randomly. There was nothing he could do even to predict their arrival, much less prevent it.

All he knew was that once the whispers came there was no point in trying either to ignore or fight them. If he tried to return to sleep, the whispers would still be there, insistent as ever, not quite inside his head, not quite outside it. If he tried to close his ears to the sound, it would seem to grow – not louder, he thought, but somehow more present, more invasive.

There was no solution other than to get up. Go downstairs, busy himself with something else. Something that required a degree of attention, though he knew from experience that the whispering would not allow him to focus on anything too demanding. The whispering wouldn't cease, not tonight, not until the first light of morning was filtering through the blinds downstairs.

He dragged on his dressing gown and stumbled downstairs, pausing in the kitchen to make himself a mug of coffee. He was resigned now to no further sleep before morning, and made his way to the corner of the living room he used as an office. There were a couple of charts he was working on for clients. It was work that required some concentration but which, after all these years, he could carry out even when his mind was partly elsewhere.

The whispers were quieter down here, or at least a little less insistent, but they were still there. Still telling him something he couldn't quite discern. He was accustomed to this by now, knowing he would be capable of focusing on the work. He turned on his laptop and waited for it to boot up.

It had never occurred to him to wonder about the source of the whispers. This was just how his life was. Filled with unexplained and, as far as he was concerned, inexplicable phenomena. Moments when he felt or saw or heard something that lay outside the physical world. Sometimes the moments were significant. More often, they were not – or, if they were, their significance passed him by. Some, like the whispers, were recurrent. Others occurred once and then never again.

He only knew that whatever lay behind these experiences was also what made him good at his work. For that reason alone, he was never inclined to question or analyse his experiences. He had a semi-superstitious fear that, if he applied too much rationality, everything would simply evaporate to nothing. It was better to accept it, and work with it as best he could.

He opened the relevant files and began to work on the charts. This was another quality he couldn't begin to explain. It was a mix of learnt knowledge – he'd read the books and acquired the qualifications, such as they were – and something he could only call intuition. Perhaps it was simply a different form of knowledge, the experience he had accrued through his years of working with countless clients. But it was somehow more than that. He could look at this mass of data and see through it or beyond it to some more profound truth. That was what distinguished him from many of his more workaday competitors.

Not that his qualities were always appreciated. Many of his competitors were successful precisely because they didn't offer the insights he could provide. They simply trotted out what they knew their clients wanted to hear. He could do that too, of course, and quite often did. If a client was seeking reassurance, you offered them reassurance. If a client wanted good news, you gave them good news. You might add a few reservations or conditions, but those were only to provide an excuse if events subsequently turned out badly. But, by and large, you played the game. That was why clients returned.

But he was capable of much more than that. Not always, but often enough. He could offer insights the client didn't expect. He could challenge their expectations, and at times he could accurately predict a future they wouldn't otherwise have foreseen. Few of his clients fully appreciated his talents. But the astute minority who did understand returned to him again and again, and were prepared to pay premium rates for what he could offer. For the moment those clients were relatively few in number, but he knew that, as he learned to use his talents to the full, he could gradually grow that client-base and finally make some real money. It was only a matter of time.

The two charts he was working on at the moment did not fall into that category. This was just routine work at his basic rate, applying the standard principles, going through the motions. Churning out the same formulaic anodyne nonsense as all his competitors. Vague assertions that could never be fully verified or denied. Ambiguous predictions that resonated with the recipients' own wishful thinking. It was the game they all played, and he was skilled at it.

He worked away at them assiduously, trying to ignore the whispering voices around his head. Tonight, they seemed more insistent than ever, more intrusive than he could recall. It wasn't exactly that they were louder. It was somehow as if their message was growing more urgent, more pressing.

For an hour or so he fought against them, forcing himself to focus on the task at hand. He looked over at the clock on the mantelpiece. It was still not yet 4.00am. It would be a while yet before first light. He rose and returned to the kitchen, intending to make himself another coffee.

His unease was growing. Tonight was feeling different, as if something had changed, as if the whispering, whatever it might be, had shifted to a new level, a new intensity.

Seeking respite, he unlocked the back door and stepped out into the garden at the rear of the house. It was still early in the year, but he could smell the first scents of spring in the air. It was a mild night, although the sky was clear, with a sickle moon visible above the swaying woodland behind the house. The sky was dotted with stars, though many were lost in the pale orange glow of Manchester in the north.

He had hoped that the intensity of the voices might reduce as he stepped outside, but their urgency seemed only to have increased.

He took another step forward into the darkness, pulling his dressing gown more tightly around him. The ground was cold through his thin slippers.

It was only then that he sensed he wasn't alone. The whisperers were there, of course, but they were incorporeal, insubstantial. But suddenly, he felt that someone else was present.

He peered into the darkness. He could see nothing but the movement of the shrubbery along the edges of the garden. 'Is anyone there?'

His voice sounded feeble in the darkness. He hadn't wanted to call loudly for fear of disturbing the neighbours in the houses that were clustered around in the cramped estate. When he finally started to make some real money from all this, he'd find himself somewhere decent to live. Somewhere that was his own rather than rented. Somewhere where he could have some space.

He walked cautiously over to the corner of the house, where the narrow entryway led out to the main road at the front. Of course, there was no-one there.

But the whispers were growing louder, and he still couldn't shake the feeling of another presence. He took a few steps along the passage, looking out towards the main road. It was as if the whisperers were warning him now, trying to draw his attention to something. He glanced back over his shoulder, but the passageway behind him remained deserted.

He hesitated for a moment, then walked towards the road, unsure what was motivating him. The whispers were growing increasingly intense, more than he'd ever previously experienced. He felt as if they were almost inside his head, invading his thoughts.

He reached the end of the narrow passage and gazed out across the tiny front garden towards the street. There was nothing, of course. Just the rows of surrounding houses, the road lined with cars, the pale orange of the streetlights.

He was growing cold, wearing only shorts, t-shirt and dressing gown, his legs bare to the morning chill. He turned to make his way back into the house and, as he did so, he heard a movement behind him. He had no opportunity to react. The whispering rose to an unexpected climax in his head, suddenly almost painfully loud, as if someone were screaming silently into his ears.

Then the whispering stopped and there was only silence and darkness.

CHAPTER TWO

'Aye, aye. Love's young dream.'

There were times, Murrain thought, when Paul Wanstead behaved and spoke as if he were thirty years older than he really was. He said the kind of things your father might have said, using idioms that most people had forgotten years before. Murrain recalled his own father adopting the same tone of voice when criticising the 'lack of tunes' in his son's teenage record collection, a combination of disapproval and mild bemusement at how the world was changing.

His father had been sincere enough, Murrain supposed, but with Wanstead it was mainly an act. Part of his dull but dependable Detective Sergeant persona. He'd very successfully carved out a niche for himself here as the one who held everything together. Others might have more creativity, imagination or even simple intelligence, but Wanstead was the one who'd keep the show on the road.

He was good at it, too. Murrain knew only too well that, when it was really needed, you couldn't find a safer pair of hands. If Wanstead said he'd do it, it would get done – thoroughly, on time and in budget. In a place that sometimes felt like a barely functional madhouse, it was a rare gift.

Wanstead's current focus of attention was the apparently burgeoning relationship between two other members of the team, DI Joe Milton and DS Marie

Donovan. If it was indeed burgeoning, it had been doing so very slowly and over a very long time. But maybe they both had reasons to be cautious, Murrain thought. Milton was still on the rebound from an equally protracted but still painful breakup with his partner. Donovan was a young widow with a complicated history as an undercover officer that Murrain knew had left her scarred in numerous ways.

If Wanstead was right, at some point Murrain ought to have a chat with the two of them. It always complicated matters when two officers were in a relationship, although Murrain had every confidence that Milton and Donovan were sufficiently professional not to allow it to affect their work. Even so, it wouldn't do any harm to check where things stood and remind them of their responsibilities. So far, he'd chickened out of initiating any discussion partly because he wasn't even sure if Wanstead was right. Although, in fairness, Wanstead was rarely wrong when it came to appraising his fellow human beings.

'Love's young dream?' Murrain echoed. 'That's what you reckon, is it?'

'Well, youngish. Younger than me, anyway.'

'That's a low bar. You reckon it's getting serious, then?'

'What do you think? They turn up at pretty much the same time every day.'

'That's your only evidence, is it, DS Wanstead? Punctuality?'

'Nah. You can tell. Just look at them.'

Milton and Donovan had just returned from making coffees in the small kitchen down the corridor, and were now engaged in an animated conversation at the far end of the open-plan office.

Murrain watched them for a moment from behind his own desk, before turning back to Wanstead. 'They could just be discussing business.'

'They probably are,' Wanstead conceded. 'But it's the *way* they're discussing it.'

'They're both smiling, I'll grant you that,' Murrain said. 'Not something you see much of round these parts.'

'There you go then. Case proven.'

'If you say so, Paul.'

'Anyway, I thought you were the one with the magical insights.'

Murrain allowed Wanstead a smile in response. He always felt uncomfortable when people raised that subject and all the more so when they did so humorously. But he'd known Wanstead long enough to be confident no mockery was intended. 'I don't have any insights about this team, magical or otherwise. You're all unreadable enigmas to me.'

That was true enough. Even Wanstead had turned out to have unexpected hidden depths in the case they'd dealt with over the previous winter. They were still dealing with the repercussions of that one, and there'd been a hell of a lot to untangle. Murrain was not looking forward to it going to trial, but that was a worry for another day. For the moment, all they could do was ensure they did their job in terms of collating and managing the evidence.

As always, they were juggling a seemingly impossible workload – the usual mix of ongoing enquiries, cases that were being prepared for trial, cases that had come to trial, and the usual endless administration that underpinned all that. They were somehow more or less keeping the show on the road, but sooner or later someone would mess something up. Then the powers-that-be would be looking for a scapegoat, rather than recognising the impossible demands they were placing on officers and staff. The last thing they needed was yet another major enquiry, but that was what they seemed to be faced with.

'Okay, enough office gossip,' Murrain said. 'Let's get back to the important stuff. When was this called in?'

'Early this morning. About seven.'

'Who called it?'

'We've got the details, but just some passer-by, apparently. On their way to get the train to work.'

'Nice way to begin your day. With a dead body.' Murrain paused. 'Even I'm not keen on it, and it's my job.'

'I'd have been tempted to walk on by,' Wanstead said. 'Leave some other poor bugger to deal with it.'

'You know as well as I do that you'd be the last person to walk on by, Paul.'

'True enough. I'm a nosy so-and-so.'

'What else do we know before I get over there?'

'Not much. Victim was stabbed, apparently. No confirmed ID yet, but they're working on the assumption it was the householder. Wearing only a dressing gown and nightwear, so it looks as if they'd just come out. White male. That's about all.'

'So what do we reckon? Burglary that went wrong? Some kind of affray outside the house?'

'Something like that. It's a quiet estate, well off the main road, so burglary seems the most likely. Maybe the victim was in pursuit of the intruder.'

'We'll no doubt discover more when we get there. Assume the scene's been protected properly?'

'Should have been. Uniforms are there. Neil Ferbrache is already in place, so he'll have everything under control.'

'I don't doubt it.'

Ferbrache was one of the senior CSIs, with a well-deserved reputation for rigour in all aspects of his work. Murrain always felt a slight sense of relief when he learned that Ferbrache was involved, because it meant everything would be done by the book.

'I'll get everything set up at this end,' Wanstead said. 'You taking Joe with you?'

'Reckon so. He can do the legwork on this one. That is, if you think it's safe to break up the *ménage á deux* over there?'

'You might have to get a bucket of cold water. They seem to be having a good time.'

'Can't be having any of that in my team.' Murrain pushed himself to his feet. 'Still, if there is something going on between them, I imagine the prospect of a freshly murdered corpse should act as a suitable anaphrodisiac.'

CHAPTER THREE

'Look, how many times do I have to say it? I'm not interested.'

'But, Geoff, at least think about it. Listen to what they have to say. It's doesn't have to be cheap and sensationalist.'

'No, it doesn't. It never does. Yet somehow it always is.'

'That's not fair—'

'If anything, it's an understatement. I should never have let you talk me into this stuff in the first place.'

'Oh, come on, Geoff. It's made you a household name—'

'Only in your household. And in mine because my wife takes the piss every time she sees me on screen.'

'She loves it really. Celebrity.'

'You reckon? Geoff Nolan, Ghostbuster. I bet her friends take the piss as well. I know my colleagues here do. You know, Darrell, there was a time, not so very long ago, when I was considered to be a serious scientist.'

'You still are. What you do is serious enough, even if it's presented in an accessible way.'

'Accessible? Some former kids' TV presenter, a bunch of celebrities jumping at shadows, some charlatan who comes on and does some blindingly obvious cold reading and then pretends he's communing with the spirits. And me there, as some joke TV scientist, to point out how it all works and why it's all bollocks.'

'It'd be a much worse show without you, Geoff.'

'You reckon? I'm just there to give it a thin veneer of respectability.'

'Anyway, this would be different. This would be focused primarily on you.'

'Thus completing the job of screwing up what's left of my increasingly tattered academic career.'

They were sitting in Geoff Nolan's office, high up in one of the shiny-looking office blocks that increasingly dominated the south end of the city. Nolan had envisaged that when he finally attained the dizzying heights of Professor, his office accommodation would be commensurate with his new status. This room was a small improvement on some of those he'd previously occupied, but the difference was marginal. He had a half-decent view out over the city centre, and the room was perhaps a metre or so larger than any he'd had before. But it was still an anonymous office space, a blank box he hadn't really managed to personalise, other than by filling the bookshelves that dominated one wall with his own idiosyncratic collection of esoterica.

Darrell Conway, sitting opposite Nolan's desk, was, supposedly, both a friend and a professional advisor. It had never occurred to Nolan that he was the kind of figure who might require a talent agent. Sure, he had already had a literary agent, but that made sense for a relatively high-profile academic figure, particularly as his books had increasingly crossed over from academia into the mainstream. His early books had been relatively dry tomes, aimed primarily at the hordes of psychology students who passed through this place and every other university in the land. But after he'd made a few appearances on television and radio as a supposed 'expert' in his field, he'd been approached by a generalist publisher about the prospect of writing something aimed at a lay readership.

Nolan had always believed that academics should do their utmost to reach out to the public at large, and had jumped at the opportunity to introduce his work to a wider audience. In the event, the book had garnered some favourable coverage in the media and had sold relatively well. From that point his career had changed direction, perhaps irrecoverably.

He wondered whether, if he'd known how this would turn out, he would still have accepted that original book commission. The answer was probably yes, because he still believed in the value of reaching out to a non-specialist public. But some of his subsequent decisions might well have been different.

On the other hand, maybe he was just deceiving himself. Many of his colleagues looked on with envy at the relative wealth he'd accrued from a string of best-selling books and associated TV appearances. Some of them might mock the populist aspects of his work, but he guessed most of them would happily trade places, given half a chance.

'Okay, Darrell,' he sighed, 'tell me what they've got in mind.'

'The whole point of this,' Conway said, 'is that it's a more serious, more academic examination of the whole field.'

'Yeah. Sure.'

'Come on, Geoff. Give me a chance. I wouldn't encourage you to do this if I didn't think it was right for you.'

'You'd encourage me to sell my own grandmother if you could take 15% on the deal. But go on.'

'What they've got in mind is a kind of "Geoff Nolan looks into..." programme. A documentary series where you investigate unexplained phenomena.'

'So me debunking the usual stuff, then? Ghosts, UFOs, spiritualism, astrology...'

'I think the topics are largely up to you. In consultation with them, obviously.'

'Obviously. We wouldn't want to include anything that wasn't sufficiently sensationalist, would we?'

'I'm not sure this cynicism really suits you, Geoff. One of the reasons they're interested in you is that you're capable of offering a nuanced view.'

'I'm sometimes gullible, you mean?'

'Like hell you are. But you're prepared to keep an open mind. That's the point. More things in heaven and earth, and all that.'

'Well, up to a point. Most of this stuff is just tosh, and I'd have to be able to say so. But, yes, there are no doubt phenomena we don't yet fully understand.'

'There. That's exactly what I mean. Fair but rigorous.'

'All this flattery – well, it probably will get you somewhere because you're good at it. But you still haven't convinced me this isn't the usual sensationalist nonsense.'

'Look, they want to do a serious programme. Entertaining, yes, but with enough real meat to make it worthwhile. They want you to examine various phenomena, explain all the potential causes, and look at some of the more problematic cases – those where there doesn't seem to be an easy explanation.'

'And I get to decide which topics we look at?'

'Exactly. The whole show is yours. You'll be in the driving seat. Obviously, they'll have the expertise to take whatever ideas you come up with and turn them into entertaining telly, but the direction and focus of the show will be for you to determine.'

'I don't believe that for a second. They'll pay some token attention to what I suggest, then they'll do whatever they were planning anyway.'

'That's not how it works, Geoff. They want you on board for your expertise. You know what topics are worth looking at and which aren't.'

'They want me on board because I'm a bit outspoken and a bit of a character. Not your usual academic, as if all academics still wear tweed jackets and smoke pipes. And of course what they really mean is an academic who isn't white. I tick one of their diversity boxes.'

'I've warned you about the cynicism, Geoff. That's not the reason, and you know it. You know your stuff, and you're good at presenting it on TV.'

'If you say so, Darrell. But, okay, you've worked your usual magic. You've talked me into it. Or at least into taking it a bit further.'

Conway eased back in his chair and smiled. 'Great stuff, Geoff. You won't regret it.'

Nolan shook his head. 'You know what, Darrell. Call it intuition or second-sight or whatever you like, but somehow I've a horrible feeling that I really will.'

CHAPTER FOUR

'Bit of a warren,' Joe Milton commented as he made the fourth turn in less than a few hundred metres. 'Even the SatNav's getting confused.'

'I hadn't realised there was so much housing down here,' Murrain said. 'Must have all been built in the last two or three years.'

'You remember when this was all fields?'

'Not exactly. But I remember when it was fewer houses.'

'What always amuses me,' Milton said, 'is that they build them all as detached houses, even though you could barely slip a cigarette paper between them. Surely it would be cheaper and more environmentally sound if they just went back to good old-fashioned terraces.'

'But then they'd sell for less. Everybody wants to live in a detached house.'

'I know. It's the same where I live. Right, I think it's the next right.'

Murrain peered at the street name as they turned, but he could see already that Milton was right. Ahead of them on the right, a substantial crime scene tent had been erected immediately in front of one of the houses. Outside the house, there were two patrol cars, lights still pulsing, and a couple of vans, presumably belonging to the CSI team.

'Doesn't look like the area for a stabbing,' Milton said. 'But I guess that's par for the course these days.'

'Can happen anywhere. And you never know what might be going on in all these innocent-looking houses,' Murrain said. 'Though I'm guessing that the burglar theory is the most likely explanation. Poor guy was probably just unlucky.'

'Burglars usually try to avoid killing people. It's one thing to go down for housebreaking. It's another to go down for murder or manslaughter.'

'Happens, though, doesn't it? Usually not premeditated. Burglar has knife for self-protection. Never intends to use it. Moment of panic and there you are.'

'Oh, I know,' Milton agreed, as he pulled the car in behind one of the marked vehicles. 'And I know we've had stabbings that are entirely random and apparently motiveless. Just some pissed guy who loses his rag in the kebab shop or at the bus stop. I just find it all baffling. Why would you *do* that?'

'It's modern life, Joe. Anyway, that's my line. You're supposed to be one of the youngsters.'

Milton offered a derisive snort in return, and then climbed out of the car. Murrain followed and they made their way across to the police cordon. The two uniforms outside the house were both familiar to Murrain, and they nodded him and Milton through to the scene.

Murrain approached the tent just as Neil Ferbrache emerged, clad in his full protective suit. 'Morning, Kenny. Fine day for it.'

'Spring in the air,' Murrain agreed. 'Just the day for a murder. How's it looking?'

'Fairly nasty one. Stabbing in the lower abdomen. A lot of blood and my guess would be that he died pretty quickly.'

'Any ID?'

'Looks like it's the householder. No ID on him because he was only wearing a dressing gown over nightwear, but the back door was wide open. We've done a quick once over of the house. No sign of a break-in as far as we could see, though could easily have missed something. We'll need to do a proper check once we're done with the body.'

'We don't have a name yet?'

'Not definitively, but there's various mail in the hall addressed to a Mr Andrew Gorman, so I'm guessing that's our man here.'

'What do you reckon then?' Milton asked. 'Burglary gone wrong?'

'You know me, Joe. Never speculate beyond the available evidence. But, yes, that looks the most likely explanation. Either someone who'd already broken in and he interrupted them and pursued them out here. Or he heard something outside and went to investigate.'

'I suppose it could just have been some fracas out here that he interrupted,' Murrain said. Sometimes, at moments like this, he caught a sense of something – some feeling or sensation triggered by his proximity to the scene or to the victim. Something that might help steer him towards a clearer understanding of what had happened and why. It might be a half-glimpsed image or a snatch of some barely audible words, both seemingly implanted in his mind by an external power. It was never something he could explain or control.

Today, though, there was nothing. Just a mental blankness. Almost strangely so, he thought. Usually there was at least some cerebral white noise, something generated by the event or the location, even if it told him nothing. Today, even that was absent. It felt almost as if any signals were being blocked, as if he was being held in some kind of invisible Faraday Cage.

Murrain could never explain any of this to his colleagues, though he'd occasionally tried to discuss it with Joe Milton. Even his wife, Eloise, struggled to understand, though she'd come closer than most. It was something Murrain barely understood himself. Just something that he'd learned to accept as part of his mental make-up.

'Fracas?' Ferbrache said. 'I suppose so. I wouldn't have thought it was the kind of area for that, but I suppose you can't tell these days. Doesn't take much to set people off.'

'You and Joe should get together to reminisce about the good old days,' Murrain said.

'When you could go out at night without fear of being stabbed?' Milton said. 'Sounds like an improvement on where we are now.'

Murrain was looking around him. 'But, either way, we're assuming that our man here is just the unlucky random victim of a crime perpetrated by person or persons unknown, who presumably made themselves scarce as soon as the deed was done.'

'I'd have said so,' Ferbrache said. 'There's nothing so far in the crime scene evidence to suggest any degree of premeditation. Although, as I say, I don't believe in speculating ahead of the evidence so that might change as we proceed, so don't go jumping to conclusions.'

'Wouldn't dream of it, Neil,' Murrain said. 'But we have to start somewhere. The first question is whether anyone witnessed either the incident itself or its aftermath. What time do you reckon death occurred?'

'That's really one for the docs,' Ferbrache said. 'But he'd not been dead long. I'd guess only a few hours. Maybe around four or five in the morning? Is anyone likely to have witnessed anything at that kind of time?'

'Depends,' Murrain said. 'If there was some kind of disturbance in the street – I don't know, kids causing trouble, a drunk making a lot of noise – others might have been disturbed too.'

'If so, they've not rushed down to make themselves known to us,' Ferbrache said. 'Though we've had a few nosy neighbours asking what's going on.'

'People don't always rush to introduce themselves to the police,' Milton said. 'For all kinds of reasons.'

'True enough,' Murrain agreed. 'And they don't always realise the significance of what they're seeing.'

'You'd think a bloody big crime-scene tent might be a clue, though,' Milton commented.

'You'd think. But maybe they'd already headed out for the day before we arrived. Or maybe they're still in bed. Who knows? A witness would be invaluable, so I think we have to start there. I assume whoever did this would have had some sort of vehicle, so again did anyone either here or in the surrounding streets see a vehicle leaving at around the time we're talking about? We need to check for any CCTV footage, too, either on this estate or in the surrounding area.' Murrain turned to Ferbrache. 'What about the murder weapon?'

'Some kind of knife or dagger,' Ferbrache said. 'That's about the best I can do for the moment. But you should get more from the size of the incision, the nature of the wound, and so on. There's no sign of anything in the immediate surrounding area.'

'We'll have to do a more thorough search of the garden and surroundings,' Murrain said. 'What about the blood? Would you have expected the killer to be heavily stained?'

'From the bloodstain patterns, I'd have said so. Difficult to know precisely, but I can't see how they'd have avoided it entirely.'

Murrain nodded. 'Okay, sounds like we've enough to start with, anyway. First thing is to find out more about the victim, assuming it is Andrew Gorman. Most likely he was just unlucky enough to be in the wrong place at the wrong time, but we can't make any assumptions. We'll leave you to it for the moment, Neil.'

'I'll keep you posted if we come across anything of immediate interest,' Ferbrache said.

'Thanks, Neil.' Murrain turned to Joe Milton. 'Okay, let's head back and get everything kicked off.'

Milton nodded, his expression distracted. 'Poor bugger, though. You go to bed as usual, and then this. Probably doing nothing but trying to protect his own property.'

'It's the world we're in, Joe. Lots of reasons for it, but most of them are outside our control. All we can do is make sure we find whoever did this.'

'I know. But it just seems so – I don't know, random. As if people don't even value human life any more. Not a world you'd want to bring kids into.'

'You must be getting old, Joe. Old and philosophical. But you're right, in some ways it's the mundane ones that get to you. The ones where it all just seems senseless. I know that better than most.'

Milton looked up, clearly recognising the significance of Murrain's words. 'Oh, God, Kenny. I'm sorry. I wasn't thinking.'

'No, you're right. That's what seems so awful. That there's just no need for it. No reason for it. A moment's anger or panic, or whatever.' Murrain paused, now apparently lost in his own thoughts. 'Okay,' he said, finally, 'let's go and do what we can.'

CHAPTER FIVE

'I'd like to keep that.'

Donna Fenwick sighed. Her mother had said the same about virtually every object in the house. She had at least been realistic enough to accept that most of the larger items of furniture had to go, but that was pretty much where her co-operation had ended. Since then, she'd been insisting that virtually everything needed to be kept. Her justifications had largely fallen into two categories – either 'your dad would have wanted it' to 'it'll come in handy one day'. In most cases, Donna sincerely doubted that either was true.

The truth was that her mother simply didn't really want to move. She'd accepted the idea because she knew all the practical arguments were sound. She'd recognised that ultimately she had no choice. But that didn't mean she had to like it or make the process easy for everyone else. And, as Donna knew from long experience, if her mother wanted to make things difficult, she knew exactly how to do it.

'You won't have room for it in the new flat.' Donna held up the vase they were discussing and peered at its uneven contours. 'It's not even very nice. I don't know where it came from.'

'Your dad bought it for me,' Irene Fenwick said. 'He'd have wanted me to keep it. I can just stick it in a cupboard somewhere. It might come in useful.'

'But you know how limited the cupboard space is there, mum. We could give this to one of the charity shops.'

'They wouldn't want it. Anyway, I want to keep it.'

That was always what it came down to. Her mum knew full well that, in the end, Donna wasn't going to contradict her mother's wishes. Not on something as trivial as a vase, anyway. She had to conserve her energies for the battles that really mattered. Such as making sure her mother really did move out of this huge shell of a house and into a place she could cope with. They still hadn't exchanged contracts with the sellers, and Donna still had a lingering fear that, at the very last moment, her mother might decide to pull out of the deal.

So, for the moment at least, Donna was treading very carefully. They needed to get this place cleared out before the sale, and Donna needed to persuade her mother to be realistic about what could be accommodated in the new flat. Meanwhile, her mother would continue to believe – or at least argue – that she'd done enough simply by agreeing to the move. She surely couldn't be expected to give up all her treasured possessions as well. Donna had to keep up the pressure while not antagonising her mother to the point where she decided to pull the plug on the whole thing. 'Okay,' Donna said now, 'we'll put that one aside for the moment. What about the books?' Donna gestured towards the room's extensive shelving. 'You can't keep all those.'

Irene blinked, with an expression that suggested she might be on the edge of tears. 'But those were your dad's. He wouldn't have wanted to get rid of them.'

That was the most frequent form of emotional blackmail. Donna knew full well that, although her father had been a prodigious reader, he'd had very little sentimental attachment to the books once he'd read them. There were a few exceptions – books that might have held a special place in his life or his academic career – and Donna had no intention of getting rid of those. But the vast majority of the books had been read once, then stuck back on the shelves and forgotten. After his retirement, in that brief period before his unexpected death, her father had himself begun to take boxes of books either into the local secondhand book store or to charity shops, perhaps already recognising that this clear-out process would eventually be needed.

'He wouldn't have cared, mum. Not about most of the paperbacks, anyway. We can try the secondhand bookshop. He might give you a few pence for them.'

'It won't be more than a few pence,' Irene said, probably accurately. 'It's not worth it.'

It was clear that Donna was getting nowhere. 'You just can't keep all this stuff, mum. There won't be room.'

'Do you think I don't know that?' There was a dangerous edge of bitterness in Irene's tone. They almost always reached this point in these exchanges, and it was the point where Donna knew she'd have to back off. But it couldn't continue indefinitely. At some point, Irene would have to make some decisions.

Donna's current expectation was that it would be another three or four weeks before her mother was in a position to exchange contracts on both the sale of the house and the purchase of the new flat. Even if Irene didn't get cold feet, there was always the risk that someone else in the short chain might pull out or delay. But if they could get to that point, the plan, accepted by all parties, was that completion would take place a month afterwards. If she couldn't make progress before then, Donna would have to use that month to force her mother to accept the reality of her position.

For the moment, all she could do was to carry out her own informal survey of the contents of the house, and try to make her own decisions about what could best be done with the various items. Once or twice, in their more acrimonious moments, Irene had accused Donna of wanting to appropriate the best items for herself. 'You'd have inherited them in due course, anyway,' she'd said, acidly. 'Can't you even wait till I'm dead?'

Her mother hadn't really meant it – or at least Donna hoped she hadn't – but it was nonsense anyway. The small terraced house she and Peter owned wouldn't accommodate any of this stuff. Donna sincerely wished she'd been able to make use of the heavy Victorian wardrobe and dressing table that adorned her mother's bedroom, but they wouldn't even fit through the doors of her house. As it was, they'd be offloaded for a few pounds to some unscrupulous dealer who'd no doubt sell them on for a tidy profit.

Donna left her mother watching television in the living room, and continued her examination of the rest of the house, jotting down thoughts in her small notebook as she went.

It was a huge place, she thought. Every time she returned here, it surprised her. She would have expected her childhood memories of the place to have exaggerated its size. Surely, for a small child, these rooms would have seemed even more overwhelmingly large? For some reason, the opposite seemed to be true. Her hazy recollections were of a place that was cosy and snug and welcoming. It was only now, returning as an adult, that the sheer scale of these Victorian rooms really struck her.

She had wondered from time to time what had possessed her parents to purchase such a house in the first place. She'd occasionally even asked her mother this question, but the replies had been vague and non-committal. Perhaps that was unsurprising. Donna assumed that, as a pair of more-or-less practising Catholics, her parents had expected to produce a large family, and that the house had originally been bought in anticipation of that.

As it had turned out, for whatever reason – and Donna had never had the nerve to enquire – Donna had been the only offspring. The three of them had rattled about in this huge place, until eventually Donna had headed off to university, after which her parents had continued to live here alone. Prior to her father's tragic death a couple of years before, there had never been any suggestion they might sell the place and move to somewhere smaller.

It was none of her business, Donna supposed. Her parents had been happy here, and she'd been happy enough here herself for her first eighteen years. Her parents, both academics, had done well enough for themselves financially. They could afford to buy and maintain a place like this without too much difficulty, so why shouldn't they, if that was what they wanted?

Even so, she had always felt that the house was really wasted on them. It felt as if they had made use of barely half the rooms, though in practice that hadn't really been the case. As Donna made her way round now, she recalled how the various parts of the house had been utilised.

They had had, in effect, two living rooms downstairs, one relatively informal where they had spent most of their time and another – which her father always semi-jokingly referred to as the 'drawing room' – which tended to be used only if they had guests. There was a small dining room, a large, well-used kitchen with a utility room, and a room which had been allocated to the young Donna as a playroom which she later turned into a teenage 'den'.

Upstairs, there had been a grand total of six bedrooms, on two floors. Two of those had been occupied by Donna and by her parents, and two were designated as 'guest' rooms, to be used by visiting friends and family. The remaining two, which were attic rooms on the second floor, had been used by her parents as what her father referred to as his 'study' and her mother called her 'office' – that is, the rooms in which they worked at home.

All in all, then, they had found a practical use for all of the rooms. Even now, as she looked around, the available space seemed almost decadent. She and Peter managed to exist quite contentedly in a house which, in effect, was little more than a slightly extended 'two up, two down' terrace.

Donna made her way up the stairs to the first floor. She had achieved a little more success with her mother up here, in that they had managed to clear some of the furniture in the two guest rooms. A local dealer had taken away the two Edwardian dressing tables and a couple of bedside tables in return for a sum that had no doubt been considerably less than they were worth. The increased space only served to highlight the size of the rooms.

She stood for a moment, looking round her, wondering when these so-called guest rooms had last been used for their intended purpose. Even when she was a child, her parents had received relatively few visitors, and even fewer who had any need to stay overnight. As far as Donna was aware, in her father's latter years, the number of visitors had been fewer still. The rooms had a slightly desolate air now. The decor wasn't exactly shabby, but it looked outdated, in need of refreshment.

That was true of the whole house. Her mother was by no means badly off, but following her husband's death and her own retirement, she didn't really have the money needed to spruce up the place. That was another good reason for her to move. The house had always been well maintained, but problems would continue to arise in a building of this age. Given the size of the place, any kind of maintenance or repair work would be costly, and would increasingly eat into her mother's limited income.

Donna left the guest rooms and stepped back out on to the landing. Some vague sense of propriety prevented her from entering her mother's bedroom, though she knew that Irene wouldn't mind. Instead, she made her way up the further flight of stairs to the second floor and pushed open the door of her father's former study.

She found this room even more melancholy than the guest rooms, mainly because it had been left largely untouched since her father's death. For many months, her mother had simply been unable to enter the room and in the end Donna had come in herself to tidy away the papers and books her father had left strewn across the desk. She suspected that was the last time that anything in the room had been touched.

At some point soon, they would have to decide what to do with the heavy mahogany desk, the row of filing cabinets and their contents, the bookshelves lined with books. Donna suspected that her father wouldn't have been sentimental even about these books, but here Donna had more sympathy with her mother. There were books here that Donna wanted to keep because she knew they were volumes that her father had treasured. Some were potentially valuable first editions, some were works that had influenced his own writing, and some were simply attractive objects in their own right. They comprised only a small proportion of the total collection, but Irene would still struggle to accommodate them in her new home.

That was yet another problem for another day. Donna took a final look around the study, and then made her way across to her mother's office, a room of broadly equivalent size across the landing. Even though she'd formally retired, Irene continued her academic work, as well as contributing to various non-specialist publications. The office remained very much a place of work, with Irene's laptop on the desk surrounded by piles of working papers. Irene had fewer books than her late husband, but even so there were likely to be more than she could take to the new flat. That might be the biggest battle of all, Donna thought. Her mother would be very reluctant to give up any of these books.

Irene had positioned the desk so that, as she worked, she could look out of the window across the rear garden to the hills beyond. It was one of the best views in the house, and her mother had always claimed that it was inspiring and distracting in almost equal measure. Donna stood by the desk to gaze out at the imposing landscape. It was a gloomy day, and the hills were partly obscured by low cloud. In clear weather, Donna knew the view could be spectacular.

Irene had never been the tidiest of workers, and the desk was covered in piles of paper relating to whatever she was currently working on, along with numerous personal documents. Donna had entered the room without any qualms, perceiving it to be a different and less personal environment than her mother's bedroom. Now she wondered whether that had been a mistake. There were documents in here that were just as personal as anything that might be found in the bedroom.

As if to prove this, Donna's gaze involuntarily shifted back to the top of Irene's desk. It really was a mess. There was a small pile of books, mostly academic textbooks, at least three notebooks, and a stack of personal mail, which appeared largely to comprise a mix of bills and junk. Donna idly picked up a handful of the documents and skimmed rapidly through them, separating out the junk-mail and other material that could easily be discarded. Most of it was uninteresting rubbish – flyers from the local supermarket, advertisements for double glazing or conservatories, or takeaway menus from local restaurants.

Then something caught her eye. A glossy leaflet with the face of a smiling male dressed in a smart-looking suit. At first, she thought it was a political flyer from the recent council elections, but then she saw the text at the bottom of the front cover, 'Justin Bannerman. Medium and Spiritualist.'

It wasn't the kind of thing that was likely to interest her mother, who, orthodox religion aside, had always held a deeply sceptical view of anything involving the paranormal. Presumably the leaflet had just been delivered along with all the other junk mail, and Irene hadn't yet got around to weeding out the rubbish. Donna opened up the leaflet and, for her own amusement, skimmed through the text.

It seemed that Justin Bannerman was a 'star of TV and radio', though Donna couldn't recall ever having heard of him. The leaflet contained details of what was apparently his latest national tour, including an appearance at a local theatre the previous week. The date of the performance was highlighted in yellow marker.

Donna's first thought was that the local date had been highlighted prior to the leaflet being delivered in the area. Presumably Bannerman produced the leaflet for national use, and then had it customised by hand in each locality.

The back of the leaflet indicated that, in between his no doubt numerous TV, radio and stage appearances, Bannerman was also available for private consultations 'in person or by telephone or Skype'. There was a contact number and e-mail address, as well as details of Bannerman's website. All the details had again been highlighted in yellow marker. Next to them, in what was undoubtedly Irene's hand, were written a time and a date the following week.

Donna frowned. She couldn't envisage her mother taking anything like this seriously. Perhaps the leaflet had just been conveniently at hand when she'd been making a note during a phone call.

She pushed the leaflet to one side, and continued working her way through the mail, ending up with a satisfying pile of documents to be dropped into the recycling bin. It occurred to her that she was mainly trying to justify her presence in Irene's office. She took one last look around the room, but knew that, for the most part, these were the items that would remain untouched by the move. Her mother would want to retain the desk, the office chair and the vast majority of the books. That was reasonable enough, given her continuing post-retirement work. But it meant there would be even less space for everything else.

Donna gathered up the documents to be recycled and then, hesitating for a moment, she picked up the Justin Bannerman leaflet and added it to the pile. Then, still feeling as if she'd been unintentionally voyeuristic, she made her way back downstairs. Her mother was watching some BBC4 documentary on contemporary art, and scarcely looked up as Donna re-entered the living room.

'I'm just going to throw away this junk mail,' Donna said, holding up the stack of papers. 'I noticed you'd jotted a note on this one and wondered if you still need it.' She held out the Justin Bannerman leaflet for her mother to see.

There was an unexpected hesitation, and for a moment Donna thought that her mother might be about to lose her temper. Instead, after a few seconds, she said mildly, 'I think I might want that. Could you pin it to the noticeboard in the kitchen?'

Donna wanted to ask her mother why on earth she might want to keep Bannerman's leaflet, but could think of no way to phrase the question that wouldn't sound either patronising or provocative. She knew Irene well enough to be sure that if she wanted to say something she would, and if she didn't then nothing would drag a response from her. In any case, Donna reminded herself, the note might have nothing to do with the leaflet.

But she already knew, from the way her mother had failed to meet her eye, that that really wasn't the case.

CHAPTER SIX

'We've got a confirmed ID on the victim, anyway,' Joe Milton said.

'It's a start, I suppose,' Kenny Murrain said wearily. 'It's always toughest when you don't even know who's been murdered.' He looked up as DC Will Sparrow laughed. 'I'm not joking, Will. We've had that a few times.'

Sparrow nodded, clearly chastened. He was an ambitious young man, keen to impress his superiors, but he somehow often ended up saying or doing the wrong thing. Even so, Murrain had a suspicion that he might progress a long way in the force. There was something about Sparrow's dogged seriousness that suggested, at least to Murrain's cynical eye, that he was destined for the senior ranks. Good luck to him, Murrain thought. Plenty of worse coppers had made it to the top.

'So who's our man?' Murrain asked Milton.

'It's the householder, as Ferby thought. Guy called Andrew Gorman. There were pictures of him on his website, so we're certain it's him.'

'Website?'

Milton nodded. 'Would you believe he was an astrologer?'

'Astrologer? Not astronomer?'

'Very much not an astronomer, no. A crystal ball rather than a telescope would be the tool of choice.'

'Isn't that fortune tellers?' DC Roberta Wallace asked. 'Who use crystal balls, I mean.'

Milton grinned. 'No-one likes a smartarse, Bert. Especially when they're as smart as you.'

Wallace was another younger member of the team. Murrain was finally beginning to train himself to call her by her nickname, Bert, which had long been adopted by everyone else. He'd struggled with it at first, worried that he might seem patronising or simply straightforwardly rude, but he'd finally accepted that she liked the name. It was perhaps because it offset what could sometimes seem an unexpectedly intimidating manner. In Murrain's view, Wallace had more creativity and imagination in her little finger than Sparrow had in his whole, slightly corpulent body. Which probably meant she'd end her career languishing in the middle ranks.

'I wonder whether he predicted his own fate,' DS Marie Donovan said. 'Though if he had I imagine he wouldn't have gone out to meet his murderer.'

They were sitting in the room that Milton, with the usual help from Paul Wanstead's infallible knowledge of the force systems, had commandeered as the Major Incident Room. Space was increasingly at a premium in the building, and it was often only through Wanstead's experience and cunning that they managed to secure the space they needed to work effectively as a team. Milton and Wanstead had also done a typically excellent job in setting up the team itself, begging, borrowing and occasionally stealing the people needed from the increasingly tight staffing numbers. Murrain had just kicked off the first briefing meeting, with a brief introduction before handing over to Joe Milton to report on the detail.

'So what do we know about Gorman?' Murrain asked. 'Other than seeing stars.'

'I've been trying to track down what I can,' Milton said. 'There's a brief bio on his website, though it doesn't say much about his background. He's a professional astrologer, and from what we've found so far in his house, it looks as if he does it full time. Maintains the website, and then provides individual horoscopes on a subscription service. Impressive client base. Even one or two celebrity endorsements on the website.' Milton looked down at his notes. 'He has a short Wikipedia entry, which tells us that he was born and educated in Sheffield, went to Leeds University. No indication of what kind of career, if any, he had before he became a full-time astrologer. Also no mention of any spouse or other family, which ties into what we've found at the house. All the signs are that he lived alone. So one of the next tasks is to try to track down his next-of-kin.'

'We've no reason to think anyone had a particular reason to kill him?' Murrain asked.

'Nothing so far. We need to know more about him, though. People can make enemies for all kinds of reasons. But at the moment the working assumption has to be that he was just in the wrong place at the wrong time. That he either interrupted a burglary or he tried to intervene in some fracas in the street. We're interviewing all the neighbours in case anyone saw anything, but we've had no luck so far. I'm not optimistic. The neighbourhood seems to be mainly young professionals with or without families. Doesn't feel like the sort of place where people will twitch their net curtains at any time of day, let alone at night. But we'll see.'

'Okay,' Murrain said. 'So that's where we stick most of our resources, at least in the immediate term. Interview the neighbours. Check for reports of any other break-ins. Check out some of our local known housebreakers. We know the kinds of people who might be in the frame for a burglary like this, if that's what it was. Check all the CCTV and traffic cameras in the immediate area. That's a fairly quiet estate, so there shouldn't have been too much traffic at that time of the morning. Anyway, you know the drill.'

'What about Gorman himself?' Donovan asked.

'Why don't you and Bert take that one?' Murrain said. 'Find out what you can about him. Finding the next of kin is a priority, but any family or friends could be useful. Anything you can find out about him. It might be worth checking out his finances. Anything in the house that might tell us more about him.'

Donovan nodded. 'This feels like one of those that either get cracked very quickly or turn into a long-running pain in the backside. We only need a bit of luck, but we do need that bit of luck.'

'Let's just hope the stars are aligned in our favour then,' Wallace said.

Once the others had dispersed to their various allocated tasks, Murrain sat with Milton and Wanstead to plan out the detail of the investigation. 'I think Marie's right,' Milton said. 'This feels like one of the mundane, straightforward ones. But we all know those can be the hardest to resolve, because the crime's essentially random. There's no real motive. Nothing to connect the killer to the victim. So if it doesn't turn out to be one of our local housebreaking fraternity, and if we don't happen to get anything useful from the neighbours or the cameras—'

'Then we're stuffed,' Wanstead said bluntly. 'You always know how to cheer a person up, Joe.'

'Just being realistic. And chances are we'll get an early breakthrough. But if we don't...'

'We get the point, Joe,' Murrain said. 'And that's assuming this is just a random killing.'

'You seriously think it might not be?'

'I'm keeping an open mind. But I've an odd feeling about it.'

'Is this one of your usual odd feelings?' Wanstead asked.

Murrain knew this was one of the few environments in which he could talk openly about what he usually referred to as his 'feelings'. He'd never been able to describe them any more precisely than that, and he'd long given up trying to. Some might think of them as intuition or premonitions or even second-sight. Murrain didn't feel any of those descriptions really captured it. It was simply the sense that, on occasions, he knew or felt things in ways that didn't seem straightforwardly rational. It was an entirely unpredictable skill. Sometimes it provided useful information or insights he couldn't have gained any other way. Sometimes it remained opaque, ineffable, the mere suggestion of something that made no obvious sense and couldn't be deciphered. It was ultimately frustrating because, although it had sometimes served him well, it was unreliable. If he placed any faith in it, it would simply dissolve away to nothing.

He shook his head. 'No, not yet. In fact, that was one of the things that felt odd about the crime scene.'

'How do you mean?'

'There was nothing there. None of my feelings, I mean.'

'Is that unusual?' Milton asked.

'Normally, no,' Murrain said. 'I mean, I'm not feeling anything much at the moment, for example. But it's odd at a crime scene. Especially a murder scene. There's normally something, however vague it might be. I don't know why, but something usually talks to me.'

'You think the radio silence might be significant?' Wanstead said.

Murrain smiled. 'I hope you're not humouring me, Paul.'

'You know me better than that, Kenny. I've no idea what it's all about, but I'm happy to accept that there's something there. Or not, in this case.'

'As to whether it's significant,' Murrain said, 'I've no idea. It was just strange. There was just nothing. Dead air.' He paused, thinking. 'It disturbed me, somehow, though. It felt – wrong. As if something was interfering with the reception.' He often found himself using radio analogies when trying to describe his feelings. It wasn't exactly right, but it was the closest comparison he could find. 'As if it was being blocked somehow.'

Milton was frowning. 'There's something about all of this that doesn't quite sit right with me. I don't share your gifts, Kenny, but I've an uneasy feeling about it.'

'The burglary theory, you mean?' Murrain said. 'I was wondering about that.'

'It's the most likely explanation,' Milton said. 'He interrupted the break-in, gave chase, maybe caught up with the intruder, intruder pulls a knife…' He trailed off.

'But?' Murrain prompted.

'But, according to Ferby, there was no sign of any forced entry. The back door was unlocked. There was no obvious sign that Gorman had been involved in any kind of struggle.' Milton shrugged. 'Doesn't prove anything either way, obviously. Maybe Gorman had accidentally left the door unlocked. Maybe he heard a noise outside and went to look. Maybe he interrupted them before they'd actually broken in. It's not difficult to find explanations. It's just that somehow – well, like I say, I feel uneasy.'

'Always worth following your instincts,' Murrain said. 'At least till you can prove they're wrong. Let's see if we dig up anything interesting on Gorman. If we do, it might just change the picture.'

Milton nodded. 'I don't want to send us off chasing shadows. Just thought I should raise it. The chances are it's exactly what it looks like.'

'No, you were right to raise it, Joe.' Murrain rubbed his temples with the air of one trying to coax his brain into action. 'We'll do it all by the book. But there's a part of me that's feeling uncomfortable about this one too.'

'Bloody hell,' Wanstead said. 'It's a good job there's one of us here keeping our feet firmly on the ground and making sure the admin gets done.'

'That's always your role, Paul,' Murrain said. 'Keeping me at least loosely tethered to reality.'

CHAPTER SEVEN

Geoff Nolan looked around him and smiled. He'd chosen this place deliberately, because he always enjoyed the effect his presence had on the other diners. Not all of them, obviously. The vast majority were no doubt oblivious to his presence. But there was generally a small but significant minority, usually the more elderly, who would spend their lunchtime glancing in his direction.

It wasn't that they were hostile or resented his presence here – or at least that was only occasionally the case. It was more that they were simply surprised, perhaps even taken aback, that he should be in a place like this. This, in Nolan's experience, was the contemporary, middle-class form of racism. There were many other kinds, of course, and most of them were more threatening than this. But this politer form was still all too prevalent and pernicious, and was equally self-perpetuating. People of colour too often felt uncomfortable coming to places like this, and so this became the sort of place they didn't go.

Nolan himself was long past worrying what others might think of him. He enjoyed causing a mild stir, and told himself he was making his small contribution to changing societal attitudes. That and getting himself a very decent lunch at the production company's expense.

He looked at his watch and took another look around the restaurant, identifying those who were already casting curious if surreptitious glances in his direction. He tended to arrive a little early for these appointments, partly because he also enjoyed imagining the speculation that would be prompted by his apparently lone presence. At times, he could almost hear his fellow diners as they whisperingly shared ideas about his identity. He imagined their first thought might be that he was perhaps a professional footballer – there were a few of those lived in the vicinity – but then they'd conclude he was too old for that. They might then move on to less flattering speculation, particularly given his tendency to mildly flamboyant clothing. And, after a while, one or two of them might recall that they had seen him on television at some point, although they'd most likely be unable to recall where or when. Every now and then, Nolan would look across to one of these tables, and offer them a polite smile and nod. The individuals concerned would always look embarrassedly away, as if they had been caught out in some illegal act.

'Geoff?'

The voice had come from behind him, and Nolan turned to see a middle-aged man hovering near the table. There was little question that this was Lyle Christopher, the owner of the production company responsible for the proposed series. He looked like almost every male television production person that Nolan had ever dealt with. He was a tall man, with his expensive-looking suit, designer glasses and sculpted facial hair. Nolan rose to shake his hand. 'You must be Lyle.'

'Guilty as charged.' Christopher was looking around the chintz-heavy dining room. 'Nice place, this, though thought you might have preferred somewhere in town?'

Nolan shrugged and gestured for Christopher to take a seat. 'Nice to get out in the country now and again. And I don't drink, so driving isn't an issue.'

'I suppose that's true.' Christopher looked as if this might be very much an issue as far as he was concerned. 'And this place does have an excellent reputation.'

'Well deserved, too.' Nolan took another look at his watch. He imagined that Darrell Conway would be a few minutes late, simply because Darrell was always a few minutes late. Nolan had long ago recognised that this was a deliberate tactic, a way of demonstrating that his time was more important than yours. Well, fair enough, if it kept him happy.

Christopher seated himself opposite Nolan. 'I assume Darrell's given you an idea of what we have in mind?'

Nolan was impressed by the absence of small-talk. Too often in these meetings he'd had to sit through half an hour of meaningless blether before they'd actually got down to business. Nolan preferred to get the business out of the way so he could enjoy the meal uninterrupted. 'I've had Darrell's version of it,' he said. 'Which may not be the same as yours.'

Christopher smiled, his expression suggesting that Nolan had just made a joke he didn't fully understand. 'The aim is to build on the television profile you've already established.'

'Geoff Nolan, ghostbuster?'

'If you want to put it that way. People see you as the voice of reason. Open-minded, fair, but with your feet firmly on the ground.'

'While all around me are in screaming hysterics. I suppose that's sort of accurate. It's all set up, though. They get these celebrity guests or members of the public, wind them up so they're in a completely suggestible state, and know they'll react to the tiniest bump in the night. Then they bring me in to calmly talk them down—'

'Selling yourself short as usual, Geoff? Good job you've got the best agent to speak on your behalf.' Darrell Conway sat down beside Nolan and nodded to Christopher. 'Afternoon, Lyle. I hope you've not been taking anything Geoff says seriously?'

'It's all very interesting—' Lyle began.

'It's more than interesting,' Conway said. 'What you need to understand is that Geoff really is the best at what he does. He knows his stuff better than anyone. He really understands what makes people tick and, more to the point, what makes them go cuckoo. He knows all the tricks.'

'I'm a Professor of Psychology,' Nolan said. 'Not a fairground magician.'

'That's the point,' Christopher said. 'We want that academic credibility. We want someone with your authority for this.'

Nolan was silent for a moment as the waiter arrived to distribute menus and take orders for drinks. Nolan and Christopher opted for sparkling water. Conway, characteristically, ordered a glass of an expensive-sounding red, gesturing towards Nolan. 'He keeps a clear head, so I have to drink for both of us.'

Nolan smiled. 'I'm hoping,' he said, 'that you don't intend to exploit my academic credibility to justify any kind of unscientific nonsense. That's always been my concern even about the ghostbuster format. I've stuck with it because it gives me a chance to show people how some of these psychological tricks work, to demonstrate that we're often not as rational as we think we are. But I'm very conscious that's not why people watch the programme. They watch it to see celebrities wetting themselves because they've just heard someone cough in a darkened room.'

'It makes very good television,' Christopher said. 'Entertaining, yes, but also educational.'

'If you say so, Lyle,' Nolan said. 'I worry that we too often end up focusing on the former at the expense of the latter.'

'In any case,' Christopher went on, 'what we have in mind is something considerably more serious.'

'But not dull,' Conway added. 'I'm assuming.'

'That's the balance we have to strike,' Christopher said. 'And again that's why Geoff appealed to us. He's a serious expert in the field, but he's also someone who knows how to present himself on TV.'

'I'm willing to make an arse of myself,' Nolan said, 'if that's what you mean.'

'I mean that you take the subject seriously, but you don't take yourself seriously. You're prepared to do what it takes to communicate effectively with the viewer. People respect you, but they also enjoy watching you.'

'Enough of the flattery,' Nolan said. 'For the moment, anyway. Let's get to the details. What exactly is the concept of this show?'

Christopher glanced at Conway, clearly wondering whether his account was going to match what Nolan had already been told. 'We're seeing it as a series of investigative reports. Each week you'd look at a different aspect of the paranormal. You'd talk to people who claimed to have experienced the relevant phenomena. You'd interview people who claimed to be exponents or experts in the area. You'd perhaps look at some well-known or well-documented cases. Then you'd give us your verdict, providing where possible a rational explanation but also, where appropriate, highlighting the limits of our current understanding or knowledge.'

'Where appropriate?'

'Well, if you feel that there are aspects of cases that can't be straightforwardly or adequately explained by science.'

'There are very few, if any, of these cases that can't be adequately explained by science. That doesn't mean that the supposedly scientific explanation is the only one possible, but then we're drifting into the realms of faith.'

'That's exactly the line we'd want you to take. We'd want you to take the viewers seriously, to have confidence in their ability to understand that kind of nuance.'

Nolan smiled. 'In my experience, you may be over-estimating the perspicacity of the average viewer. Many of them seem only too happy to believe any old tosh you might throw at them.'

Christopher shrugged. 'We want to make a serious programme. Nothing sensationalist. We think you'd be perfect for it.'

Nolan had spent enough time with television executives to recognise this kind of flattery for what it was. This was how they talked to the 'talent', at least till they got you on board. What happened after that depended on the success or otherwise of the programme, assuming it actually ever got made. He'd had plenty of these discussions which, for all Darrell Conway's unfailing optimism, had ended up going precisely nowhere. That was why Nolan always tried at least to get a decent lunch out of it.

'Okay,' Nolan said. 'I'm up for it in principle. Obviously we'll all have to see how it pans out in practice. But I do quite fancy the idea. It's the kind of stuff you can make interesting without the sensationalist bullshit. Do you have particular topic areas in mind?'

'That's partly up to you,' Christopher said. 'I know you've some particular areas of interest.'

'If it's all the same to you, I'd rather steer away from the haunted house stuff, at least initially. I think I've become a bit typecast as the ghostbuster man.' The truth was that Nolan didn't care too much about this, but he thought it would be a good way to test the seriousness of Christopher's commitment to 'serious' television.

As Nolan had expected, Christopher hesitated before responding. 'It's what the public associate with you, of course. So I don't think we should reject it out of hand. I was wondering whether we should start with something that's along those lines but different from the ghostbuster stuff.'

'Such as?'

Christopher waited until the waiter had brought their drinks and taken their orders. 'We were wondering about spiritualism. Mediums. All that stuff.'

Nolan nodded. 'I'd be happy with that. My highly nuanced opinion is that it's all utter bollocks. I don't get too worked up about this stuff usually – people can believe whatever they want to, as far as I'm concerned – but I do get angry about so-called spiritualism. Preying on people at their most vulnerable. Most of it's pretty straightforward, too. It's not even clever psychology.' This was one of Nolan's familiar hobbyhorses, and he suspected Darrell Conway might have primed Christopher to suggest it.

'I'd be only too pleased to expose some of the charlatans.'

Christopher nodded. 'Obviously, we have to be a little careful how we present it. We don't want to find ourselves being sued by some irate medium.'

'I'd be only too happy to strike an unhappy medium,' Nolan said. 'But, yes, I take your point. I think the important thing will be to expose the kind of techniques they use. It's even easier for them now we all lead so much of our lives on-line. It used to be just cold reading. You know, using prompts to get people to reveal things about themselves. But these days if they're dealing with someone one-to-one, they can often dig up a lot of the material beforehand, just using social media and the like. The same goes for astrologers and fortune tellers. It can be a pretty sophisticated business.' He was conscious he was on the point of embarking on one of his pat routines, the kind of material he sometimes used, in a slightly more structured form, as the basis of his student lectures.

Christopher seemed happy enough, though. 'This is what we want. We can decide how best to present it. We could even get you to do a performance as a medium – you know, actually conducting a séance. Then, when the clients are singing your praises, we reveal how it's done.'

'You'd have to do it sensitively, though. I don't want to end up doing exactly what I'm accusing these frauds of doing. The effects on them could be even more traumatic if we then expose it as fake.'

'Yes, of course,' Christopher responded airily. 'We wouldn't want to do anything that you'd see as unethical.'

He sounded about as sincere as Nolan would have expected, but that was fine. Nolan knew full well that if he sold his soul to the television devil, it was up to him to protect his own reputation. The production team would be interested only in making the programme they wanted to make – whether that was serious or sensationalist – and would care about his profile only in so far as it affected that. As long as he never forgot that, he knew he'd be fine.

The rest of the lunch went as he'd expected. The food was as good as ever. Christopher talked with mounting enthusiasm and increasing flattery. Darrell Conway largely kept his own counsel as he tended to in these situations, preferring to keep his powder dry for the more formal negotiations that would no doubt follow. He chipped into the conversation only occasionally, usually to add some endorsement of Nolan's qualities.

'Well, that was very pleasant,' Nolan said afterwards, as he and Conway stood by Nolan's BMW in the car park. Christopher had left a few minutes earlier, letting them know that he was already running late for a production meeting back in town.

'You did okay, Geoff,' Conway said. 'They're keen to get you for this, and it'll do wonders for your profile.'

'That's what worries me,' Nolan said. 'But I'm sure you'll look after my interests.'

'I always do, Geoff. You know that.'

'So you tell me, Darrell. Right, I'd better get back into town. This is all very glamorous, but until the day you finally make me very rich I've still got some students   to   teach.'

CHAPTER EIGHT

'What have we got so far?' Marie Donovan asked.

Bert Wallace lowered herself on to the seat opposite Donovan's desk. 'Bit of a mix, to be honest. It's not difficult to find out stuff on Andrew Gorman's public profile. He's got – that is, he had – a fairly comprehensive website. Free daily, weekly, monthly and annual horoscopes, with just enough detail to get punters to stump up for more. The daily ones have continued to update since his death, so he obviously had them set up to post automatically.'

'That seems a bit creepy,' Donovan said. 'Predictions from beyond the grave.'

'Technology rather than magic, I suppose,' Wallace said. 'But a bit beyond my abilities. We've got the IT people looking at his laptop to see what else might be on there. It looks as if he had a portfolio of paying subscribers who received a customised report from him every month.'

'What? Personal predictions?'

'Something like that, I suppose. I had a look at a few. They all seemed pretty vague. You know, "you may be going on a journey" or "something unexpected may turn up in your life". And those flattering but meaningless personal profiles. "You have very high standards and you're sometimes intolerant of others". That kind of stuff.'

'Amazing what people will pay for,' Donovan said.

'I suppose it provides them with reassurance. I suppose I can understand it. He seems to have had different levels of subscription, though. The premium ones received much more detailed reports. In fairness, those seem much more specific.'

'Though probably still with plenty of wriggle room, I imagine.'

'I imagine. Anyway, as I say, there's plenty of stuff on his professional life, but we're struggling to get much about his personal life. There's a short bio on the website, as Joe said, but it's really just bigging up his astrology credentials. So that and the Wikipedia entry are pretty much all we have at the moment. We don't even have a next of kin, so far, but we're chasing that up. I'm hoping we might find some stuff on the laptop that will give us some personal leads, especially in his e-mails.'

'We've found nothing useful in the house?'

'Not really. There's no sign that Gorman was in any kind of a relationship. We've not found any personal mail – just the usual bills and circulars. There don't really even seem to be any personal photographs.'

'What about his phone?'

'Now that's a little odd. We've not been able to find one.'

Donovan looked up. 'Really? Doesn't everyone have a mobile these days?'

'My nan doesn't,' Wallace said. 'But then she still gives her phone number when she answers the landline. It seems odd for someone of Gorman's age. He was only early forties. It might be that he had it tucked away somewhere we haven't found, but the house has been searched fairly thoroughly. It's certainly not in any of the obvious places, like his desk or by his bed.'

'Seems a bit odd,' Donovan said. 'Is it possible the killer took it?'

'It's possible, obviously. But there's no sign of anything else in the house being taken. Maybe Gorman took it out with him if he was thinking of calling 999.'

'I take it we've checked that he didn't?' Donovan was conscious that this was one of those basic details that might easily get overlooked in the pressure of an investigation.

Wallace smiled. 'Must admit, the thought only occurred to me belatedly. But, yes, I've checked with the enquiry desk and there's no record of any relevant call in the likely time-slot. So if he was thinking of calling us, he obviously didn't get round to it. We've done a search for the phone outside, in case he dropped it in the struggle or when he gave chase. I suppose it's possible that it might have got kicked somewhere in the undergrowth away from the body. Or that the killer just took it opportunistically.'

'Or took it deliberately because Gorman had managed to get a photograph?' Donovan suggested. 'Whatever, it doesn't help us very much.'

'It's frustrating,' Wallace said. 'A phone might have given us some personal leads. Calls or texts.'

'Maybe it'll turn up,' Donovan said. 'What about his landline?'

'We're checking on that. We've found no signs of any paper bills, so my guess is that the account was on-line. Once we know the provider, we should be able to get details of any calls.'

'Assuming he used the landline much,' Donovan said. 'Most of us don't these days.' She sighed.

'There's not a lot for us to report back to Kenny, is there?'

'Not so far. We've interviewed the immediate neighbours. Nobody seemed to have seen or heard anything, and nobody seems to have known Gorman, except as someone to nod to in the street. Usual "kept himself to himself" stuff. Doesn't seem to have had many visitors, or at least none that anyone noticed.'

'So he didn't do face-to-face consultations?'

'Doesn't look like it, or at least not many. Most of the business seems to have been done on-line.'

'Modern life really is rubbish, isn't it?' Donovan said, wearily. 'There would have been a time when someone like Gorman would have known all his neighbours, would have family and friends living nearby. Would have been part of the community. Now he was just some bloke who lived in the house across the street, and we're struggling to find anyone who actually knew him.'

'It's early days,' Wallace pointed out. 'We'll find someone.'

'We could be wasting our time anyway. Chances are that this has nothing to do with who Gorman was. I can't imagine that he was killed because one of his clients was unhappy with his predictions.'

'You never know, though, do you?' Wallace said. 'Strikes me it might be a sensitive area. People have a reason for wanting to know the future. Usually because they're scared or worried about something.'

'You might be right,' Donovan said. 'I don't know why anyone would want to contact an astrologer – I mean, pay money for it, rather than just read a column in a newspaper or magazine. But it might be because you're anxious. Whether that could lead to murder – well, it doesn't seem likely. But who knows? We've encountered weirder motives.' She paused. 'Joe thinks there's something odd about this one. And he's not normally the over-imaginative type.'

Wallace gave her a curious look. 'I'd have said he was the down to earth kind. Keeps Kenny tethered to earth, anyway.'

'Don't let Joe hear you say that. He's very sensitive about his relationship with Kenny. Always reckons that Kenny's a lot less fanciful than the rest of us believe. He'd much rather be your standard solid down-to-earth copper. It's one of the reasons the feelings stuff tortures him so much. Yes, it sometimes helps, but it makes life more complicated.'

'Is this what Joe told you?' Wallace was clearly making an effort to keep a straight face, but there was a smile playing at the corners of her mouth.

'What do you mean?' Donovan didn't actually have much doubt what Wallace meant, but she was wondering what was being said behind her back.

Wallace finally allowed herself to smile. 'I was just wondering whether you and Joe are really an item now?'

'Is that what people are saying?'

'Well—'

'I know Paul's being dropping his usual subtle hints for ages, but I didn't know the rest of you were talking about us.'

'I didn't mean—'

Finally, Donovan decided to let Wallace out of her misery and smiled back. 'I know you didn't. And I don't mind, really. I just wondered what people were saying. I mean, the ones who aren't inveterate gossips like Paul.'

'Nobody's really saying anything. We're all curious, though.'

'I don't know what to say, really. I don't think we are an item. Not quite, not yet. We've both got too much emotional baggage to jump straight into it. But, well, I guess we're heading in that direction. Let's put it that way.'

'That's good,' Wallace said, sincerely. 'Everyone would like to see you and Joe get together.'

'You reckon? I think there are one or two people who might have reservations.'

'I can't see why.'

'Not in the immediate team, maybe. We're a pretty tight-knit bunch. But some of the higher-ups might have concerns. Even Kenny.'

'Oh, come on,' Wallace said. 'Kenny's like a father to Joe.' They both knew that there was more truth in this than was immediately apparent. Joe had also been the name of Murrain's son who had died some years before in circumstances that ultimately had almost derailed Murrain's career.

'I don't know,' Donovan said. 'Maybe that's part of the problem. Fathers don't always approve of their son's choices of partner.'

'That's ridiculous. Kenny has huge respect for you.'

Donovan shrugged. 'If you say so. I mean, I know he respects me professionally. But it complicates things, doesn't it? Joe's a higher rank than I am. That raises questions about our working relationship. Not that we'd ever exploit it, but there are people out there who'd think we would.'

'Kenny's wife's a higher rank than he is.'

'I know. But they've always made a point of working in very different fields. Eloise isn't really even an operational officer any more.' Eloise Murrain was a Chief Superintendent, but now spent most of her time working on strategic change management projects for the force. 'If Joe and I really do get together, we'd have to consider whether we can realistically carry on working in the same team.'

'That would be a pity,' Wallace said.

'I guess it's a bridge we'll cross when we come to it,' Donovan said. 'But I don't think that time's too far away.'

'Has Joe spoken to Kenny about it?'

'Not yet. We both feel we want to be sure where things stand before we set too many hares running. But Kenny must have a good idea what's going on. He's not a fool.'

'I hope it works out for you.'

'It'll work out, I'm sure. I'm just not sure in what way. We both have to decide what we want first.' Donovan felt as if she'd already said too much. 'Okay, we'd better get on. We really need to know a lot more about our friend, Andrew Gorman.'

CHAPTER NINE

Eloise Murrain looked up as her mobile buzzed on the desk. She was in the middle of untangling a particularly knotted spreadsheet and would really have preferred not to be interrupted. She picked up the screen, glanced at the identity of the caller, and then thumbed the Call button.

'Don't tell me,' she said. 'You're going to be late back tonight.'

'I thought I was supposed to be the one with second-sight, or whatever it is,' Kenny Murrain said at the other end of the line. 'How did you know?'

'You've just kicked off a major murder enquiry. Your name's Kenneth Murrain. Given those two facts, I don't exactly need the gift of prophecy.'

'Oh. I suppose not. Anyway, I'm going to be late back tonight.'

'I've already started planning my meal for one. Do you want me to get something out for you?'

'Don't worry. I'll sort something when I get in.'

'Or you'll call for fish and chips on your way back. I know you.'

'I'm leaving that option open. Not sure what time it'll be. We're just trying to make sure we've got all our ducks in a row here. I've a feeling this is one that's going to need a lot of legwork. If I'm going to have to seek more resources, I need to make sure I can demonstrate we're making the best of what we already have. You know what these Chief Superintendents can be like.'

'Utterly reasonable and generous to a fault, in my experience,' Eloise said.

'You might be. But you're not Marty Winston.'

'Marty's all right. I'm known worse.'

'Oh, so have I. But that's a low bar. Present company excepted,' he added hurriedly. 'Marty's okay, but he's not a soft touch.'

'You wouldn't want him to be.'

She heard Murrain sigh. 'I suppose not. But he does love his spreadsheets.'

'Does he? That must be where we differ, then. I hate the bloody things. Especially the one that's on my screen at the moment. Maybe I should seek his help.'

'Not if you ever want to get out of his office again. It's his specialist subject.'

'He must be a wow at parties. Okay, I'd better get on. See you later.'

'Have fun.'

She ended the call and stared back at the screen. The spreadsheet was supposed to calculate the immediate and long-term costs that would result from various restructuring and relocation options, but a number of the cells were simply showing ERROR. The spreadsheet had been designed by a supposedly expert member of her team who, inevitably, had chosen this week to be on leave. The problem was no doubt something straightforward he could have sorted in a few minutes, but she'd been reduced to working through it cell by cell to work out where the issue was. If she couldn't sort it by the morning, she'd have no choice but to interrupt his holiday, but – after years of hers and Kenny's holidays being disturbed – she was reluctant to do that except as a last resort.

She was in the middle of working laboriously through yet another formula when her phone buzzed again. She cursed, assuming it was Kenny calling back with some other request. But when she picked up the phone, the screen said 'Number Withheld.'

She didn't get many junk calls on her force phone, but a few managed to get through, generally from automated dialling with nothing but silence at the end of the line. She ignored the call, waiting for it to go to voicemail. If it was anything important, they'd leave a message.

The phone eventually fell silent and she returned to focussing on the spreadsheet. A moment later, the phone buzzed again, indicating receipt of a voicemail.

With another choice expletive, she picked up the phone and listened. The speaker was male, the accent southern and noticeably upmarket. 'Chief Superintendent Murrain. My name's Derek Whitcomb. You don't know me, but I'm a senior civil servant. I'd really like to speak to you as soon as possible. It's about your husband. I'm available all evening.' He left a mobile number and ended the call.

Her first instinct was to disregard the call. What the hell did he mean by a 'senior civil servant'. If he really was a civil servant, senior or otherwise, surely he'd have said he was from the Home Office or the Ministry of Justice or whichever pen-pushing body he represented.

Unless.

Unless he was a spook. Eloise had had a few dealings with the intelligence services over the years and had concluded that they revelled in the clandestine nature of their occupation. If they were so concerned about secrecy, they'd just keep their mouths shut. Instead they tended to mouth endlessly on about just how secret it all had to be. They also almost always had a very high opinion of themselves, which in her experience had largely been unmerited.

But why would the intelligence services be interested in Kenny? Even if they were, for some reason connected with his work, surely they'd either make contact with him directly or through his own command chain. Not through his wife, even if she was a fellow police-officer.

On that basis, the sensible response would be to report the call to the Communications Team and perhaps to her own superiors. It was quite possible that this was just some tabloid journalist looking for an inside track on one of Kenny's current or past cases. If they were chasing a story, they'd try every trick in the book to get someone to talk.

On the other hand, she wasn't some junior on the enquiry desk who was going to blurt out something confidential without realising. There'd been something about the message that had piqued her curiosity. It was partly the confidence in the speaker's voice, oozing with the entitlement of someone who'd been to the right school and university. There were a few tabloid journalists like that, but there were far more spooks.

Finally, her curiosity got the better of her and she dialled the number. The phone rang twice and then the same voice said, 'Whitcomb.'

'Mr Whitcomb. This is Chief Superintendent Murrain. You left a message for me.'

'Chief Superintendent Murrain.' His tone suggested her call was somehow unexpected. 'I'm very grateful to you for calling back.'

'No problem. What can I do for you?'

'As I said in my message, I'd like to talk to you about your husband. I believe he's also a police officer. A Detective Inspector.' Whitcomb spoke the last two words as if uttering a foreign language.

To Eloise, this sounded suspiciously like someone fishing for confirmation. 'I'm afraid that's not possible, Mr Whitcomb.'

'I'm sorry?'

'I don't think it's appropriate for me to talk to you about a third party.'

'But—'

She sensed he was about to embark on some emollient attempt to persuade her, so she cut him off abruptly. 'I don't know who you are, Mr Whitcomb. I don't know who or what you represent. You claim to be a senior civil servant. May I ask from which department?'

There was an almost imperceptible pause. 'You probably already know that, Chief Superintendent.'

'I know what you'd like me to think. But I've no grounds for believing it to be true. Can you provide me with any evidence of your identity?'

'You'll appreciate that's rather difficult over the phone.'

'I do. That's making me wonder why you contacted me this way. Rather than, for example, speaking through my senior officers here.'

'I can do that if necessary. I thought you might prefer a little discretion at this stage.'

'At this stage?'

'I'd prefer not to have to handle this formally, if possible. At least at the moment. I think that's in all our interests.'

'Is that right? Then I don't think I can help you, Mr Whitcomb.'

There was silence for a moment. 'I was going to suggest we might meet face to face, Chief Superintendent. Then I could confirm to you that I am who I claim.'

'You haven't actually claimed to be anyone,' she pointed. 'You've just allowed me to infer it. I'm not in the habit of meeting with complete strangers.'

'I'm not suggesting anything clandestine. I'm happy to meet somewhere very public. A cafe, say. Wherever suits you.'

'I'm afraid not. I don't think it would be appropriate for me to meet you, whoever you might be, to talk about my husband. I don't know what I could tell you that would conceivably be of interest to you. If you need to know something about him, I suggest you either speak to him directly or make appropriate contact with the senior team here.'

'I'm sorry you've responded in this way, Chief Superintendent.' The words sounded vaguely threatening. 'I was hoping for more co-operation.'

'I really can't understand why.' Eloise found herself bridling at his tone. 'I'm a police officer. I'm not accustomed to talking to strangers about any of my business. You'll appreciate the reasons why. If you need information, I can only suggest you make use of the appropriate formal channels.'

'I would ask you not to mention this conversation to your husband.'

'Ask whatever you like. Don't expect me to take any notice.'

'So be it. As I say, I'm sorry. Thank you for your time.'

Before she could respond, he ended the call. She sat for a moment, staring at the phone as if expecting it to provide some explanation of what had just taken place. Then she thumbed down the contacts list and dialled Kenny's number.

'Eloise?'

'I've just had the oddest call.'

'Go on.'

She briefly outlined her conversation with Whitcomb. 'He sounded almost threatening at the end. Not in anything he actually said, but his tone.'

'You think he really was a spook?'

'He sounded convincing enough. I mean, I've had one or two dealings with the intelligence services over the years, and he definitely sounded the type.'

'Sounds a bizarre way of doing things, if he's genuine.'

'I don't know. They love the cloak and dagger stuff. But he could have been anybody. Some tabloid journalist trying to get an inside track on one of your cases, maybe?'

'You'd have thought there were more promising ways of doing that than approaching a senior officer because she happens to be my wife. He must have known you'd react the way you did.'

'I shouldn't have called him back really. Curiosity got the better of me. Maybe he thought that would be enough to make me play ball with him. I got the impression he wasn't accustomed to having his requests refused.'

'I know that type well enough,' Murrain agreed. 'If he was the real thing, I can't envisage why they'd have any interest in me. I'm just a provincial middle-ranking police officer.'

'Maybe you've trodden on someone's toes without realising it. It happens. Though more usually it's some issue with the NCA. Tripping over some operation they've not bothered to tell us about.'

'I suppose if there's anything in it, he'll try a more formal route next, so I guess we'll know soon enough.'

'I guess so. I didn't like his tone, though.' She laughed. 'Mind you, in fairness, he probably didn't like mine either. I'll report it up the line in case he starts causing any trouble. And I'll let the Comms team know. If he wasn't for real, we should probably warn people to be on their guard, in case he tries it on some other way.'

'Thanks for letting me know, anyway. Maybe he'll contact me directly. If it's me he wants to know about, I'm the most reliable source of information.'

'You reckon? He probably called me because he knew I'd tell him what you're really like.'

Murrain laughed. 'Just don't go revealing that to anyone, will you?'

'My lips are sealed. Right, I'll let you get on with that fascinating admin stuff. Give my regards to Joe and Paul.'

'I will. And I'll let you get back to your spreadsheet.'

They finished the call, and Eloise sat for a moment staring out of her office window. Kenny was still based in Stockport, although there were constant rumours about the whole Major Crime Team being centralised in Manchester. The only reason it hadn't happened yet was the constant pressure on space, increasingly the focus of her own work. She'd moved up to the central HQ in Newton Heath some years before, and her office offered an uninspiring view of the business park. She supposed it at least prevented her being distracted by the beauty of her surroundings.

She was still feeling uneasy. Although she kept telling herself that Whitcomb could have been anyone – her force mobile number was in the public domain – her instinct was that he was exactly what he'd led her to believe. There'd been something about his manner that had felt exactly right for a spook, though she'd have struggled to pin down quite why that was.

If he really was a spook, that left her with one question. Why the hell would the intelligence services have any interest in Kenny Murrain?

CHAPTER TEN

Irene Fenwick looked at her watch for the fifth time in ten minutes. Still a few minutes to go.

He'd said he'd call at ten. That was how it worked apparently. You booked the appointment on line, and then Justin Bannerman, or one of his assistants, contacted you by Skype at the specified time. To her slight surprise, she'd had a call at 9.45am from one of those assistants to check she was there and ready to take the call. It was made clear to her that she would have her allotted 30 minute slot and no more, and that she would have only one opportunity to accept the call. If she failed to answer, Bannerman would not call back.

The underlying message was that Bannerman's time was precious. Well, she already knew that. It had cost her enough to have this short consultation. It had all been a very slick operation. She'd had to pay by card at the time of booking the appointment using Bannerman's highly functional website.

She was already beginning to feel slightly foolish about the whole thing, like a supposedly intelligent mark who's been taken in by the oldest trick in the book. She knew full well what Donna would say if she found out about this. She might well think that her mother was beginning to go gaga. But she told herself that Gordon would have understood. He was always sceptical, but he would never scoff at this kind of thing. After all, it was only through Gordon that she'd heard of Bannerman in the first place.

In any case, why should she care what Donna might think? It was Irene's own money, to spend as she wanted. If she wanted to give this a go, why shouldn't she? She had no real expectation it would work. She kept telling herself she didn't really believe in any of this kind of stuff. But what if it did? What if, if only for a few minutes, she could regain what she'd lost?

That was what Donna didn't understand. She simply didn't realise how much Irene missed her late husband. That wasn't surprising. Irene herself hadn't expected to miss him as much as she did. She'd loved him, of course. That had, usually quite literally, gone without saying. But they were both successful professionals. They'd lived largely independent lives. Of course, she'd supported him in his career, and he'd done the same for her. But, through a combination of work and their various other commitments, they'd probably spent more time apart than together.

So she'd expected that, although Gordon's death would undoubtedly remove one important element of her life, the rest would come flooding in to fill the resulting vacuum.

But she'd realised, as soon as his death was finally confirmed, that everything was different. It felt, suddenly and shockingly, as if part of her own self, her own body and soul, had been torn from her. A hole in her life that nothing else could ever fill.

As for throwing herself into her work, she'd felt unable to work at all. She was officially retired, so there was no requirement for her to turn up to an office each morning. She had various commitments, of course, but for the most part she had to motivate herself to continue her writing and research. For many months after Gordon's death, the motivation simply had not been there. She'd sat in her chair, watching endless inane daytime television, unable to persuade herself even to boot up her laptop, let alone carry out any serious work.

She had never told Donna this, of course, though she suspected Donna knew something was wrong. It was at this point that Donna had begun agitating for her mother to move out of this absurdly large house and into something more suited to Irene's new single status.

Irene hadn't been too resistant to the idea. She'd been wondering herself whether what she really needed was a change of scene, an opportunity to move from this place that she and Gordon had made into a family home. A clean break, that was what she needed.

At the same time another part of her was terrified at the prospect of severing her last links with Gordon. If she moved away from this house, she'd have nothing left of Gordon, other than the few books and other gifts he'd bought her over the years. Without that link, her memories of Gordon might just dim and fade to the point where she could no longer even recall the man he had been.

In the end, she'd gone along with Donna's plan and placed the house on the market. She'd hoped that the sale might take some time, enabling her to come to terms with what had happened. But to her dismay she'd received an attractive offer almost immediately. 'Houses like this don't come on the market very often,' the agent had said, 'so they get snapped up very quickly.' And here I am, she'd thought, voluntarily giving the place up.

By that stage, she felt she had no option but to continue. She accepted the offer and put in an offer on an upmarket new flat in the city centre. She'd liked the new place, with its impressive views of the distant Pennines, and it would be much more convenient for many of her commitments. But she still hadn't managed to convince herself she was doing the right thing.

That was what she wanted really. Reassurance. She wasn't seriously expecting that Gordon's spirit would be magically conjured up to offer his views about her moving. It was more like tossing a coin to make a decision. You didn't necessarily obey what the coin instructed. But your own reaction to the result helped you understand what you really wanted.

She looked at her watch again, and then at the screen of her laptop. She wasn't exactly a Luddite, and she understood the basics of using a computer. But whenever she had to do something like this, she was always convinced she'd get it wrong. The call should come any moment now.

Even so, the ringing tone took her by surprise. She hesitated for a second, trying to calm herself, and then took the call. She hadn't been sure what to expect, but she found herself gazing at Justin Bannerman's smooth features. He was a good looking man and was obviously aiming to extract maximum value from the fact. His skin was smooth and well-shaven, his pale blue eyes shimmered with interest and energy, his lengthy fair hair was stylishly swept back away from his face. There was something slightly androgynous in his features, but she could easily imagine some female clients being seduced by his appearance.

'Mrs Fenwick,' he said. The voice was deep and accentless. 'May I call you Irene? Please call me Justin.'

At first, she could hardly bring herself to respond. 'Yes. Yes. Of course. Irene.'

'Now, Irene, how can I help you? I believe it's in connection with your late husband. Gordon?'

For a moment, she was taken aback by his knowledge. Then she recalled that, when completing the on-line form, she'd been asked to indicate briefly what she wanted to achieve through the consultation. She had written, feeling rather foolish as she did so, that she was seeking her late husband's advice on a potential house move. As far as she could recall she hadn't mentioned Gordon's name, but he'd had a reasonably high public profile. She imagined even a cursory internet search would have quickly revealed his name.

'Yes, Gordon. He died a couple of years ago.'

'I sense that his death was unexpected,' Bannerman said.

'It was,' she said. She reminded herself that this information would also be readily available on line. Gordon's death had received some coverage in the local and specialist media.

The set-up around Bannerman looked very professional, suggesting he was sitting in a studio with proper lighting rather than, as she was, staring at a laptop in the gloom of her office. She suspected Bannerman had also been made up. His complexion looked too smooth to be true.

'So you'd like to make contact with Gordon?' he said. 'You're considering moving house?'

She was already concluding that this had been a mistake. Her only consolation was that Donna would never find out about it. 'The place I'm in – the place where Gordon and I raised our daughter – is really too big just for me. I'm considering moving to a smaller flat in the city. But I'm afraid I'll be cutting off my remaining links with Gordon.' She hesitated before continuing. 'I suppose I really just want Gordon's blessing. That he's happy for me to do this.'

That was it, she thought. That was all she really wanted. She didn't really want Gordon's advice, even though she would never previously have made a decision without consulting him. She just wanted him to tell her he didn't mind. That he accepted it was for the best. That he would, in some sense, be with her wherever she might live.

'I understand. These decisions are always difficult.' This was Bannerman's style, she thought. He never said anything substantive. He just echoed your own words in a platitudinous way. 'It's always a challenge to do this remotely, but let me see if I can make contact with his spirit.' He spoke as if about to send a vaguely contentious e-mail.

He closed his eyes, and his expression changed subtly but noticeably. The effect was as if consciousness had left his body, as if he'd become an empty vessel that another spirit might fill. It was clearly a trick, Irene thought, but an oddly impressive one. She could almost feel herself being sucked into this.

There was a long silence, and she had almost begun to think that Bannerman was genuinely unconscious. Then, unexpectedly, his eyes opened. Again, the expression in the eyes seemed to have changed. He's just an actor, Irene told herself. This is all just a pretence, though he's very good at it.

Finally, he spoke. 'Irene?'

Irene took a breath. The voice wasn't Gordon's. It didn't sound like him. But another part of her brain was telling her that it did. That she could detect his intonation, even in that single word.

'Gordon? Is that you?' She felt an idiot even for playing along with this, but somehow couldn't help herself.

'It's me, Irene. Not for long. But for the moment.'

It doesn't sound remotely like him, she thought. But there was something that did. Some trace of the flat northern vowels that underlay his educated accent. She was just being suggestible, falling for the oldest trick in the book. Being encouraged to believe something because you wanted it to be true, even while telling yourself not to be gullible.

'What do you want from me, Irene? I can't stay long.'

'I'm thinking of moving, Gordon. Selling the house. It's too big for me now. I'm considering moving to a small flat in the city centre. Donna thinks it's a good idea. But I wanted so much to know what you would have thought.'

'You have your own life now, Irene. You must do what you think best.'

'But it's the house we shared, Gordon. I don't want to lose that.'

'That's in the past, Irene. I'm still here. I'm always here. It doesn't matter where you're living.'

'Where's here, Gordon? Where are you?' She wasn't sure why she'd even asked the question. She was feeling foolish enough already. She wasn't some credulous old biddy. Yet here she was, talking to a dubious fraudster impersonating her dead husband.

'I'm going now, Irene. I'm losing contact. It's hard to sustain. But go ahead and move with my blessing...'

With my blessing, she thought. The words she'd used herself in explaining to Bannerman what she wanted. He was just echoing back what she wanted to hear. That was how this always worked.

Even so, she found herself saying, 'Gordon. Don't go...'

Bannerman had closed his eyes again and gradually his expression softened. Again, the effect was startling. It was as if Bannerman was slowly regaining control of his own body. Finally, he opened his eyes and blinked at her. 'I know he came. Did he answer your questions?'

You utter charlatan, she thought. You know full well what he said because it was you saying it. Out loud, she said, 'He came. He gave me his blessing.'

'I'm so glad.' Bannerman sounded absolutely sincere. 'I'm delighted that you can get on with your life.'

She wanted to object, tell him he was exploiting the vulnerable. She wanted to expose him for the fraud he undoubtedly was. But she couldn't bring herself to do it. Somehow, he'd convinced her. He'd persuaded her she really had just had a conversation with her dead husband. Rationally, she knew that was nonsense. But emotionally she had already accepted it. She had received what she wanted.

'Thank you,' she found herself saying. 'I'm very grateful to you.'

Bannerman smiled. 'I am merely the conduit. It's a simple gift, but if I can use it to help people like yourself, I'm very pleased. Is there anything more I can do for you today?'

'I don't think so. I have what I needed.'

'That is good. And a good day to you, Irene. Best wishes.'

The call ended, more suddenly than she'd expected. She was still under Bannerman's spell. She kept telling herself it was all nonsense. It didn't matter. It had given her what she wanted.

She took another look at her watch. She had been talking to Bannerman for barely ten minutes, rather than the thirty she'd supposedly booked. She wondered if that was always the way, whether Bannerman's spirits always struggled so conveniently to sustain their presence on earth. She could imagine Bannerman might have had another appointment booked in for 10.15.

Somehow it didn't matter. Whatever her rational mind might be telling her, she no longer cared. She'd communicated with Gordon. She'd received his blessing. That was all that mattered.

CHAPTER ELEVEN

'So what have we got?' Murrain looked round the table. 'I'm really hoping for good news.'

It was the familiar morning briefing. Murrain had gathered those in charge of the various enquiry work-streams in the conference room along the corridor from the incident room. He hadn't formally booked the conference room, and he expected that at any moment some group from HR or Finance would come striding in, tutting profusely, to inform him that, actually, they already had this room booked. If so, they'd return and convene in a corner of the MIR, but for the moment he was pleased to be somewhere where he could at least hear himself think.

Murrain had had a bad night. As so often these days, his sleep had been disturbed by dreams he couldn't recall. He had a vague sense that last night's dreams had been Kafkaesque, that he'd been trapped in some insoluble bureaucratic maze, but could remember no more than that. Perhaps it had been that call to Eloise the previous evening. Whatever their reasons, the thought of the intelligence services poking their noses into his business left him feeling uneasy.

He'd risen early, leaving Eloise sleeping – no-one could quite sleep like Eloise – and after a quick shower and coffee had made his way into the office. Eloise wouldn't be surprised and would know where he'd gone. It wasn't the first time, and they knew each other only too well. He'd used the extra couple of hours to catch up with yet more administration. He had the hope that one day he'd actually get on top of it, but he knew it would never happen. It just kept coming.

Something else had been disturbing him all morning. It was a return of the familiar sixth-sense that had been unexpectedly absent at the murder scene. As always, he would have struggled to describe it. It was as if a film was playing in the gloomier recesses of his head, some scenes or narrative he could barely discern, let alone understand. But, as so often, he felt it was trying to tell him something. Whether it was something about the case or whether it was something else entirely, whether it was likely to be meaningful or helpful, only time would tell. But it was there and it was troubling him.

'Not sure if it actually constitutes good news,' Joe Milton said, 'but we do seem to be making some progress.'

'That's what I want to hear,' Murrain said.

'Actually quite interesting progress.' Milton had attached his laptop to the conference room projector – one reason they'd decided to commandeer the conference room – and now flicked through a series of images. 'Traffic cameras. As we expected, the area around Andrew Gorman's house is very quiet overnight. It's a largely residential neighbourhood so there's not much coming and going after midnight. No cameras on the backstreets, of course. But we've got one on the A6 junction that catches a lot of the traffic that comes out of that area. Obviously, the A6 is fairly busy even overnight, but there aren't that many vehicles turning on to it at that point. We've collated all the ones that loosely match what we understand to be the period in which Gorman might have been killed—'

'This is turning into War and Peace, Joe,' Wanstead said. 'Get to the point.'

'Just wanted to make sure you were fully up to speed, Paul. I know it sometimes takes you a while to catch up.' Milton gestured up at the screen. 'We're gradually going through all the vehicles we've caught. We'll be interviewing all the registered keepers, of course, but this is the one that's caught our attention.' The image showed a small white van, its registration plate clearly visible. 'It's a fake plate.'

As Milton spoke the last words, Murrain felt the sensation he often experienced at significant moments in an enquiry. It was as if the distant voices that had been muttering away in the recesses of his mind suddenly became audible. He was still unable to distinguish what was being said, but he knew it was significant. 'And this fits the likely timing of Gorman's death?'

'Looks like it. We haven't had the pathology results back yet, but for once we can actually be relatively precise about the time of death. We've started going through Gorman's laptop. He'd obviously been working on some horoscopes – stop grimacing, Paul – and the timing on the files indicates he was working up to about 4.45am. The body was found at around 6.00am, so it looks as if the killing took place in that 75 minute window.'

'And the van?' Murrain said.

'Caught on the camera just after 5.00am. So that would work perfectly.'

Murrain nodded, thinking through the implications of this. 'Most of our local housebreakers wouldn't go to the trouble of fake plates, would they?'

'I checked it out with the neighbourhood team in case I was behind the times,' Milton said. 'The answer was basically that most of them aren't bright enough to get hold of fake plates. It's not impossible – there are one or two more organised gangs – but it's not the norm.'

'Have we had any reports of other break-ins in the area?' Marie Donovan asked. 'On the same night, I mean. If they didn't reach Gorman's house till that time, you'd have expected them to have done a few others first.'

'Doesn't look like it,' Milton said. 'There were reports from other parts of the city, but nowhere near Milton's place.'

'Intriguing,' Murrain said. 'So if we assume this vehicle was connected to Gorman's death, we can probably rule out anything purely opportunistic. If these were house-breakers, they were obviously more professional than average. The pros usually try to avoid doing more harm than they need to. Too much police attention is bad for business.'

'If they weren't house-breakers,' Bert Wallace said, voicing what they were all clearly thinking, 'that might mean that Gorman was targeted for some reason.'

'I'm not jumping to any conclusions,' Milton said. 'Maybe this vehicle wasn't even connected to Gorman's death. We've had more unlikely coincidences. Maybe they were pros, but something went wrong that resulted in Gorman's death.'

'But it's a line worth pursuing,' Murrain said. 'Have we identified any subsequent sightings of the van anywhere else?'

'Not yet,' Milton said. 'But we're checking all the other cameras, in case it was caught on the way in or out. Depends on how much it stuck to the main roads, I guess.'

'If they really were pros,' Wanstead said, 'I'm surprised they allowed themselves to get caught at all.'

'Might have just been unlucky,' Milton said. 'The camera on that junction is a temporary one. Only been there a few days because there'd been reports of people jumping the lights.'

'Let's hope their bad luck is our good luck,' Murrain said. 'It's a useful lead anyway. As Bert says, it at least means we still can't rule out the idea that Gorman was targeted for some reason.' He turned to Donovan. 'Have we any more on Gorman himself?'

'We're gradually getting somewhere,' she said. 'We're hoping the laptop might give us some more leads, but there's a hell of a lot of stuff on there so it won't be easy to sort the wheat from the chaff. We've done a quick search through the e-mails using all the obvious key words we could think of. We've found a few e-mail exchanges with what appears to be Gorman's brother. Called Simon, lives over in Glossop. Not found any reference to other relatives so far. We've tracked down an address for the brother. I was planning to head over to talk to him when we've finished here.'

'Paul, can you let the powers-than-be in Derbyshire know, just so we don't get accused of treading on anyone's toes?' Murrain said. 'But sounds a decent lead. How recent are the e-mail exchanges?'

'It doesn't look as if they were in contact all that often,' Donovan said. 'Not by e-mail anyway. But that doesn't mean much these days. I'm old enough to use e-mail a fair bit, but there are countless other ways they can communicate.'

'They could just talk on the phone,' Wanstead said. 'Or even meet face to face. That's how old I am.'

'The last e-mail's from a couple of weeks ago,' Donovan went on, 'so pretty recent. There isn't much of substance in the e-mails themselves. Looks as if the brother's a GP, and he spends a fair bit of the time making fun of Gorman's line of work. But all good humoured as far as I can see, and Gorman responds in kind. There's a bit of stuff about football – looks as if they were both City fans – and the odd bit about films they've seen. But not much else. None of it's particularly intimate.'

'Even so, he may be able to tell us a bit more about Gorman's life and background. We'll also need to get him onside in respect of investigating Gorman's flat and possessions. Can't imagine he's likely to object, but you can never tell how people will react in this kind of situation.'

The remainder of the meeting was more routine, with updates that confirmed how much activity was taking place across the various work-streams. They'd interviewed most of Gorman's immediate neighbours, but had uncovered little of interest. No-one had seen or heard anything unusual on the night of Gorman's death, and most of them claimed hardly to know Gorman. He had apparently moved into the house the previous year, but had made little effort to introduce himself to any of the neighbours. Not that there was anything unusual in that, Murrain thought. He and Eloise had been living in their current house for a couple of decades, but they still had only nodding relationships with most of their neighbours. It was the way people lived today. He and Eloise both worked long and irregular hours, and many of their neighbours commuted into Manchester, Stockport or elsewhere. Their paths just didn't cross, and no doubt it had been the same with Gorman. The neighbours who had encountered him had formed generally positive impressions – he'd been friendly and pleasant enough – but could offer few other insights.

They were looking into Gorman's finances but from the information they'd so far found on the laptop and in the house there was no sign of anything out of the ordinary. He'd presumably made a living through his astrology business. Murrain couldn't quite imagine how that might be possible, but he'd keep an open mind until they'd checked out the details.

Beyond that, for the moment, it was the usual legwork. More interviews, more checking of CCTV footage, the hope of further leads from the forensic reports. It wasn't exciting, but it was probably how they were most likely to achieve the breakthrough they needed.

It wasn't until Murrain was in the process of winding up the meeting that the conference room door burst open. It was a woman who Murrain vaguely recognised as one of the more officious Human Resource Business Partners. He'd only had a few dealings with her because he was more than happy to leave that kind of stuff to Milton and Wanstead, but the encounters had not generally been easy ones.

'I think you'll find,' she said now, 'that we have this room booked from 11.30.'

Murrain glanced up at the conference room clock. It read 11.28. 'No worries, Barbara. We'll be out in two minutes. Exactly.'

CHAPTER TWELVE

'Not a part of the world I know, really,' Bert Wallace said, as they took the right turn that would lead them into the centre of Glossop. 'Driven through it a few times heading over to Sheffield, but never had reason to stop.'

'It's a nice little town.' Marie Donovan lived on this side of Greater Manchester, and she'd had a few weekend trips out here. Most recently for lunch with Joe Milton. 'Decent shops. You know, proper independent ones. One or two good restaurants. Not the most exciting place, but pleasant enough.'

They'd waited until late afternoon before heading over here, having checked out the operating hours of Simon Gorman's practice. The practice was open late several nights each week, but today fortunately it closed at 6.00pm. Donovan didn't know what hours Gorman worked, but, having found both addresses, she hoped they'd be able to catch him either at the practice at the end of the working day or subsequently at home. Despite the urgency of their enquiry, she hadn't thought it appropriate to break the news of his brother's death while he was still likely to be engaged with patients.

The practice was at the far end of the town. It was a small, modern building with an adjacent car-park which, at this time in the afternoon, was largely empty. The sign by the entrance indicated that the practice comprised five GPs, the first on the list being

Dr S Gorman. The door was locked, so Donovan pressed the bell and waited. After a moment she heard a movement inside and the door opened a crack. An anxious-looking female face gazed back at her. 'I'm sorry. We're closed. If it's an emergency—'

'Police,' Donovan said, holding out her warrant card. 'We're trying to get hold of Dr Gorman if he's here.'

'Simon? I think he's still here. He was finishing some paperwork.'

'May we come inside?'

'I don't know—'

'It is rather important.' Donovan had the impression that, like medical receptionists everywhere, this woman would be skilled at protecting the medical staff from unwanted visitors.

'In that case, I suppose...' The woman opened the door and ushered them inside. 'I'll track him down.' She hurried through a set of double doors at the far side of the reception area.

Donovan looked around. It was the usual doctors' waiting room, with the standard rows of chairs, the walls lined with posters promoting health initiatives, a rack of medical leaflets.

'These places give me the creeps,' Wallace said. 'Not as bad as hospitals, but the same kind of feeling.'

'Why's that?' Donovan turned back to her, immediately wondering whether she should even have asked the question.

'It was just my dad's last couple of years. Cancer. We spent more time in medical establishments than we did at home.'

'I'm sorry.' Donovan had never heard Wallace talk about her private life. It wasn't that she was secretive, but she rarely volunteered information about herself.

She was a highly professional officer, but Donovan sometimes felt that Wallace concealed her real personality behind that professional facade. Donovan didn't much mind – with her own background, she was the last person to criticise others for separating their private and professional lives. But she wanted to know Wallace better. Not for the first time, it occurred to her to wonder about what secrets might lurk even in the most mundane of lives. After all, even Paul Wanstead had turned out to have some unexpected skeletons in his family closet.

'Can I help you? I'm Simon Gorman.'

Donovan turned to see a man standing by the double doors. The receptionist hovered just behind him, clearly keen to know what this was all about.

Gorman was a tall man, clearly a little older than his brother had been. Perhaps late forties, Donovan estimated. He was good-looking, with a neatly trimmed thatch of dark hair, and he peered at them curiously through a pair of thick-framed glasses.

'Good to meet you, Dr Gorman. Is there somewhere we could talk in private?' Donovan glanced momentarily at the receptionist.

Gorman turned to the receptionist. 'We could use the rest room, couldn't we, Carol? That's probably more comfortable than the consulting rooms.' He didn't wait for a response, but led them back through the doors. 'In here,' he said, gesturing to a door on the left.

The rest room turned out to be a small room with a scattering of low chairs and a small kitchenette with a kettle and a microwave. 'It's not much,' Gorman said. 'It's where we come for coffee and lunch. When we get the opportunity. Now, how can I help you?'

'Perhaps you'd better sit down, Dr Gorman. I'm afraid we have some bad news.'

Gorman lowered himself into one of the armchairs, gesturing for them to sit opposite. 'Bad news?'

'Can I ask when you last heard from your brother Andrew?'

'Andy? Couple of weeks ago, I suppose. Why?'

'I'm afraid he's been found dead.'

'I—' Gorman stopped, as if unable to articulate what he wanted to say. 'How did it happen?'

'He was killed.' Donovan knew there was no point in prevaricating. 'We believe murdered, although the full circumstances aren't yet clear.'

'Murdered?'

'We can't be entirely sure. But certainly an unlawful killing. I'm sorry.'

'I can't believe it. Andy.' He looked at Wallace as if expecting her to contradict what Donovan had just said. 'But how? When?'

'Outside his house,' Wallace said. 'He was stabbed. It was in the early hours of the morning so our initial assumption is that he interrupted a burglar or some other kind of disturbance outside.'

'Jesus,' Gorman said. 'How can that sort of thing even happen?'

'We'll make it our business to find out, Dr Gorman.' Donovan paused. 'We also have to ask whether you know of anyone who might have had a reason to want to harm your brother.'

'Andy? Why would anyone want to harm Andy?'

'It's a possibility we have to consider, as I'm sure you'll appreciate. As my colleague says, most likely your brother was simply in the wrong place at the wrong time. Unfortunately, that happens. But we do have to consider other explanations.'

'You mean that somebody targeted Andy? That's nonsense.'

'Do you feel up to answering a few questions about your brother, Dr Gorman? I appreciate this is a difficult time, but the more we know about your brother the more quickly we'll be able to make progress.'

'Yes, of course. Anything I can to do to help catch the bastard who did this.'

'Can you tell us a little about your brother? We believe he made his living as an astrologer?'

Gorman gave a mirthless laugh. 'Yes, and I used to mock him mercilessly about it.'

'How did he get into that line of work?'

'I don't really know exactly. He got interested in it when he was at university. I used to tell him it was all bollocks, but he couldn't be persuaded. In fairness, he accepted that most of the stuff we see in newspaper and magazines was nonsense. But he reckoned that serious astrology was different. If the forecast was done properly based on the actual time of birth, it could be remarkably precise and accurate. That was what he claimed. There were plenty only too happy to believe it.'

'You didn't?'

'I don't know. I mean, not really. I'm prepared to accept that there may be more things in Heaven and Earth, and all that. I don't really believe he could predict the future, but there were times when Andy had insights I couldn't really explain.' He stopped again. 'Jesus, I can't believe I'm talking in the past tense.'

'What about his clients? Did your brother tell you anything about them?'

'Not really. He wouldn't have told me any personal details, any more than I'd have told him about my patients. But from the little he told me, I had the impression they were a fairly mixed bag. Some no doubt sincerely wanted guidance and thought he could provide it. I imagine others just consulted him out of curiosity or for a laugh. But you surely can't think that one of his clients…'

'We're just keeping an open mind at the moment, Dr Gorman. We need to explore all avenues however unlikely they might appear. I'm sure you wouldn't want us to do otherwise.'

'I suppose so. But from what you've said you might be better off looking at your local housebreakers.'

Donovan smiled in a way that she hoped was reassuring. 'That's our primary focus at present, of course. But we can't discount other possibilities.'

'I really can't believe anyone would have wanted to harm Andy.'

'Even so, if would be helpful for us to know more about your brother. We understand he lived alone. Was he in any kind of a relationship?'

'Not at present.' Gorman suddenly looked uncomfortable, Donovan thought, as if he'd been caught out some misdemeanour. 'Look, you're going to find out one way or another, so I might as well tell you straightaway. Andy was gay.'

Donovan frowned. 'Many people are, Dr Gorman. But thank you for telling us. We need to know as much as possible, in case any facts are relevant to our enquiry.'

'That's my worry,' Gorman said. 'I don't want you to jump to any conclusions. Like, I don't know, that Andy might have been killed by someone he'd picked up. Just because he was gay, that doesn't mean he was promiscuous.'

Donovan exchanged a brief glance with Wallace. 'Of course not. We try very hard not to jump to any conclusions. We simply gather the evidence to make an informed judgement. But it helps us to have as much knowledge as we can about your brother. It's impossible for us to judge in advance what might be relevant.'

'I'm sorry. Yes, of course. It's just that Andy's sexuality was a big issue in the family. He didn't really come out till he was in his early twenties, though I don't think it was a big surprise to me or anyone else who knew him well. Except for our parents. That was the reason it took him so long. They were – well, let's say conservative types. My mum was probably more "live and let live" but my dad was old school. As far as he was concerned, homosexuality was simply a perversion. When Andy came out, he literally disowned him.'

'Really?'

'Really. Andy had already left home by then. Had left university, got a job with one of the local councils in Manchester. This was before he started dabbling more seriously in the astrology stuff. Anyway, my dad made it clear he was *persona non grata*. I sided with Andy, so I was *persona non grata* too. It was a hell of a mess.'

'I'm sorry.'

'It's a good few years ago now. But we never really rebuilt the relationships. Mum was okay. We kept in touch with her, but neither of us succeeded in making contact with my dad. He wouldn't talk to us. The first time we went back to his house was for his funeral.'

There was silence for a few moments, as Donovan and Wallace absorbed this. 'And your mother?'

'She died a year or so back. Luckily, we were both able to get to know her again after dad died. She was as old-fashioned as dad in some ways, but she didn't allow that to stop her loving Andy.' Gorman took a breath. 'It affected Andy badly, though. His mental health took a knock. He'd never been the most resilient type, and this just knocked the stuffing out of him. He had a year or so of really bad depression. Luckily, I was able to pull a few strings to help him get some treatment. But it was the astrology that really seemed to help him come through it.'

'In what way?'

'Like I say, he'd been interested in it since his university days, but only as something he'd dabbled with out of curiosity. He began to take it more seriously, and it was as if it gave him a sense of purpose. He'd found something he could do that others couldn't. I tried to discourage him at first because I was worried he might end up pinning his hopes on something that, well, I thought was nonsense. But I realised how seriously he was taking it, and also that, actually, he was very good at it.'

'Good at it?'

'At two levels, really. The first is just the way astrology tends to work in newspapers and magazines and the like. Most people don't take it very seriously, or claim they don't, but they still read their horoscope for fun or out of curiosity. Then they'll tell you that such-and-such an astrologer is surprisingly accurate. What that usually means is that the astrologer in question is very good at writing predictions which feel very precise but which are actually widely applicable. It's a real skill. Anyone can say "you're going to meet a tall dark stranger". It's much more difficult to persuade a reader that you've predicted exactly what's going to happen to them.'

To Donovan's ears, this sounded not much different from a con-trick, but she supposed there were readers who were looking for that kind of affirmation or reassurance. 'And your brother was good at this?'

'Very good. He managed to get a column in one of the local papers, started to build a reputation. Then he set up an on-line business. He was actually pretty good at all the on-line marketing stuff, and it all took off from there.'

'You said two levels,' Wallace pointed out. 'What was the other one?'

'It was what I said earlier. There were times when he seemed to come up with insights I couldn't really explain. I mean, maybe it was just another example of his skill at presenting the predictions, or maybe it was just confirmation bias on my part. But a few times I was genuinely gobsmacked. He knew it too. He had two types of subscriber. Those who paid the basic rate got the clever writing. Those who were prepared to stump up for the premium rate got what I know Andy thought of as the real stuff.'

'He really believed he had a special gift?' Donovan said.

'Definitely. He never doubted it. He couldn't explain it. Didn't know exactly how he did what he did. There are plenty of books on astrology, plenty of guides on how to do it. He learnt from all those, obviously. But he reckoned this was something more. Some way that he could look at the results generated by a standard astrological projection, or whatever they call it, and see things others couldn't.'

'And this helped him rebuild his mental health?' Donovan said, unsure how to respond to what Gorman had just told them.

'There were other factors, of course. But I'd say it was a big one. It gave him a focus. The sense that he was doing something useful. Whether he really was, who knows?'

'And more recently? You said he wasn't in a relationship currently. Had he been in one in, say, the last year or two?'

'He had a partner for a year or so. I thought it was going to be a long-term thing, but they split up a few months back. I don't really know why. Andy reckons they just decided it wasn't working. I had the sense that it might have been something more specific than that. I asked him if he wanted to talk about it, but he claimed he wasn't troubled by it.'

'Do you think that was true?'

'I'm honestly not sure. It wasn't always easy to read Andy.' He looked up at Donovan. 'It still hasn't really hit me, you know? I mean, I'm talking to you as if this is all perfectly normal. As if there's nothing unusual about sitting with you talking about my brother's murder.' He shook his head. 'It's how shock works. It'll hit home later.'

'Do you have someone to go home to?' Donovan asked, conscious of quite how far they'd pushed him.

Gorman smiled. 'Married, two kids. Exactly as my father would have wished it. Jenny'll be there for me.'

'Do you have contact details for your brother's former partner?'

'I don't think so. His name was Bernard Craigie. Lecturer at Manchester Uni or Manchester Met, I think.'

'We'll track him down,' Donovan said. 'Any other close friends or relatives we should speak to.'

'No other close relatives, now our parents are gone.' Gorman stopped, as if the implications of that statement had only just struck him. 'As for friends, I don't know, really. Andy and I had a good relationship, but we didn't see each other that often. We'd invite him round for dinner every few months, and we'd usually see him at Christmas and the like. We'd drop each other e-mails or texts quite often, as well. But we really lived pretty separate lives. I had the impression he had a circle of friends, but I couldn't have told you who they were. I'm sorry I can't be of more help.'

'Of course. I presume from what you've said that you were his next of kin?'

'There's no-one else.'

'We'll need you to come in to provide a formal confirmation of the identity. We don't really have any doubts, given the location and the photographs on his website, so it's really a formality, I'm afraid. We're also currently conducting searches on his laptop and in his house. We don't know who actually owns those now.'

'As far as I know, he didn't have a will,' Gorman said, 'so it'll probably end up going to probate, but I'm the next of kin. I've no problem with you continuing, if that's what you're asking. Do whatever you need to catch whoever did this.'

'Thank you, Dr Gorman. It just makes things slightly simpler if we know we have your support.'

'You have it in spades,' Gorman said. For the first time, it looked as if the reality of the situation might have struck him. 'Jesus. Poor Andy. Who'd do something like that?'

Donovan reached out and took his hand. 'All we can do is offer our sympathy and promise you that we'll do our utmost to find out.'

CHAPTER THIRTEEN

'Can I get you some coffee?'

'Thank you. That would be good. Just milk, please.'

'Bear with me.' Justin Bannerman gestured towards an informal meeting area at the far end of the room. 'Take a seat and I'll be back in a jiffy.'

Geoff Nolan walked the length of the room and lowered himself into one of the stylish-looking armchairs. He hadn't known what to expect, and he still wasn't entirely sure what to make of what he'd encountered here so far.

He hadn't even been convinced this meeting was a good idea. It had been Lyle Christopher's suggestion, and Nolan had initially resisted, arguing that something formal would have been a better idea. He'd have preferred a more distant relationship with Bannerman to help ensure objectivity in the proposed programme. But Christopher had insisted that a degree of personal chemistry would be critical to the programme's impact. 'It doesn't matter whether you love each other, hate each other or somewhere in between,' he'd said, 'as long as the viewer gets a sense of an interaction between you.'

Christopher was already worrying Nolan. It wasn't exactly that he was sensationalist – he seemed quite sincere in wanting the show to be serious. But his ideas did seem at odds with the way Nolan preferred to do things. Nolan didn't see himself as particularly precious or difficult to work with, but he did want his professional views to be listened to. For the moment, though, he was prepared to go with the flow.

Nolan looked around him. This was clearly Bannerman's own office, an elegant modern space in one of the newly-built business blocks that increasingly ringed the city centre. It looked like the nerve-centre of an up-and-coming IT start-up rather than the offices of a spiritualist. But then, whatever else he might be, Bannerman was clearly a businessman. At the far end of the room, there was a large work-station with a high-specification desktop on it. The near wall was lined with office cabinets, and the far wall with glass-fronted shelves filled with copies of Bannerman's books and CDs, interspersed with what appeared to be awards. Nolan wondered what sort of awards might be applicable to a medium. Manifestation of the year, maybe? Best original ectoplasm?

Nolan's musings were interrupted by Bannerman's return. 'Right, coffee will be with us in a few minutes. In the meantime, we might as well get down to business.' He took the seat opposite Nolan.

'It's good of you to spare the time to see me.'

'On the contrary. My reasons for agreeing to be involved in this aren't exactly altruistic. I hope to gain some personal benefits from it. That is, if I don't allow you to shaft me.'

'I've no desire to do that,' Nolan said. 'I'm approaching it with an entirely open mind.'

Bannerman smiled. 'Of course you are. But exposing the tricks of the charlatan always makes for better television, doesn't it?'

'You'd have to ask Lyle Christopher about that. My job's just to give a professional view.'

'As a Professor of Psychology?'

'Pretty much. I've largely specialised in examining the irrationality of the human mind. The ways in which we can be tricked, or can trick ourselves, into believing almost anything.'

As he was speaking, a young woman had arrived bearing a tray with a cafetiére of coffee and a plate of expensive-looking biscuits. Bannerman nodded his thanks and leaned forward to pour the coffees. 'So you think I'm a trickster?'

'I didn't say that, and I don't think it,' Nolan said. 'At the moment, I know almost nothing about what you do or how you do it, other than the initial background research I've conducted, which was little more than reading a few articles about you and your background. I deliberately avoided looking at anything that might have influenced my views of you.'

'Very commendable,' Bannerman said. 'I assure you you could have found numerous sceptical articles if you'd looked. We live in a sceptical age.'

'I tend to think we live in an over credulous one. But I'm open to persuasion.'

'The simple fact that I'm prepared to take part in this proposed programme should indicate to you that I've some confidence in what I do. Yes, I'm sure that if you wished you could find psychological explanations for some of it. I'm very aware that it's all too easy to play tricks on the mind, and I don't for a moment deny that I use some of those techniques as part of my showmanship. I believe I provide a genuine service, but I also want to entertain people.'

'Like any good stage magician?'

'If you will. I want people to come and see me. And, to be honest, I want people to come who don't initially believe in what I do. If they come to my shows out of curiosity or because they simply want to have an enjoyable evening out, that's fine. But I hope that while they're there, they'll experience some things that will leave them surprised. Some things they're unable to explain.'

'Any good stage magician would aim to do the same.' Nolan was conscious he was gently goading Bannerman, but he was intrigued to discover more about what the man really believed – or claimed to believe.

'Most stage magicians will happily acknowledge that what they do is nothing more than sleight of hand and misdirection. I claim rather more than that.'

'You claim to commune with the dead?'

Bannerman was silent for a moment. 'That is not terminology that I would use, though I suppose it is how others would characterise it.'

'What terminology would you use?'

Bannerman frowned, and for a second looked almost as if he was in some kind of physical pain. 'In truth, I don't have the words for it. I can't describe exactly what I do. I present it as spiritualism because that's a language the public understands. I even cloak it on stage and in my consultations as channelling the spirits, as if your grandma or uncle was inhabiting my body. But that's not really it. That's not really what happens. It's something different from that. It's as if I'm tuning into something I can't really describe. Some source of knowledge. Of insight.'

Bannerman was turning out to be a more interesting subject than Nolan had originally expected. When Christopher had suggested opening the series with a spiritualist, Nolan had been more than happy to go along with the idea because of his strong feelings about the subject. At the same time, he'd expected that the topic would provide easy pickings. Nolan thought he knew pretty much everything he needed to about how spiritualists worked. Their techniques were all largely the same. Some research and cold reading, some smart questions to elicit information and smarter answers to suggest unexpected insights, a bit of showmanship, a little misdirection, and there you were. Some were more sophisticated than others, but otherwise they were all the same.

His only real worry had been that it would be too easy. Fish in a barrel stuff. His preference was that the show should investigate some genuine mysteries. He wanted to encounter some phenomena he couldn't immediately dismiss or rationalise. In that sense, Nolan's claims to open-mindedness were sincere enough. He didn't doubt that, ultimately, he'd be able to come up with at least probable explanations for everything he might come up against, but he genuinely wanted to be challenged. He hadn't expected to find anything approaching that kind of challenge in spiritualism.

Most likely, he still wouldn't. But he was already concluding that Bannerman was smarter than most practitioners he'd encountered in the field. It was interesting that Bannerman had dismissed most of the traditional claims for spiritualism even if he retained the trappings of them in his stage show. Nolan suspected he was already being misdirected, that the mind-games had started immediately. 'So what are you claiming?' he asked Bannerman now. 'Some kind of telepathy? Second-sight?'

Bannerman appeared to hesitate, as if the question had been genuinely unexpected. 'I'm not sure. I think either or both terms could apply. When I tap into this sense, it's partly as if I'm intuiting part of what the individual is thinking, but it's also as if I'm drawing inspiration from somewhere else, from information the individual couldn't possibly have.'

It was clear to Nolan that Bannerman wasn't going to allow himself to be pinned down to anything as clear as a definition or explanation. 'Can you do this with any individual, any subject?'

'No, I can't. It's relatively consistent. But it isn't something I can control. Sometimes I sit down with a subject and it's simply not there. There's nothing I can do to force it. Sometimes it works intermittently even with a given individual. One time it's there, and the next nothing.'

This sounded very convenient to Nolan. 'That must be awkward if you're on stage?'

'On stage I just cover for it. That's one of the times when I resort to the usual tricks. A bit of cold reading. A bit of background research where I've been able to do it. I'm experienced enough to have that as a safety net if it doesn't work.'

'So then you lie to them?'

Bannerman laughed. 'If you like. But I don't like people to go away disappointed. If they'd paid to come and see me, and then paid a little more to be one of the subjects on stage, I don't want them to be short-changed.'

So instead you give them false information and false hope, Nolan thought. 'What about in your private consultations? What if it doesn't happen then?'

'That's a different matter. I explain to all my private clients that I can't guarantee results every time. If it doesn't work, I simply refund their payment.'

It was a useful get-out clause, Nolan thought. If the subject doesn't go for your cold reading or simply isn't providing the information you need, you simply claim that the spirits aren't willing today. Ironically, that approach would often help convince people of your authenticity because they saw that you were not simply grabbing the money regardless. Bannerman knew what he was doing.

'Does it worry you that many of your clients will be people who are vulnerable? The recently bereaved or those suffering from severe loneliness.'

'Of course. But I wouldn't do this if I didn't think I could genuinely provide a service to those people.' Bannerman shook his head. 'I've read some things about you, Geoff. I know you dislike spiritualists. I think, in general, you're right to do so. Many of the people who operate in this field are nothing more than frauds. Some of them are entertainers, as I am, but very few of them can offer anything more than a few conjuring tricks. And, yes, they prey on the vulnerable.'

'But you're different?' Nolan found himself unable to keep a note of scepticism out of his voice.

'I understand your suspicions, but, yes, I genuinely believe I am. I make no claims to omniscience, but I do believe that I can offer insights that would not be attainable any other way.'

'You're running a very successful business.' Nolan gestured at the office around them. 'I assume you're doing well for yourself.'

'I do, and I make no apologies for it. I provide a service, just as you do to your students, and I expect to be paid for it. I don't believe that my rates are excessive, and I do try to tailor them to what individual clients are able to afford.' He smiled. 'And you must recognise that I have staff to pay, this office to maintain, as well as all the expenses associated with my national and world tours, so I'm perhaps doing less well personally than you might imagine.'

My heart bleeds, Nolan thought. 'I wasn't offering any kind of criticism. But clearly you do have a strong incentive to do this, whether or not it's genuine.'

'Of course, and I can see that it would be easy to pigeonhole me as a fake like all the others. Perhaps you'll still decide to do that at the conclusion of your programme. But the truth is that I'm not like the others. I really can do this, whatever it is.'

Despite himself, Nolan was impressed. If you can fake sincerity, he thought, you'd got it made. And Bannerman seemed sincere enough. Whether that made what he was saying true was another question, but for the moment Nolan felt disinclined to challenge him. If Bannerman was the fraud that Nolan assumed, it wouldn't be difficult to expose that. If he really did have some gift that Nolan couldn't easily explain – and Nolan, for all his scientific rigour had encountered one or two such instances – it would be something worth investigating further. 'I'll be fascinated to see. Genuinely.'

'So how do you want to play this?'

'Lyle's idea is that I do some initial background work before we start filming anything. So I can get a sense of what you do, and we can decide how best to structure the programme.'

'And do I get a say in that?'

'You'll have to discuss the details of that with Lyle. My understanding – and my strong preference – is that you should. We obviously reserve the right to our own editorial independence, but Lyle committed to take on board your views as to how we should film and present the programme. He also told me that you'd be allowed to see it prior to the final edit, so that you have a final right of reply to anything that's said or claimed. The aim's not to stitch you up, but to present you fairly and objectively.'

Bannerman was smiling. 'It's not been my experience of the way television generally works. But that all sounds more than acceptable. If I were more cynical, I might say almost too good to be true.'

'I can't comment on television in general,' Nolan said. 'I can only comment on the way I work. I've insisted on certain conditions in the way the programme is produced.'

'In that case, I hope they don't shaft you as well.'

'Me too. To go back to your original question about how we should play this, what I'd like first of all is to come along to one of your stage shows. Just to get a feel for what you do and how you do it.'

'Just as a member of the audience?'

'Pretty much. It might be good if we could have a brief chat after the show, if that's appropriate. In case I've any questions about aspects of the performance.' Nolan smiled. 'If that's the right word for what you do.'

'I don't deny it's a performance. And, yes, that's fine. As long as you recognise that I'm generally fairly drained afterwards. I'm not usually in the best mood for idle chatter.'

'I'll stick to business then.'

'You wouldn't like to be one of my subjects. On stage, I mean. We could arrange that.'

'I don't think so. Not just yet. It might be one of the things we include in the programme. It would be interesting to be on the receiving end of your techniques.'

'Techniques,' Bannerman echoed, as though questioning Nolan's use of the word. 'Well, that would certainly be possible. You'd also be welcome to sit in on one or two of my consultation sessions, obviously subject to the client's agreement. That would give you the chance both to see what I do, and to speak to the clients about their perceptions of it.'

'That all sounds excellent. Probably best if I get Lyle to contact you to set things up. Then we can be sure he's getting what he wants out of this as well.'

Bannerman laughed. 'Of course. That is the most important thing. We must ensure that Lyle gets what he wants. Though Lyle strikes me as the sort who almost always do.'

CHAPTER FOURTEEN

'Mr Murrain.'

The voice was quiet, scarcely more than a whisper in the darkness. Murrain turned from locking his car and peered back down the drive. It was a gloomy night, with heavy low cloud and the threat of rain. He'd just arrived home after another lengthy night in the office running through the latest developments on the enquiry with various members of the team. The last thing he needed was a news reporter badgering him on his own doorstep.

His first instinct was simply to ignore whoever was calling his name, but he knew the media could be tenacious if they were after a story. The Comms team had issued a media release about Gorman's killing earlier that afternoon, though detail had been kept to a minimum. Presumably this man was after something more.

Murrain took a step down the drive. 'If you have a media query, I'd suggest you talk directly to our Communications Team. I'm sure they'll be only too pleased to assist. In the meantime, I'd really like to request you don't bother me at home. I won't make any comment except through the appropriate formal channels.'

'I'm not a journalist, Mr Murrain.' The speaker's voice was as quiet as ever, but Murrain could discern every word, despite the rustle of the rising wind through the trees. Some severe storms had been forecast for the coming days, and Murrain could sense their impending arrival.

'In that case, there's probably even less I can do for you.' Murrain turned to make his way back up to the house. He wasn't physically scared of the man – Murrain was tall, heavily built and more than capable of looking after himself, but he was beginning to recognise that some caution was necessary. Strangers didn't turn up at the houses of serving police officers without a reason.

'I spoke to your wife earlier,' the voice said from behind him.

Murrain stopped and turned. 'You're this Whitcomb character then?'

The man had emerged from the shadows and was now standing in the bottom of the drive, his features caught in the light of an adjacent streetlamp. He was tall and slim, with a gaunt face and slightly cadaverous features.

There was no response, so eventually Murrain went on, 'My wife made it clear she didn't want to talk to you. I'd like to make it clear that I don't want to talk to you either. Not until you go through the appropriate formal channels. Goodnight, Mr Whitcomb.'

He started to turn again. Then he heard Whitcomb say, 'It's about your gift, Mr Murrain.'

'My what?'

'Don't be coy, Mr Murrain. You know exactly what I'm talking about.'

'I've no idea what you're talking about. I've also no desire to talk with a complete stranger about anything. Goodnight, Mr Whitcomb.' This time he really did turn away. He made his way back to the house, rummaging for his house-keys as he did so. As he turned the key in the lock, he heard Whitcomb's voice, as clear as before. 'I just want a brief conversation, Mr Murrain.'

Murrain ignored him and stepped inside, locking the front door firmly behind him. 'Eloise?'

'Here.' She emerged from the living room, clutching her mobile phone. 'You're not going to believe this,' she said. 'But I've just had that Whitcomb guy on the phone again.'

'I believe it,' Murrain said. 'He's outside.'

'He's what?' Eloise blinked in incomprehension. 'What, outside here? You're kidding.'

'Wish I was. He seems very determined to speak to me.'

'Then he needs to go through the proper channels. If he's on the level, he shouldn't have any difficulty getting them to listen to him.'

'Which is one reason I suspect he's not who or what he says he is.'

'Do you think we should call it in?' Eloise said. 'Get whoever's on patrol to swing by. It might stop him bothering us again.'

'Last resort, I suppose,' Murrain said. 'But for the moment we're probably better off ignoring him. I'll check in a bit to see if there's still any sign of him. If he's still hanging about, we can call it in. He obviously knows who we are and what we do, so I wouldn't have thought he'd want to have to explain himself to a couple of bolshie uniforms.'

'You'd have thought so,' Eloise agreed. 'All a bit weird, though. Why's he insisting on this cloak and dagger approach?'

'If he's a spook, it's probably second nature. Maybe my first instinct was right and he really is a reporter trying a creative approach to getting an inside track.'

'Could be. Anyway, you must be exhausted. Do you want something to eat or drink?'

'Just something quick.'

'There's half a big pizza I didn't finish earlier, if that'll do.'

'Sounds perfect. That and an equally big glass of wine.'

'I'll stick the pizza back in to warm up. How's the enquiry going?' She and Murrain generally made a point of not discussing police business beyond this very general level.

'We're making progress. Slowly and not very surely, but we should get there eventually.' He followed her into the kitchen. 'How was your day?'

'Oh, you know. Meetings about meetings. Finance nitpicking on every aspect of the costs. Senior ranks challenging anything that's likely to inconvenience them personally.'

'The usual, then?'

'Pretty much.' Since her most recent promotion, Eloise was leading what was designated as the force's Change Management Unit. Its basic remit was to find ways of responding to the ever evolving challenges facing policing across the city, while also determining how this could be achieved in the face of ever-reducing funding. It was a continuing challenge, and the previous incumbent, a civilian member of the police staff who had been expensively headhunted from a major management consultancy, had lasted less than a year in the role. Impressively, in that short time he'd made more enemies across the force than Eloise had managed in her whole career. She'd already been working on various change projects and had built a reputation as a credible, fair and thoughtful operator. By the time the previous jobholder left, she'd been the obvious candidate for the role, or at least the only candidate prepared to take it.

So far, as far as Murrain could see, she'd done a characteristically excellent job. She'd made things happen, in a way that her predecessor had not, and she'd done so without incurring too much animosity across the force. That wasn't to say that everyone was happy with the proposed changes and their outcomes, but most recognised that they were necessary and that Eloise would at least try to manage the interests of all those involved in a fair and open way.

She seemed to thrive on it, too. Murrain poured both of them a glass of wine and watched as she busied herself putting the pizza back in the oven. She'd always had a sane approach to work, much more so than Murrain himself. She worked hard and she worked long hours when she needed to, but she made a point of not letting it become a habit. She had the enviable knack of being able to focus intensely on work while she was there, but switching off almost completely when she wasn't in the office or on call.

It was a quality that Murrain wished he shared. For him, work was always there, always lurking in the back of his head. Sometimes that could be useful. He'd often gain unexpected insights into cases at the most unlikely times, and not always as a result of his indefinable 'gift'. Almost without realising he was doing so, he'd mull over the issues while engaged in some other mundane task, and an idea or thought would suddenly pop unbidden into his brain. Once or twice, that process had even proved critical in the breaking of some investigation. Even so, Murrain would have welcomed the ability just to switch off completely in the way that Eloise could.

While he was waiting for the pizza to heat through, Murrain walked back into the living room, turned off the light, and pulled back the curtain to peer out at the front garden. There was no sign of anyone out there, although the trees and shrubbery were being tossed wildly by the still-rising wind. It was beginning to rain too, drops pelting heavily against the window, so it was difficult to imagine that Whitcomb would be still out there braving the elements.

'Are you worried about him?'

Murrain turned to see Eloise silhouetted in the doorway.

'Whitcomb? I'm not worried about him personally. Whoever he really is, he's not likely to be much more than a nuisance. But I'm a bit concerned about what might lie behind it.' He followed Eloise back into the kitchen. She topped up their wine while he retrieved the pizza from the oven. 'When he spoke to me outside, he mentioned my "gift". That made me uneasy.'

'It's not exactly a state secret.'

'It's not exactly common knowledge either. I'm not secretive about it, but I make a point of not talking about it. Mainly because I never know what to say.'

'But a lot of your colleagues are aware of it. At least as part of your reputation.'

People gossip about it. Some of them take the piss out of me, though usually only behind my back. Nobody takes it very seriously.'

'Joe does. And Paul too, though he'd never admit it.'

'Maybe. But they'd never talk to anyone outside the immediate team.'

'Even so, word's bound to get around. Maybe someone in the media thinks there's a story in it.'

'Christ, I hope not. That's the last thing I want plastered all over the media in the middle of a murder enquiry.' Murrain cut himself a slice of pizza and chewed it morosely. 'You don't really think it's likely to be that, do you? There's no real story there. It's not like I've ever made any claims for it as a detection aid.'

'It's given you some useful insights from time to time,' Eloise pointed out. 'Occasionally critical ones.'

'Maybe. But all it's ever done really is allow me to cut the odd corner or save some time. Importantly so, in a couple of cases, yes. But I've never used it as a substitute for straightforward detective work. I couldn't. It doesn't work like that.'

'I know. But they might not know that.'

'I can just see the headlines. "Psychic Cop". Jesus.'

'If he is a journalist, the fact that he's been trying to talk to you and me suggests he doesn't have much to go on. If he had the basis of a story, he'd be telling you that and asking you for your comments.'

'But suppose he does find someone who's prepared to talk to him. Someone in the force, I mean. There are a few people out there who wouldn't be sorry to see me humiliated by the tabloids.'

'Fewer than you think. I'm the one who makes enemies. Usually of the Chief Officers.' She took a sip of her wine. 'If that's the case, there's probably not much you can do about it. If you talk to Whitcomb, that'll only make it worse. However carefully you try to play it, he'll get some quotes he can twist out of context. Better just to keep your powder dry and, if something does appear, get Comms to respond and say it's nonsense.' She paused. 'Anyway, we don't even know that Whitcomb is a journalist.'

'What else would he be? If he really is a spook, why would he be interested in me? If it's something to do with one of our cases, surely he'd go through the formal channels. I might joke about how the security services behave, but this would be unnecessarily convoluted even for them.'

'I don't know. I just think we're best ignoring Whitcomb unless he starts to make a real pest of himself. If it gets to the point of harassment, we can take more formal action. My guess is he'll disappear back into the woodwork. Or, if he is genuine, he'll come to his senses and make an approach for whatever he's after through the proper channels.'

Murrain nodded. 'You're right, as ever. The whole thing just troubles me. It's the last thing I need right now.'

'What you probably need right now is another glass of wine and then an early night.'

'Okay. You're right about that as well.'

'How many years have we been married, Kenny? Have you not learnt by now that I'm always right?'

CHAPTER FIFTEEN

The storm had arrived overnight, and they'd woken to the sound of gale-force winds battering the house and fierce rain hammering against the windows. Joe Milton's house was a new-build on an estate in Sale. Looking back he wasn't even sure why they'd bought it. He suspected Gill hadn't been any more enthusiastic about the place than he was. They'd just drifted into it, just as they'd drifted into so many things. Just as they'd eventually drifted out of their relationship.

That seemed a long while ago now, though it was really only a couple of years. Gill was living apparently happily in Paris working for the OECD. They still had to sort out the ownership of the house, but neither of them were in any hurry now Milton had taken on sole responsibility for the mortgage. It was more than he could really afford just on his own salary, so he was intending to sell up before too long with the aim of repaying Gill her share of the value and moving somewhere smaller.

Now, he was waiting to see which way the dice would fall next. His relationship with Marie Donovan had progressed beyond friendship into something more serious. For the moment, he still wasn't sure how serious. He was conscious they'd spent the last few months dancing round the question. Milton was still on the rebound from what had been an amicable but, from his perspective, unexpected split. Donovan was a widow, her husband having died tragically young. He knew, without knowing any of the details, that she had a complicated history as a former undercover officer. The question was whether either of them was ready to step back into a long-term relationship.

Even so, they'd found themselves moving in that direction. A few casual dates had become regular get-togethers. She'd stayed at his place a few times, and he'd stayed at hers, whichever was most convenient for wherever they'd been out. That had gradually become something they both took for granted. The next step, he guessed, would be for them to move in together. The only question was whether it was a step they both wanted to take.

This morning had been typical. They've been out for a meal in some local pub and then spent the night at Milton's. Breakfast had been the usual hurried affair of a slice of toast and a hastily swallowed coffee, and then they'd hurried out to their separate cars to make the journey into the office. They'd more than once discussed the absurdity of this, but for the moment felt inclined to maintain the illusion that they were living separate lives.

'We should say something to Kenny,' Milton had said, but he recognised that, once he broached this openly, they were committing themselves to a future they still weren't fully sure of.

'I reckon Paul's already guessed,' Donovan said. 'He's been raising an eyebrow when we keep arriving at roughly the same time even though we're in separate cars.'

'Paul doesn't miss much,' Milton said. 'And what he does miss he's happy to make up.'

'Let's have a proper talk about it this evening. If we don't come clean, people are going to make up even more lurid rumours.'

So that was how they'd left it. Milton gave her a few minutes head start as he generally did when they stayed at his place and then set off after her. The rain was still hammering down, and the traffic was even worse than usual. He was only a few minutes into the slow trek to Stockport when his mobile rang. He took the call on the hands-free.

'Joe? It's Kenny. You on your way in?'

'Just set off. You're in early.'

'Keep waking up too early, and I can't think of anything better to do with the time other than come into the office. I need to get a life.'

'Don't we all? What can I do for you, anyway?'

'Can you take a detour on your way in? Last thing we need, but it looks like we've another body.'

'Whereabouts?'

'Bramhall. Just by Bramhall Green roundabout.'

It took Milton a moment to recall the traffic island in question, midway between Bramhall and Cheadle Hulme. 'Yes, I know the spot. Roughly, anyway.'

'Area around the roundabout's apparently been badly flooded this morning, so the roundabout itself and the surrounding roads are all closed. The body was spotted on the east side, on Bridge Lane. Not clear yet if it was washed up by the floods themselves or whether it's just been dumped there.'

'Dumped? So we're talking foul play?'

'Not much doubt about it. Apparently the victim was stabbed in the stomach. Not dissimilar to Gorman, funnily enough, though I'm not jumping to any conclusions.'

'Who found the body?'

'Some numpty of a motorist who thought it would be smart to remove the safety barriers so he could disregard the warnings and try to get through the flooding. In fairness to him, he made it about three meters into the water before he drowned his engine. At least we've got the satisfaction of knowing he got his feet very wet when he eventually climbed out of the car to see what a mess he'd made. The body was on the pavement, almost concealed in the water, but our man recognised it for what it was and called it in. We're in the process of protecting the scene, but Ferby's just arrived there. He gave me the good news about the stabbing. Just in case we were getting bored, he said.'

'Ferby needs a body to kick start the day.' Milton commented. 'Everyone else is happy with a coffee. Who else is on the scene?'

'The two uniforms originally called out, plus a couple of others who were available. They're sealing off the scene, no doubt under Ferby's watching eye. I was going to ask Bert or Will to join you, but they've both got witness interviews scheduled so I've asked Marie to meet you there.'

There was no suggestion of any subtext to Murrain's words. Milton wasn't sure if that was the result of Murrain's famously deadpan manner, or because he really didn't share Paul Wanstead's evident suspicions about their relationship. 'That's fine. I'll see her there, then. Anything else I should know about it?'

'Male. White. Bit older than Gorman, probably late forties. That's all from Ferby, so likely to be sound enough. Beyond that, nothing else so far.'

'Ferby's obviously slacking. I'll get on over there.'

'You'll need to loop round to avoid the floods. Probably down the A6 then back along Jacksons Lane.'

'I'll find it,' Milton said. 'I'll keep you posted once I get there.'

He ended the call and continued his journey, heading up on to the M60 so he could circle round to Bramhall. This is going to be a fun one, he thought. The rain showed no sign of abating, whipped hard against his windscreen by a buffeting strong wind. The wipers were struggling to cope, and visibility was deteriorating by the minute. Milton hugged the inside lane, keeping a decent distance from the car in front. As always, there were a few idiots racing past, hanging on the tail of the car in front as if engaged in some life or death chase.

Eventually, he reached the turn off that would enable him to make his way down through the centre of Stockport on to the A6. Milton always found himself confused by the twists and turns of the town, but eventually found his way through to the main road and headed south. The weather was getting even worse, but he was at least now travelling against the flow of traffic and was able to make a reasonable speed.

Even so, it was another ten minutes or so before he reached Hazel Grove and turned off in the direction of Bramhall, and another five minutes before he finally saw the pulse of blue lights ahead of him. There were a couple of marked cars, the CSIs' white van, and behind them the car he had last seen pulling out of his driveway some forty-five minutes before.

He pulled up behind Donovan's vehicle and took in the scene. A few yards ahead, the road disappeared into flood water. Two uniformed officers were cordoning off the scene with police tape. Marie Donovan stood with Neil Ferbrache under cover of a large golfing umbrella emblazoned with the name of a local car dealer, Ferbrache struggling to hold it steady against the force of the wind. Milton could see a dark shape in the water beyond where they were standing, which he presumed was the body.

He pulled up the hood of his heavy waterproof and climbed out into the rain. Donovan turned to greet him. 'You took your time,' she said, her face expressionless.

'Traffic was awful,' he said. 'You're that bit nearer.'

Her face revealed nothing, although Ferbrache was watching them with some curiosity. 'We're just trying to work out what to do.'

'It's a bloody mess.' Ferbrache raised his voice to make himself heard above the wind. 'I'm not even sure we can get the tents up in this wind. There's not much point in trying to protect the scene anyway. The water will have destroyed any evidence that might be there.' He paused. 'In any case, we don't really even know where the scene is.'

'Not here?'

'I don't think he was killed here. Not from the way he's dressed.'

'Go on.'

'Funnily enough, the MO seems very similar to our killing the other day. Whether that's significant or just coincidence, well, that's your job. But he was stabbed in the stomach, with very similar puncture wounds. And, like our guy the other morning, he was dressed in nightwear.'

'Nightwear?'

'Dressing gown, t-shirt, boxers. Bare feet, but there may have been slippers that were lost in the water.

Maybe it's become fashionable in Stockport to go out for a stroll in your nightwear,' Ferbrache said. 'Actually, from what I've seen in my local supermarket, that wouldn't surprise me. But I don't think that's the case here. My guess is that the body was washed down from somewhere in the Ladybrook.' He gestured over the road. 'The river's over there beyond the houses – well, it is normally – and it runs east to west. Given how full it must have been last night, my guess is that the body could have been carried some distance.' He turned and gestured behind them. 'So from anywhere in that kind of direction. There are houses up there that overlook the river at the rear. If, say, the body was dumped from one of the rear gardens, it could have ended up in the swollen water and been carried round to this point.'

Milton nodded. 'I presume we've no idea of the time of death yet?'

Ferbrache looked pointedly at where the body was still lying in the water. 'What do you reckon, Joe? You think I'm likely to have even the vaguest idea?'

'Sorry, Stupid question.'

Ferbrache grinned. 'Well, not entirely. I've had an initial look at the body. The doc'll have to confirm obviously, but I'd say it's unlikely to have been in the water for more than twelve hours. Which most likely means that death occurred sometime last night.' He paused. 'Unless of course the body had been lying somewhere for a day or two before being picked up as the water levels rose.' He shrugged. 'Best I can do, I'm afraid. Don't know if the doc'll be able to give you anything more definitive.'

'It's a start anyway,' Donovan said. 'So what's the plan?'

'Buggered if I know,' Ferbrache said. 'Unless you can do something about the weather.' He paused, and looked around. 'Okay, my feeling is that we should try to get the tent up over there.' He gestured to a spot on the other side of the road where there was a small parking area that offered some relative shelter and was clear of the flood waters. 'That'll at least give us somewhere to work. I'll get the body moved out of the water. Like I say, I can't see too much point in worrying about the scene itself. We can check out the immediate location once the water levels have receded, but I don't imagine there'll be anything useful there. Your first challenge will be to find out where the killing actually took place.'

'We should be able to narrow it down fairly easily,' Donovan said. 'We can check on when the waters started rising, so that should give us an idea of how far the body might have been carried. There must be a fairly limited number of options. Assuming that the body wasn't brought here from somewhere else to be dumped.'

'You think that's possible?'

'Anything's possible. But I think it's unlikely. The injuries look severe. There'd have been a lot of blood. My guess is that, if you were going to the trouble of moving the body, it would be to dump it somewhere it wouldn't be found. And that wouldn't be in the Ladybrook. But that's all supposition.' A sudden gust of wind caught the umbrella and Ferbrache struggled to hold it in place. 'We'd better get on. Doesn't look like the weather's going to improve any time soon.'

'You could do with some more resources down here,' Milton said. 'I'll get on to the office and get things organised. Anything else you need from us for the moment?'

'Not unless you can do something about the rain.'

'Above my pay grade, mate. Okay, we'll leave you to it for the moment, while we have a think about next steps.'

Ferbrache strode away, carrying the umbrella, to join the rest of his team in setting up shop in the relatively sheltered area over the road. Donovan grimaced and pulled up the hood of her waterproof. 'God, this is awful.'

'Forecast to continue for the rest of the day,' Milton said. 'Suspect the waters here are going to get even higher. Come on, let's head to the car and work out what we do next.'

Once they were safely sitting in the front seats of Milton's car, watching the rain pouring down the windscreen, Milton said, 'This is getting a bit silly, isn't it? I'm sure Ferby suspected something.'

Donovan took Milton's hand. 'I don't see why he should. And it doesn't really matter if he did. It's not as if we've anything to hide.'

'So why are we hiding it?'

Donovan was silent for a moment. 'I'm not sure, to be honest. I suppose at first I just wanted to be sure we were doing the right thing. You know my history, or some of it at least—'

'I don't care about your history.'

'I know that. That's not what I meant. You're the first decent man I've met since Liam, and I didn't exactly treat him well.' Liam had been her first husband. 'I don't want to end up treating you as badly.'

'From what you've told me, you weren't going through the easiest of times.'

'That's a bit of an understatement. But it doesn't excuse some of the things I did, even if it helps to explain them. I just wanted to make sure I wasn't going to make the same mistakes. I don't want to hurt you.'

'You're a different person now.'

'I genuinely think I am, in many ways. I've been through a lot, one way or another, and I'd like to think I'd learnt from it. But who knows? Maybe we can't help being the people we are.'

'So? Where does that leave us?'

'I want to give it a go. You and me. A serious go. If you're up for it.'

'Christ, I'm more than up for it.'

'In that case, let's go for it. Properly, I mean. You need to sell your house. So do it. Move in with me. My place is plenty big enough for us. That would mean you could pay Gill what you owe her, and we'd still have a few quid behind us.'

He laughed. 'That sounds very pragmatic.'

'Well, if we're going to do this, we might as well be sensible about it. But what I mean is, I want us to be together.' She leaned forward and kissed him unexpectedly on the lips. 'Openly, I mean.'

Milton found himself glancing over his shoulder to see if Ferbrache or any of the uniforms were watching them, though he knew the chances were remote. 'Okay,' he said. 'Let's do it.'

'There we go. One problem solved,' Donovan said. 'Now all we have to worry about is this potential double murder.'

CHAPTER SIXTEEN

Murrain knew he couldn't really justify this. He was Senior Investigating Officer on the enquiry. His job was to sit back in the office and co-ordinate everything, making sure, with Wanstead's help, that every detail was accounted for, keeping an eye on the overall investigative strategy, making sure they were focusing on the right priorities, allocating resources appropriately. All the stuff, in short, that mostly bored him rigid.

What he wasn't supposed to be doing was accompanying a junior member of the team on what was likely to be nothing more than a routine interview.

The original plan had been for Marie Donovan and Bert Wallace to interview Bernard Craigie, Andrew Gorman's former partner. It hadn't taken them long to track him down. He was a lecturer in history at Manchester Metropolitan University, and Wallace had called him first thing that morning to arrange the meeting. She'd left a message on his office voicemail to call her back, which he'd done within the hour.

'This must be about Andy,' he'd said. Gorman's name had been released to the media that morning with his brother's permission.

'I'm afraid so.'

'I hadn't seen him for a few months but it's still a huge shock. Especially the circumstances.'

'I'm very sorry. And I'm sorry we have to bother you at a time like this.'

'You've got your jobs to do, and I'm only too glad to help you if I can.'

Wallace had arranged to meet him later that morning at the university. By that stage, it was becoming clear that Marie Donovan would be caught up with the second murder enquiry for some time. In her absence, Murrain had volunteered to accompany Wallace to the interview.

He'd told Wallace he just felt like a break from the bureaucracy, get himself out of the office. All of that was true as far as it went, but he wasn't sure he'd really fooled her. As Eloise had pointed out, most of his colleagues were fully aware of his distinctive 'gift', even if most of them rarely talked about it.

When Wallace had approached him to ask about the interview with Bernard Craigie, he'd felt something as she'd been talking. As always, it was nothing he could pin down. On this occasion, it was little more than a mental tremor somewhere in the back of his head, a mild alarm bell that suggested a potential focus of interest. But it was enough to make him want to meet this Bernard Craigie face to face.

Murrain had driven them into the city centre, and they'd parked in one of the multi-storeys close by the university. Now, they were waiting in the reception area of one of the university buildings, watching as fresh-faced students paraded past them.

'Makes me feel old,' Wallace said.

'How do you think it makes me feel? Some of these kids look young enough to be my grandchildren.' Murrain was silent long enough for Wallace to recall that Murrain was now never likely to be a grandfather. 'They look as if they're having a good time, though.'

'Don't suppose you've too many worries at that age,' Wallace said. 'Though I don't recall it exactly feeling like that.'

'It never feels like that at the time, does it?' Murrain said. Then he nodded towards a figure apparently approaching through the streams of students. 'Looks like our man.'

'DS Wallace?' The man blinked at them through thick glasses. He was tall and thin, with swept-back fair hair beginning to recede from his forehead. He carried with him a mild air of disorganisation, though Murrain noted that he'd appeared precisely on time. 'I'm Bernard Craigie.'

'DS Wallace.' She reached out to shake his hand. 'This is my colleague, DCI Murrain.'

'Come through. I've booked us a small meeting room down here. I have to share an office so it's not ideal for anything of this nature.'

He led them to the security barriers, gesturing for the receptionist to allow them through, and took them down a corridor to a suite of rooms evidently used for seminars and tutorials. He hesitated for a moment, peering at the room numbering, then opened the door of one of the smaller rooms. 'This one. I think.'

The room's furnishing was basic, comprising little but a central table, four chairs and a small side table with a telephone. The single window looked out over a car park at the rear. 'Meeting rooms are like gold dust in this place. Can I get you a coffee? There's a machine just round the corner.'

Murrain registered that Craigie was talking too quickly, clearly anxious about the impending conversation. That might be significant, but most likely it was nothing more than the usual nervousness people felt at talking to the police. There might be benefit in giving Craigie a few more moments to calm his nerves. 'If it's no trouble,' he said, 'I wouldn't mind one. Just milk please.'

Wallace exchanged a look with Murrain. 'Just black for me, please.'

Craigie nodded. 'Back in a sec, then.'

He exited the room, and Murrain nodded to Wallace. 'Bit nervous.'

'His ex-partner's been brutally murdered,' Wallace said. 'It must have been a shock, even if they were no longer together.'

'Be useful to know a bit more about the relationship. Wonder how long they were together.' Murrain had asked Wallace to lead the interview. He knew that she was more than capable of doing a good job, and he wanted to be able to focus on his own responses in Craigie's presence. The sensations he experienced were sometimes so subtle as to be almost imperceptible, and it was always difficult to determine their significance.

Craigie reappeared after a few moments, balancing three steaming cardboard cups. 'There,' he said, depositing them carefully on the table. 'Can't promise anything except that they'll be wet and warm.'

'All I ask for is a dose of caffeine,' Wallace said. 'Thanks.'

The task of fetching the coffees seemed to have relaxed Craigie a little. He took a sip of his own coffee and said, 'It was all a bit of a shock, I must say. I could hardly believe it when I heard it on the news. Thought it must have been a different Andrew Gorman at first.'

'I'm very sorry, Dr Craigie. We very much appreciate you agreeing to see us at what must be a difficult time for you.'

'Nobody deserves that kind of fate, but Andy probably deserved it even less than most people. He was a very gentle soul.' He paused. 'The radio report didn't give very much information. My impression was he tried to stop an intruder?'

'That's our working assumption at the moment,' Wallace said. 'But we're not taking anything for granted. That's one reason why we want to find out more about Mr Gorman's background.'

'If you think someone might have targeted Andy for some reason, I'm sure you couldn't be more wrong. He wasn't that sort of person.'

Even as Murrain was wondering what that sort of person might be, he felt the first mental ripple. It was little more than the softest of tremors in his mind, but he'd no doubt it was there. It suggested some significance to what Craigie had said, even if Craigie himself had been unconscious of it.

'In my experience,' Murrain said, 'the most unexpected people can make enemies. Sometimes without even realising it.'

'Anything's possible, I suppose.'

'If it's not too intrusive, Dr Craigie, I wonder if you could tell us a little about your relationship with Mr Gorman,' Wallace said.

'I hope you don't think I had anything to do with his death.'

'We're just trying to gain a fuller picture of Mr Gorman. Anything that helps us understand his background could potentially be relevant to our enquiry.'

'No, of course. I understand. You'll appreciate I'm still struggling to get my head around what's happened to him.' Craigie paused for a moment. 'We split up about six months ago. We'd been together for a couple of years. We got on well enough, and we enjoyed each other's company. That would have been enough for me, to be honest, but I'm not sure it was quite enough for Andy.'

Wallace momentarily caught Murrain's eye, signalling that she intended to follow this up. 'How do you mean?'

Craigie shifted awkwardly in his seat. 'I'm not exactly sure how to put it, without giving you the wrong impression. Basically, all I wanted was someone I could spend time with. I'm happy to live a pretty quiet life. I just want to sit in and read a book or watch TV, maybe go out for a meal or drink now and again. But I prefer not to do it alone.'

'And that was the nature of your relationship with Mr Gorman?'

'Makes me sound really middle-aged, doesn't it? It wasn't quite like that. We did a lot of different stuff together. But I was much more of a domestic creature than Andy was. My ideal night is to sit and read a book, with some decent food and a glass of wine. He preferred to be out on the town.'

'That's why you split up?'

'In the end, yes. We kept talking about moving in together, but we never actually got around to doing it, which probably tells you something. We got on really well when we were together, which helped disguise the differences. But really we just wanted different things. I think we'd both known it for some time, but it took us a while to acknowledge it.'

'Was there something specific that brought it to a head?' Wallace asked.

'You mean was he seeing someone else? No, nothing like that. We just finally managed to bring ourselves to talk about it one day. If I'm honest, Andy forced us to talk about it. I'd probably have kept on putting it off. But we both knew he was right.'

'Was it an amicable split?' Murrain asked.

'I wasn't left feeling murderous towards him, if that's what you're asking. No, it was perfectly amicable. We remained good friends. We went out for the odd beer or bite to eat.'

Murrain had wondered if he might experience some sensation during this exchange, indicating perhaps that Craigie wasn't telling the whole truth. But there had been nothing. That didn't necessarily mean that Craigie was being honest, but Murrain was left with no immediate reason to doubt it.

'When did you last see him?' Wallace asked.

'Three or four weeks ago, I think. Hang on.' Craigie reached into his pocket and pulled out his phone. 'I put it in the diary at the time.' He spent a moment flicking back through the calendar then said, 'The 24th. So just over three weeks ago. We went for a couple of beers in town after work.'

'How did he seem?' Murrain asked. As Craigie had given the date of the meeting, Murrain had finally felt something more – that same familiar mental juddering in the back of his head. Slightly stronger, he thought. This time also with something close to an image, an unfocussed scene that flickered momentarily behind his eyes, too brief to be discernible. He could sense Craigie hesitating before giving his response to this apparently innocuous question.

'Looking back, I think he didn't seem quite his usual self.' Craigie paused. 'But it changes things, knowing what's happened.'

Murrain understood that only too well. It was one of the common problems they had in taking witness statements. People misremembered events, their perceptions coloured by their knowledge of how things turned out. If your team wins a football match, you focus on the moments they played well in the game and downplay the times they played badly. If we know someone's been murdered, everything they said or did gains a new significance.

Eventually Craigie went on, 'But it definitely struck me, even at the time. He seemed anxious, jittery. As if something was troubling him.'

'He didn't give you any indication what that might have been?'

'Not at all. He clearly didn't want to talk about it. And I couldn't bring myself to ask him outright. I wish I had now. But he'd just have denied it. He could be very stubborn when he wanted.'

'And you've no idea of what might have been troubling him?'

'Not really.'

Not really, Murrain thought. The answer you give when you're trying to avoid just saying 'Yes'. He'd felt the same sensation again at the moment, the patched-through message not quite loud enough to be audible. 'Can I ask you about Mr Gorman's occupation?'

Craigie smiled. 'I was wondering how long it would take you to get round to that. You're presumably expecting me to disapprove of it. Me being an academic and all.'

'Did you?'

'Initially, yes. I thought it was nonsense. When he first told me, I struggled to believe it. It didn't really seem to tie in with the kind of man he was.'

'In what way?' Wallace asked.

'He always came across as Mr Rational. He was completely down to earth in most things. He was normally sceptical about anything that smacked of the paranormal.'

'But he believed in astrology?'

'To be honest, I'm not sure he really did. He did all the usual chart paraphernalia, and he'd learnt all the disciplines. But I was never sure how seriously he took all that stuff.'

Murrain raised an eyebrow. 'His clients presumably took it seriously?'

'Yes, and Andy never shortchanged them. He'd do the charts in what I presume is the orthodox way, and he'd give them advice or information based on the outcomes. If you believe astrology works, then you got what you paid for. It's just that I was never entirely convinced Andy believed it himself.' He laughed. 'He wrote the reports skilfully, though. Gave the client enough to satisfy them without ever committing himself too far.'

'You didn't disapprove of that?'

'I might have been wrong. He was never openly sceptical. But the way he talked about that side of his work made me suspect he didn't take it as seriously as he claimed. I think he felt differently about the other work he did.'

'Other work?'

'His so-called premium clients. He gave them a different kind of service.'

'We're still talking about astrology clients?'

'Ostensibly, yes.'

'Ostensibly?' Wallace said.

'He went through all the same motions with this group. Produced the charts and all that stuff. But he seemed to do something more. I never knew or understood what, and it wasn't something he ever really wanted to talk to me about. But he gave this group of clients more than just clever writing. He believed he was giving them insights that they couldn't have gained any other way.'

Murrain had read Wallace's summary of the previous interview with Gorman's brother, and was aware that the brother had said something similar. 'But these insights, as you call them, weren't from his astrological work?'

'I don't think so. They seemed to come from somewhere inside Andy himself. From the little he told me, they could be remarkably accurate. Or at least Andy thought so.'

'You didn't believe it?'

'I don't generally believe that kind of thing. Magical powers. Telepathy. Second sight. Whatever you want to call it.'

'Second sight?' Once again, Murrain could feel that odd mental stirring in the back of his brain.

'It seemed to be something like that. As I say, I never really discussed it with him. He probably thought I'd just mock him.'

Murrain made a mental note to examine some of the reports that Gorman had prepared for his so-called 'premium' clients. Whatever the truth of Gorman's gifts, it sounded as if Gorman himself had believed in them.

'You said that Mr Gorman was less of a domestic creature than you,' Wallace said. 'Do you know if he was in a new relationship?'

'Not that I'm aware of,' Craigie said. 'Although I'm perhaps the last person he might want to tell about any development of that kind. He certainly didn't give me that impression when we last met. In all honesty, Andy was more the "good time" type, happier playing the field than settling down.'

'Do you know what kind of places he might have frequented?' Wallace asked.

'If you mean gay clubs and the like, there are one or two places we used to go to. Not really my scene, but Andy seemed relatively happy there. I can dig you out details if that would help.'

'Please,' Wallace said. 'It may well be a dead end, but it's one we have to check out. What about other friends? Was there anyone else he was particularly close to.'

'Again, not that I'm aware of. He just wasn't good at all the friendship stuff. It required too much investment on his part. Investment of time. Investment of emotion. He preferred to keep things at a more superficial level. That was just the way he was.'

'We have to ask this,' Wallace said, 'but do you know of anybody who might have wanted to harm Mr Gorman.'

'I can't imagine it. He was a decent guy, on the whole. He could be a bit cavalier in the way he behaved, and some people might have found him infuriating.' It was clear from Craigie's tone that he'd been one of those people. 'But he was also the kind of person you can't help liking, sometimes despite the way they've behaved. There was no malice in him. Quite a lot of thoughtlessness at times, but no malice. So, I can't really imagine anyone would have any serious reason for wanting to harm him.'

'I'm not sure how to phrase this,' Wallace said, tentatively, 'but did he have a lot of casual encounters?'

'One night stands, you mean? I don't know really. He wasn't really the promiscuous type. But equally he wasn't really looking for any kind of long-term relationship, so I imagine there'd have been a few brief liaisons, as it were. Are you thinking his killer might be someone he'd brought back?'

'It's a possibility we have to consider,' Wallace said blandly.

'It just seems unbelievable to me. That Andy should have died like that. I'm sure you know what you're doing, but it seems to me to be overwhelmingly likely that he just happened to be in the wrong place at the wrong time.'

Murrain nodded. 'We understand that, and that's the major focus of our investigation. But we can't discount other possibilities.'

'Yes, of course. And I suppose it is a possibility. Andy was far from the reckless kind, but you can't exactly vet everyone you bring back. I can't really help you with any names, though. I've no idea who Andy might have been seeing since we split up. Not something I was ever inclined to enquire into.'

'Do you know of anyone else we should be talking to?' Wallace asked. 'Other family members? Other friends?'

'Not really, I'm afraid. As far as I'm aware, the only family Andy had was his brother. He wasn't the type for close friends. As I discovered to my cost.'

Murrain felt it more strongly then. As if something was almost coalescing in front of him, some image he couldn't quite interpret, frustratingly close to emerging into focus before dissolving back into nothing. 'Why do you say that?'

'He wasn't keen on commitment. The thought of being in a long term relationship seemed to disturb him somehow. But it went further than that. He was a very private individual. There were things he didn't want to share.'

'What kind of things?'

'I don't exactly know, obviously. But there were aspects of his life he kept compartmentalised. Things he wasn't prepared to talk about. Some of it was to do with whatever he drew on to prepare those "premium" reports. He never wanted to talk about that. If I tried to discuss it, he just changed the subject or clammed up. And he never really wanted to talk about his past. Anything more than superficial details, anyway.'

'His brother told us a little about it,' Murrain said.

'I know he had a falling out with his father about his sexuality,' Craigie said. 'And he'd had some mental health issues. But that's about all I know. I used to try to talk to him about it, because I had the sense there were things he hadn't fully resolved.' Craigie shrugged. 'I never really knew him. Not properly. He preferred it that way. So, no, as far as I know he didn't have any other close friends.'

'Thank you, Dr Craigie. That's really been most helpful,' Wallace said. She looked over at Murrain. 'Do you have any further questions, sir?'

Murrain felt as if there was something more he wanted or needed to ask, but he had no idea what it might be. 'I think that's all for the moment. We're grateful for your time, Dr Craigie.'

'I'm not sure I've been terribly useful. But I've told you what I know.'

'Thank you,' Wallace said. 'I don't know if we'll need to talk to you again. Obviously that depends on the direction our investigations take. If anything else occurs to you that you think might be useful to us, please do give me a call.' She handed over one of her business cards.

Craigie escorted them back down to the reception area. Outside, the rain was hammering down harder than ever, the skies leaden above the city. 'Manchester, eh? I should have stayed in Leeds. Always drier that side of the Pennines.'

'Is that where you're from?' Murrain asked. As Craigie had spoken, he'd experienced another tremor, another mild electric shock to the brain.

'Down south, originally,' Craigie said. 'But I taught in Leeds until a couple of years ago.' He seemed to hesitate, and Murrain had the impression that he was wondering whether to say more. 'That was where I met Andy, in fact. A good few years ago now. When he was an undergraduate. I was doing my PhD there.' He laughed. 'Then I didn't see him for years. Happened to run into him when I moved over here. Funny how things turn out.'

Murrain wasn't sure whether Craigie was referring to the coincidence of meeting Gorman in Manchester or to what had happened subsequently. 'Life's full of twists and turns. Thanks again for your time, Dr Craigie.'

Murrain and Wallace remained in the reception for a few minutes after Craigie had left them, in the vain hope that the rain might lessen before they had to make a dash for the car.

'What did you make of that?' Murrain asked.

'I'm not sure exactly. Everyone seems very keen we should treat Gorman's death as some sort of opportunist killing, rather than anything to do with Gorman himself.'

'It's still the most likely explanation,' Murrain said. 'But I know what you mean. I had the sense that both the brother and Craigie were trying to steer us away from delving too deeply into Gorman's background or private life. Craigie was very keen to let us know how little he knew about it.'

'Can I ask…?' Wallace said hesitantly.

'Whether my spider sense was tingling, as Joe would put it? Yes, it was. At various points.' He shifted awkwardly on his feet, feeling uncomfortable as he always did when discussing this topic. 'Whether it meant anything, who knows? But it made me feel that Gorman's relationship with Craigie is in some way significant. Leeds, too. That felt important somehow.' He shrugged. 'But it might all be nonsense, obviously. It doesn't change anything in terms of the investigation.' As he spoke these words, he wondered if this was true. He wouldn't say anything to the rest of the team and he certainly wouldn't change the formal priorities of the enquiry. But, though he was reluctant to admit it even to himself, he recognised that something had shifted. He had no idea what his brain was telling him, but he knew it was significant. He couldn't disregard it. Even if it changed nothing else, it would change his own attitudes.

It might well be that Gorman's death was opportunistic, or at least partly so. But Murrain was becoming increasingly convinced it was not simply random. There was something in Gorman's background or his private life, perhaps something linked with Craigie or Gorman's brother, that was pertinent to their investigation. It was little more than a hunch, maybe based more on the familiar copper's instinct than his own unique gifts, but he couldn't disregard it.

That rain's showing no sign of lessening,' Wallace said. 'I reckon we're just going to have to run for it.'

'Fine by me,' Murrain said. 'Nobody ever said this job was going to be easy. Especially not in Manchester.'

CHAPTER SEVENTEEN

'Mum?'

Donna Fenwick stood in the hallway and looked around her. She'd held on to her keys to the house from the days when she'd lived here, and was accustomed to letting herself in when she came to visit. Her mother didn't mind as long as Donna never turned up unexpectedly. Donna couldn't imagine what she might interrupt if she arrived without warning, but that was her mother's business.

In any case, it was an easy enough condition to abide by. She usually came over at pre-arranged times, as today. If she had reason to call at other times – once or twice she'd just found herself in the area and thought she ought to pop in – she just phoned her mother and asked if it was okay to visit. To date, her mother had never said no.

Today, she'd been surprised not to find her mother in the living room or kitchen. These days, Irene spent the majority of her time down here. Although she still notionally worked in her office upstairs, she'd bring her laptop downstairs and sit at the dining table, tapping away while the television played at low volume across the room. Donna had wondered whether her mother felt uncomfortable spending time in the room opposite where Gordon used to work. It was yet another subject her mother would never acknowledge, much less discuss.

'Mum?' she called again.

'Up here.' Her mother's voice was coming from somewhere upstairs.

Donna made her way up. The door of Irene's office was open, but there was no sign of her inside. 'Mum?'

'I'm in Gordon's study.'

Irene's voice sounded odd, slightly raw and strained as if she'd been shouting. Or perhaps crying. Donna pushed open the door of the study and peered inside.

The sight that met her eyes left her aghast. The last time she'd been in this room, when she'd been conducting her informal inventory of her mother's possessions, it had looked poignant and slightly neglected. Now it was reduced to chaos. Her father's books were scattered across the carpet, as if dragged off the shelves. The drawers of his desk and filing cabinets were pulled open, and papers and files had been scattered across the floor. The whole room had been subjected to what appeared to be systematic vandalism. Irene was sitting in the middle of the chaos, her back to the door.

Donna's first thought was that her mother was responsible for this, that it had been some kind of response to her impending move. But as Irene turned to face her, Donna saw the shock etched on her mother's face.

'Why would someone do this?'

'I don't understand,' Donna said. 'What's happened?'

'It was this morning,' Irene said. 'I was out for a couple of hours. One of my meetings. When I came back, I came upstairs to get a book I wanted. I saw the door of your father's study was open. I was sure I'd left it closed – I almost always do – so I came in to check and...' She trailed off.

It took Donna a few moments to absorb this. 'You mean someone broke in?'

Her mother stared at her. 'Well, obviously. How else do you think this happened?'

'I…' Donna moved to sit on the floor beside her mother, putting her arm round Irene's shoulders. 'I'm sorry, mum. I'm just trying to take it in. What about the rest of the house? Has anything been taken?'

'I don't know. I've not had chance to look yet. I was just so devastated by this.'

'I'll go and have a quick look. We need to call the police.'

'Can I leave that to you, love? I'm not sure I feel up to talking rationally at the moment.'

'Are you okay?'

'It's a shock. But I'll survive.'

Donna made her way back out on to the landing, and glanced briefly into Irene's office. As far as she could see, it looked undisturbed. She frowned, and then walked downstairs to her mother's bedroom. Again, it appeared not to have been touched.

She hurried down to the ground floor and quickly checked the living room, dining room and kitchen. The back door was slightly ajar, though from her superficial examination it looked undamaged. She assumed that the intruder had somehow been able to force open the single lock without damaging it or the door itself. Donna had worried previously that this rear door was vulnerable to a break-in, although her parents had always ignored her advice.

It was clear that her mother was right, that someone had broken in and ransacked her father's former study. The bigger and odder question was why they had only targeted that single room. As far as she was aware, there had been nothing of value in the study. Nothing more, in fact, than her father's old books and papers.

If you were looking for valuables, she thought, surely you'd look first in the living room and the bedrooms. As far as she was aware, her parents had had few items of substantial value, other than one or two items of jewellery Irene kept in a locked cabinet in her bedroom. From her brief survey of the room, that appeared to have been left untouched.

Donna pulled out her phone and dialled the police enquiry number. It took her just a few moments to explain the situation to the call-handler, and she was advised that an officer would visit later in the day. Donna had made a point of explaining that only one upstairs room had been affected, but the call-handler had seemed uninterested.

She ended the call and made her way back upstairs. Her mother was still sitting where Donna had left her, surrounded by the scattered books and files. She looked up as Donna entered the room. 'How does it look?'

Donna lowered herself back on to the floor beside her mother. 'I've called the police. They're sending someone round later.'

Her mother gave a cynical laugh. 'How much later?'

'They didn't say. I didn't get the impression it was a priority. They just don't have the resources to deal with this kind of thing. It's small beer to them.'

'It's devastating to me,' Irene said. 'I mean, look at this. All your father's stuff. Why would anyone do this?'

'I can't begin to imagine.' Donna paused. 'As far as I can see, nothing else has been touched.'

Her mother looked up. 'Really?'

'You might spot something I've missed, but from a quick look all the other rooms look undisturbed.'

'What about my jewellery?'

'I'll go and double-check, but as far as I can see the cabinet hadn't been opened.'

'But why would they just come in here?'

'Maybe they were interrupted. Perhaps they heard your car coming back and just legged it.'

'They must have been quick,' Irene said. 'I didn't hear anything when I opened the front door. But why would they start up here? I mean, they look as if they've been pretty thorough in messing up this room. Why not start downstairs?'

'I don't know,' Donna acknowledged. 'It looks as if they got in through the back door. It's been forced open. So I don't know why they'd have then headed up here first. Maybe they just thought there'd be more chance of finding something valuable.'

'Maybe.' Irene sounded doubtful. 'But why would they be so thorough? They seem to have gone through everything systematically. All the files. All the papers. All the books pulled on to the floor. Why would you do that? I mean, once you open those filing cabinets, it must be obvious there's nothing in there but papers.'

'Maybe it's the kind of place where people usually hide valuables. I don't know. It's a bit weird.'

'I should tidy it all up.'

'You should probably leave it till the police have been. They'll probably want to see it as it is. And there might be fingerprints or other evidence.'

'Yes, you're right. I'm not thinking straight.'

'Let's go downstairs and make a cup of tea. It's been a shock for you.'

Donna helped her mother climb slowly to her feet. 'I still don't understand why you'd do this,' Irene said. 'It's as if they just wanted to wreck the place.'

It didn't look quite like that to Donna. Her impression was that her mother's previous words had been more accurate. That they had gone through the room systematically, as if they'd been looking for something. But she couldn't begin to imagine what anyone would want with anything in her father's posthumous papers. 'Does anything seem to be missing?'

Her mother looked slightly bewildered. 'Not that I can tell. But I wouldn't really know. Your father's papers were always a bit chaotic. He said he'd tidy them up and get rid of anything he didn't want, but he never really got round to it.' She gave Donna a weak smile. 'At least, whoever did this hasn't messed up a rigorous filing system.'

'They might even have improved it,' Donna laughed. The initial shock of seeing her mother in the middle of that ransacked room was beginning to wear off, and she was able to consider the matter more rationally. At least, her mother hadn't been deprived of anything valuable, and maybe this incident would help persuade Irene it was time to move on from this place.

'Come on. Let's go and get that cup of tea.' She led Irene across to the door, then stopped and peered back at the room. She still felt that whoever had done this had been looking for something. But she couldn't begin to imagine what.

CHAPTER EIGHTEEN

Murrain narrowed his eyes and leaned back in his office chair. They were sitting in a corner of the MIR, having a quick catch-up after Milton had completed the afternoon briefing with the rest of the team. Murrain was a large man and the chair creaked alarmingly under his weight. 'So what do we think? Are these killings linked?'

'I don't think we can discount the possibility,' Joe Milton said. 'If that helps.'

'Not much.'

Milton smiled. 'From what we know so far, the MOs are remarkably similar. Stabbings in the stomach with an at least broadly equivalent sharp instrument. Both victims were in nightwear, suggesting that they'd been disturbed at home.'

'We still don't have an ID for the second victim?'

'Not yet, but we're optimistic we'll get one soon. Our assumption is that the body was carried by the flood waters to the spot where it was discovered. If that's the case, it can't have come far.'

'No-one's been reported missing?'

'We're keeping an eye on that, but nothing so far. We've got officers doing door-to-doors in the relevant areas, so fingers crossed we'll identify him before long.'

Murrain was stretched almost horizontal on his chair, his eyes nearly closed. 'If the two cases are connected, it rather blows the "opportunistic killing" theory out of the window.' As if suddenly waking up, he sat forward, his eyes wide open.

'Are you okay?' Milton said.

Murrain shook his head. 'It hit me then. Suddenly. Like a bloody electric shock. And I saw something…' He was silent for a long moment, thinking. 'Whitcomb,' he said, finally.

'What?'

Murrain blinked. 'Nothing. Just thinking out loud. But I'm increasingly coming to the view that Gorman's death wasn't just random. It's nothing more than a hunch, so we shouldn't stop following up that line. But we also need to be looking at Gorman more closely. Have we got the stuff off his laptop yet?'

'Getting there. There's some stuff on there that's pretty well protected. The IT people aren't sure they're going to be able to get at it.'

Murrain tensed again, as though someone had passed a mild electric shock through his bulky body. 'Tell them to keep at it. If there is anything significant on Gorman's computer, that's where it's likely to be. Have we identified any other contacts of Gorman's?'

'There are a number of e-mails we're following up. One or two of them look like people Gorman might have met for dates. The others mainly look like professional contacts or clients from the astrology stuff. We're tracking them all down and making contact, although it's been slow going in some cases. We'll interview any that look as if they might be useful.'

'I take it we're following up all our usual chums in the house-breaking fraternity?'

'We are, but no joy in that direction so far. To be honest, with maybe one or two exceptions, I don't see any of them as potential killers. Not even if they were panicking. But I suppose you never know what people are capable of.'

Murrain was about to offer a response when he registered that Will Sparrow was hovering a yard or two behind Milton, clearly eager to catch their eyes. 'Will. You look like a man bearing news.'

'It's the killing in Bramhall. We think we might have identified the victim.'

Milton gestured for Sparrow to take a seat. 'Go on.'

'We've been checking out the various roads that adjoin or back on to the flooded area. We spoke to a woman in one of the houses who's just arrived back after a few days away on business. She'd been trying to contact her husband for the last day or two, but there was no answer from his mobile. She'd thought at first there must be some problem with the phone but had started to get worried so asked one of her friends to go round yesterday and check at the house, but again no answer. She'd tried phoning round various other friends and family, but no-one had heard from him. So eventually she cut short her trip and headed home.'

Murrain exchanged a glance with Milton. 'And?'

'When she got back to the house, she found the back door had been left open. There was no sign of her husband. She found his phone sitting on the table by their bed, switched on with endless missed calls from her.'

'Sounds like it could well be our man,' Milton said.

'Eerily similar to Gorman's circumstances,' Murrain added. 'Though this time the phone's not gone missing.'

'How have things been left with her?' Milton said to Sparrow.

'The uniform's still with her. Has told her not to touch anything else till we get there.'

'I'd better get over there,' Milton said. 'We need to get the house sealed off as a potential crime scene. First thing is to confirm that this guy really is our victim. I'll get some photos from Ferby. The body wasn't in a condition to show the widow, if that's what she is, but if she's got any photos of her husband I'll be able to compare them. But it seems probable. Do we have their names?' he asked Sparrow.

'The wife's called Judy Clayburn. The husband's called Gareth.' Sparrow paused. 'There's one other thing. I don't know if it's relevant or not.'

Murrain stiffened. It had hit him again, this time like a spasm in his forehead, like the first foretaste of a migraine. Another image. A face, a half-familiar face, that dissolved before he could grasp its contours. 'Go on.'

'I was thinking about our first victim,' Sparrow said. 'The astrologer.'

'And?'

'Well, it just seemed a coincidence. I mean, it's not exactly the same, but it's the same ballpark.'

'You've lost us, Will,' Milton said. 'What's the same ballpark?'

'What this Gareth Clayburn does for a living. He works for Justin Bannerman.'

Murrain was feeling increasingly baffled, his brain still buzzing from the previous sensations. 'Who's Justin Bannerman?'

'He's on TV sometimes,' Milton said. 'He's a modern-day Doris Stokes. A spiritualist. A medium. Communes with the dead. That sort of thing.' He looked at Sparrow. 'It's an interesting coincidence, certainly.'

Murrain nodded, his brain already trying to recall and collate what it had experienced. 'Isn't it just? I'll come with you to see this Judy Clayburn. She sounds as if she might be well worth meeting.'

CHAPTER NINETEEN

Geoff Nolan stopped outside the door of the office and listened. He hadn't intended to eavesdrop, but it was impossible to ignore the raised voices inside. It didn't seem an appropriate moment to intrude, so he found himself hesitating.

'So where the hell is he?' Nolan recognised the voice as Justin Bannerman's.

'I don't know. I'm not his bloody keeper.' The second voice was unknown to Nolan, presumably one of Bannerman's team.

For a moment, Nolan wondered if he might be the subject of the argument. He looked at the watch. He wasn't actually due here for another ten minutes. It was possible that Bannerman might resent Nolan's presence, but he could hardly complain about him not being there.

'Somebody needs to be,' Bannerman went on. 'I assume you've tried to contact him?'

'Of course I've bloody tried to contact him. What do you think I've been doing for the last forty-eight hours? No response on his mobile. I even went round to his house. There seemed to be a couple of lights on, but I stood there ringing his doorbell and hammering on his door for the best part of fifteen minutes. Nothing.'

'So where the hell is he?' Bannerman said again.

'It's not like him,' the other speaker said. 'I mean, he can be difficult because that's the kind of guy he is, but he's normally reliable. He wouldn't just not turn up and not phone in.'

'Except that's exactly what he has done,' Bannerman said.

Nolan hesitated a second longer, then decided he couldn't just hang around outside the office. Deliberately fumbling with the handle to announce his arrival, he pushed open the door.

Bannerman and the other speaker – an eager-looking young man in his mid-twenties – were standing in the centre of the office, clearly surprised by Nolan's appearance. Bannerman regained his poise almost immediately, and turned to greet Nolan with a smile. 'Geoff, great to see you. I'm just hoping we've not given you a wasted journey.'

'I've only come across town. Is there a problem?' He'd arranged to sit in with Bannerman on a selection of his one-to-one client consultations. Nolan had suggested this because he wanted to gain some understanding of Bannerman's methods before seeing him on stage. In Nolan's experience, it was harder to pull off psychological game-playing in a small-scale setting than when supported by the dynamic of a large crowd.

He'd half-expected Bannerman to say no, most likely citing client confidentiality as the reason. But Bannerman had seemed enthusiastic about the idea, and had managed to talk a number of his clients into agreeing to Nolan's presence. Nolan suspected that some of them were hoping to get themselves on television. That might ultimately happen, he supposed, although for the moment he was here only to familiarise himself with Bannerman's approach. Nolan was due to meet with Lyle Christopher in the next couple of days to start discussing the proposed format of the programme.

Bannerman led him across to the informal meeting area they'd used on Nolan's previous visit. 'At least let me get you a coffee.'

That didn't sound promising, Nolan thought. But he wouldn't be surprised if Bannerman had had cold feet. If Nolan was going to expose him as a charlatan, it would most likely be during these intimate sessions. 'Thanks.'

Bannerman gestured to the young man to bring them coffees, and then turned back to Nolan. 'White, no sugar, wasn't it?'

'Exactly right.' Nolan imagined that Bannerman made a point of memorising these kinds of details. It was one of the techniques that helped make you an effective cold reader.

Bannerman took a seat and invited Nolan to do likewise. 'Is it still raining?'

'Absolutely bucketing it down. It's impressive even by Mancunian standards. I'm glad you were able to provide me with a parking space downstairs.'

'One of the benefits of this building. We can usually manage to organise one with a bit of notice.' He paused, clearly done with the small talk. 'I'm afraid we're having a few technical problems.'

'Oh dear. Nothing serious, I hope?'

'We don't think so. Just a glitch in the studio. We've got the techies looking at it, but I think we might have to postpone this afternoon's consultations.'

I bet you might, Nolan thought. 'That's a shame. I was looking forward to getting a sense of how you work.'

'And I was looking forward to showing you. I'm sure we can rearrange it all. I'm just sorry you've come over here for nothing. I'd have called you but the technicians have only just given us the bad news. It's what I was discussing with Gwyn here when you came in.' He waited while the young man set down the mugs of coffee on the low table. 'Isn't that right, Gwyn?'

'Something like that,' Gwyn agreed.

Nolan knew full well that Bannerman was lying. He'd heard the conversation himself. He didn't know who they had been discussing, but it hadn't been anything to do with technical problems. He found himself feeling slightly disappointed. He hadn't really expected that Bannerman would be anything but a fraud, but he'd hoped for at least a higher class of duplicity. As it was, Bannerman seemed to have tripped at the first hurdle, bottling out of the first even semi-serious scrutiny of his work. 'We'll have to find another date, I guess. Assuming that's feasible.'

'I'm sure we can. How are the filming plans going? I'm very keen to get this moving.'

'I'm sure. Lyle's working on the overall structure of the show. I'm meeting him later this week to discuss things so I can get started on the script. Then we'll need to have a chat with you about how we should best put it all together. Who we need to interview. What we should film. I'm assuming we'll want to film some of your stage work and also, if the clients agree, some of the one-to-one sessions. We might also want to talk to some of your team.'

'The team? Who would you want to talk to?'

'We'd obviously want your views on that. I just thought it might be interesting for the viewers to get a sense of the professionalism of your set-up here. It's probably not what people would associate with spiritualism.'

'People just think we're eccentrics in a world of our own? You might be right. It might be good to give people a feel for that. We take this all very seriously. I'm sure we can come to an agreement on all that.'

'Of course, the primary focus of the programme will be on you. How you work. How you interact with the clients. The kinds of techniques you use—'

'Whether I'm a fraud?'

Nolan laughed. 'As I've told you, this isn't intended to be sensationalist. But equally I have to be appropriately challenging and sceptical. You're making some large claims about your abilities.'

'Yes, of course. I'd expect nothing less.'

'If it's not possible for me to observe any of your sessions this afternoon,' Nolan said, 'would it be possible for you to describe to me how the sessions typically work?'

'I'm not sure there really is a typical session,' Bannerman said. 'But I'll do my best to describe how I work. I make contact with the client through Skype. I can do it by telephone if necessary – and we have a few older clients who struggle with the technology – but I prefer to be able to look them in the eyes. It makes the connection stronger somehow.'

'Connection?'

'I'm not sure what you'd call it. A psychic link, I suppose. It's something that I have to – well, tune in to, I suppose. I have to almost literally get on to their wavelength.'

'And you can still do that remotely?'

'Apparently so. It's generally easier if the person is sitting there in front of me, as they are in the stage shows. But it works very well at a distance.'

'And you know nothing about the clients in advance?'

'Very little. We ask them to fill in a short on-line form. But it's not much more than name, age, marital or other status, and a short summary of what they're hoping to get from the session.'

In other words, Nolan thought, you ask for sufficient information to enable you to do an on-line search for any information that might be available. Very few people had no kind of on-line presence these days, so the chances were that you'd be able to dig out a few useful nuggets from the various social media platforms. Any information about the individual, however trivial, was likely to be invaluable in convincing the client of Bannerman's authenticity.

'So what happens once you've forged this – psychic link?' Nolan was trying hard to keep any note of irony out of his voice.

'It varies from client to client, of course. It depends on the connection I've formed with them – sometimes it's stronger than others – and it depends on the client's personality and needs. I try to be flexible and respond to each person as an individual, rather than just adopting a production line approach.'

'Of course.' Nolan imagined this was probably true. It would no doubt depend on how much information Bannerman had been able to glean beforehand, how responsive the client was to his cold reading techniques, and how open the client was in general. He'd watched these kinds of people operate over many years, and he knew the best of them were very skilful operators indeed. It probably wasn't even always fair to call them charlatans. Some seemed scarcely aware of what they were doing or how effectively they were doing it, and perhaps had genuinely come to believe that they had some kind of psychic powers.

It occurred to Nolan that he was already becoming more sceptical about Bannerman. He'd begun this with at least the vague hope that, for once, he might stumble upon something different. He had always tried to keep his mind open to that possibility, even though he recognised that the chances of it happening were infinitesimal. Bannerman had struck him as different from the norm. He seemed serious, not just a grifter. That didn't mean he wasn't just a highly effective conman, but it might mean there was something more there.

The cancellation of today's sessions had demolished any lingering hope that Nolan might have had. Bannerman hadn't even managed to come up with a convincing excuse. A technical glitch, for goodness sake. What kind of glitch would prevent him from contacting his clients by Skype? In any case, someone like Bannerman would surely have back-up arrangements in place to ensure he could always maintain his services to clients. The only real mystery was why he'd agreed to let Nolan observe in the first place.

'But the first step,' Bannerman went on, 'is to ask the client to explain, as clearly and briefly as they can, what they hope to achieve through the session.'

'I thought they'd already given you that information on the form.'

'They have, although sometimes they don't complete that field. Some are reluctant to raise very personal issues until they see me face-to-face. In any case what they tell me is often very different from what they've written on the form. Sometimes it's because they don't really understand what it is they want. Sometimes it's because they've been embarrassed to talk about it. Sometimes it's just a matter of emphasis. They don't realise what's really important to them. So we often have a brief discussion about it, and I can tease out what they're really looking for.'

I bet you can, Nolan said to himself. Out loud, he said, 'And then what? I mean, do you actually channel the spirits of their loved ones?' He tried to keep his voice steady, but it was difficult to prevent his words from sounding facetious.

Bannerman seemed to hesitate. 'It's hard to describe. And it varies from session to session, depending on the client. For me, it's as if I'm surrendering to something, something outside myself. I've no control over what I'm saying. I can hear myself, but it's as if I'm observing everything from a distance. As if another consciousness has taken over my body. Whether that's channelling the spirits of the dead or something else, I've no idea.'

'How long does it last?'

'Again, it depends. Quite often just a minute or two. Sometimes quite a lot longer – maybe fifteen to twenty minutes. Once in a while, it doesn't work at all. Either I just can't make the link or nothing comes through.'

'What do you do then? With regard to the client, I mean.'

'We tell them in all the literature that there are no guarantees. If I've been able to do nothing, I apologise and offer them the chance for a second session. Sometimes it works when I try again, sometimes it doesn't. If they don't want a second session or if there's nothing when I retry, then we simply refund their payment.'

'You've no idea why that happens? Why it sometimes doesn't work?'

'Not really. It's partly to do with the client, with that psychic link or whatever you want to call it. But sometimes even when that seems strong, nothing comes through.'

Nolan nodded. He sensed that Bannerman was feeling uncomfortable with his questioning. That might be because he was afraid of being exposed or simply because, if he really did believe what he was saying, he found it hard to describe what he experienced. Nolan was inclined to believe the former, but he knew from previous investigations that those involved in spiritualism could sometimes delude themselves as effectively as they deluded their clients. 'Very interesting,' he said. 'That's really helpful, Justin. I'm really looking forward to seeing how that works in practice.'

'Once we've got everything back up and running, that won't be a problem,' Bannerman said. 'I'm really sorry to have wasted your time today.'

'No worries. At least we've had a chance to discuss things. That'll be helpful.' Nolan pushed himself to his feet. 'I'd better get on, though. Good luck with sorting the technical issues.'

'I'm sure we'll be fine. Just a bit frustrated it's taking so long.'

Nolan couldn't think of a response that wouldn't have sounded at least mildly sarcastic. He didn't like to think of his professional encounters as competitions, but he had hoped that Bannerman would prove to be a more convincing subject than most. Eventually, he said, 'I guess Lyle or I will be in touch over the next few days to discuss next steps.'

He smiled. 'We both very much look forward to working with you on this.'

Bannerman nodded. He looked suddenly distracted, Nolan thought, as if his thoughts were elsewhere. It was a moment before he responded. 'Yes,' he said. 'That's great. Look forward to it.'

CHAPTER TWENTY

'Christ,' Marie Donovan said. 'It's getting worse.'

She and Murrain were sitting in one of the pool cars outside Judy Clayburn's house. The rain was hammering down harder than ever, the windscreen a steady stream of water. Flood warnings had been issued for much of the area, and Murrain was conscious that police resources were becoming stretched, even without two major murder enquiries to deal with. 'We just seem to have continuous extreme weather these days,' Murrain said. 'At least this is less restrictive than the snow last winter.'

Donovan nodded. 'I wouldn't want to go through that again.' She, Murrain and other members of the team had been trapped by snow up in the neighbouring hills during a murder investigation some months before.

'Judy Clayburn's still here then?'

'For the moment. We've been trying to organise somewhere else for her to go, partly just so she's not on her own and partly so forensics can get the house properly checked, assuming her husband is our victim. She's got a sister down in Congleton, but she's not managed to get hold of her yet.'

'Must be awful for her,' Murrain said. 'Imagine coming back to find all this waiting for you.'

The Clayburns' house, like its neighbours on this road, was an imposing detached residence, with a sizeable front garden divided between a gravelled driveway and a lawned area. Murrain imagined that there would be an even larger rear garden which would overlook the Ladybrook. The houses here weren't as large as some in the area, but they wouldn't come cheap. 'Must have a bob or two,' Murrain commented.

'Judy Clayburn works for a local pharmaceutical company, apparently.' Donovan said. 'Some sort of senior marketing role, hence all the travelling. So probably paid pretty well. Husband had this job with Justin Bannerman—'

'The medium? I get the impression I'm supposed to have heard of him.'

Donovan smiled. 'You don't watch much TV, do you?'

'Not if I can help it,' Murrain said. 'Not that kind of stuff, anyway. He's on TV, then?'

'I've seen him in a few things where he tries tastefully to commune with the dead.'

'I imagine he generally succeeds.'

'Well, supposedly. He's certainly a good showman. He's just kicking off a big stage tour, with a couple of nights at the Palace Theatre. He must have a decent following if he can fill that, even if he is a local boy.'

'He's from Manchester?'

'Apparently. Was looking him up earlier. Born and brought up in Wythenshawe. Still lives up here and has an office in town.'

'What did Clayburn do for him?'

'I'm not entirely sure. Something on the creative side, his wife said.'

'Do mediums needs creatives?' Murrain said.

'It's a show, isn't it? Whatever the substance or lack of it to what he does, it's all going to be a performance on stage. I guess he needs scripts, stage management, all that kind of stuff.'

'Someone to provide the ectoplasm.' Murrain peered out at the rain. 'We can't sit here forever, can we? Better make a run for it.'

They'd had to park on the road as the Clayburns' drive was filled with vehicles. The two cars nearest the house presumably belonged to the Clayburns themselves, and behind these were ranked a couple of police vehicles and the CSI van. Even in their heavy waterproofs, the hurried jog from the car to the front door left Murrain and Donovan dripping. They clustered together in the small porchway while Murrain pressed the doorbell.

The door was answered almost immediately by a PC who Murrain knew slightly.

'Afternoon, Bill. Can you allow in a couple of drowned rats?'

'Since it's you,' the PC said. 'Assume you're here to talk to Mrs Clayburn?' He led them into the hallway.

Murrain unzipped his waterproof, conscious of how much water they were dripping on to the carpeted floor. 'Is there somewhere we can put these?'

'I'll take care of them for you,' the PC said. 'Judy Clayburn's in there.' He gestured towards a door on the right of the hallway. He lowered his voice, 'She was in a state when we got here, but she seems to have a recovered a bit.'

'Thanks, Bill.'

Murrain led Donovan into what was clearly the main living room. The woman he took to be Judy Clayburn was sitting on a large sofa in the centre of the room. Murrain recognised the uniformed officer sitting beside her as PC Anita Parker. A good choice, he thought. He'd had a few dealings with her and knew her to be a sensitive and reliable officer, who was skilled at handling difficult or emotional conversations.

Judy Clayburn looked up as they entered, her eyes red-ringed.

'Mrs Clayburn?' Murrain said. 'I'm DCI Murrain and this is my colleague DS Marie Donovan. Do you feel up to talking to us?'

Judy Clayburn looked across at Anita Parker as if seeking her permission, then nodded. 'Do you know what's happened to Gareth?'

Murrain lowered himself on to the sofa beside her. Donovan took one of the armchairs. 'I'm afraid it doesn't look like good news. We've found a body—'

Clayburn shook her head. 'It can't be Gareth. He should be here.'

'The body was found nearby. Do you have any photographs of your husband?'

She stared at him blankly for a moment, as if having no idea what he was asking. 'I–I think so. On my phone.' She picked up her mobile phone from the coffee table in front of them, and flicked through a selection of photographs and eventually held one up to Murrain. 'That's a clear one.'

It was a photograph taken on some past holiday. Gareth Clayburn was standing on what was presumably the terrace of some hotel, a blue-green sea stretching behind him. Murrain had studied the CSI photographs of the body before they'd set off, and he had little doubt the smiling face in front of him was the same man. He handed the phone to Donovan. She scrutinised it for a moment and then nodded.

'I'm very sorry,' Murrain said. 'I'm afraid that does seem to confirm what we thought.' They would need to obtain a formal identification at some point, but this wasn't the time to raise that.

Judy Clayburn's expression suggested that she was struggling to absorb what he was saying. 'But–where did you find the body?' she said, finally.

Murrain decided it would be better to be straightforward. His instinct was that Judy Clayburn was a resilient woman who would cope with this better than her current demeanour might suggest. She struck him as the kind of person who preferred the truth, however painful, rather than being fobbed off with platitudes. 'The Ladybrook's very swollen,' he said. 'Your husband was found in the flood waters. We assume he must have somehow entered the water at the rear of these houses and been carried along. I'm very sorry.'

'I don't understand. Why would Gareth have gone into the water? What are you suggesting?'

Murrain took a breath. 'We don't believe he entered the water voluntarily. We believe he was murdered.'

'Murdered? Gareth?'

'I'm sorry, but that looks to be the case.'

'But why would anyone want to murder Gareth?'

'We don't know,' Donovan said. 'Not yet. We know nothing about the circumstances of the death, except that it's clear it was inflicted by a third-party and wasn't accidental.'

'That's why we need to talk to you, Mrs Clayburn,' Murrain said. 'We need to know as much as possible about your husband. His likely movements while you were away. His friends and other contacts. Anything that might help us understand what happened. Do you feel up to talking to us now?' Murrain always felt bad at pressing bereaved relatives, but he knew that, in a case like this, every minute could be valuable.

'You are sure this is Gareth?'

'On the basis of the photographs you showed us, I'm afraid I don't have much doubt. I'm very sorry.'

'But why Gareth? He wouldn't hurt a fly.'

'We've no reason to think he was targeted personally,' Donovan said, 'though clearly we have to consider that possibility.'

'He was dressed in nightwear,' Murrain added. 'A dressing gown, t-shirt and shorts.' He described the items that the body had been wearing.

Judy Clayburn nodded. 'That sounds like Gareth's dressing gown. And he generally used to wear a t-shirt and boxers in bed.' Her voice was flat and hollow-sounding.

'One possibility is that he interrupted an intruder. Perhaps following someone outside into the garden, tried to stop them…'

'To be honest, that doesn't sound like Gareth. He wasn't a coward, but was pretty sensible. He wasn't a "have a go" type. I can see how something might have happened in the house, but I can't imagine him chasing someone out into the garden. He'd have stayed in here and called 999.'

Murrain nodded. Ferbrache and his team would be trying to identify where the death had actually have occurred, but it seemed unlikely that Clayburn would have been killed inside and the body then dragged outside. Murrain also couldn't imagine that the nature of the stabbing wouldn't have made the crime scene very obvious. On the other hand, the intensity of the recent rain could well have compromised any forensic evidence in the garden, so they might never know for sure exactly where death had occurred. 'We don't yet know where it happened. But people can sometimes behave unexpectedly if they're taken by surprise.'

'Gareth was a bit of an insomniac,' she said. 'He was often up and working in the small hours. So if someone did break in, he might have disturbed them, I suppose.' She shuddered, as if envisaging the scene.

'Can I ask you about your husband's work?' Murrain said.

'His work? Do you think that's relevant?'

'At this stage, we can't discount the possibility that this wasn't just accidental or opportunist. It may help us to know more about your husband and his background.'

'Gareth wasn't the kind to make enemies.'

Murrain couldn't recall how many times he'd heard this sentiment expressed by close relatives of victims. 'I don't imagine he was. But sometimes people have enemies they're not even aware of. I understand your husband worked for Justin Bannerman.'

'That's right.' Judy Clayburn suddenly laughed, though there was no evident humour in her tone. 'It just occurred to me. Maybe I should get Justin to contact Gareth to find out what happened.'

Murrain glanced at Donovan. Judy Clayburn's tone was as calm as ever, but her words and tone suggested she shouldn't be pressed much further. 'What did your husband do for Mr Bannerman?' he asked, gently.

'Gareth's background was in theatre. Direction and stage management, mainly, though he also did a bit of acting and writing. Justin headhunted him to help develop his stage shows. Justin had only ever done very low-key stuff before, but when he started to develop a bit of a profile on TV, he wanted to exploit it. Gareth helped him, not just to develop the mechanics of the show, but also to develop Justin's stage persona, write the scripts and so on.'

Murrain had felt something as she'd been speaking. He'd seen a momentary image of two men, one tall, the other shorter, standing in a spotlight. Was that an image of Bannerman and Clayburn on stage? 'I didn't realise that mediums needed scripts?'

'You'd think not, wouldn't you?' Judy Clayburn said. 'But it's entertainment at the end of the day. A lot of it's showmanship. That's what Gareth helped him with.'

There was an edge of cynicism in her tone, Murrain thought. 'Did you disapprove of your husband's work?'

'Not at all. He did a good job. He was one of the big reasons why Justin had become so successful. I'm just not sure I approve of what Justin is doing in the first place. Gareth and I had a few debates about it.' She shook her head. 'I suppose the question is whether you think what he does provides comfort to the vulnerable or simply exploits them.'

'You don't believe that Mr Bannerman is genuine?' Murrain had tried to phrase the question as delicately as he could.

'What do you think?'

'I don't know,' Murrain said, honestly. His own intangible gifts had taught him not to be unduly sceptical about so-called paranormal phenomena. 'What were your husband's views?'

To her surprise, she hesitated before responding. He had assumed that Clayburn would have shared his wife's doubts, and that any disagreement would have been about the ethics of working for Bannerman. 'To be honest, I'm not sure. He'd sometimes make jokes about what Justin did. But I don't think he ever fully discounted it.' She paused. 'He was always a bit odd about it, to be honest. He could get very defensive if I questioned Justin's work. Told me he'd seen Justin provide insights that I wouldn't believe. He reckoned he didn't necessarily believe Justin talked to the spirits, or whatever, but he'd seen enough to make him think that Justin had some kind of skill or gift.' She shrugged. 'I don't know whether he really believed that, or if it was just something he told himself to justify working for Justin.'

Murrain felt as if he'd pressed Judy Clayburn as far as he could. She'd been remarkably calm so far, but he could sense that her emotional state was growing increasingly brittle. He suspected the reality of her husband's death would hit her fully before too long. 'Thank you, Mrs Clayburn, that's been most helpful. I'm sorry we've had to do this now, but we need to get things moving as quickly as possible. We'll need to talk to you again, but that can wait for the moment.'

'Of course. I'll do anything I can to help. I still can't believe this.'

'Is there someone who can be with you?'

'I've been trying to contact my sister. I've left a message for her, but she's not good with her mobile.'

'We'll get someone to help you with that,' Murrain said. 'We'll ensure that someone stays with you until we can sort something out. I'm afraid our forensics team will need to conduct a full examination of the house, so we'll have to seal off most of the rooms until that's done. If you're able to stay with your sister for the next day or two, that would probably be better for you and for us.'

'I'm sure that'll be possible. I'm not sure I'd want to stay here just at the moment, anyway.' She looked around as if suddenly realising where she was.

'We'll make sure there's someone to stay with you until we can sort that out.' Murrain leaned over and placed his hand gently on Judy Clayburn's shoulder. 'I'm very sorry,' he said, again. 'We'll do everything we can to bring whoever did this to justice.'

It was the kind of meaningless reassurance you had to offer at a time like this. Murrain was always conscious of the emptiness of the words, but knew it was what people wanted and needed. In this case, though, he felt she'd hardly heard. Her mind seemed elsewhere.

That was understandable, but at that moment he'd felt another internal tremor, another echo of a voice whispering in his ear. It felt to him, at least in that moment, that Judy Clayburn's mind was focused on something specific. Something she hadn't told them. Something that might prove to be important.

CHAPTER TWENTY ONE

'Hang on. I'm still getting the hang of this.'

Lyle Christopher was standing in front of an impressive-looking espresso maker which stood on a sturdy oak cabinet in a corner of his sizeable office. The cabinet looked as if it might be an antique, but Geoff Nolan guessed that it was no more genuine than anything else in the room, including Christopher.

'Nice place,' Nolan said.

Christopher finally worked out which button to press and stood back to watch the flow of dark coffee drip into the cup below. 'There. Are you happy with an espresso or would you prefer something with milk?'

'Espresso's fine.'

'Probably just as well. I've no idea how to operate the foamer. I'm beginning to think we should go back to instant.' He looked around the office, as if Nolan had just made him aware of it. 'We're pleased with the place. Only moved over here a few weeks ago, and there are one or two teething issues, but it seems pretty ideal for us.'

The office in question was situated in a newly-built block on the edge of the Northern Quarter. It was exactly the kind of place that Nolan had expected, full of elegant if impractical architectural features and largely resembling a cross between an upmarket cafe and a kindergarten.

He'd phoned Christopher on his way back from visiting Justin Bannerman. On reflection, Bannerman's apparent delaying tactics had troubled him. If Bannerman was going to get cold feet, it would be better if they cut their losses quickly and found another subject. Although Nolan was keen to do the programme, he was conscious he hadn't yet signed a formal contract. Darrell Conway was supposed to be sorting that, but seemed to be doing so at his usual glacial pace. The last thing Nolan wanted was to waste his time on something that might be going nowhere.

Christopher finished preparing his own coffee, and then sat down opposite Nolan. 'So you think Justin decided against letting you sit in on his sessions today?'

'That's what it looked like. I didn't really believe the stuff about a technical glitch. I think he had second thoughts about whether he really could pull the wool over my eyes.'

'So you're concluding that Justin's a fraud?' There was a faint note of disapproval in Christopher's voice, as if Nolan had somehow disappointed him.

'I'm concluding nothing,' Nolan said. 'So far I've no evidence either way. But the intimate stuff is much harder to pull off than something on stage. It's like conjuring. It's relatively easy to fool people with a big stage illusion. They can't examine what you're doing and they're caught up in the collective moment. But effective close-up magic is much harder.'

'So why invite you in the first place? As I recall, it was his idea.'

'I don't know. Maybe he thought he could do it, and then bottled it.'

'So what do you think?'

'There are two issues for me,' Nolan said. 'The main one is whether he'll just pull out of the whole thing. This has always been high risk for him. If he's getting cold feet, he might just pull the plug. I don't want to be wasting time if he doesn't want to go ahead.'

'And the second issue?'

'That I might be shooting fish in a barrel. I'd assumed that, with his reputation, Bannerman would have something more to offer than the usual transparent nonsense. But this suggests to me that he might be just like all the rest. I was hoping he might at least give me some food for thought. Maybe leave me with a few unanswered questions. But if I can just pull him apart at the most basic level, it won't make great TV.'

Christopher nodded thoughtfully. 'I can see that. But I wonder if you're underestimating Justin?'

'You reckon?'

'We didn't pick him by accident, you know. We looked at a lot of options before we suggested him.'

'I assumed you'd gone for him because he's relatively well known.'

'That was a consideration, of course. But we also heard much more positive feedback on Justin than any similar figure. His fanbase really rates his work.'

'I'm sure they do. That probably just means he's a more effective conman than his competitors.'

'It may well do. But that's what you're interested in, isn't it?' Christopher smiled. 'I know you say you keep an open mind, but you don't really believe that Justin has psychic powers, do you?'

'I'm genuinely open to any possibility. But I've watched clips of Bannerman's act, and I've seen nothing to persuade me so far. He's slick, but it looks to be the usual stuff.'

'His fans would say differently. That he offers insights they can't explain.'

'Of course they do. That's how it works. But most likely it's a not very sophisticated conjuring trick.'

Christopher took a sip of his coffee. 'Well, it's your call, Geoff. If you really think we should look elsewhere, so be it. But we've invested a lot in this already. If we have to start looking for another subject for this programme, it'll push back the whole schedule. It might make it all unviable.'

'We'll have the same problem if he pulls out.'

'I'm sure he won't.'

It had already occurred to Nolan to wonder if Christopher's connections with Bannerman were stronger than he was letting on. They had sold the idea to Nolan on the basis that it would be his show, a pilot that would most likely lead to a series. But now Nolan was wondering who was actually being set up here. Was this really all about generating publicity for Bannerman? If he did somehow succeed in fooling Nolan, that would be a perfect 'man bites dog' story. 'You seem quite wedded to using Bannerman.'

'Like I say, it's your show, Geoff. I'm just advising you of the practicalities. But, yes, personally I believe Justin's a good subject. I think he'll give you a run for your money.'

Nolan couldn't see much point in arguing further. He'd just make sure Darrel Conway got the contract tied down as soon as possible so at least he wouldn't end up doing all this for nothing. 'I'm happy to go with your judgement, Lyle. Let's see how this pans out. I guess if Bannerman is going to have cold feet, it'll happen pretty soon.'

'I imagine so. But I'm sure he won't.'

'Okay. Well, I've registered my concerns.'

'Heard and understood, Geoff. Look, I have every confidence in this project. And I really do think you and Bannerman are well matched. I wouldn't underestimate his abilities. I've seen demonstrations of it myself. He surprised me.'

Nolan nodded. Perhaps that was the more straightforward explanation, he thought. Perhaps it wasn't that Christopher had cooked this up with Bannerman. Maybe Christopher had actually fallen under Bannerman's spell. Nolan had seen how charismatic Bannerman could be, particularly in his stage act, and he could imagine that even someone as supposedly smart as Christopher could be taken in. 'He gave you a consultation, did he?'

'I wanted to test him, obviously. I'd seen the stage act. I'd researched what he was supposedly capable of. But I wanted to see it for myself. My father died last year. I wondered if it was possible to communicate with him.' He laughed. 'It sounds stupid, doesn't it? But my dad worked in the industry. I just thought it would be interesting to get some career advice.'

'What happened?'

'I'm as sceptical about this kind of stuff as you are. But I can't easily explain what happened. He actually seemed to be channelling my father. I mean, not an impression as such. But there was something about the way he spoke that echoed the way my dad talked.'

Nolan nodded. He knew how easy it was to persuade people they were hearing from their departed loved ones. People heard what they wanted to hear. 'And did he give you the advice you were seeking?' Nolan wondered whether perhaps the spirit of the departed senior Christopher might have advised his son to make a programme about Justin Bannerman.

'That was the thing. He knew things about my business that Bannerman couldn't have known. His advice was basically to be bold in my work, to take some risks. He even referenced specific projects we'd been looking at. I couldn't quite believe it. I don't know how he could have known those things.'

'It sounds impressive.' To Nolan, none of this sounded much different from what he'd seen with other mediums. A mix of some specific information dug out from public domain sources with some anodyne advice to the bereaved. The specific stuff made it sound credible, while the advice could be interpreted in whatever way best suited the recipient. 'I look forward to seeing it in action, as long as he'll let me.'

'I'm sure he will, Geoff.' Christopher had risen to his feet, in a manner that suggested the discussion was over. 'I'm sure we're going to produce a really exciting and informative programme here.'

Nolan had noted the brusque nature of the dismissal. He was beginning to recognise that, whatever platitudes Christopher might offer, the only person who really mattered here was Lyle Christopher. 'Okay, Lyle. I'm sure you know best. I'll leave it in your very safe pair of hands.'

And, he added to himself, I'll make bloody sure you take responsibility for anything that goes wrong.

CHAPTER TWENTY TWO

'How's it looking?' Murrain asked. He and Marie Donovan had just emerged from the interview with Judy Clayburn and had encountered Neil Ferbrache, fully suited, emerging from the kitchen.

Ferbrache removed his helmet before responding. 'To be honest, we haven't found much inside so far. There's no sign of any struggle. No evidence the killing took place in here. We've found a few fingerprints that don't match either of the Clayburns, but they have a cleaner who comes in three times a week so they'll probably turn out to be hers. The rear door was left open but it hadn't been forced, so it looks as if it was probably opened from the inside. There's no sign of any other break in. The front door was locked from the inside, so it looks as if no-one came in or went out that way, and none of the downstairs windows seem to have been disturbed.'

'What about in the garden?' Donovan asked.

'That's where it gets a little more interesting. There are some patches in the back garden that look as if they're probably blood. It's difficult to be definitive at the moment because the evidence has been degraded so much by the weather. We've now set up a protective tent over the area, so we can at least prevent it getting any worse. We've taken samples and will get them tested. But it looks probable that the killing took place somewhere in the back garden.'

'So how would the body have ended up in the water?'

'The land behind here drops pretty steeply down towards the stream. There's only a fairly low fence at the rear of the garden. From the position of the bloodstains – if that's what they are – the body might have either fallen or been pushed over the fence and dropped down the slope. At another time, it would have ended up on the bank, but with the waters so high it could easily have rolled all the way in from up here.'

Murrain nodded. 'Do you think it was an attempt to hide the body?'

'I'm guessing not. If the killer knew how high the waters were, I suppose the aim might have been to let the waters take it. But it's really just an overgrown stream so, even at a time like this, it wasn't going to take the body very far. More likely the body either toppled over by itself or was pushed to help keep the blood off the killer's body.'

'What do you reckon, Ferby? To me, this feels too much like Gorman's killing for comfort.'

'That was my thinking. The circumstances are almost identical. The body's found outside, having probably left the house in the small hours. No signs of any kind of break in or struggle. The nature of the stabbing looks very similar. Just looking objectively at all of that, I think you'd be struggling not to link them, at least tentatively.'

'What's even more weird,' Donovan added, 'is the similarity between the two victims' occupations. One a supposed astrologer, the other working for this spiritualist guy. That's presumably just a coincidence, but it's a bloody strange one.'

'The whole thing's bizarre,' Murrain said. 'Apparently motiveless killings. No sign of a break in. Victims for some reason heading out of the house in the middle of the night.' He nodded to Ferbrache. 'We'll let you get on, Ferby. Look forward to seeing the results.'

'I'm here to serve. Anything else interesting pops up, I'll let you know.' He replaced his helmet and disappeared back into the kitchen.

'So what next?' Donovan said.

'I think we have to keep an open mind,' Murrain said. 'We can't discount the idea of some sort of interrupted break-in here, any more than we can with Gorman.' He shook his head. 'Maybe we've even got ourselves some kind of psychopathic housebreaker. Who knows? This is the kind of area where a lot of the houses are likely to be equipped with security cameras so worth seeing if there's any evidence of intruders or attempted break-ins among the neighbours. Joe can get all that stuff moving. But it does begin to feel as if there's something more to this. Once she's in a state to talk more, we need to get whatever further information we can from Judy Clayburn. Anything about her husband's private life, friends, acquaintances. We should probably check his finances for any signs of debts or other issues. Check out his phone and laptop, if he had one. And we ought to speak to this Bannerman guy.'

'You think this might be somehow connected with his work?'

'I've no idea. But you were right just now. It may mean nothing, but it's odd that both victims are working in similar fields. And pretty esoteric fields at that. It might just be a coincidence, but it's one that merits probing further. I suppose Bannerman's a pretty public figure. If you're in the public eye, particularly doing something as sensitive as spiritualism, I'm guessing you can attract some pretty odd types.'

'Even so, why would they go after Clayburn rather than Bannerman himself?'

'It feels as if there's too much we don't know. I'm all too conscious I might just be chasing ghosts here, but it does feel to me as if there's some kind of underlying pattern.'

'When you say feels…?' Donovan asked tentatively.

Murrain grimaced. 'There's a bit of that. But also just a big dose of copper's gut.'

'I'd trust both of those, as it happens.'

'Maybe you shouldn't. But in any case it doesn't change what we're doing. Let's not get deflected.' He grinned. 'Yes, and I know I'm the worst for doing that. Shall we brave the rain and take a quick look at the rear garden. I'd like to get the lay of the land.'

Outside, the rain hadn't lessened, drumming heavily on the sodden grass and earth in the front garden. Donovan pulled up the hood of her waterproof and stepped into the deluge. 'Feels like it's never going to stop.'

'Forecast reckons we've got at least another couple of days of it,' Murrain said. 'Don't like the look of it. A lot of the rivers are already at bursting point. Won't take a lot to cause some real problems.' He peered along the house. 'Assume we can get to the back down there if the gate's not locked.'

He led the way to the corner of the house, from where a passageway led down to the back garden. There was a full-length gate, but it was open and there was no sign of a lock. 'Ferby reckoned the front door was locked, so if anyone did break in they'd have presumably come down here,' he said to Donovan who was following close behind him. In the lee of the house they were a little more sheltered from the pounding rain and could talk more easily.

Donovan looked up. 'Can't see any security cameras, but we can double check that with Judy Clayburn. There's a security light up there which I guess would have been set off by anyone coming down here. But you'd be fairly sheltered from the road here, so it might be attractive to a house breaker.'

They made their way to the end of the passageway. Murrain looking round for anything that might help them understand what had happened on the night of Clayburn's death. The passageway was not directly overlooked, bounded on the outside by a high fence, with more garden and the neighbouring house beyond. There were windows in the Clayburns' house that looked out over the passage, but anyone passing by here would be invisible from the upper floors.

The end of the passageway was sealed with a line of police tape. Murrain stopped at that point and looked into the rear garden. It was a fairly sizeable patch of land, stretching perhaps fifty or sixty metres to the low fence Ferbrache had described. The white CSI tent was set up at the far side of the garden, close to the fence. Visibility was poor in the driving rain, but it was evident that, past the fence, the land fell away towards the valley below. Past that, there was parkland, thickets of trees standing at a lower level to the house.

'Decent garden,' Donovan commented.

'I imagine it's a decent view on a clear day—' Murrain stopped abruptly, feeling a sharp pain in his temples. It felt as if something had just physically struck him across the side of the head. He staggered backwards.

Almost immediately, he heard it. A continuous whispering, somewhere in the lower registers of his hearing. A choir of unearthly voices trying to impart some information, some news to him. He had never quite experienced anything like that before. The closest he could recall were on occasions when he entered the mortuary at Stepping Hill. He had never thought of his 'gift', whatever it might be, as any form of communing with the dead, and he didn't really believe that was the case. But somehow, when he was standing alongside those rows of preserved human remains, it was as if he could sense a rabble of voices trying to communicate with him.

For a moment, he felt almost overwhelmed by the sensation. The voices were almost below the threshold of his hearing, but the sheer intensity felt almost as if someone was screaming at him. He dropped his head, pressing his hands to his ears.

'Are you okay?' Marie Donovan's voice sounded as if it was coming from somewhere far away.

The voices ceased as suddenly as they had begun, and there was nothing but the endless rasp of the rain on the leaves around them. Murrain opened his eyes. 'I— Yes, I think so. I don't know what happened.'

'Was it…?' Donovan left the question hanging in the damp air.

Murrain stared at her, as if he couldn't understand the question. 'I suppose it must have been. I've never experienced anything quite like that before, though.' He paused, trying to find some way of articulating what he had felt. He never liked discussing this topic, but now felt he needed to talk about it, to share what he'd experienced. 'It's hard to describe, but sometimes it feels as if I'm hearing someone whispering to me. Like a very insistent voice in my ear that I can barely hear. It was like that but – I don't know – as if it was a whole rabble of voices…' He trailed off, conscious how difficult any of this was to articulate.

'Do you think it means anything?'

Murrain hesitated. He was aware that Marie Donovan had good reason to take all this much more seriously than some of her colleagues. It had, after all, once contributed to saving her life. 'You know my pat answer to that question. That I don't know. If I'm honest, what I really think is that it almost always does mean something, but I usually don't have a clue what it might be. When it's as intense as I've just experienced, I'm convinced it must be significant. But I still don't know what it might mean.'

'You couldn't hear what the voices were trying to tell you?'

'I rarely can. That's what so frustrating. Occasionally I pick up what seems like a word or two. Sometimes I see images, though I can't usually make out anything clearly. It's like trying to tune into some distant radio station, but you can't quite capture the signal.' He was aware that he was speaking more openly than he normally ever did to anyone other than Eloise. 'Actually, that was the thing here. It normally feels as if my brain is trying to tune into something. That was why this felt different, I think. Just then, it felt more as if someone was targeting me.'

'Targeting you?'

'I know. It sounds absurd. And I don't know if I'm quite capturing it. Targeting suggests that it was being directed at me personally. That's not quite right, either.' For a moment, Murrain felt almost despairing at the difficulty of articulating any of this. 'It was as if

I'd walked into something. Like when you're dazzled if you accidentally walk into the beam of a spotlight. It was like that.' He paused. 'Something like that.'

'But then it stopped? As if – what? Someone had turned off the light?'

For a moment he thought she was mocking him, but he could see she was serious. 'I'm not sure. Maybe I just stepped back out of the beam, as it were. To be honest, I'm not particularly inclined to try again.' He shook his head. 'I'm probably talking complete nonsense.' He took a tentative step forward and looked out across the garden again, wondering whether the sensation would recur. There was nothing.

'It doesn't sound nonsense,' Donovan said.

'I don't know,' Murrain said. 'But it's an interesting question, isn't it? If Clayburn was killed over there we have to ask what brought him out into the garden. Once we've got some idea of the rough time of death, we'll have an idea what the weather would have been like at the time, but it's not been great for a couple of days. So something quite probably brought him out into the rain. Maybe he was chasing an intruder, though his wife thought that was out of character. So maybe something else lured him out here…'

'Like what?' He realised that Donovan was watching him curiously, as if expecting that he might have some solution to offer.

'I really haven't a clue. I'm not even sure why I said that.' He turned to face her. 'But that's how this sometimes works. I don't pretend to understand the process. But what I have learnt over the years is that if it brings a question or an idea into my mind, it's worth taking seriously.'

CHAPTER TWENTY THREE

Donna Fenwick opened her eyes, unsure what had awakened her. She lay in the darkness, bewildered, unsure where she was. She felt as if she'd been unexpectedly thrust back into her own past.

That was it, of course. She was back in what she still unwillingly thought of as home. Her mother's house. She'd been reluctant at first, but had realised how rattled her mother had been by the break in. As always, Irene had denied it and insisted she was quite capable of looking after herself. But her tone had belied her words, and Donna had seen that her mother was genuinely frightened.

Donna had no idea whether her mother's anxiety was justified. The police had done their best to be reassuring, but had been unable to offer any guarantees. They had a visit in the afternoon from a PC, who'd made dutiful notes about what had happened, agreed the break-in had almost certainly been through the back door, and asked whether anything appeared to have been taken. When Irene had confirmed that, as far as she could judge, nothing significant was missing, he'd seemed largely to lose interest, advising only that a crime scene officer would visit later in the afternoon.

As she'd been leading the police officer out of the house, Donna had asked him discreetly whether there was any risk of the intruder returning. The officer had shrugged, saying that it wasn't unknown for housebreakers to make a return visit. 'But that's usually when they've stolen house keys or the like. The housekeeper doesn't realise the keys are missing so doesn't know they're vulnerable. It doesn't happen often, but it does happen.'

Thanks for that, she'd thought. She couldn't imagine that any house keys would have been taken without her mother realising, but it wasn't impossible. There might have been a set of house keys in her father's study that Irene was unaware of. In any case, Irene's anxiety seemed less rational than that. She wasn't concerned that the intruder might return, she was simply concerned that her security here had been breached. Her safe haven had suddenly become less safe.

In the longer term, that might prove beneficial. It might help to convince Irene that she really would be better moving out of this place. In the immediate term, though, it meant that she would need some support. In the end, Donna had phoned Peter and said she'd stay overnight at her mother's. Peter had taken that in his stride, as he generally did, asking only whether this was for one night only. She hoped so, but she had no idea of her mother's real state of mind.

That was why she was here, waking up in the small hours back in the bedroom she'd last slept in during her university vacations. She rolled over in the single bed and looked at her watch. Three am.

She was normally a sound sleeper unless disturbed by some external factor, but perhaps sleeping in an unfamiliar bed had made her more sensitive to the nightly settlings of this old house. She turned over and tried to settle herself back to sleep.

Then she heard something. The sound of someone moving on the landing outside. She lay for a moment, wondering whether she'd imagined it. But there was no doubt. There had been the sound of soft footsteps on the carpet, and then the sound of someone climbing the stairs to the second floor.

As far as Donna was aware, her mother was also a sound sleeper, though that might have changed as she'd grown older. The main bedroom had en-suite facilities so she wouldn't have needed to leave the room to visit the bathroom. Given her anxiety earlier, it was difficult to imagine that Irene would have ventured out into the darkness for any other reason.

Donna had popped back home briefly earlier to pack an overnight bag, and she felt grateful now that she could slip into her familiar dressing gown. She pulled it tightly round her, then felt her way to the bedroom door, opening it as quietly as she was able.

The landing was still in darkness. Donna peered into the semi-darkness and saw that her mother's bedroom door was closed. Donna turned and began to climb slowly and silently up towards the second floor. As she reached the top of the stairs, she saw there was a light showing from her father's study which stood slightly ajar.

Donna was conscious of her heart pounding and she felt on the edge of genuine panic. The sensible response would be to return to her bedroom and call 999, but she also knew she couldn't leave this situation unresolved. She could now hear noises from inside her father's study, and had no doubt someone was in there.

She took several deep breaths to calm herself, and then, moving as gently and silently as she could, crossed the landing to her father's study. As she reached the door, she stopped and listened.

The sound was that of someone turning the pages of a document – perhaps a large book or a file. The sound recurred relatively frequently, as if whoever was in there was skimming through the document rather than reading it thoroughly. Was this last night's intruder returning to continue his enigmatic search?

Donna slowly pushed open the door, poised to flee if her presence should be detected. She inched open the door a little more, praying it would make no noise. Then she leaned further forward to see what was inside.

Her mother was sitting on the carpet, in the same position Donna had found her earlier in the day, systematically leafing through one of the scattered files. A pile of other files was positioned beside her.

'Mum?' Donna whispered the word quietly, trying not to startle her mother.

Irene looked up, her expression one of surprise and mild guilt, as if she'd been caught out in some illicit act. 'Oh, Donna. You made me jump.'

'Sorry. I tried not to.'

'Did I wake you?' It wasn't clear from her tone whether Irene was concerned about Donna's interests or her own.

'I'm not sure. I just woke up. Maybe it was just sleeping in an unfamiliar bed.'

'It shouldn't have been unfamiliar. You slept there for enough years.'

Donna knew better than to respond to that one. Irene had never quite forgiven her for not returning home, at least temporarily, after leaving university. 'What are you up to, mum? It's the middle of the night.'

'I couldn't sleep. It's not like me. I'm usually out like a light till morning, but tonight I woke up and couldn't get off again. I kept thinking about the person who broke in. What they wanted. Why they'd targeted your father's work.'

'We don't know they did,' Donna pointed out. 'They might have just started in here for whatever reason, then been interrupted by your return.'

'I don't believe that, and neither do you.'

Donna knew her mother was right. They had tried to persuade themselves that this was just another break-in, that the intruder had picked her father's study because it was the most likely location of any valuables. But why would you start with a room at the top of the house before searching the downstairs rooms? There had been no sign of any disturbance – not even the opening of a drawer or cupboard – except in this one room.

'So what do you think?'

'I think they were looking for something,' Irene said. 'Something that belonged to your father.'

'But what would dad have that would be of any remote interest to an intruder? It's not as if he'd have had a hidden treasure map or a secret nuclear formula.'

'I haven't the faintest idea. But I'm convinced there was something.'

'I'll get us both a cup of tea, mum. Then we can have a chat about it.'

As she made her way downstairs, it occurred to Donna to wonder if they were both still in a mild state of shock, letting their anxieties persuade them of something that couldn't possibly be true. Her father had been an academic. A clinical psychologist as far she understood it. He'd never been the type to talk about his work. Not that he was secretive, or at least he'd never seemed to be. If she'd asked him a question about what he did, he'd always given her a full answer. Sometimes a little too full, she'd thought as a child as she struggled to make sense of the jargon and acronyms. But, though he'd answered her questions in general terms, he'd never revealed much about the detail of his work. Was that significant? It was difficult to believe that he was involved in anything clandestine. He'd published books and papers, he'd spoken at public conferences, he'd been a low-key public figure.

She turned on the light in the kitchen. They'd found a local locksmith who'd been able to add a new deadlock and bolts on the back door that afternoon, which had at least provided her mother with some reassurance.

Donna filled the kettle, staring out of the kitchen window into the darkness. The rhythmic movement of the raindrops down the window felt almost hypnotic.

Absurdly, as she waited for the kettle to boil, she could feel herself growing nervous. She was struck by the thought that someone might be out there in the darkness, watching her caught in the brightness of the kitchen lights. It was a ridiculous idea, of course. Who would be standing out there in the pouring rain?

Nevertheless, she couldn't quite shake off her anxiety and she hurriedly pulled down the kitchen blinds. She couldn't recall ever previously seeing them closed. She had expected the room to feel safer and cosier, but instead it seemed oddly claustrophobic.

When she returned to her father's study, Donna found Irene still sitting on the carpet, working rigorously through the stack of files. Donna sat down beside her and handed over the tea, 'What are you expecting to find, mum?'

'I don't know,' Irene admitted, 'and to be honest I've no idea whether I'll recognise it even if I find it. But I don't know what else to do.'

'Tell me about dad's work. I don't really know anything about it.'

Irene closed the file she was holding. She looked impatient, as if Donna was interrupting some urgent task. 'He was an academic. A professor by the time of his retirement. You know that.'

'But that's about all I know. I mean, I know he was a clinical psychologist, but I know nothing about the work he did.'

'Does it matter?'

'It might,' Donna pointed out. 'If you're right and whoever broke in was looking for something among his papers, presumably it might be linked to his work.' She gestured to the file her mother was holding. 'Those are work files you're looking at, presumably.'

'They're a mix, actually. As far as I know, Gordon's work files were largely kept in his offices in the university. Most of what's here is the stuff he amassed personally, although some of it seems to be copies of work-related material. Your dad was always scrupulous about drawing the line between home and work, so he kept anything sensitive or confidential in the office. But he did a lot of work at home.'

'Doesn't that mean there's unlikely to be anything of interest here?'

'Our intruder didn't seem to think so. But I don't know. At home, your dad used to work on the things that really interested him, which sometimes diverged from the formal focus of his university work.'

'What sorts of things?'

Irene was silent for a moment. 'He wanted to take his university work a bit further. In the formal context, he was obviously constrained by needing to adhere to academic standards.'

'Isn't that what he was supposed to do?'

'Yes, of course. And he did. He had to ensure academic rigour, transparent methodology, replicability of outcomes, all that. Without that, any research becomes meaningless. But he was interested in experimenting outside those constraints. He thought it was the only way to open up our thinking, to generate new ideas, to identify new areas for investigation. The way to stop yourself becoming too hide-bound or prone to group-think.'

'But the results wouldn't have any academic credibility.'

'That's not the point. If you do come up with new ideas, you can test them rigorously. But you can't do that without the ideas.'

'And do you subscribe to this? As a academic yourself, I mean.'

'I don't know. My field's very different. I'm looking at the past. Your dad was more interested in pushing the boundaries.'

'In what ways?'

'His personal interest in recent years was in some of the more esoteric stuff. Things like telepathy, precognition, second-sight, that kind of thing.'

'Really? I'd no idea.'

'He never talked about it much, because he thought that people wouldn't take him or it seriously. It was one of those really controversial areas. As I understand it, there'd been various academic studies over the years – some stuff at Stanford in the '60s and various subsequent ones, but there were big question marks over the methodology and results. The intelligence services in the US became interested, but ultimately the whole thing was largely discredited.'

'But dad thought there was something in it?'

'He felt it was an area worthy of investigation. He had a personal interest too. He'd had a few experiences himself of what you might call second sight. Nothing very startling and probably nothing that couldn't have been explained in some way, but enough to make him intrigued. It was supposedly some kind of family trait, going back to his ancestors in the Highlands, but he never took that side of it very seriously. He'd have liked to have raised the funding for a really serious study. I remember him getting quite excited at one point – this was a few years ago – because he thought the intelligence services here had reignited their interest in it, but that came to nothing. I know he ran a few small studies, but he was never happy with the resources available.'

'You think this is what the intruder might have been interested in?'

'I don't know. I mean, it wasn't the main focus of his formal work. Most of that was related to the psychology of serious criminality. That was fairly high profile. He was on various Government committees, and he did a lot of work with the Ministry of Justice and other criminal justice agencies. So that could have attracted external interest, but I'd imagine most of the work would have been in the public domain anyway. I'm just trying to think about anything he might have stored here rather than at the university. Most of the material I've been looking through has been related to his personal interests rather than his work on criminality. Funnily enough, most of that material doesn't seem to have been touched in the break-in, though that might be just because they hadn't got to it when they were interrupted.'

'That's assuming they were interrupted.' A thought had struck Donna. 'If you're right and they were looking for something, how do we know they didn't find it? You said you heard nothing when you got back, so perhaps you didn't interrupt them. They might have already left because they'd found what they were looking for.'

Irene looked dismayed. 'I suppose that's possible. If so, we'll probably never know what it might have been.' She looked around at the randomly scattered files and papers.

'I don't want you sitting up all night if this is all a wild goose chase.'

'It's all speculation,' Irene said. 'We don't know that there isn't something here.'

'It's a long shot, though. And you don't even know what you might be looking for.'

'I've got to do something, though.'

That was what this was really all about, Donna thought. Her mother's usual equilibrium had been disturbed by the break-in. She wanted to be able to do something and this was no doubt providing a form of displacement activity. Perhaps she should simply leave her mother to it. 'It's your choice, mum. If you think there's any point.' She paused. 'Can I ask you something?'

'You can ask anything,' Irene said. 'As long I can reserve the right not to answer.'

Donna laughed, relieved to see that her mother's spirit hadn't been entirely quashed. 'Okay. It's about Justin Bannerman.'

Irene's gaze was fixed firmly on the file she was examining. 'Who?'

'Don't play the innocent with me, mum. I found that leaflet with the date circled and a time written on it. You told me it was just a bit of scrap paper you'd made a note on. That wasn't true, was it?'

'I'm not sure it's any of your business.'

'I'm not sure either. Except that you're my mother, and I want to make sure that no-one's taking advantage of you.'

'I may be getting older, but I'm not an idiot.' At the precise moment, Irene had the demeanour of a sulky child, Donna thought.

'Nobody's saying you're an idiot, mum. And if you don't want to talk about it, that's fine.'

After a long silence, Irene said, 'I came across him because of your dad.'

'Dad? Really?'

'He was interested in all of that stuff. Clairvoyants, spiritualists, astrology. An academic interest. He wanted to know how they worked or at least what made people think they worked. What sort of psychological levers were being pulled.'

'But he didn't believe in this stuff?'

'He approached it sceptically, but he kept an open mind. Bannerman impressed him. His act was a mix of fairly standard cold reading and similar techniques along with some elements that seemed distinctive. There were aspects that, at least on the surface, he couldn't easily explain. He told me he'd come across a few like that, but they were very rare. He could generally see through the charlatans.'

'Seriously? He thought that someone like Bannerman might actually have some kind of special gift?'

'He was just open minded about anything that he couldn't easily explain. He'd have loved to have conducted some kind of proper study with Bannerman and others. See how much of what they did could be replicated in laboratory conditions.'

'Why were you interested in Bannerman?'

Irene was staring at the carpet, avoiding Donna's eyes. 'It was this bloody move. I can see it's sensible, but I felt as if I was betraying your father. Leaving here will feel as if I'm separating myself from my last tangible link with him.'

'That's not true, mum. You'll be able to keep whatever possessions of his you want to. In any case, that's less important than your memories of him, surely?'

'You know that's not the point. I'd always envisaged Gordon and I would have a good few more years living here after we retired. I hadn't planned for any of this.'

'It must have been a shock. Dad's death, I mean.'

'It was out of the blue. We were both getting on and your father wasn't in the best state. You accept you're not going to live forever. But that—'

'I know, mum. It was such a stupid, unnecessary death.' Donna was aware their conversation had drifted away from Justin Bannerman, but she was also conscious that this was the first time she and Irene had discussed her father's death. At the time, the shock had simply been too great. After that, Irene had largely clammed up about it, insisting she was fine, that she just wanted to get on with her life. She'd thrown herself back into her various unpaid and volunteer projects. Donna wondered now if she'd been cowardly in not pressing her mother to seek some bereavement support, but she knew Irene would not have accepted any interference.

For the first time Donna could recall, her mother had tears in her eyes. 'I don't want to think about it, even now. I can't imagine how someone could have done that and then just driven off.'

There was nothing Donna could say. She had been round this conversation often enough with Peter at the time, venting her fury at the bastard who had been responsible for her father's death. 'I know, mum. It's awful. But they probably weren't even aware of what they'd done.'

'They got away with it,' Irene said. 'That's what I don't understand. How they managed to get away with it.'

'They were lucky,' Irene said. 'Simple as that. There's no justice. The police reckoned that nine times out of ten they'd have identified the vehicle. They'd have picked him up on a traffic camera or CCTV. They did everything they could.'

'I'm not blaming the police. I know they did their best.'

It was nearly some months since her father's death, but Donna wondered whether what she was witnessing now was the delayed psychological impact of that event on her mother. Perhaps the grief had finally hit her. 'You were talking about Justin Bannerman.'

There was silence for a moment, as if Irene had forgotten their conversation of just a few minutes before. 'I was just feeling guilty. Almost as if by leaving here I was walking out on your father. I wanted his approval for what I was doing.'

'That's why you contacted Bannerman?' Donna could hardly believe what she was hearing. She'd always thought of her mother as a bastion of rationality.

'I booked an on-line consultation with him. I thought there was no harm in it.'

'But you didn't seriously expect to – what? To speak to dad?'

'Not really, I suppose. That wasn't the point. I suppose I thought that if Bannerman really did have some gift, he might be able to give me some – I don't know, some kind of insight into what your father felt about the move. But I also thought that, even if he was a complete charlatan, whatever he told me would help me to work out my own feelings…' She trailed off. 'If that makes any sense.'

Donna nodded. 'I think so. Did it help?'

'It did, actually. He told me Gordon approved of the move. It was a convincing – well, performance, I suppose, but that wasn't really the point. It was more that when I heard him say that, I felt convinced he was right. That Gordon would approve.' She smiled sheepishly. 'Maybe it was just what I wanted to hear. But I still believe it's true. He wouldn't have wanted me stuck in this huge place on my own. I was just using that as an excuse not to make the changes I need.'

'That's good to hear, mum,' Donna said, sincerely. She had no doubt Bannerman was a fraud, but if he'd helped Irene come to terms with reality, that could only be good.

Irene was smiling now. 'You can't believe how difficult it was for me to tell you that.'

'I think I can.' Donna gestured to the stacks of documents beside her mother. 'You still think it's worth going through all this?'

'I'm probably being stupid.' She hesitated. 'But I suppose this is about not betraying your father. If there's the smallest chance that this is connected to his work, I want to know. Maybe I won't be able to find anything or recognise it if I do find it, but I'd like to try.'

'I'm happy to help you if you want.'

'Why don't you go to bed?' Irene said. 'I'll carry on for a bit, but I'll get some sleep when I'm ready. Then we can have another chat about it in the morning.'

'If you're sure?'

'I'll just feel guilty if I keep you up. I know I'm just chasing shadows, but I'm old enough to be allowed the odd crazy obsession.'

'As long as you don't allow it to drive you too crazy.' Donna pushed herself to her feet, knowing there was no point in arguing further. 'I'll leave you to it. If you need me, come and get me. I won't mind.'

Irene nodded absently and picked up the file she'd been working through. It was clear her mind was already back focused on the task. Donna quietly left the room, pausing momentarily on the threshold to look back at her mother, who was sitting, head down, working steadily through the files.

CHAPTER TWENTY FOUR

'Can you spare me a few minutes?'

Murrain was already halfway out of the door on his way to update Marty Winstone. They'd just finished the morning briefing, and the team were already dispersing either back to their desks or out to whatever tasks they'd been allocated. Murrain had decided that, although the two murder investigations would still be treated as separate, it was worth coordinating the briefings. He knew how even the most trivial detail could sometimes open up an investigation, so felt it was important that the knowledge and information relating to the two enquiries should be shared across all those involved.

The meeting had gone well. The teams seemed energised and enthused, and the group discussion had identified a couple of potential new lines of enquiry. So far, their progress was relatively limited, but Murrain remained optimistic.

He glanced at his watch. He hadn't committed to a time to see Winstone, but had said he'd pop up once the meeting was finished. 'Sure. I'm due to see Marty shortly but he won't miss me for a few minutes.'

'Can we go somewhere private?' Milton said.

Murrain looked around the crowded MIR. 'Are you suggesting this isn't? Let's see if we can find one of the meeting rooms. We'll get into trouble for going in there without booking, but I'm prepared to live dangerously.' He led them along the corridor to the small suite of meeting rooms and found one sitting empty. 'We're in luck. What can I do for you, Joe?'

Milton waited until the door had closed behind them before responding. 'It's about me and Marie.'

'I had a suspicion it might be. Go on.'

'I know there's been a lot of gossip.'

'There always is, especially from Paul. I try to disregard it.'

'In this case, there's something in it. Marie and I are in a relationship.'

'I'm not quite sure how to say this, Joe, but I don't think that's exactly going to constitute breaking news among the team. I suspect most of us already had an inkling.'

'And we thought we'd been so discreet, as well.'

'What can I say? We're detectives. What is it that you wanted to tell me, other than that.'

'Marie and I have been together for a little while, but neither of us was sure how serious it really was.'

'She's been through a lot, and so have you, in a different way.'

'That was just it. We've been dancing round it for weeks now, neither of us quite prepared to take the big step.'

'And?'

'Now we have. I'm moving in with her. We've talked it all through. I imagine I'll end up selling my place so I can give Gill what she's due. But, well, we're going to set up home together.'

'Congratulations,' Murrain said. 'I mean, seriously, congratulations. You both deserve a bit of happiness.'

'Thanks. That's kind of you. Obviously, we'll take it a step at a time, but we're both over the moon about it, now we've finally made the leap.'

'It's great. The only question is why you're telling me.' Murrain paused. 'In what capacity you're telling me, I mean. Are you telling me because I'm a friend or because I'm your boss?'

'Both, I suppose. I obviously wanted to tell you anyway. You and Eloise have been really good to me. But I also thought I ought to let you know officially.'

'Of course. And you're right. You ought to communicate this through the appropriate channels. You'll need to let HR know your change of address in due course, so I'd also inform them of the circumstances.'

'Do you think one or other of us will have to move teams? I'm conscious there's a bit of potential awkwardness about the fact we'll be working together.'

'It's why Elly and I have taken different career paths,' Murrain agreed. 'That and the fact that she's infinitely more capable that I am. But I don't think there's anything in the rules that explicitly forbids you from working with a partner. The requirement's just that you're open about it, which you are being, and that you make efforts to avoid any potential conflicts of interest. You should check with HR, but that's how I understand it. I can do what I can to make sure neither of you is put in a difficult position.' Murrain smiled. 'To be honest, I wouldn't want to lose either of you from the team. Top quality officers aren't exactly thick on the ground. If HR prove difficult, I'm happy to fight on your behalf. And I'll make sure Marty's on-side too.'

'Thanks, Kenny. That's a relief. This is the work we both want to do.'

'More fool you, then, I'm tempted to say. But all the best to both of you. Are you going to let the rest of the team know?'

Milton smiled. 'I thought if you mentioned it to Paul, it would get around quickly enough.'

'Fair enough. I'll do my duty. What's your next step with the Clayburn enquiry?'

'I want to talk to this Justin Bannerman. Not sure whether he'll have much to tell us, but if there is any link between this and the Gorman killing, it could be related to their occupations.'

'It feels a bit tenuous,' Murrain said. 'But we found no other links between them so far.'

'He might be able to shed a bit more light on Clayburn, anyway. Obviously, Judy Clayburn will be able to give us more as well as directing us to other family or friends, but I don't think she's up to talking in detail about him yet.'

'I shouldn't have pushed her so far yesterday. I knew I was taking it to the limit.'

'I doubt it made much difference. You probably did well in getting something from her in that brief window before the reality hit home.'

'This is why I want you around, Joe. You stop me feeling guilty.'

'Anyway, from what I'm told, she seems a pretty tough cookie. But however strong you are, something like this stops you in your tracks.'

'Tell me about it,' Murrain said. He recalled all too vividly the day, many years before, when he'd been told about the death of his young son. His intemperate reaction at the time had been almost enough to cost him his job. 'But, yes, Bannerman sounds worth speaking to. Apart from anything else, I presume that's where Clayburn would have been most in the public eye. Bannerman's a high profile figure, and Clayburn seems to have been a big player in his team.'

'The whole thing's a bit outside my experience,' Milton said. 'I don't think I've ever interviewed a medium before.'

'Every day's a school day in this job,' Murrain said. 'I must say, Bannerman's someone I wouldn't mind seeing in the flesh.'

'See what your spider sense tells you, you mean? You're welcome to come.'

'I'd love to. But I can't really justify another excursion. I only do it because I'm not built to be a pen-pusher.'

'Shouldn't have got yourself promoted, then,' Milton said. 'I must say, it's one of the things that makes me have second thoughts. I feel as if I spend too much time behind a desk already.'

'Well, think on. That's all I'll say. Speaking of which, I'd better go and brief Marty. He's already getting jittery about the prospect of a double murder. And the Bannerman link will give the media something to get their teeth into.'

'Doesn't take much to get Marty jittery,' Milton observed. 'But we need to start making some progress soon. I'm a bit surprised the press haven't already run with Gorman as a "have a go hero".'

'We've been vague in the details we've given to the media. If they start taking that line, it'll make our job that much harder.' Murrain rose, with a feigned air of weariness. 'Right, we'd better get on.'

Milton followed him out into the corridor. 'Thanks again for the support, Kenny. We both really appreciate it.'

'No worries. I hope it all works out for you.'

Milton smiled. 'I'm sure it will.'

CHAPTER TWENTY FIVE

'Swanky building.'

Milton followed the instructions he'd been given and turned off the main road into the smaller service road. 'Be interesting to see what Bannerman's offices are like.'

'I imagine he does well for himself,' Marie Donovan said. 'I was looking up his management company on the Companies' House site. Looks very profitable. The TV appearances, stage tours, expensive private consultations. All very lucrative, I imagine.'

Milton was concentrating on finding his way into the basement car park. When he'd contacted Bannerman earlier to break the news of Clayburn's death and set up this meeting, Bannerman had told him there'd be a parking space reserved for them. That was a luxury Milton had never experienced in his years of driving in the city, but it was more than welcome given the rain showed no sign of lessening. 'I wonder why he's remained up here rather than decamping to London.'

'Maybe he's just another proud Mancunian. A lot of people resist the idea that they have to move to London to develop their careers.'

'Quite right,' Milton said. 'Ah, this looks like the one.' He pulled up in front of the barrier. 'Hang on.' He leaned out to speak into the intercom beside the car. 'Detective Inspector Milton. Here to see Justin

Bannerman. I was told there'd be a space reserved for me.'

There was a buzz of static before a metallic voice said, 'That's fine. Take Space 18 then follow the signs up to reception.'

'Thanks.' Milton drove past the raised barrier into the car park. The interior was filled with expensive-looking executive cars, presumably belonging to the various business types occupying the building. 'I feel as if I shouldn't really be allowed in here,' Milton said. 'Lowering the tone.'

'Story of my life,' Donovan said. 'But at least you don't get your money by ripping off the vulnerable.'

'Some might say otherwise. You reckon that's what Bannerman does.'

'I've never had a lot of time for these quacks. I've seen Bannerman on TV a couple of times. It's superficially impressive, but it's just the usual type of trickery. People want to believe it because they want to be in touch with their loved ones.'

Milton found the designated parking space, and they made their way up to reception. The car park had been spartan, with bare concrete walls and exposed pipework, but the public areas of the building were plush and glossy, with airy, architect-designed spaces and what Milton took to be designer furniture. The receptionist directed them to the fourth floor where Bannerman had his offices.

Milton hadn't been sure what to expect. In the event, Bannerman's offices resembled an upmarket estate agent or perhaps a private medical practice. The wall outside the office was decorated with Bannerman's logo, and they were greeted by a young female receptionist. Bannerman himself appeared almost immediately and ushered them through to his office. He looked ashen-faced and worried, as he gestured for them to take a seat.

'You're sure about this?' he said, once they were settled. 'I mean, you're sure it's Gareth?'

'He hasn't yet been formally identified,' Milton said. 'But we've good reason to believe it's him, I'm afraid.'

Bannerman looked genuinely shocked, Milton thought. 'I can't believe it. Who'd want to hurt Gareth?' He looked up at Milton. 'How did it happen?'

'That's what we're trying to find out. I can't go into detail at present, but the circumstances of his death are something of a mystery.'

'But you're sure he was killed?'

'There's not much doubt about that. What we don't know is why and in what circumstances. It's possible that he interrupted a break-in, but we can't discount the possibility that he was the intended victim. You can't think of anyone who might have had a reason to harm Mr Clayburn?'

Bannerman hesitated. 'I can't imagine it.'

'Can I ask about the nature of Mr Clayburn's work here?'

This time the hesitation was more obvious. 'Is that likely to be relevant to your investigation?'

'At this stage, we don't know what's likely to be relevant or what isn't,' Donovan said. 'We can't discount the possibility that Mr Clayburn's death was in some way linked to his work.'

'I can't imagine how.'

'Nevertheless, we have to explore every avenue,' Milton said patiently. 'And it's also helpful for us to know as much as possible about Mr Clayburn's background.'

'Yes, of course. Forgive me, this is all just such a shock. I haven't really processed it yet.' He lowered his head into his hands and rubbed his temples. For a moment, Milton thought that Bannerman might actually be weeping, but eventually he raised his head and continued. 'I've known Gareth for a long time. He worked freelance originally mainly on polishing the scripts for my TV and radio appearances. But he was a skilled theatre director. I'd seen some of the work he'd done for other people in the business – mainly stage magicians and the like – and been impressed. I had a guy who did that stuff for me, though I'd been thinking for a while that Gareth might do a better job. In the end, the other guy moved on and I approached Gareth to see if he'd like to come on to the payroll. He wasn't sure at first – I think he liked the flexibility of being freelance – but I talked him into it.'

'And he worked on your stage shows?'

'Mainly, and any TV appearances I did. There's been talk of a TV series for a while now, but these things always seem to take forever. He worked on the stage design, the structure of the shows, the scripts we used and so on.' He gave a weak smile. 'Before you ask, the use of scripts doesn't imply it's all fake. A lot of people come to the shows for a night out, and we want to entertain them as well as providing the services we do.'

Milton exchanged a glance with Marie Donovan. 'Of course. And how was Mr Clayburn to work with?'

There was another noticeable hesitation. 'He was a decent man. He could be a bit of a perfectionist, but that's what I paid him for.'

'When you say he was a perfectionist, does that mean that he could rub people up the wrong way?'

The question felt blunt, but Milton could think of no other way to ask it.

'He had a few run-ins over the years. Backstage staff at the theatres we were playing. TV directors who wanted to do things their way and didn't really understand what we do. But nothing serious. You have a free and frank exchange of views, as they say, and then you get on with it. At the end of the day, we're professionals. That kind of thing's pretty much par for course in the business.'

Milton had noted that Bannerman kept referring to himself as being in 'the business'. He supposed that told him everything he needed to know about Bannerman's attitude to his work. Whatever gifts he might or not possess, he clearly saw himself primarily as an entertainer. 'What about within your own team? Were there any tensions there?'

'What are you suggesting? That someone here was responsible for Gareth's death?'

'I'm not suggesting anything, Mr Bannerman. I'm just trying to get a sense of what kind of man Mr Clayburn was.'

'There were tensions sometimes, as there are in any workplace. But again nothing serious. Just the odd spat that we'd soon put behind us. Gareth was someone who had strong views about how things should be done. He didn't always suffer fools gladly. But overall everyone got on well with him.'

This didn't exactly sound like a ringing endorsement. Milton was beginning to suspect that Gareth Clayburn was a more difficult character, at least at work, than his wife had indicated. Not that that in itself was a motive for murder, but it might be a consideration. 'Were there any particular colleagues Mr Clayburn argued with?'

There was silence for a moment. 'I think one or two of them resented his prominence here.'

'How do you mean?'

'We've never formalised it, but Gareth was effectively my number two. What he did was integral to our work here. He took my – well, my gifts and turned them into something special. To be honest, I'm not sure what we'll do without him. When we joined us, he effectively pushed a couple of people down the pecking order. Not deliberately, of course, and I hope I treat all the team in the same way. But it's just how it was.' He was silent for another moment. 'To be honest Gareth could sometimes throw his weight about. Like I say, he was a perfectionist, so he sometimes put a few people's noses out of joint.'

'Anyone in particular?'

'Colin Drury is the obvious one who springs to mind. Colin looks after all my admin stuff – liaising with the theatres, buying props and other items we need, looking after the finances, that sort of thing. He's just as integral to our work, but in a different way. Without him, we wouldn't have a show on the road in the first place.'

'There were tensions between him and Mr Clayburn?'

'At times. I don't want to give you the wrong impression. It's not as if they were daggers drawn. But Colin keeps a tight grip on the purse-strings, and that could sometimes lead to disputes between him and Gareth. Gareth's view was that we should spend whatever it took to make the shows as impressive as possible. They were both doing their jobs and doing them well. But that sometimes brought them up against each other.'

'Was there any personal animosity between them?'

'They weren't exactly bosom buddies, but they had a decent working relationship, as far as I could see. They respected each other's professionalism. You're not suggesting that Colin could have anything to do with this?'

'At this stage, we just want to understand the background. I think it would be helpful for us to talk to Mr Drury.'

'Of course. You'll appreciate that this has all been a huge shock. I thought of Gareth as a friend rather than just an employee. So it's a personal blow as well as a blow to the business. I'm sure we'll find a way to carry on, but Gareth will be a massive loss. I'm not sure we'll easily be able to operate at the same level as before.'

'I'm sorry,' Milton said. 'We'll do everything we can to bring the person who did this to justice.'

Bannerman's expression suggested he had little faith in their ability to deliver this pledge. 'We'll co-operate with you in any way we can. Would you like to see Colin Drury now?'

'I think we should while we're here. We'll need to speak to the rest of your team, too, Mr Bannerman. There may be other information they can provide about Mr Clayburn. We'll get that set up before we leave.'

'No problem. I'll introduce you to Colin.'

He led them through to an adjoining room. This was a larger open-plan office, occupied by two men and a woman, all tapping at computers. Milton wondered what all this had to do with communing with the dead. It was clear that this was a highly commercial operation. 'In other circumstances, I'd give you the tour,' Bannerman said. 'It's an impressive set-up. We've a studio we use for the on-line consultations, and a consulting room I use for face-to-face sessions.'

'Do you do a lot of those?' Donovan asked.

'Not the face-to-face ones. It's something I do occasionally for – well, for our more exclusive clients.'

This all seemed a far cry from Milton's notion of some elderly spiritualist conjuring up fake ectoplasm in a Victorian parlour. Marie was no doubt right that this was just a sophisticated way of separating the vulnerable from their savings, and he could imagine that this outfit managed that very slickly.

Bannerman led them over to the man sitting at a desk in the corner. He looked in his mid-thirties, with balding swept-back black hair. He blinked at them through thick, heavy-rimmed spectacles.

'Colin. This is DI Milton and DS Donovan. I've afraid they've come with some bad news.'

Milton was impressed that Bannerman had remembered their names. He imagined that a well-trained memory was a necessary quality if you were trying to impress the bereaved with your supposed insights into their loved ones.

'Bad news?' Drury gazed up at them with a baffled expression.

'It's about Gareth Clayburn,' Bannerman said, before Milton could respond. 'He's been found dead.'

'Gareth? Really? But how?'

He looked genuinely shocked, Milton thought. He couldn't bring himself to believe that Clayburn had really been killed by one of his colleagues. Even the most vicious office feud didn't generally end with one party being stabbed, although he'd encountered more trivial motives for murder. His primary hope was that Drury might give them a most honest assessment of

Clayburn's character than they'd so far obtained from either Bannerman or Clayburn's wife.

'We believe he was murdered,' Milton said. 'Beyond that, we're not able to say much more at this stage. We're trying to gain an understanding of the circumstances of his death.'

'That's awful, though. Gareth. I can't believe it.'

'We wondered whether you could spare us a few minutes. We understand you worked closely with Mr Clayburn?'

Drury glanced at Bannerman. 'Well, we all worked closely together in different ways, but I suppose he and I had a lot of interaction. But I don't know what I can really tell you.'

'You can use the consultation room, Colin,' Bannerman said. 'I'll make sure you're not disturbed.'

'Okay.' They followed Drury back out into the reception, then into a smaller room opposite. The receptionist was on the phone. From her expression, Milton guessed that their news was already being shared by one of Drury's colleagues.

The room was designed to offer comfort and a sense of calm, with a tasteful mix of pastel colours and a selection of paintings depicting a range of attractive landscapes. Milton suspected that the interior design had been as costly as the furniture. He wondered how much the so-called exclusive clients paid for the privilege of visiting here, and what they received for their money.

Milton waited till they were all seated and then asked, 'We wondered if you could tell us a little about Mr Clayburn.'

'What is it you want to know?'

'The circumstances of Mr Clayburn's death aren't entirely clear. We're trying to find out as much as we can about his background and character. Could you tell us a little about your work with him?'

'I'm not sure how this is going to help you, but we used to work together mainly on planning the stage shows. Gareth worked on the structure and scripts, as well as on the stage design.'

'Do the shows require much stage design?' Donovan asked.

Drury gave what sounded like a cynical laugh. 'You'd think not, wouldn't you? But it's all theatricals. Justin's idea was to bring mediumship into the twenty-first century. It's a tricky balance. You don't want it to be too showy, so that people think it's just another stage magic show. But equally you've got to entertain those who've come mainly just for a night out.'

'And Mr Clayburn helped him do that?'

'He was good at what he did.' Drury's tone sounded grudging. 'Had some genuinely good ideas about how to present Justin on stage. Took it a long way from the old "anyone here missing a relative called Charlie" stuff.'

Milton could sense a 'but' coming. 'How did he do that?'

'Expensively, usually. We had a few bust-ups about that. All expenditure is supposed to come through me – I oversee all our purchasing – and has to be signed off by Justin. But Gareth could be a law unto himself. He'd go off and commit us to something without consulting anyone. Usually it was stuff he knew Justin would be happy with, but not always. There were times when I could have got us a better deal or negotiated a lower price. He didn't care about any of that.'

'And you fell out about it?'

'Sometimes. Not enough to murder him, if that's what you're getting at. Though there were times I was tempted.' He stopped. 'Sorry, that was a joke. Not a very funny one. It hasn't really sunk in yet.'

'How was he to work with generally?'

'Bloody difficult, to be honest. I hope I'm not incriminating myself by saying that.' He laughed, uneasily. 'But it's the truth. Anyone in here will tell you. Anyone but Justin, anyway. He thinks the sun shone out of Gareth's backside.'

'In what way difficult?'

'He was an arrogant bugger. Loved ordering people around. Didn't think the rules applied to him. Believed he was special in some way.' Drury stopped, as if he'd suddenly realised how vehement he sounded. 'He was talented, but that didn't justify him being rude to his colleagues. He just ordered people about. Even those of us who'd been around here a lot longer than he had.'

'You said that Mr Bannerman had a different view of him?' Donovan asked.

'That was something we could never understand. Once or twice, when Gareth had been particularly high-handed, I complained to Justin. I didn't particularly mind him being rude to me. I can give as good as I get. But I got incensed when he treated the junior staff badly. They weren't really in a position to respond or to make a fuss about it. Anyway, I approached Justin about Gareth's behaviour and he just couldn't see it. Sometimes he seemed to ignore what happened right in front of him.'

'Why do you think that was?'

'There's no doubt that Justin owed Gareth a lot. He'd helped Justin build on the profile he began to develop from his TV appearances and leverage it into something much more substantial. So he didn't want to risk losing Gareth. God knows what he'll do now. But it seemed to be something more than that. Gareth used to give the rest of us the impression he had some kind of hold over Justin.'

'What kind of hold?' Donovan asked.

'I've no idea. It was probably just bullshit. Gareth was prone to that. He liked us to think Justin needed him for something more than just the obvious reasons. As if he had something that Justin needed, and that it wasn't just his theatrical talent.'

Milton had no real idea whether or not this meant anything, but it sounded as if, at least on the face of it, they might have stumbled across a potential motive for murder. 'Did Mr Bannerman ever suggest anything like that?'

'Not in so many words. But there was always something slightly odd in their relationship I thought. Look, you'll treat this in confidence, won't you?'

'As far as we can, Mr Drury. But this is a murder enquiry. We can't make any promises. But we want you to talk honestly and openly to us. We'll use our discretion in respect of any information you provide to us.'

'It's not much, to be honest. But the relationship between Justin and Gareth always seemed – well, back to front, somehow. Justin's good at playing the slick frontman, but behind the scenes it always felt as if Gareth was the one pulling the strings. As if this was his show, and Justin was there to do his bidding. Justin seemed weirdly subservient, and Gareth would effectively order him about. None of us could quite understand it.'

'This was in public?'

'It varied. Gareth tended to be better behaved in front of the more junior members of staff – though he wasn't averse to bullying them himself. But when they were dealing with me, he didn't try very hard to pretend he wasn't in charge. That was why we had so many arguments about the finances. I'd try to apply the rules Justin had supposedly set, and Gareth would simply ignore them. If I complained to Justin, I was over-ridden.'

'And this was because Mr Clayburn was so critical to the success of the show?'

'It felt like more than that to me. Gareth had done a good job in helping to establish Justin's image, there's no question about that. But no-one's irreplaceable. The hard work of building Justin's profile's already largely been done. There are plenty of talented scriptwriters and theatre directors who could take it forward from here. Sure, it wouldn't be easy to change, and I'm sure we'll go through some tricky times now as Justin looks for a replacement. But the basics are all in place. So I don't think it can just have been that. But I don't know what else.'

'From your knowledge of Clayburn, is there anyone you think might have reason to harm him?'

'Other than me, you mean? Seriously, I don't know. Like I say, he was a difficult man to deal with, so I wouldn't be surprised if he'd managed to rub somebody up the wrong way. And I suppose there are some nasty people out there.'

'Do you have any reason to suppose he mixed with people like that?'

'No, not at all. But I know the kind of person he was. Let's just say he wasn't one to ingratiate himself.'

'Thanks, Mr Drury. That's been very helpful. Is there anyone else in the team who was particularly close to Clayburn?'

'I wouldn't have said so. Other than Justin, obviously.'

'We'll talk to everyone in due course and I imagine we may want to talk to you again as the investigation proceeds. But we won't take up any more of your time for the moment.'

'I've probably told you all I can,' Drury said. 'But happy to help if I can. Gareth and I didn't exactly see eye to eye, but he didn't deserve this.'

They concluded the interview, and Drury led them back through to Bannerman's office so they could say their farewells.

'I hope that was helpful,' Bannerman said, when Drury had left the room.

'Very,' Milton said. 'Can we ask you about your own working relationship with Mr Clayburn?'

Bannerman looked surprised. 'Mine?' His eyes involuntarily tracked towards the door, as if he were looking for Drury, wondering what might have been said.

'I just wondered how you got on with him? At a personal level, I mean.'

'He was – well, as I said, he could be a bit of a perfectionist, and his high standards applied to me as much as to anyone else. If he thought I wasn't doing justice to something he'd written or some set-piece he'd designed, he wasn't afraid to say so. Just as I wasn't hesitant to say so if I thought something he'd written or designed wasn't up to scratch. But that was the point. That was how we refined the act. We both wanted that kind of honest feedback. How else do you improve?' He stopped, as if conscious he'd been talking too quickly. 'We respected each other's professionalism.'

'Did you ever have arguments? You said that he sometimes had rows with other members of the team. Did the same apply to you?'

'Are you trying to imply that I might have had a reason to murder Gareth?'

'I'm just trying to build up a picture of what he was like as a person.'

'And no doubt Colin's given you his view on that.'

'Mr Drury described his experiences of working with Mr Clayburn, yes. I just wondered how Mr Clayburn interacted with you.'

'We had the odd falling out, yes. But, as I say, it was always about work. It was never personal.'

'I can imagine that at times this must be quite a pressurised environment.'

'When we're preparing for a tour, it can be. And obviously when we're on tour, too, but in a different way. But that all goes with the territory.'

Milton nodded. 'If it's not an indelicate question, what will you do now? I have the impression that Mr Clayburn was central to your work here.'

Bannerman's expression indicated that this was exactly what he had been thinking about since they'd first broken the news to him. 'That's the question. We're okay for the moment, because all the work for the next tour has been done. Although there are parts of the show where Gareth's active involvement was still needed, so we're going to have to rethink those. The bigger question is what we do beyond that. I just don't know at the moment.'

'You don't think you'll easily be able to find a replacement?'

Milton sensed that Bannerman was struggling to hold himself together. It wasn't clear whether he wanted to burst into tears or explode in anger, but there was some simmering emotion just below the surface. 'If you had any understanding of what Gareth actually contributed to our work,' he said finally, 'you'd realise what an idiotic question that is. No, I don't think I'll easily be able to find a replacement. In fact, I don't think I'll be able to find a replacement at all.'

CHAPTER TWENTY SIX

'You're sure you'll be okay, mum?'

Donna Fenwick stood in the kitchen doorway, watching her mother eating breakfast. It was perhaps the third or fourth time she'd asked some variation of the question that morning.

Irene swallowed her mouthful of muesli. 'How many times do I have to tell you? I'll be fine.'

'You must be tired, though. You were up all night.'

'I wasn't up all night.'

'What time did you go back to bed, then?'

'I don't know. Fourish?' Irene lied. The truth was she hadn't been back to bed at all. She'd continued working through Gordon's papers for the rest of the night and finally, just before she knew Donna would be rising, she'd returned to her room for a shower before getting dressed. She'd been sitting in the kitchen drinking a mug of coffee by the time Donna had appeared.

'Make sure you have a lie down if you're feeling tired, won't you?'

'Of course I will. Stop nagging.'

'The tables have turned, haven't they?' Donna said. 'I can remember when you'd have nagged me for staying up all night.'

'It's my second childhood,' Irene said. 'And I'm making the most of it.'

'Do you want me to come back tonight?'

'No. You've got your own life to lead. I'll never hear the last of it from Peter if I steal you away for a second night. I'm not worried now. The back door's secure, as is the rest of the house. I can't really see our intruder having a second shot at it.'

'If you get worried or you change your mind, just give me a call.'

'I will. You'd better get off.'

Donna hesitated a moment longer, then said a final goodbye. A moment later, Irene heard the front door closing behind her daughter and breathed a sigh of relief. She'd been fearing that Donna would start to interrogate her about what she'd found during her overnight search through Gordon's papers. But clearly Donna had simply taken for granted that her mother had found nothing.

Irene wasn't sure what she really had found. She'd continued to plough assiduously through the files after Donna had returned to bed, but for a long while had found nothing of interest. The files all related to Gordon's interest in the esoteric – to telepathy, astrology, second-sight, and a range of related phenomena. But the assembled documents were a jumbled mishmash of materials – copies of articles Gordon had taken either from academic journals or from more popular sources, his own notes or summaries of books he'd read, accounts of the limited experiments he'd had the opportunity to conduct outside his mainstream academic research. Gordon had never been the most organised of individuals, and Irene had struggled to make sense of the files. To her eye – inexpert as it was in this field of research – it was difficult to understand why the files had been collated as they had, or why different sets of documents had been filed alongside one another. She presumed the significance of each file would have been clear to Gordon, but as so often he'd made no effort to communicate that significance to anyone else.

It was difficult to imagine why any of this material would be of potential interest to any third party, let alone justify a housebreaking. As the hours had worn on, she'd become increasingly convinced she was engaged in a wild goose chase. There was nothing here of value.

It was only as the clock was approaching 6.00am, and she saw the first signs of light through the uncurtained window of the study, that she finally came across a file which seemed a little more interesting. Compared with many of the others, it was a relatively slim file, which related to a series of experiments that Gordon had conducted as a younger man, while employed at a previous university.

Reading between the lines, Irene concluded that the experiments had been conducted unofficially and it was unclear how the work had been funded. Irene wondered whether Gordon had somehow bent the rules to divert some funding towards work which had not been officially sanctioned. If that were the case, it was very unlike the Gordon she thought she'd known. He could be chaotic in his administrative work – and he'd occasionally received criticism from the university authorities for being so – but he'd always been a stickler for the rules. If he'd behaved inappropriately, Irene could assume only that he must have believed he had good reason.

Whatever the truth, it was also clear from the notes that the experiments had ceased very abruptly and that the outcomes had been, in Gordon's eyes, frustratingly inconclusive. As far as she could tell from the characteristically rambling notes, the idea had been to test in laboratory conditions the abilities of a group of individuals who had supposedly demonstrated various forms of extra-sensory abilities. Gordon had thought that the initial results had been promising, and had been keen to proceed further but was unable to secure additional funding.

Her impression from Gordon's account was that there had been some controversy among the research team about the results, but that there was general agreement that the study was worth progressing further. It appeared that at least some of the subjects had demonstrated potentially genuine abilities, although the level of performance had been very varied.

Towards the back of the file, Irene found a list of the participants in the experiments. Her eye was caught immediately by the security classification - Confidential: Top Secret. The wording immediately struck her as odd. There were areas of university work that dealt with highly confidential material, sometimes with national security implications. But she'd never come across that kind of classification in respect of her own area of work, and she wouldn't have expected it to relate to Gordon's. Clearly, the names of the subjects were confidential in so far as they represented personal data – and there was no question that Gordon should not have stored them in a file kept insecurely at home. But she couldn't envisage why the list of names would have justified such a high level of classification.

Was this what the intruder had been seeking? It seemed unlikely. This document had been sitting in this file for over a year since Gordon's death, and for goodness knows how long before that. Why would anyone come looking for it now? Indeed, how would anyone even know it was here?

But the classification continued to nag at her. Why would a list of participants in a psychological experiment be treated as 'Top Secret'? She looked again down the list. It included the individual's name, address, occupation and some notes of their supposed 'abilities'. There were around 30 names, and they seemed a very mixed group. Some were students. Others ranged from accountants to police officers. Some had clearly volunteered in response to advertisements placed in unspecified journals. Some had apparently been identified and 'recommended', although the document did not specify by whom. In some of these cases, there was an asterisk next to the individual's name. A note at the bottom of the document indicated that this represented an individual identified by 'Government sources'.

Government sources. That was interesting, she thought, taken alongside the 'Top Secret' classification. Was it possible that the security services had somehow been involved in the study? Had they been the mysterious source of funding?

It wasn't impossible. Gordon had told her about CIA interest and involvement in similar studies in the US, though she understood that their enthusiasm for the concept had waned relatively quickly.

She wanted to tell herself that Gordon wouldn't have brought this information home if it had remained genuinely sensitive, but she'd known Gordon well enough to be aware that such considerations hadn't always figured in his thinking. It wasn't that he'd been irresponsible as such, more that his mind tended to be focused elsewhere. She could easily envisage him bringing this material home without really even thinking about its content. He might even have brought it here specifically to avoid it being destroyed or discarded within the university system.

But it was still a stretch to imagine that the sensitivity of this document might have resulted in someone trying to acquire it through house-breaking. The real question was whether she was likely to stumble across any more likely candidate among Gordon's papers. Finding this document had simply confirmed how futile her search really was. Her reservations about its likely significance applied equally well to anything else she might find. All of this material had been sitting here since Gordon's death, and probably for years before that. Why would anyone break in now to try to access them?

As her thoughts reached that point, Irene had looked at her watch. It was nearly seven. The day was growing light outside. Donna would be awake and up before too long. Reluctantly, she'd left Gordon's study, intending to return to her room to shower and get dressed.

Before she'd done so, though, she'd removed the list of names from the file, folded the document in half, and taken it through to her own office. She'd hesitated a moment and then, rather than locking it in any of the secure cabinets in the room, she'd taken a book at random from the shelves and slipped the list between the pages. She'd replaced the book back in its original place, taking care to leave no sign that it had been moved. It wasn't exactly an impregnable hiding place, but she reasoned that it would take any intruder longer to find it there than anywhere else.

Not, she had added to herself, that any intruder was really likely to be interested in it. She knew she was just wasting her time. Gordon would no doubt have told her that it was linked to the psychology of moving out of this house. That she was trying to give some meaning to her recollections of her late husband, trying to perform one last act in his memory before she finally moved on. Something like that, anyway, she'd laughed to herself. That had been one of the things about Gordon. He'd had a theory about everything.

CHAPTER TWENTY SEVEN

As a Superintendent, Marty Winston had somehow managed to blag an office to himself, which was relatively unknown even for the more senior ranks in the 'open plan' culture of the building. It was a tiny room with glass walls, but it still constituted a private space that allowed Winston to separate himself from less privileged members of the team.

Not that Winston was particularly aloof. Murrain had had various relationships with his managers over the years, ranging from the amicable and productive to the downright hostile. His relationship with Winston was closer to the former end of the spectrum. From Murrain's perspective, Winston had his faults but generally did a decent job. He no doubt thought much the same of Murrain. They respected each other and generally rubbed along pretty well.

In any case, Murrain's attitude to the senior ranks had softened as he'd grown older. That was partly due to general mellowing but mainly due to his marriage to Eloise, who had now reached the dizzying rank of Chief Superintendent and was tipped to rise further still, assuming she wanted to. Eloise was hardly a typical senior officer, but she'd made him aware that the stresses and challenges at that level were no less than those he faced closer to the front line. Murrain was conscious, for example, of how much effort Winston put into shielding his team from all the demands emanating from the upper ranks.

As he arrived outside Winston's office for their scheduled meeting, he was surprised to see that Winston was sitting talking to another visitor, the office door firmly closed.

'Marty tied up?' Murrain asked one of the administrative staff stationed in the adjoining open-plan office. 'I was due to see him, but I can come back.'

The young man looked up from his screen as if he'd only just registered Murrain's presence. 'He said just to go in when you arrived.'

'You're sure? I don't want to interrupt anything.'

The young man shrugged. 'What he said.' He returned to tapping away at his keyboard in a way that indicated he had nothing further to add.

Murrain knocked gently on the door, and Winston waved for him to come in.

'Kenny. I've someone here who apparently wants to talk to you.'

The man sitting opposite Winston looked familiar, but it took Murrain a moment to place him. He'd last seen this man standing in the darkness outside his house. The man who called himself Derek Whitcomb.

Before Murrain could speak, the man rose and held out his hand for shaking. 'Good to meet you, DCI Murrain. I'm Charles Barnett. Ministry of Justice.'

Murrain nodded. 'Good to meet you, Mr Barnett. What can I do for you?' He looked at Winston, hoping some explanation might be forthcoming from that direction. In response, Winston gave a barely perceptible shrug.

'It's a private matter. I was just asking Superintendent Winston if there was somewhere where I could talk to you alone.'

'I'm sure that's not necessary,' Murrain said. 'If it's an official matter, surely Superintendent Winston needs to be party to it. I'd be very uncomfortable talking about any issues without his input.'

'I've been explaining to Superintendent Winston that it's a rather complicated and delicate personal matter. I'd rather talk to you alone in the first instance.'

'If it's a matter of police business, we have a duty to be completely above board. Don't you agree, Marty?' Murrain said, directing the last question directly to Winston.

To Murrain's slight surprise, Winston looked uncomfortable. 'It might be better for you to talk privately to Mr Barnett in the first instance. There seem to be various – interests involved.'

Murrain had no idea what was going on here, but he assumed Winston had received his orders from on high. Winston was a cautious man and he wouldn't normally go along with anything substantially outside normal protocols. 'I see.'

Barnett smiled. 'I promise you I'll say nothing that will compromise you or Superintendent Winston. If it were possible for me to handle this in some other way, I would, believe me. But it's probably better if we err on the side of caution for the moment.'

Whatever the man's name might be, he was the consummate civil servant, Murrain thought. Capable of generating a string of portentous sounding verbiage without actually saying anything. 'If Marty's happy, let's talk.'

'You can use the small meeting room over the corridor,' Winston said. 'I'll make sure you're not disturbed.'

Murrain gestured for Barnett to follow him across to the designated meeting room. As he closed the door of the room behind them, Murrain said, 'Charles Barnett?'

'I'm grateful you went along with my little charade. I assumed you would, at least until you knew more, but I had a nervous moment.'

'Is there any reason why I shouldn't just walk back into Marty's office and tell him that you've been apparently stalking both me and my wife, calling yourself Derek Whitcomb?'

'Because it would make things very awkward for all of us. Including Superintendent Winston. I know you're a smart man, DCI Murrain. It would be better for all of us if you just listened to what I've got to say before you take any precipitate action.'

'Go on, then. Fire away.' Murrain sat himself at the meeting table, gesturing for Barnett to do the same. 'So what do I call you? Whitcomb or Barnett?'

'It doesn't really matter. Let's stick with Barnett while we're here. Then there's less risk of us tripping up over it.' Barnett smiled, as if this were some kind of standard joke in his profession.

'Okay, Mr Barnett. Fire away.'

'First of all, DCI Murrain, I apologise for causing you any embarrassment in the workplace. I would have preferred to handle this some other way. I'm sorry you and your wife wouldn't talk to me privately.'

'When somebody approaches a police officer to talk "privately", that's usually a signal to talk to Professional Standards,' Murrain pointed out. 'We can't afford to be compromised or even to risk possible compromise. Everything we do has to be above board.'

Barnett's expression suggested that Murrain was talking a foreign language. 'I understand that now. The culture I work in is perhaps a little different.'

'I imagine so. Why did you approach my wife first?'

'I thought she might prove more receptive to my request. I generally find that, when I'm talking to police officers, the more senior ranks are more responsive to co-operating with us. I thought she might at least listen to what I had to say.'

'So what is it you have to say?'

'I understand that some years ago you participated in a university-based psychological study?'

'I've no idea what you're talking about.'

'This was some twenty years ago. 2002, to be precise.'

Murrain frowned. 'Right. I'd almost forgotten. It was something I volunteered for out of curiosity. It looked interesting.'

'Out of curiosity? Can I ask you about the nature of the study?'

'You seem to have more information about it than I do,' Murrain said. 'I wouldn't have remembered it if you hadn't mentioned it. You're presumably well aware of the nature of the study. Can I ask you what this is all about?'

'Our understanding is that the study was examining a number of subjects who claimed to have some kind of – I'm not sure what the word is – extrasensory abilities.'

Murrain could feel himself bridling. This was a subject he felt uncomfortable discussing at any time. He certainly had no desire to talk about it with some pseudonymous spook who seemed unprepared even to put all his cards on the table. 'Mr Barnett, I've no desire to be difficult about this, but I've really no idea why any of this is your business. Whether or not I attended some academic study twenty years ago is surely of no interest to anyone.'

Barnett picked up the laptop bag he'd been carrying with him. He unzipped the bag and rooted inside for a few moments. Then he pulled out a slim file. He flicked through the pages and eventually settled on a page. He pushed the file across to Murrain. 'This is your name, DCI Murrain?'

The page appeared to be a list of those who had participated in the study. His own name was there, with his occupation shown as 'police officer' and some brief notes based on his own description of his experiences with his so-called 'gift'.

It occurred to Murrain that he'd experienced no sensations since he'd first encountered Barnett in Marty Winston's office. He wondered about the significance, if any, of that. Perhaps it reflected Barnett's own skills in concealing his thoughts and emotions.

'I do wish you'd stop playing games, Mr Barnett, and simply tell me what this is all about. Why on earth are you interested in my participation in this study? It was a weekend's event, and as far as I'm aware it went nowhere. I don't think I even received any feedback on the results.'

He recalled now his disappointment that the study had apparently proved so inconclusive. He'd been attracted to it because he'd hoped that it might provide some insights into what he experienced. At that point, as a rookie cop in his early twenties, he'd been struggling with the intensity of the sensations he'd been experiencing. He'd been aware of his 'gift' for as long as he could remember. In his childhood years, he'd just assumed that it was something shared by everyone. It was only as he entered his teenage years that he first became aware that what he experienced was unique to him. When he'd tried to describe it to others, they'd expressed bafflement which quickly evolved into ridicule. That was just how teenage boys were, and he'd rapidly learned not to talk about it.

For his own part, he'd found the sensations not unpleasant. Sometimes they were useful, for example warning him not to involve himself with certain individuals or activities. Sometimes they were simply baffling, with no significance he could easily discern. In short, it was the same pattern that had continued through most of his subsequent adult life.

However, when he'd first joined the force, the nature of the sensations had changed. Looking back, he suspected that it was because he was dealing with situations and individuals that were more intense and emotional than those he had previously encountered. Even as a probationary officer, he was often dealing with people at the extremes, and his waking and sleeping hours were filled with disturbing images and sensations – sudden flashes in the forefront of his mind, those endless whispering voices clamouring at his ears, dreams that woke him drenched in sweat. This was in the days shortly before he'd met Eloise, and there was no-one with whom he could share what he was experiencing. There were days when he became convinced that he had some kind of mental health problem, that the stresses of the job were proving too much for him.

Murrain couldn't recall now where he'd seen the advertisement for the study. He assumed it must have been in one of the national or local newspapers. It had caught his eye initially because it was being conducted in a local university. Volunteers were being sought from among those who believed that they had had some significant experience of 'telepathy, precognition, extrasensory perception or similar phenomena'. Murrain had assumed initially that his own apparently haphazard experiences would not qualify him for the study. Even so, he'd called the telephone number provided.

To his surprise, the researcher he spoke to had sounded enthusiastic about his participation. He later discovered that many of those who had volunteered had either been judged to be frauds or able to offer only very limited experiences. Murrain's recurrent, if frequently inconclusive, sensations were judged to be both more credible and more interesting. So he'd duly spent a weekend participating in a range of experiments conducted under laboratory conditions.

He couldn't recall much of the detail now, except that he'd found the majority of the experiments largely incomprehensible. He'd taken part in the hope that the study would provide him with some insights into his condition, but he'd come away only with a feeling that he'd failed to live up to the researchers' expectations. They'd assumed he could somehow conjure up coherent and consistent answers to their questions, whereas in reality he often struggled to explain the nature of his experiences even to himself.

As far as he could recall he'd heard nothing more about the study after he'd left the university campus on the Sunday afternoon. There'd been no feedback on his own contribution, no update on the results of the study, not even a letter of thanks for his contribution. It had all seemed rather discourteous, but he'd quickly put the experience behind him. He'd barely thought about the study since then.

'What can you tell me about the study, DCI Murrain?' Barnett asked now, as if reading Murrain's train of thought.

'Almost nothing, I can barely even remember what exercises they put us through. I remember there were the usual ESP type tests, and various interviews.'

'Can you recall who was running the study?'

'Not their names, I'm afraid. There was some older professor who, as far as I could judge, was leading the study, and several younger researchers.' Murrain shrugged. 'I'm afraid that's all I can tell you.'

'What made you volunteer in the first place?'

'I'm afraid that, once again, that's really none of your business, Mr Barnett.'

'My understanding is that you believe you do have some kind of – well, let's say extrasensory abilities.'

'I'm not sure where you get your information from. But, as I say, that's really my business.'

Barnett nodded, as if Murrain had confirmed his views. 'Do you apply your talents in your police work, DCI Murrain?'

'I've really no idea where this is going, Mr Barnett. Why on earth are you interested in this twenty year old study? For that matter, why are you interested in me? I'm just a humble copper. As far as I'm aware, I've never had any dealings with your kind of people.'

'Nor do you want to. I understand that. A lot of people feel that way. But you don't really have a choice.' Barnett's smile had returned, but now there was no sign of humour or goodwill in his eyes.

'I'm not sure why you're threatening me or what you're threatening me with, but I'm not easily intimidated.'

'I'm not threatening you,' Barnett's smile was unwavering. 'I'm afraid, if anything, I'm warning you.'

'Warning me?'

'And quite possibly helping you.'

'I'm afraid you really have lost me now.'

Barnett tapped the file on the table between them. 'Have a look at the list of participants again. Under G.'

Baffled, Murrain ran his finger down the list as Barnett had indicated. It took him a moment, but then he saw it. Gorman, Andrew. Student. Potential 'skills' were listed as 'potential telepathy, precognition.' He looked up at Barnett. 'Andrew Gorman was one of the participants?'

Countless questions were already beginning to run through Murrain's head. They had issued a media release about Gorman's murder a few days earlier, so his name was in the public domain. But he was wondering quite what Barnett knew about the case, and why he'd taken such a convoluted route to get to this point. 'You're aware that Mr Gorman's death is the subject of a current investigation?'

'That's one reason I'm here, DCI Murrain, as you may have surmised.'

'What I'm surmising, Mr Barnett, is that I'm in the middle of a major murder investigation, and you seem to be here playing incomprehensible games. Do I understand from this that you have some information pertinent to Andrew Gorman's death? If you do, I'd suggest you start sharing it immediately before I think about charging you with obstructing a police investigation.'

'I really don't think that would be wise. And the position is a little more complicated than you're suggesting.'

'I'm sure it is. I'm just sick of listening to you playing your enigmatic games when I've got a job to do.'

'I'm sorry if I've appeared enigmatic. Force of habit, I'm afraid.' He tapped the file again. 'But we do have some concerns about the provenance of this study and about the people who were involved in it.'

'I don't understand why you think a twenty year old study is likely to have any relevance to a current murder investigation.'

'It's conceivable that it doesn't. But, if not, we have an unlikely coincidence on our hands. To be frank with you, Chief Inspector, when I first approached your wife I was unaware of Mr Gorman's death. That was drawn to our attention only in the last few days. That was why I felt it necessary to make a more formal approach.'

'You could just have contacted us in the usual way,' Murrain pointed out. 'If you have information that's relevant to our enquiry, you have an obligation to share it with us as a matter of urgency. This isn't a time for your smoke and mirrors operations.' Murrain paused, conscious that news of Gareth Clayburn's death wasn't yet in the public domain. 'It's quite possible that time really is of the essence in this case. We already had a second death which we think may conceivably be linked to Gorman's.'

'A second death? Can I ask the name of the victim?'

Murrain's first instinct was tell Barnett that any sharing of information had to be reciprocal. He'd had more than enough of Barnett's game-playing. But he saw that Barnett's eyes were fixed on the file in front of Murrain.

Murrain looked down at the list of names. He couldn't understand now why he hadn't spotted it when he'd first looked at the list. It was only a few lines above Gorman's entry, but of course he hadn't been looking for it.

Clayburn, Gareth. Student. Supposed talents included potential telepathy, precognition. Almost an identical entry to that for Andrew Gorman.

Murrain looked up from the file. 'I don't know what this is all about, Mr Barnett. But I've had enough of this cloak and dagger approach. I want to get Superintendent Winston in here now, and I want to do this by the book.'

'As you wish, Chief Inspector. I understand your position, and I hope I can rely on yours and Superintendent Winston's discretion if necessary.'

Murrain stared at him for a moment. 'That,' he said, 'rather depends on what you have to tell us.'

CHAPTER TWENTY EIGHT

Geoff Nolan turned off the kitchen light and peered out through the window into the night. It was pitch black out there, although only early evening. He reached to his left to turn on the pair of spotlights that he'd had installed over the rear garden. They were security lights, primed to be turned on by any movement, but the constant buffeting of the wind and rain had caused him to turn them off earlier in the evening. Now he wanted to see what was going on out there.

When they'd first decided to buy this place, it had seemed the best of ideas. On a fine summer's day, the place was idyllic, with its rear garden backing on to the river. They'd held barbecues and summer parties out on the large lawn, even fancy-dress parties with the guests dressed up in mock Edwardian boaters and crinolines. Those parties were an example of what made some of his colleagues resent him. Academics weren't supposed to have enough money to live in a place like this and to throw parties like that. Even so, they rarely refused his invitations.

They'd first begun to see the downsides of the house the previous winter. When they'd bought the place, he'd asked about the risk of flooding and had been assured that, in all the house's hundred or so year history, the river had never risen sufficiently high to give any cause for concern. With no confidence in estate agents or even surveyors, he'd checked back through the history himself and confirmed the claim to be true.

Until the previous winter. Then they'd watched the waters slowly rise far above their usual levels. It had been an eerie and unnerving experience. The river had gradually breached its banks and gradually, inch by inch, encroached along the lawn. The rains had continued to fall for a couple of days, and the line of the water had drawn ever closer to the house. Even when the rain had finally ceased, the waters had continued to rise, the river swollen by the flow from the hills behind them.

They had escaped disaster only by a few yards, saved by the gradient of the lawn. If the river had risen just another few inches, Nolan had thought, it would have been sufficient to send the waters cascading across the ground floor of the house. They had already taken the precaution of moving the more valuable and irreplaceable furniture to the upper floor, but even so the damage would have been considerable.

That had been last year. It had rained torrentially for two days and finally stopped, to be succeeded by several weeks of relatively dry weather. The waters had quickly receded and the river had returned to its usual level.

This year, it had already been raining for two days and, according to the forecasts, the weather showed no sign of changing. As yet, the river hadn't quite risen to match its previous highest point, but it was likely only to be a matter of time.

All in all, it was not looking good.

Nolan stood now staring at the waters, as if he might drive them back through sheer force of will. A large segment of the lawn was already lost to the river, and in the beam of the spotlights he could see the rushing water pitted by the hammering rain. The trees were thrashing in the strong wind.

They had done everything they could. There were sandbags lined across the rear of the house, and, as in the previous year, they had moved everything they could to the upper floor. Tonight, though, he was feeling much more fatalistic. It was going to happen. The waters would eventually come pouring in here, creeping their insidious way through the sandbags and the locked doors and windows, spreading slowly across the carpet, gradually encroaching through the house.

As yet, there was no suggestion that they should evacuate. There had been a visit from two police officers earlier, who had issued them with an unnecessary warning about the rising waters but had not suggested abandoning their homes. That was probably sensible. The roads at the front of the house were likely to be safe. If they needed to get out of here, they could do so easily enough. For the moment, all they could do was sit here and await the slow motion destruction of their home.

Nolan turned the kitchen lights back on, and walked back through to the living room. His wife, Bred, was sitting on the sofa watching one of the news channels. 'How's it looking?' she said.

'Not good.' He lowered himself on to the sofa beside her. The sofa was one of the few items of furniture they'd not managed to move upstairs, as its size wouldn't allow them to navigate the stairway They'd moved the main television upstairs and Bred was watching a portable model Nolan mostly used for computer gaming. 'Still below last year but rising. I'm not hopeful.'

'Shit.'

'Quite. Nothing much more we can do, though.'

'Just wait and pray.'

'Or, in my case, just wait.' Nolan had never been the religious type. He sat beside Bred, feeling increasingly restless. Finally, he rose again and wandered over to the front window. He pulled back the curtain and gazed into the night, hoping to gain some comfort from the relative normality at the front of the house.

It was a wild night out there, the wind roaring through the trees and shrubbery in the front garden. Beyond, Nolan could see the road, slick from the rain, smeared with the orange of the streetlights. Although it wasn't late, it seemed deserted.

He was about to pull the curtains closed when something caught his eye. He pressed his face to the glass, peering into the darkness. 'There's someone out there.'

'What?' Bred said from behind him.

'I'm sure there's someone out there.' In fact, he was less certain now. What he'd taken to be the silhouette of a figure standing inside their driveway now looked like nothing more than a pattern of leaves and branches. 'Hang on.' He turned off the lights, then returned to the window. Whatever he'd thought he'd seen, it was no longer there, if it ever had been. He couldn't now even identify the patch of shrubbery he might have mistaken for the motionless figure.

'Any sign of anyone?'

'No. I must be going stir crazy.' He turned the lights back on.

'Why would anyone be standing outside in this weather?'

'That's why I thought it was so strange.'

'Less strange if you've imagined it.'

'Well, yes.' He sat back down beside her. It was at moments like this that he realised why he still loved Bred so much. She was perfect in most respects, of course, but what he appreciated was her calm in the face of almost any kind of crisis. She coped quite happily with almost any challenges life was likely to throw at her.

It was ironic that he was just about to embark on a television series about a bunch of people with supposed paranormal abilities, all of whom were likely to turn out to be charlatans of various kinds, while the most promising subject of any such study was sitting right beside him. He'd had little doubt, from the first time he'd met her, that she had some kind of unique ability. He still didn't know what those abilities actually comprised, but he was sure they were real enough.

If he was honest with himself, that was one reason why he'd initially been attracted to her. There were many other reasons, of course, which had proved more important in the longer term. But at that first meeting, he'd simply been intrigued by her.

Even her name had been baffling. 'Bread?'

She grinned, having no doubt faced this countless times before. 'No, Bred. B-R-E-D.'

'Right. That's…unusual?'

'I'm not even entirely sure where it comes from. My real name's Brenda, though I hate that. My mum tells me I was nicknamed Bred because when I was small I used to spell my name Bredna. But my sister tells me it was because I wouldn't eat anything but bread. It's possible she was just winding me up.'

He hadn't known what to make of all that, so he'd just nodded politely. At that stage, he'd found her amusing and intriguing. It was only when they'd begun to test her abilities that he became more interested in her. They'd quickly come to the conclusion, that weekend, that most of the volunteers had little to offer them. It wasn't that they were frauds, or at least not for the most part. Most of them sincerely believed they had experienced some kind of paranormal event, but these had generally been isolated instances most likely attributable to coincidence. Many had been familiar phenomena – dreams which appeared to predict real life events, thinking about friends or relatives at the point of their deaths, the apparent remote sharing of thoughts between relatives.

Their tests of these individuals had proved predictably disappointing, with no convincing evidence that they had any kinds of unusual abilities. Perhaps unsurprisingly, the most interesting candidates seemed to be those who were most tentative about making any strong claims for their abilities. Bred had been one of those. In the initial interview, she had described a range of experiences she'd had over the years, many of which had proved inconclusive. But on a number of instances she had had insights about people or situations, which appeared inexplicable in any conventionally rational way. Her test results had still been highly inconclusive, but had yielded results with a greater statistical significance than most.

There had been a handful of similarly promising subjects over the weekends they had run. Some had appeared more in control of whatever abilities they possessed, but all had been able to offer something more than the norm.

Nolan had been unsurprised when the funding for the project suddenly dried up. He'd known they were operating out on a limb, and he'd already had some concerns about the potential impact on his burgeoning career if their work had leaked to the tabloids, even though they were operating under the leadership of a relatively eminent academic. Professionally, however, he'd been disappointed. He'd genuinely felt that there was scope for the studies to produce some interesting results if they'd been allowed to work further with the most promising subjects.

He'd never been privy to whatever internal politics had resulted in the closure of the project, but he'd known there had already been some controversy about the impact of the work on some of the subjects. Most of those who seemed to have some potentially interesting capabilities, including Bred herself, struggled to articulate exactly what it was they experienced. It was clear that some of them were troubled and disturbed by their sensations, and Nolan had had some reservations about the possible impact of their study on these individuals' mental health. Even in those early sessions, some had behaved oddly.

Whatever the reason for the termination of the study, it had happened suddenly and unequivocally. The research team had been disbanded, and Nolan and others had returned to their core work. The group of subjects were sent home at the end of the last weekend, and there had been no contact with them.

Except that Nolan had exchanged telephone numbers with Bred, and they'd met again soon after, initially for a drink and then for a series of dates that had turned into a relationship and finally into marriage. Nolan had told himself at the time that there was nothing unethical about this. Once the study had ceased, there had been no professional relationship between the two of them. Within a few weeks, the question had seemed irrelevant.

Looking at Bred sitting beside him now, Nolan wondered how much of his initial interest in her had been related to whatever unique abilities she possessed. She was an attractive woman, of course, and they'd known immediately they made a very compatible couple. It hadn't taken Nolan long to realise he was in love with her, and she'd appeared to feel the same about him. They'd been happily married now for the best part of twenty years, and he hadn't regretted a moment of it. But he still wondered whether any of that would have happened if he hadn't been fascinated by her supposedly psychic powers.

The real irony was that, once they were in a relationship, he felt no desire to probe further into the nature of those powers. Bred herself had clearly had no desire even to discuss them, much less to try to dissect what lay behind them. She had volunteered for the study because she had felt disturbed by her abilities and wanted to understand more about them. But the outcome of the experiments had left her feeling even more uneasy about what her mind might be capable of, and she'd quickly decided she wanted simply to leave it behind. Once in a while, she'd relate to Nolan some sensation or experience she'd had, and quite often those events had proved apparently significant. But each time that had simply left her feeling more uneasy.

Now, almost as if she were reading his thoughts in the most literal sense, she said, 'I had one of them this afternoon.'

He didn't need to ask what she was referring to. 'Oh, yes?'

'Like – I don't know – an image. A vision, even.'

It was unlike her to use such direct language to describe her experiences. 'What sort of vision?'

She hesitated. 'I'm not sure. I'm never sure, you know that. But it was something to do with the river, with the waters rising. I could sense a rising darkness.'

'That's real enough.' He tried to keep his tone light. 'Just a question of how far it rises.'

'That wasn't the part that disturbed me. There were figures. People. I don't know how many exactly. Three or four. Maybe more. The rain was falling, the wind was howling. It was pitch black and they were fighting with the weather, with the rising waters. I'm not sure what was going on, but I think there was someone – at least one person – in the water. Maybe the others were trying to save him. But I think there was also some conflict between them. As if they were fighting each other, as well as the elements…'

It was rare for her to discuss her experiences in this level of detail, so he knew that this must be troubling her. 'This felt – significant to you?'

'It was stronger and clearer than my usual sensations. But that doesn't necessarily mean anything.' They'd occasionally talked about this in the past, on the rare occasions when she'd been prepared to talk about it. Her experiences were very varied – ranging from momentary impulses to more intense sounds and visions. Although he hadn't, after that first weekend, ever subjected her abilities to any kind of formal study, his impression was that there was some correlation between the intensity of her sensations and their ultimate significance. But it was far from straightforward. Occasionally, her experience seemed to provide a relatively obvious prediction of some real life outcome. More commonly, her sensations appeared to offer a more oblique insight into some subsequent event, only recognisable in retrospect. And in many cases her feelings seemed to have no relevance at all to the real world.

Nolan was conscious of the risk of confirmation bias in his response to all this. It was easy to give undue weight to the instances where Bred's sensations seemed to relate to some real life event, and to disregard the cases when they came to nothing. Even so, over the years he had seen enough to make him take her experiences seriously. 'So what do you think?'

She was silent for a moment. 'It wasn't just what I saw. It was the feeling behind it. The emotion. I don't often get that. The whole scene felt drenched in it. An intense feeling of – I don't know – malevolence. Anger, maybe. Something really dark and unpleasant, anyway.'

'You think it was here?' Nolan said. 'The river, I mean.'

'I think so. Somewhere close by, anyway.'

He reached out to take her hand. 'Are you worried? By this vision, or whatever it is, I mean.'

'I am, actually. It's a long while since I had one of these experiences that really disturbed me. Maybe it's just because I'm worried about the flooding anyway. But this felt different from anything I've experienced in recent years. I didn't even want to talk about it. It shook me.' She was clutching his hand more tightly now. 'There's something wrong out there, Geoff. Not just the flooding. Something else. Something very wrong.'

CHAPTER TWENTY NINE

'How does it feel then?' Joe Milton asked.

Marie Donovan was lying beside him, her head on his lap, her feet draped over the arm of the sofa. She was reading a crime novel he'd recommended to her. 'How does what feel?'

'Living together.'

'Is it official now then?'

'Well, I've told Kenny. So I guess that commits us.'

'I suppose so. I'm not sure it feels any different, to be honest.'

'No, well. We were pretty much doing it anyway.'

'So what's the plan? We sell your place?'

'If you're happy with that.' They'd discussed this on numerous occasions, and always reached the same conclusion, but it seemed more real now.

'It makes the most sense,' Donovan said. 'This is nearer the office and a bit bigger.' She grinned. 'Nicer, too.' Donovan's house was an Edwardian terrace in Hale. Whether it was nicer than Milton's place was debatable, he supposed, but it certainly had more character.

'If you say so,' he said.

'But it's up to you, too.'

'I'm only too happy to move out of that place,' Milton said. 'To be honest, I never much liked it. Gill and I just drifted into it. It was convenient, the right price, supposedly low maintenance.' He laughed. 'It seemed like a good idea at the time, but I don't think either of us really ever settled there.'

'And you want to put it behind you,' Donovan said. 'Start afresh.'

'I suppose so,' Milton said, doubtfully. 'I hadn't really thought about it like that.'

'It was how I felt after Liam died. I mean, it was complicated because that was tied up with a whole lot of other stuff. But I knew I needed a new start. That was why I moved up here.'

'Just as well,' Milton pointed out. 'We wouldn't have met each other if you hadn't.'

'You don't know that. I've have tracked you down somehow.'

He laughed. 'You're probably right, though. I don't feel comfortable in that place any more. It feels like a different part of my life. Probably best if I draw a line under it.'

'There we go, then. It's settled.'

'So you're comfortable we're making the right decision, then?'

'Aren't you?'

'Pretty sure we are. It's taken us long enough, after all.'

'So now we just have to look forward.' She paused. 'I'm not sure it seems right to be this happy when we're in the middle of a major murder enquiry.'

'If we wait until we're not in the middle of a major enquiry before we allow ourselves to be happy, we might be waiting a long time. You think this really is just one enquiry? Not two separate murders?'

'I don't know,' she said. 'It feels that way to me. There are too many coincidences between the two killings.'

'From what we heard at Justin Bannerman's offices, it sounds as if Clayburn might have been more than capable of making enemies. Less clear why anyone would want to kill Gorman. Unless you think we've just got a homicidal house-breaker on our hands.'

'What does Kenny think?' Donovan asked. 'What's his spider sense telling him?'

'I'm not sure. I was going to try to grab a word with him before I left this afternoon to update him with what little progress we've made. But he was tied up in some earnest looking discussion with Marty Winston and some other guy.'

'Probably budget cuts,' Donovan said. 'It's usually budget cuts.'

'God, I hope not. We're stripped to the bone as it is.'

'You do realise we've only been living together for half a day and we're already talking shop, don't you?'

'We've a lifetime of this ahead of us.'

'Now there's a cheery thought.'

Milton grinned. 'I can't think of anyone I'd rather do it with, though.'

'Well, that's something.' She pulled herself up to a sitting position. 'I think this calls for a glass of wine, don't you?'

'What? Us talking shop?'

She picked up one of the cushions from the sofa and threw it at him. 'I was thinking more about celebrating moving in together. Or at least telling Kenny that we've moved in together.'

'Fair enough.'

'Pity we haven't got any fizz. It'll have to be a bottle of red.'

'I can cope with that.' He followed her through into the kitchen. While she busied herself opening the wine, he walked over and opened the back door.

The cold wind hit him like a blow, soaking his exposed face and hands. Donovan's small garden was relatively sheltered from the weather, but even here the force of the storm was considerable. He could hear the thrashing of the rain in the shrubbery that lined the boundaries of the garden.

Donovan moved to stand behind him, pressing her warm body against his. 'Glad we haven't got to go out in that.'

'You're not going to send me home at the end of the evening, then?'

'Depends how well behaved you are.'

'I'll do my best.' He turned and pressed his lips against hers. They kissed deeply for a moment, then he said, 'It's going to be all right, this, isn't it?'

'I reckon so,' she said. 'Mind you, if you don't shut that door, I might have to push you out into the night.'

'Fair enough.' He pushed the door shut, feeling the force of the wind resisting him. When it was finally closed, he turned the deadlock, and pulled across the two heavy bolts. Good solid security, which he suspected reflected Marie's experiences of a few years before.

'That's better,' she said. 'Just the two of us together, and the world shut out.'

'Let's keep it like that,' he said, 'for as long as we possibly   can.'

CHAPTER THIRTY

'You're kidding,' Eloise said. 'Whitcomb actually came in to see you?'

'Exactly. Except his name's Barnett. Apparently,' Murrain said.

'Whatever his name might be, I'm willing to bet that it's neither Whitcomb nor Barnett.'

'Quite.'

'So he's a spook then?'

'I'm assuming so, though he still didn't say so in so many words. But then he never seems to say anything in so many words. He's clearly someone with influence. The instruction came down from on high that he wanted to see me.'

'So what was it all about?'

Murrain hesitated for a moment. In general, he and Eloise made a point of not discussing their respective police business. This was partly because both of them ideally wanted to maintain a separation between their work and their domestic lives. There was always a danger that two old coppers living together ended up talking about nothing else. But it was mainly because neither wanted to risk compromising the other. It was all too easy to end up revealing something inappropriate about an ongoing investigation or, in Eloise's case, about some impending organisational change. Even as it was, everyone assumed they both gained advantageous information through their shared pillow talk. If only they knew, Murrain thought.

Eloise's idea of pillow talk generally involved telling him to shut up because she was trying to sleep.

This, though, felt different to him. It was partly because, in his discussions with Barnett and Marty Winston, he'd had to open himself up much more than he was prepared to do. He'd been forced to talk openly and in a work context about subjects that he normally kept very much to himself. The other two had clearly been oblivious to his feelings, but there'd been moments in their meeting when he felt as if he'd been figuratively stripped naked, exposed in ways he'd found almost physically painful.

Having been through that, he decided he was damned if he was going to be less open with the person he loved most. 'It's a weird one,' he said, finally. 'Barnett wanted to talk to me about my – well, my gifts.'

He had never known how to describe his unique abilities, whatever they might be, to Eloise. Eventually, they had settled on referring to it as his 'gift'. He had used the term semi-ironically initially, because he'd always felt that, whatever it might be, it was as much a curse as a benefit. But the term had stuck and become their shared shorthand.

'That was what he told me on the phone,' Eloise said. 'I assumed it was some gossip he'd picked up about you on the grapevine.'

'It was a bit more than that. He was interested in some academic study I was involved in twenty or more years ago.'

'What?'

'It's a long story. It was something I volunteered for. I thought it might help me gain a better understanding of – well, what I was experiencing.'

'Why on earth was this Barnett interested in some academic study from years ago. Even by the arcane standards of the security services, that's a bit of a stretch.'

That was the way it had seemed to Murrain too. Barnett had reluctantly agreed to Murrain's demand that Marty Winston should join them in the meeting. Winston himself had seemed equally baffled as Barnett had outlined the reasons for his visit.

'You're telling me you're here because Kenny took place in some kind of university study twenty years ago?' Winston had said to Barnett. He'd looked initially at Murrain, as if expecting that some explanation would be forthcoming from that direction, but Murrain had simply shrugged.

'We're interested in all the individuals who participated in that study,' Barnett said. 'Not least because we think they may be in danger.'

'Two of them are already dead,' Murrain pointed out.

Winston blinked. 'What?'

Murrain slid the file, still open at the list of participants, across to Winston. 'Read down the list.'

Winston ran his finger down the names and then stopped. 'Shit.'

'Quite.'

'If you've got something you want to share with us,' Winston said to Barnett, 'I think you'd better begin talking PDQ.'

Barnett sighed, his demeanour suggesting the whole meeting was just an unnecessary interruption to his valuable time. 'As DC Murrain rightly says, it's a long story—'

'Then I suggest you give us the abridged version,' Winston said.

Barnett glared at him for a moment. 'The study DCI Murrain was involved in was funded by the intelligence services. One of our former senior officers had something of a bee in his bonnet about this kind of thing, unfortunately.' He shrugged, as if embarrassed by the gullibility of his predecessor. 'We weren't the only ones. The CIA had spent a lot of money on exploring so-called "remote viewing" back in the 1990s, though even they'd given up on it by the time we got involved. There were some other government studies going on at the time—'

Winston noisily cleared his throat. 'I hope this is going somewhere.'

'The point is that the study was an unofficial one. We channelled the money through an appropriately eminent academic to ensure any positive results would have credibility. He organised the sessions himself. I assume he used university facilities and staff, but we left it to him to arrange all that. We kept our distance.'

'Deniability,' Murrain said.

'I think even our former boss recognised that if this were exposed in the media it might be somewhat awkward for us. Anyway, the study went ahead over several weekends. It attracted a rather motley assortment of individuals—'

'Thanks,' Murrain said.

'Present company excepted, obviously.' Barnett smiled. 'But I'm afraid the project did attract several apparently rather disturbed individuals.'

'I was probably one of them at the time, to be fair,' Murrain said. 'I was struggling with what I was experiencing. I thought I'd grown accustomed to it but it intensified when I joined the force. There were times when I thought I might be going mad.' He smiled at Winston's expression. 'This was a long time ago, Marty. I'm not like that any more.'

'That's a matter of opinion,' Winston said.

'Judging from the notes, there were a mix of people participating in the study,' Barnett went on. 'Some of them were like yourself, DCI Murrain. People who felt they'd had experiences they couldn't easily explain. Some, I suspect, were little more than fantasists. I imagine that any study of this kind attracts a few people like that.' He paused. 'And there were a handful of genuinely disturbed individuals.'

'Disturbed in what way?' Murrain said.

'People who were experiencing some form of psychosis,' Barnett said. 'I don't claim to be any kind of expert in the field, but I'm told these were people experiencing various forms of hallucination. Seeing things that weren't there. Hearing internal voices.'

'That's the point.' Murrain was never comfortable discussing this, and he knew that Winston shared his discomfort. Murrain had never known what Winston really thought about Murrain's supposed 'gift' – whether he believed what Murrain had told him or whether he was just prepared to go along with it for a quiet life. 'It does feel something like that. That was why I was so worried at the time. I'd grown used to it as a kind of background noise in my life. When it suddenly intensified, I began to worry I was losing my reason.'

'If it's any belated consolation,' Barnett said, 'the notes of the study suggest that there was something in your – abilities. Your positive results are well above the norm, to the point that the researchers had provisionally concluded that they were statistically significant, at least. The notes are all couched in typically cautious academic speak, but there were only a handful – half a dozen or so – of the subjects they felt merited further examination. You were one of them.'

'Pity they didn't tell me that at the time,' Murrain said. 'It might have helped put my mind at rest.'

'The study was rather hurriedly terminated. There was an incident on what turned out to be the final weekend.'

'An incident?'

'One of the subjects, a man called Edward Crichton, became convinced that others – it's not clear if this was directed at other subjects, the researchers or both – were listening into his thoughts. He was clearly paranoid and probably psychotic. Some time towards the end of the first day, he attacked another of the participants.' He paused, apparently for dramatic effect. 'He stabbed the other person.'

'Stabbed?' Winston said.

'In the stomach. Several times. With a knife that he'd brought in with him.'

'In the stomach,' Murrain echoed.

'Quite so.' Barnett tapped his fingers on the table. 'I understand your Mr Gorman died in the same way.'

The details of Gorman's death had not been released to the public, but Murrain was unsurprised that Barnett had been able to access this information. 'As did our Mr Clayburn,' Murrain said.

Barnett nodded. 'That doesn't surprise me.'

'So what is it you know, Mr Barnett?' Winston said. 'So far all you've given us is a history lesson. If the killings really are linked to this study twenty years ago, what's prompted this now?'

'There was one other facet of the study I've not yet mentioned to you,' Barnett said.

'Then perhaps it's about time you did.' Winston gave Murrain a barely perceptible grimace. Murrain knew Winston well enough to recognise that he was tiring of Barnett's circumlocution.

'One of the factors that prompted my predecessor to sponsor the study was that we believed some of our competitors had made some progress in this field.'

'Competitors?'

'I'm sure you don't need me to spell this out,' Barnett said. 'The opposition, if you like.'

Winston nodded. 'And had they?'

'They wanted us to think so. Personally I think it was nonsense. But our life is always one of smoke and mirrors. We had a supposedly credible source who led us to think they'd had some success. But we always have a credible source when it suits us. In this case, it was enough to persuade the powers that be to release some funding so that one of our leaders could ride his personal hobbyhorses. Apart from anything else, we no doubt wanted the opposition to believe we were making progress in the same area. It's all a game.'

'A game that seems to have resulted in two deaths,' Winston said, acidly. 'So far.'

Barnett nodded, suddenly looking weary. 'Quite. Anyway, after the stabbing, the whole study was immediately terminated. Fortunately, the victim, although badly injured, ultimately survived. Crichton was arrested, charged with grievous bodily harm, but was judged unfit for trial and ended up in a secure hospital. He was there until he was judged fit for release some five years ago.'

'What's he been doing since then?' Winston had picked up a pen and was doodling on a note pad, drawing spirals that started on the outside and then gradually circled in on themselves. A sign of his growing frustration, Murrain thought.

'That's something of a mystery,' Barnett said. 'He wasn't on our radar. There was no particular reason he should be—'

'He committed a violent assault as a result of a study your people had commissioned,' Winston pointed out. 'Given how many people you lot keep tabs on, I'd have thought he ought to have been on the list.'

'The study was seen as something of an embarrassment,' Barnett said. 'The individual behind it was quietly pensioned off, and there seems to have been a collective unspoken agreement to act as if it had never happened.'

Winston gave a snort of disgust. 'So you've no idea what this person's been up to?'

'We believe that our – competitors may have taken an interest in him.'

'Why would they do that?' Murrain was already beginning to suspect he knew the answer. 'If he was just a violent psychotic.'

'They wouldn't have, if that was all he was,' Barnett said. 'But I think they suspected, as did the original researchers, that he was something more. That he did have some kind of unique abilities.'

'He wasn't just psychotic?'

'Quite so. He was one of that small number of subjects – like yourself, DCI Murrain, as I say – who the researchers felt were producing significant results. In fact, they were genuinely excited by him, even more so than the others. I hope that doesn't offend you, DCI Murrain?'

Murrain allowed him a smile. 'I've never seen it as a competition. Or, if it is, it's one I'd have preferred not to have to participate in.'

'It seems as if Crichton might have had some genuinely interesting talents. I suspect if our man had been allowed to remain in post, he'd have tried to follow it up, despite the attack. But, as I say, the whole thing was immediately suppressed. The lead researcher was sufficiently mortified by what had happened that he raised no objections. Just shut the study down and sent the research team back to their day jobs. Meanwhile, our competitors maintained their interest in what we'd been doing.'

'How were they even aware of it? I mean, I know you lot leak like the proverbial sieve but even so…' Winston said.

'Who knows? As you imply, some of my colleagues seem more interested in the smoke and mirrors than in the national interest. It's possible that our man leaked it as a revenge for his enforced retirement. What we do know is that they've maintained an interest in this ever since. I'm a little surprised you've never had an approach from them, DCI Murrain?'

'Not that I'm aware of. If they did approach me, they must have done it so subtly I didn't notice.'

'Perhaps your reputation precedes you,' Barnett said. 'I've made a point of checking out your record, and you don't appear to be a natural target for such an approach. You seem a rather – ethical man.' He spoke the last words almost with an edge of disapproval.

'There are a few of us about.'

Winston was clearly growing increasingly impatient. 'To get back to the point, what's this man been doing for the past five years?'

'We've been doing some retrospective checking,' Barnett said. 'It looks as if he's spent a fair portion of the time out of the country. We're not sure where.'

'You're not sure where?' Winston said. 'I thought you were supposed to be the intelligence services.'

'We're not infallible, Superintendent Winston. Crichton was initially released on licence, but at some stage appears to have simply vanished. Our suspicion is that he was at some point provided with a fake passport and left the UK. But that's supposition. We've not actually been able to trace his movements during that period.'

'That sounds rather extraordinary,' Winston said. 'I thought it was impossible to go completely off-grid.'

'It depends what resources you have behind you,' Barnett said. 'We're assuming that our man was shipped somewhere for – well, let's say for further examination. All we know is that he seems to have reappeared on the radar a few months ago, arriving from France via the Eurostar.'

Murrain had been trying to follow the thread of this narrative. 'I'm not sure I understand. You said you had no interest in this man. That he'd effectively been written out of your history. So why did you become interested in him on his return?'

'We didn't,' Barnett said. 'We only became interested in him again by accident.'

'That doesn't surprise me,' Winston snorted.

Barnett ignored him. 'What brought this to our attention was the death of one of our officers.'

Winston looked up, his familiar expression of bored cynicism suddenly wiped from his face. 'What?'

'What I say. You may even recall the story. About three months ago. Middle aged man by the name of Julian Stevens attacked in North London. Apparently motiveless crime. Lots of tutting in the press about knife crime out of control. He was stabbed in the stomach.'

Winston nodded. 'Of course he was. It says something about the state of the UK that I don't even remember the story. Presumably his occupation wasn't made public?'

'He was a civil servant,' Barnett said. 'Just very unlucky. Wrong place at the wrong time. Collateral damage in some gang war or some such.'

'That sounds depressingly familiar,' Murrain said. 'The wrong place at the wrong time part, I mean. It's what we've been wrestling with in our investigations.'

'Quite,' Barnett said. 'But we don't tend to take anything for granted when it's one of our officers involved. We conducted a few enquiries of our own.'

'Were the Met advised of your enquiries?' Winston said.

'I understand they were advised at the appropriate level.'

'Which presumably didn't involve telling anyone who was actually involved in the investigation?'

'I couldn't honestly say,' Barnett said. 'But I can assure you we didn't interfere with the police investigation. We were more interested in working out why Stevens might have been targeted. He was a middle-ranking officer, one of those whose career had never really taken off. He worked on cyber crime and counter intelligence stuff. Bit of a boffin, at least by our standards. Also a bit eccentric, but that's less unusual. Had something of a drink problem, which he thought no-one knew about. Nothing serious, but enough for us to keep an eye on him. All in all, though, he was an odd figure to be targeted by a foreign power. Not an obvious target.'

'I'm sure that would have been a great consolation to him,' Winston said. 'So why do you think he was targeted?'

'We can be rigorous when it suits us. This one left us uneasy. Maybe it was just what it appeared to be. But it goes against the grain for us to take anything at face value. So we tracked back through his career in the hope of spotting something that might have provided a motive for his death.'

'And?'

'There was nothing. Nothing in the last twenty years, at least.'

Murrain had already pulled the file back towards himself. He looked up at Winston and nodded. 'He's on the list. Stevens, Julian. Civil servant. Evidence of potential telepathy and precognition.'

Winston shook his head. 'You're seriously telling us that this guy Stevens, along with our two victims, was killed because he participated in an academic study twenty years ago.'

'It appears so,' Barnett said. 'Unless we have the strangest coincidence on our hands. We now have four victims who were involved in that study.'

'Four victims?' Murrain said.

'We believe so. Another London killing about four weeks ago. This one received even less coverage than Stevens's death. A homeless man found dead in a backstreet near Covent Garden. Guy in question was an alcoholic, drug-user, you name it. Police assumed he'd either got into a fight or was mugged.'

'Stabbed?' Murrain said.

'In the stomach. Exactly the same. A man called Ronnie Hargreaves, it turned out.'

Murrain ran his finger down the list and again nodded. 'On the list.'

'We don't know much about Hargreaves,' Barnett said. 'But it looks as if he was one of those who didn't cope well with – well, what his brain was doing to him.' Barnett looked at Murrain. 'I'm sorry I'm not expressing this very well. My impression is that these – qualities, whatever they might be, are psychologically challenging?'

'You might say that,' Murrain said. 'It's impossible to describe to anyone who hasn't experienced it. It can be very destabilising. I've found ways of dealing with it, but I imagine many wouldn't – especially if their experiences are more intense than those that affect me.'

'We saw that with Stevens,' Barnett agreed. 'The booze was part of his way of coping.'

'My apologies for breaking up this psychology seminar,' Winston said impatiently, 'but can I just make sure I'm clear on this.' He looked at Winston. 'You seriously think we have four killings linked to participation in an university study literally at the turn of the century And you have potential evidence about the two London victims that you've presumably not shared with the Met?'

Barnett sighed, 'Again, we've liaised with them at the appropriate level. My impression is that they didn't take our information terribly seriously. It's a mistake to think we can just snap our fingers and we have the police at our beck and call.'

'I've never laboured under that delusion,' Winston said. 'Try snapping your fingers here and see how far you get. But while you've been playing your games, four deaths have mounted up.'

'We've been as open with the police as we're able to be,' Barnett sad. 'Probably more than we ought to have been. I tried to talk to DCI Murrain informally because I thought he might be more receptive to what I had to say than if I went through the formal channels. But as soon as I became aware of the first killing up here, I put everything on a formal footing. That's why we're talking now.'

Murrain knew Winston was more than capable of getting a procedural bee in his bonnet, and felt it was time to move the discussion on. 'So we think this man is potentially responsible for at least four deaths. Is it possible there are others?'

'We've checked all the names on the list,' Barnett said. 'Other than a couple who died in unrelated ways – one from cancer, the other in a car accident – everyone else seems safe and well. So we believe these are the only victims who were involved in that study.' He shrugged. 'We don't know if there might be others, of course.'

'But why now?' Winston said. 'Okay, you say he's been out of commission for whatever reason for a number of years. But why would he return now and start killing these people? What's prompted that?'

'Other than that the man's clearly deeply disturbed, I don't have an answer to that,' Barnett said. 'But there is one other thing about the victims.'

'Go on.'

'It's not just that they participated in that study. If you check through the notes, you'll see that all those who've died have something else in common. They were all people who, like DCI Murrain here, were judged to have abilities that were at least worthy of further investigation. These were all people who were judged to have some significant gift.'

'Are there many more of those?' Murrain asked. 'On the list, I mean.'

'That's one of our problems,' Barnett said. 'We can't be sure. There are a couple we do know about, including DCI Murrain, but beyond that we don't know. Frustratingly, the official records of the study are incomplete. We don't know what happened to them. The research lead seems to have been rather chaotic, for all his eminence. We also suspect that, when the study was brought to its premature end, he may have appropriated some of the findings for his own use.'

'Have you approached him?' Murrain asked. He could see Winston was wondering why they should take any of this seriously, and Murrain had to acknowledge it sounded pretty far-fetched as a motive for multiple murder. On the other hand, ever since Barnett had started talking about this his own inner voices had been telling him to listen. There was something in this, he thought, even if he wasn't quite sure what it was.

'Too late, I'm afraid,' Barnett said. 'He died a few months back.'

'Not stabbed, I hope,' Winston said, morosely.

'Not on this occasion.' Barnett paused. 'Odd story, though. He was suffering from early onset dementia. Went missing, and his body was ultimately found on the edge of the M60 near Bredbury where he lived. Looked as if he'd been hit by a car. Verdict was accidental death.'

'You're not suggesting…?' Winston said.

'I'm just telling you the facts.'

'So where does this get us?' Murrain said. 'I mean, where's this Edward Crichton now?'

'I'm afraid we don't know.'

'You've lost him again? Have you ever thought of leaving this stuff to the professionals?' Winston said.

Murrain half-expected that Winston might have finally pushed Barnett too far, but Barnett simply smiled. 'Perhaps your people would have done a better job than we did, Superintendent, but I doubt it. We've only been tracking Crichton retrospectively, as it were. When we became interested in the study, we tried to discover what had happened to him. All we learnt was that he'd left the country and apparently vanished off the system, and that he subsequently reappeared on the system a few months back. As far as we can tell, he was living in Highbury for a month or two. We've checked his finances and he seems to have had a reasonable amount in a newly established bank account. The source of the money isn't clear. He doesn't seem to have been working. He then disappears again. Had paid his rent in advance but just walks out. Nothing after that. No access to his bank account, no use of any of his bank cards, nothing.' He smiled at Winston. 'Proving yet again how easy it is to step off the grid if you've got the resources to do it.'

'So all we know is that he's out there somewhere and, if you're right, potentially dangerous,' Murrain said.

'If he's right,' Winston echoed, his voice heavily loaded with irony. 'It sounds pretty out there to me. I'm not comfortable with us wasting our time on this.'

'We don't have much else,' Murrain pointed out. 'I'm assuming Mr Barnett's credentials are sound enough, or he wouldn't be here. I think we have a duty to take this seriously.'

'I think you should,' Barnett said. 'I wish there was something more concrete I could offer you.'

'We've got bugger all,' Winston said.

'You said there were a couple more potential targets you were aware of, including me,' Murrain said. 'Who's the other?'

Barnett leaned forward and pointed to the list. 'There,' he said, 'that one. She seems to have been one of the strongest subjects.'

Murrain looked down at the list. 'Dalton, Brenda,' he said. 'Known as Bred.'

CHAPTER THIRTY ONE

She had fallen asleep in her chair, midway through some absurd cosy crime drama on TV. Now, she'd never know which inhabitant of that chocolate box village was the unlikely perpetrator of the string of grisly murders.

She wasn't sure what had woken her. Probably just her uncomfortable posture in the armchair. Perhaps the sharp rattling of the rain against the window. Perhaps her own growing sense of unease. It had been increasing since the morning, and she couldn't pin down exactly why.

She'd been able to distract herself earlier in the day by attending one of her regular meetings in the city centre, braving the heavy rain to scurry along Oxford Road crouched under an umbrella. But when she'd returned to her home later in the afternoon, she'd immediately felt a sense of discomfort. Even the house, which had been her refuge for so long, felt empty and desolate. As she stood in the hallway, she felt lost in what now felt like nothing more than a vast barely-used space.

It was what Donna had been telling her for months. She'd resisted because this had still felt like her home. Now, unexpectedly, it didn't. She walked through into the kitchen and checked the back door. It was still firmly locked and bolted. There had been no further sign of her intruder, but she had a constant irrational fear that he was still there somewhere in the house. Donna had checked the whole house for her, and she'd been round herself that morning to double-check. But that wasn't the point. Someone had been in here, without her permission, without her knowledge, for some reason she couldn't begin to fathom. It had left her feeling exposed, vulnerable.

For the rest of the afternoon, she'd struggled to continue as normal, but she'd felt the anxiety gnawing away at her. It was what Gordon had always described, semi-jokingly, as her 'womanly intuition'. It was a quality that had always fascinated him – one of the factors, indeed, that had initially sparked his interest in extra-sensory phenomena. He'd tried a few experiments with her over the years, but the results had always been frustratingly inconclusive. She had no control over any abilities she might possess. Over the years, she'd had a few experiences of the kind of anxiety she was feeling now, often apparently linked to some distant or impending event – the death of her mother and other loved ones, even Gordon's own death. She'd never thought too much of them – she knew enough about coincidence and confirmation bias not to jump to any conclusions – and had been surprised Gordon had taken them as seriously as he had. But he 'd never been able to achieve any statistically significant outcomes in his laboratory tests, and had certainly never been able to replicate the more intense of her experiences. If she did have some kind of ability, its functioning appeared to be largely random and entirely outside of her control.

Even so, when she experienced them, the sensations were powerful. The anxiety made her sick to the stomach, the same kind of fear she might have felt if faced with an immediate and direct threat.

That was what she was feeling now.

It had faded away early in the evening after she'd eaten, and she'd felt relaxed enough to treat herself to an evening of mindless television, hoping it would distract her from whatever had been troubling her earlier. It had worked initially, and she'd relaxed to the point where the soporific programming had made her drowsy.

But as soon as she awoke the anxiety returned, if anything even more intense than before. She sat up sharply and glanced involuntarily over her shoulder, momentarily convinced someone had entered the room behind her. She forced herself to walk into the kitchen to make a cup of tea. She needed some sense of normality to help her counter her unease.

She found herself unexpectedly relieved that the kitchen door was still firmly locked and bolted. But she was already beginning to recognise that her anxiety was not – or at least not primarily – linked to her fear of the intruder. Something else was going on. It was the kind of anxiety she'd experienced before, unrelated to anything that was happening immediately around her. It was anxiety on behalf of someone else.

Someone in danger.

The thought had entered her head unbidden, and she had no idea what had prompted it. She had been able to link her previous experiences of this kind of anxiety, if only retrospectively, to something happening to a family member or a friend. An impending death, a serious illness, some kind of major tragedy. In every case she could recall, she had subsequently become aware of some event which had appeared to offer a correlation – she was reluctant to describe the relationship as causal – to her unprompted emotion. But the anxiety itself had always been non-specific. This was the first time, as far as she could remember, when she had envisioned anything as precise as a sense of danger.

Most likely, this was all just the product of her own anxieties and over-active imagination. She didn't know anyone closely who was likely to be in danger. She'd spoken to Donna earlier that evening, and she and Peter had been fine. She had no other close family members and no friends she could imagine being at risk. This was no doubt just a combination of her worries about the intruder, her continuing fears about the move, and perhaps even the stories she'd been watching on the news earlier about local flooding. The floods posed no risk to her or, as far as she was aware, to anyone she knew, but some of the reports had been distressing.

She finished making the tea, still trying to rationalise away her nagging unease. But it remained there, lurking in the back of her brain and the pit of her stomach, unshakeable. Almost without volition, she found herself taking the mug of tea upstairs into Gordon's old study. Before she'd left that morning, Donna had persuaded her to finish tidying up the detritus left by the break in. They'd carefully replaced the papers back in the filing cabinets, with Irene trying as best she could to replicate Gordon's eccentric approach to ordering the documents.

Now, she reopened the cabinets and extracted the files relating to that mysterious study of twenty years before. She had no idea what had led her back to these, or why she thought they might be relevant to her current anxiety. Except that, she told herself, the intruder had clearly been looking for something.

She carried the files through to her own office, and sat down at her desk to work through them once more. Somehow she felt that examining them in here, rather than in Gordon's study, would enable her to review them more rationally, unclouded by her own emotions about Gordon's life and tragic death.

She still had lingering doubts about Gordon's death which she'd never shared, even with Donna. She recalled waking, on the morning he went missing, to find that he was no longer in bed beside her. That had surprised but not unduly concerned her. In those latter days, she had generally tended to wake before he did, but it wasn't unknown for him to wake first and silently leave the room. That had never worried her, despite his condition. For the most part, Gordon had still been able to function relatively normally. He was often confused and highly forgetful, but he was able to find his way around the house safely – perhaps because they had lived here so long it had simply become second-nature to him. His main problem had been simple inertia. He would sit down in front of the television and apparently simply forget to get up again, unless she chivvied him. Without her support, it wouldn't have occurred to him to make himself anything to eat or drink. He did remember to go to the lavatory, but sometimes only when it was likely to be too late.

For that reason, even in those last days, she'd never seen him as a threat to himself. He'd been assessed by the local care team who'd come to much the same conclusion. He could be hard work, as Irene had known only too well, but, as long as his condition didn't deteriorate, he was unlikely to be at risk.

On the occasions when he awoke before her, he had generally just made his way down downstairs, sat himself in his favourite armchair in his pyjamas, and waited till she appeared. She had often wondered what had been going through his mind during those long minutes while he had sat waiting. The answer, she guessed, was not much. When she appeared, he would gaze blankly at her for a few moments and then say, just as he always had, 'Morning, love. Sleep well?'

She had always nodded, asked him whether he'd slept well himself, and then gone to make them both a cup of tea. That first exchange had begun to feel like something almost ritualistic – a form of words devoid of meaning but maintained for the sake of form. She was unsure whether he even really understood her response, but he'd always nodded politely and smiled. She wondered whether he would have done the same whatever she'd replied.

So, on that last morning, she'd descended the stairs confident, without really even thinking about it, that he would be sitting in the armchair waiting for her. But the armchair was empty, and the ground floor of the house felt unexpectedly chilly.

Suddenly worried, she'd checked all the downstairs rooms and headed into the kitchen. The back door had been standing ajar, just as it had been on the day of the break in. On that occasion, it hadn't occurred to her to wonder whether the door had been somehow forced. She'd assumed that somehow Gordon had managed to find and use the key that she normally kept in her handbag by the bed. However he'd done it, it appeared that he'd left the house and then set out – well, where?

That remained a mystery even after she'd called in the police. As far as she could judge, Gordon must have left the house dressed only in his pyjamas, dressing gown and slippers. His clothes from the previous day still sat in the bedroom, untouched. As far as she could tell, no other clothing had gone missing. The back garden was safely enclosed on all sides. The only possibility was that he had made his way down the side of the house to the front garden and then set off down the street.

Irene had woken herself at around 8.00am. She had no idea what time Gordon might have risen, but he hadn't normally woken before 7.00am. She had been astonished that no neighbour or passer-by, on foot or in a vehicle, had noticed this elderly man walking aimlessly through the streets in his nightwear. But the police had interviewed their neighbours, checked CCTV and traffic cameras, and ultimately launched a media appeal. No-one, it seemed, had spotted Gordon.

In the end, he was missing overnight. Irene had come to the conclusion that he must have fallen somewhere, perhaps in one of the local parks or open areas, and was lying hidden from view. She had had no illusions that, if that was the case, Gordon would have been unlikely to survive beyond the first night. It had been late in the year, the nights cold, and Gordon would almost certainly have died from exposure.

It had been a surprise when, the following morning, the police had arrived on her doorstep to advise that Gordon's body had been found on the edge of the M60, having apparently been hit by some passing vehicle. He was still dressed as she had expected, in his pyjamas and dressing gown, although the slippers were missing.

It had made no real sense to her. Gordon had been killed by the impact of the vehicle, which meant that he had been still alive at the point he'd strayed on to the motorway. The police had initially been vague about the precise time of death, and she'd wondered whether the accident might have occurred sometime on the preceding day. But that seemed unlikely. The body had been visible to passing vehicles, lying on the hard shoulder of the motorway, and it was inconceivable that it had been there for very long without being seen. Somehow Gordon must have survived through the cold night dressed only in his nightwear.

It had seemed impossible, and at the time she hadn't even wanted to think about the implications. She'd envisaged him desperately seeking shelter, unable to find his way back home, unable to make contact with anyone, until that moment when he'd somehow emerged out on to the busy motorway.

The police had seemed more interested in trying to track down the driver of the vehicle that had hit Gordon. If Gordon had been hit by a truck, it was possible that the driver had simply been unaware of the impact. If the vehicle had been a car or van, the police thought it was unlikely the driver had failed to see Gordon. In short, they'd been less concerned about the reasons for Gordon's extended survival and more about the circumstances of his death.

She'd been too confused and emotional to think much about it at the time. She supposed the police priorities had been correct. Where Gordon had spent that night was one of those mysteries that would probably never be solved, whereas the police had had a reasonable expectation they might identify the driver of the vehicle. As it had turned out, even that had proved to be vain hope.

So the circumstances surrounding Gordon's death had remained a mystery. Her impression prior to his death had been that, though he was sometimes confused, he had generally recognised where he was. His condition was typified, more than anything, by inertia, an absence of initiative. So she'd always wondered what had prompted him to leave the house that morning, what had made him wander out from the garden, and why he'd been unable to find his way back. And then how he'd managed to survive overnight, making his way the best part of a mile to the motorway without being seen. The police had offered her little more than a metaphorical shrug. 'These things happen,' one of them had said to her. 'Sometimes we just don't get to the bottom of it.'

Just thinking about those words now increased her sense of unease. At the time, in her distress and grief, she'd accepted what she was being told. She'd assumed the police knew best and been prepared to trust their judgement. In the months since then, she'd tried to put it all behind her, focusing instead on her memories of the past and her anxieties about the future. The circumstances of Gordon's death were unimportant now. The simple fact was that he was gone, and she had to face the future without him.

It was only now that the issue had resurfaced in her mind. She told herself it didn't matter, that there was nothing she could do anyway after all this time. But the concern had lodged itself in her mind, an incongruity that snagged at her thoughts.

She placed the files on the desk in front of her, and reached out to the bookshelf where she'd concealed the list of names. For a chilling moment, she had a fear the book had been moved, but after a second she spotted it tucked unobtrusively where she'd left it. It occurred to Irene, as she took out the papers and unfolded them, that Donna would think her mother had gone quite insane if she could see the lengths she had gone to to conceal this twenty year old list.

Irene still had no idea what had brought her up here, or why she'd imagined that her anxiety would be alleviated by perusing these files yet again. All she could do in the face of this was trust her instincts. And her instincts – those nagging voices in the back of her brain – were telling her that these files were important.

She looked again down the list of names, none of which meant anything to her. There had been some notes elsewhere in the files summarising the outcomes of the experiments for each individual, but frustratingly the notes had been anonymised. It was only now, as she examined the files more carefully, that Irene realised that each name on the list had been annotated, in Gordon's handwriting, with a short code which in turn related to each set of notes. She imagined that this was another example of Gordon being cavalier with the intended confidentiality standards for the study. If he'd been challenged on it, he'd have been baffled. He'd have seen it simply as a shortcut to help him carry out his work more efficiently.

Irene spent a few moments lining up each of the notes with the individuals. It was clear from the notes, which she'd only skim-read previously, that the study had not been a conspicuous success. The vast majority of the subjects had produced no statistically significant positive results, with only a handful meriting a seemingly grudging 'Worthy of further study' or similar note.

Irene made a note of the handful of names on the list which had produced apparently positive results. One of the names, Andrew Gorman, rang a vague bell, as if she'd heard it somewhere recently. She couldn't immediately recall where, so she booted up her laptop and searched on-line for the name.

As soon as she saw the news stories on the screen she remembered. Andrew Gorman had been the name of the poor man killed in his front garden, supposedly having pursued a burglar from his house. She registered the story because it had been relatively local, and it had resurfaced in her mind when she'd experienced the break-in just a few days later.

It was surely just coincidence, though. Gorman wasn't that unusual a name. There was nothing to connect the man who had been killed with the name on the list in front of her, other than that he was approximately the right age to have been a student at the time of the study. Even so, as soon as the news stories had appeared on her screen, she'd felt an odd frisson, her intuition telling her that this mattered.

She ran her fingers down her list again. None of the other names meant anything to her. On the first of the weekends, there was, alongside Gorman, a Gareth Clayburn, a Kenneth Murrain and a Brenda Dalton. There was a similar handful of names from each of the subsequent two weekends.

She redirected her attention back to the notes, in the hope something might catch her eye. She still had no idea what she was looking for, or indeed even why she was even looking.

It was only when she looked back at the list of names that something else caught her eye. Beside each of the names there was a brief note of the individual's full name, occupation, reasons for volunteering for the study, and any other points of relevance. Alongside Brenda Dalton's name was a note: 'Known as Bred.'

That rang a vague bell. She'd known, or at least come across, a Bred somewhere. She recalled having a conversation about why the woman had come to be known by that name. Some childhood misspelling of Brenda, she recalled.

It took Irene a few moments to disinter the memory. She thought this Bred had been married to some colleague or ex-colleague of Gordon's. Someone who'd worked closely with Gordon at some stage, she thought. Probably one of his research students. Gordon had been a fairly charismatic presence, for all his disorganisation, and had tended to attract keen followers. He'd been good at mentoring them too, and Irene knew a number had gone on to successful careers in the field. She could almost visualise the individual in question but the name continued to elude her.

She flicked over a few pages in the file, and found a list of the researchers who had worked on the aborted study. It was a long shot, but perhaps the person in question had been one of those. After all, she told herself, how else would he have met Bred Dalton?

In fact, she recognised that name almost immediately, not only from her recollection of meeting him a few years before, but also because he was now something of a celebrity. Dr Geoffrey Nolan. She wondered how she could have forgotten. She'd only met Nolan a handful of times, usually at university events, and recalled him as a larger than life character. That was probably why she'd not initially made the connection with Bred Dalton. From what she remembered, Nolan tended to dominate any gathering – not unpleasantly, as she recalled him as a generally likeable individual, but simply through force of personality. Others, including his own wife, faded into the background by comparison. Irene had been unsurprised when Nolan had begun to build a profile for himself as a TV academic.

As soon as she saw Nolan's name, her sense of unease reignited, a cold clutch to her stomach. Irene prided herself on her rationality, and had always gently mocked Gordon's interest in her supposed intuition. Even so, she'd always felt the reality of what she experienced, even though she'd made a point of downplaying its importance. The sense she had now was something that she couldn't ignore, however much she might want to, however foolish she might feel.

Something was wrong, she thought. Somewhere, out there in the cold, rain-filled night, something was very wrong.

CHAPTER THIRTY TWO

As he had earlier in the evening, Geoff Nolan turned off the kitchen light and walked over to the window, peering out into the darkness. It took his eyes a few moments to adjust before he could make out the shapes of the trees and bushes, swaying rhythmically against the pounding of the wind.

He considered switching on the spotlights again to gain a better view, but something made him pause. It was almost that he didn't want to see what might be out there. Bred's comments earlier had left him feeling genuinely rattled. He could see how shaken she was by the experience she'd had earlier, and he knew her too well to take that lightly. Her instinct had always been to play down any sensations she felt. This was the first time for many years that he could recall her talking so earnestly.

Something wrong out there.

Those had been her words. When he'd asked what she meant, she had simply shaken her head. She had no more idea of the significance of her words than he did. All he knew was he had to take them seriously.

The water had risen further up the garden towards the house. It was still some way from reaching them, but he knew it would eventually creep up to their back door. In the near darkness, the water looked almost as if it was boiling, its surface pounded by the constant wind and rain.

Earlier, Nolan had felt a potent sense of threat from the rising water. Now, it felt almost irrelevant. Yes, it would damage their carpets and furniture, and no doubt create a mess that would take months to sort out. But he could cope with that kind of material damage. He wasn't exactly short of money.

But Bred's anxieties had disturbed him. He felt increasingly convinced that there was something else out there, something threatening. Somewhere in the distance he could hear the sound of thunder, and every few minutes the sky shivered with sheet lightning. The electrical storm felt like a harbinger of worse to come.

He was startled by the sudden sound of the landline phone ringing in the living room, the unexpected intrusion feeling as if someone had been listening in to his thoughts. He looked at his watch. It was nearly ten. Bred had already headed upstairs with Nolan's encouragement, to calm herself by reading before trying to sleep. Neither of them had acknowledged it openly, but Nolan assumed neither of them was likely to get much sleep tonight. The ceaseless noise of the wind and rain combined with the impending threat of the floods would keep both of them awake.

Who the hell would be calling them at this time of night? Probably just some international junk call, like most of those they received on the landline now. He walked back to the living room, turning on the lights as he entered, and stood waiting for the call to go to voicemail.

He'd half expected that the call would be cut at that point, but instead he heard a slightly tentative female voice saying, 'I hope I've got the right number. I'm trying to contact Professor Geoffrey Nolan—'

He picked up the phone. 'Hello?'

'Professor Nolan?' The voice was female, probably elderly. Not a voice he recognised.

'Speaking. Can I help you?'

'You won't remember me, Professor Nolan. It's Irene Fenwick. Gordon's wife. Well, widow now, sadly.'

Nolan needed no further prompting. He had only the vaguest recollection of Irene Fenwick, but Gordon Fenwick had been a hugely influential figure at the start of Nolan's career. He'd been one of Nolan's PhD examiners, and then his first boss as a young research associate. Fenwick had had his failings but he'd been a hugely charismatic and inspiring teacher, responsible for cultivating Nolan's enthusiasm for his areas of work. They'd been good friends for a while, though they'd largely lost touch as Nolan's career had developed. Nolan had been aware of Fenwick's death and had hoped to attend the funeral, but it had clashed with some filming commitments in London. He'd made a charitable donation as requested but it had felt inadequate as a recognition of the professional debt he'd owed to Fenwick.

'Of course,' he said now. 'I was very sorry to hear about Gordon's death. I'd hoped to attend the funeral, but…' He trailed off, conscious of how feeble his excuses were likely to sound. 'How can I help you, Mrs Fenwick?' It occurred to him, as he spoke, that Irene Fenwick had also been an academic, almost certainly with a doctorate herself, and that he'd probably just committed another *faux pas*.

'Irene, please,' she said. 'Look, Professor Nolan—'

'Geoff,' he said.

'Geoff.' She spoke his name as if it were some kind of talismanic incantation. 'I'm sorry, this is going to sound idiotic. I'm really sorry to be bothering you at this time of night.'

'No problem.' It was no doubt just because of his own overwrought state of mind but he was finding something disturbing about her tone. She sounded as anxious as he felt.

There was a moment's silence at the other end of the phone, as if she were trying to find the right words. 'It's a long story,' she said, finally. 'But I've been looking through some old files of Gordon's. I found some notes relating to a study he was involved in. We're talking about twenty years ago. It was an examination of various individuals who claimed to have – I'm not sure what's the right terminology, but various forms of extra-sensory ability.'

Nolan felt an unexpected chill run down his spine. 'If we're talking about the same study, I remember it well. It was where I met my wife.'

'Brenda Dalton,' Irene Fenwick said. 'Bred.'

'I— Yes, that's right. How did you know?'

'I came across her name in the notes. I remembered meeting her with you at a few university events. That's why I phoned you.'

Nolan glanced towards the stairs, conscious of Bred no doubt still lying awake up there. 'I'm afraid I don't understand.'

There was another moment's silence. 'I'm not sure I do either. I just had a bad feeling, and it somehow felt associated with your wife. I'm sorry. I told you it was going to sound idiotic.'

The fear he'd felt when she mentioned the study was intensifying. 'When you say "a bad feeling", can I ask what you mean, exactly?' He recalled now that Fenwick had occasionally talked about what he called his wife's 'intuition', saying she'd have made a good subject for their study. If he recalled correctly, Fenwick had attempted to persuade her to participate in one of the weekends, but she'd refused.

'It's hard to explain,' she said. 'Again, it just sounds foolish. Not the kind of thing you'd expect from a hard-bitten rationalist like me. But I get feelings, emotions, which don't seem to be linked to any rational cause. Once or twice, they've proved – well, possibly significant.'

Nolan took a breath, trying to remain calm. 'It doesn't sound foolish at all. That was the kind of thing we were trying to look at in that study. Bred sometimes has similar experiences. We've never succeeded in really testing them experimentally – at least, not since that study – but she's convinced there's something in it.'

'Is she all right?' Irene Fenwick asked unexpectedly. 'I mean, just now.'

It was Nolan's turn to be silent for a moment. 'She's upstairs right now. She's been a bit anxious. We're worried about the potential flooding.'

'Are you affected by that?' Irene Fenwick said. 'I'm sorry, I hadn't realised. I wouldn't have troubled you if I'd known.'

'No, that's fine. There's nothing much we can do about it either way. Or, at least, we've already done everything we can. But if the waters continue to rise we'll be flooded. It'll do some damage, but we're not in any danger.' As he spoke the words, he wondered whether that was actually true.

'That's good to hear. But you must have more important things to do than listen to an old woman jabber on.'

He recalled Bred's anxiety earlier, her sense that something was wrong. 'Not at all. Funnily enough,

Bred had a similar sensation earlier in the evening. She had the sense that there was something wrong. That was the way she put it. Something wrong out there.' He paused. 'To be honest, it worried me. She normally plays down these experiences, but this had clearly left her feeling disturbed.' He felt slightly foolish even admitting this to another person.

'I'm still feeling it,' Irene Fenwick said. 'I'm feeling it now, talking to you. It seemed to grow stronger as soon as I heard your voice. I'm sorry, that sounds stupid.'

Nolan was still trying to make sense of what he was hearing. 'Why did you ask about the study?'

'Because it feels to me that it's somehow connected with the study. That was when the feeling first struck me. When I was looking at the notes and saw your wife's name. So I dug out Gordon's old address book and found your number. I'm sorry. This is all just ridiculous.'

'It isn't, though, is it?' Nolan said. 'You clearly trust your intuition or whatever it is, just as Bred tends to trust hers. She doesn't always know what it means, but she thinks it means something.' Bred had never quite said this explicitly, but Nolan had no doubt it was what she thought. 'That study…' He stopped, thinking back to those weekends, twenty years before, when he'd been a young research associate keen to impress Dr Fenwick. God knew where Fenwick had got the funding from – it clearly wasn't from any legitimate university sources – but he'd been eager to try something outside the mainstream and, initially at least, Nolan had been glad to assist. It was only after they'd begun that Nolan had wondered whether partnering Fenwick on this particular hobby-horse might prove detrimental to both their careers.

The study had proved a disaster. They'd sought volunteers from various sources, including some students and some members of the public who had responded to advertisements in the national press. It had quickly become clear that the vast majority of the participants had no remarkable skills. It wasn't that they were frauds. Most of them were sincere enough. But they'd typically had some single experience – a dream or a feeling about a relative or loved one – which was easily explicable by nothing more than coincidence. Only a small number of the participants had produced results which were statistically significant, including Bred, and even those had been sporadic and unpredictable. The whole thing had ended disastrously. Gordon Fenwick had still wanted to continue, even after the stabbing, but by that stage Nolan felt they were dabbling in some potentially dangerous areas. In the end, the decision was taken out of their hands. The funding, whatever its source, was withdrawn and the study had been abruptly terminated. For his part, Nolan had felt relieved.

'What about the study?' Irene Fenwick said.

'I don't know, exactly,' Nolan said. 'It felt ill-omened, somehow.' He laughed. 'I'd normally be embarrassed saying that, but not in this context. I was never clear where the money came from.' He paused, trying to recall and articulate the reservations he'd had at the time. 'To be honest, I was concerned your husband was being taken advantage of.'

'How do you mean?'

'I'm not sure how to put this, and I hope you won't take it the wrong way, but Gordon never struck me as the most worldly of men…' He hesitated, wondering what her reaction would be.

She laughed. 'You can say that again. Or if he was, it was a world of his own. But I'm not sure what you mean.'

'There was something odd about the whole study. I couldn't put my finger on it at the time, but it felt as if there was some kind of agenda. Something above and beyond Gordon's academic interests. I'm not suggesting that he was part of that. I'm sure his intentions were entirely sincere. But it felt as if they were being manipulated. Some of the exercises we were asking the subjects to undertake, for example. They weren't what I'd have expected, and Gordon was vague about their purpose. It felt as if he'd been asked to include some elements as a condition of obtaining the funding.'

'What kind of elements?'

'For example, trying to determine the contents of documents or the detail of people's thoughts. It felt like trying to run before we knew whether we could even crawl.' He stopped again. 'It was all too sophisticated. As if someone wanted a productive use from the study rather than just exploring whether there was anything there at all. There were one or two individuals in the research team I didn't recognise at all and who didn't seem like academics. Again, Gordon just avoided the question when I asked him about them. It was all a bit odd.'

'And it ended badly, I recall?'

'Very badly. The university hushed it up and it never made the press. But it was embarrassing. I was junior enough to escape unscathed but I don't imagine it did Gordon's career much good.'

'Gordon was never exactly career minded,' Irene said. 'He was a professor by then, anyway. But I'm still trying to understand the significance of the study. Why it's troubling me now, I mean.'

'I don't know,' he said. 'It never went anywhere. Like I say, only a few of the participants demonstrated any real abilities, and even those were questionable. If we'd had the chance to do more work with them, it might have made a difference.'

'I was looking at the list of names,' Irene said. 'I don't suppose Gordon should have kept them here at home, but that was Gordon. That was where I came across your wife's name. The other one that struck me was someone called Andrew Gorman.'

'The name rings a bell from somewhere,' Nolan said.

'Probably because you've heard it on the news. It was the name of that poor man who was killed a week or so back. They reckoned he'd probably interrupted a burglary or something.'

'Oh, right, yes. I remember the story. Awful business. I noticed it because they said he was a professional astrologer of all things. Astrology's one of those areas that interests me. Professionally, I mean. How it works, why people take it seriously.' He paused. 'Curious, that, isn't it? That he should be working in an area like that. Bear with me a second...'

Nolan's laptop was on the table near the phone. It was already booted up, and it took him just a moment to do an on-line search of the relevant news story. The press had managed to obtain a picture of Andrew Gorman from somewhere, and his face stared out from the front covers of most of the tabloid newspapers. Nolan suspected the picture was a few years old, and looking at it now he had little doubt. 'I've just looked at his picture on-line,' he said to Irene

Fenwick. 'I hadn't made the connection before, but now you've said it, I think it could well be him. The same Andrew Gorman who participated in the study.'

'You're sure?'

'I'm not a hundred percent certain. It was a long time ago. But we did devote quite a lot more attention to the supposed "positive" participants, and – well, he looks familiar. I think it's him.' He shivered, suddenly feeling a cold in his body that had nothing to do with the temperature in the room. 'I don't like this.'

'I don't either. I've got the names of the other positive candidates here. I don't know if any of the others rings any bells?'

'Go on?'

'There's a Kenneth Murrain, who was apparently a police officer.'

'I remember him. Big burly guy. Bit of a character. He was one of the ones who genuinely seemed to have something. He felt very uncomfortable with it, just as Bred does, I remember.' He paused. 'But I don't think I've come across him since. Who else?'

'A Gareth Clayburn?'

This time, Nolan felt a definite frisson of fear, as if a cold hand had gripped his innards. 'Gareth Clayburn?'

'That's the one. Does it mean something?'

'It does, though I'm not sure what. I thought the name rang a bell when I met him.'

'Met him?'

'That's the thing. I met him quite recently. It's a long story, but it's connected with some telly stuff I'm involved in.' He felt almost embarrassed mentioning his television work, knowing how Gordon Fenwick would have disapproved of this apparent trivialisation of their field. 'We're looking at various practitioners in what you might call the paranormal area. Examining the techniques they used, assessing whether there's anything legitimate in what they claim. That kind of thing. Anyway, one of the people we're looking at is a chap called Justin Bannerman—'

'The medium?' Her voice was unexpectedly sharp, as if he'd startled her.

'That's the one. Have you come across him?'

She didn't respond immediately. 'It's another long story. But, yes, I've come across him. Another coincidence.'

Her tone suggested she didn't want him to enquire further. 'Anyway, I was introduced to Bannerman's back-room team. And one of them – in fact, the one who seemed to be Bannerman's *de facto* number two – was called Gareth Clayburn. I only met him briefly, and the name didn't mean anything to me, but it wouldn't have done after twenty years. I wonder if I can find a picture of him on-line.' He turned back to the laptop and found Justin Bannerman's website, wondering if there might be a page devoted to the support team. But clearly Bannerman was too much of an egotist for that. There were endless posed pictures of Bannerman himself, but no mention of other names. Nolan returned to the search engine and typed in Gareth Clayburn's name in the hope of finding a reference to him elsewhere.

He pressed the Search button and then froze. 'Shit.'

'I'm sorry?'

Nolan had almost forgotten he was still holding the phone. 'I'm sorry. I've just found a stack of news stories from this evening. About Gareth Clayburn.'

'I haven't seen the news. What is it?'

'His body was found in the floodwaters in Bramhall. There's not much detail in the reports but the implication is that he was murdered.'

'My God. That can't be a coincidence, surely?'

'I'd have thought not.' He glanced over at the stairs, thinking yet again about Bred lying in the bedroom. His fear was for her rather than himself. 'It makes no sense, though, does it? Why would anyone want to kill someone just because they were involved in some psychological study twenty years ago?'

'I've no idea,' Irene Fenwick said. 'But I'm sure there's some linkage. I haven't told you the whole story yet. The reason why I became interested in this study in the first place was because I had a break-in. It was an odd burglary because they did nothing except ransack Gordon's old study. Pulled out all his files as if searching for something. No other rooms touched. I went through the files wondering what they might have been looking for, and this list was the only thing that looked remotely relevant.'

'Are there other names on the list?'

'Several. Gorman's and Clayburn's are on the first page, along with your wife's and this Kenneth Murrain's, but there are several other candidates on the other pages who were assessed as "worth further examination".'

'That was my recollection. Something like seven or eight in total. So what are we suggesting? That, for whatever bizarre reason, someone's working down that list?'

'Except they didn't get the list, obviously,' Irene Fenwick pointed out. 'It's still here. I suppose they could have copied down the names, but if you were worried about being interrupted, it would be quicker just to take the file. And that way I wouldn't have known what was missing either, though maybe they didn't realise how chaotic Gordon's filing was. In any case, Gorman's killing was before the break-in.'

'Gorman and Clayburn are relatively public figures,' Nolan said. 'Gorman because he advertised his astrological services, Clayburn because of his association with Justin Bannerman—' He stopped suddenly. 'Just occurred to me. I wonder what Clayburn's role in Bannerman's set up actually was. Bannerman was vague about it. Talked about design and scripts. But I got the impression Clayburn was pretty influential. Maybe he was the one with the real abilities and Bannerman was just the showman.' His memory was finally catching up with his train of thought. 'Jesus, that was who they were talking about the day I went in there.'

'Clayburn?'

'Yes, they'd got themselves very exercised because someone hadn't turned in to work. I wondered at the time why it was such a big deal. But if Bannerman couldn't work without him, or at least if his absence reduced Bannerman to nothing more than the usual huckster spiritualist, that would explain why he wouldn't do a face-to-face consultation with me in Clayburn's absence.'

Irene Fenwick was silent for a moment before she responded. 'You think Clayburn had some genuine ability to – what? Contact the dead?'

'I'm not saying that. But I think he might have had some genuine extrasensory abilities and that he used those to feed into Bannerman's performance. Or at least that he and Bannerman believed that.'

'That's very interesting,' Irene Fenwick said, with an edge to her voice he couldn't interpret.

'I'm just wondering whether Gorman and Clayburn were targeted first just because their killer came across their names in some public context. If you were interested in this kind of paranormal stuff you'd find their names quite easily. It would be harder to track down those who've not been professionally involved in anything of that sort. I assume this Kenneth Murrain falls into that category.'

'What about your wife?'

'I'm not sure. My wife's steered well away from anything that smacks of the paranormal. But she's married to me, and my public profile, as opposed to my academic one, is very much caught up in all of that. So I suppose she wouldn't be difficult to track down through me.' He found himself looking again at the stairs. 'Speaking of which, I ought to make sure she's all right.'

'I'm sorry, I wasn't thinking. I hadn't realised how late it was. I've probably just been wasting your time.'

'Not at all. I just don't know what to do about it. If you're right about the link between Gorman's and Clayburn's deaths, I mean. If I go to the police, I can't see that they'll take it seriously.'

'I don't know. I'm not even sure why I called you, really. It was just that bad feeling I had. That sense that something was wrong.'

'I'm grateful for that,' Nolan said. 'Bred was feeling the same. I've no idea what this all means, but I'm taking it seriously. If there's any possibility Bred's in danger... ' He stopped, not even wanting to think about what that might mean. 'Look, Irene, I'm really grateful you called. We may be worrying about nothing, but I'd much rather be safe than sorry.'

'You've more than enough on your plate,' she said. 'You should probably be worrying about the flooding, not this.'

'There's not much I can do about the flooding. But I can at least make sure Bred's all right. Let's get through tonight, and we can talk again tomorrow. Work out what's the best thing to do with this.'

'I'm probably just being a foolish old woman.'

'Whatever you might be, Irene, it's not that. I'll call you tomorrow.'

'Goodnight, then. And good luck with the floods. I hope you avoid the worst.'

'Me, too. Goodnight.'

He walked back through to the unlit kitchen and peered out into the darkness. It was hard to tell whether the waters had risen further while he'd been talking to Irene Fenwick, but the rain was still lashing down hard. The wind was as strong as ever, and the electrical storm had drawn closer to the house. He shivered, though the house was not cold.

He returned to the living room to turn off the lights. He'd been around the ground floor earlier, checking all the doors and windows were closed and locked. He was tempted to re-check everything, but told himself that he was being unduly paranoid.

He made his way upstairs to the upper landing. He could see through the open doorway that the light in the main bedroom was still on, which suggested that Bred was still awake.

It was only as he reached the doorway itself that he felt a sudden resurgence of his earlier anxiety. It had been the silence, he thought later. The absence of the usual tiny sounds of human life – a turned page, a cleared throat, a breath.

He entered the room praying he was wrong, but he knew immediately that his worst, most absurd fears had been realised.

The bed was undisturbed. The room was empty.

CHAPTER THIRTY THREE

'You should go home,' Marty Winston said.

'You're still here,' Murrain pointed out.

'More fool me, then. I'm heading off shortly. I just thought I'd head down to the Ops Room to offer some moral support. It's bedlam out there tonight.'

Murrain had his doubts about the motivational effects of a Superintendent turning up to hover over the heads of the call handlers, but he knew Winston meant well. In fairness, he was generally well liked across the force. People would no doubt take his visit in the spirit it was intended. 'The weather?'

'You'd noticed, then.' Winston gestured through the office window, as if pointing out some specific incident. 'High winds. Pouring rain. Floods. Couple of lorries jackknifed on the M60. Trees down. Roads closed. Some houses being evacuated. You name it.'

'Hadn't realised it had got that bad.' Murrain had spoken briefly to Eloise a short while before to advise her that, as so often, he'd be late home. She'd had a fairly hairy drive home herself but that had been, in her words, the result of endless half-witted drivers who didn't seem to understand the meaning of the phrase 'traffic conditions'. 'Take care when you do head back,' she'd said. 'It's no fun out there.'

'Looks like it'll get worse before it gets better,' Winston said. 'Right, I'll go down there and offer to make them all coffee. That way they'll think I'm one of the good guys.'

'Little do they know.'

'Not everyone has your insights into my true character, Kenny. Don't stay too much longer, will you? What are you doing, anyway?'

'I'd like to say that I'm working hard to progress our investigations into Gorman's and Clayburn's death, but I'd be lying. I'm just obsessing about them after our conversation with Barnett or Whitcomb or whatever the hell his name was.'

'Bloody spooks,' Winston said. 'Why can't they do anything straightforwardly? You really think there's anything in it?'

'I wish I knew. It gives us a link between Gorman and Clayburn, which we didn't have before. Hell of a coincidence that they were both killed in the same way.'

'So we take it seriously?'

'I'd say so. However far-fetched it might sound. I've set the wheels in motion to get more information on the supposed first victim, Julian Stevens. That was one of the Met's so we'll no doubt have the usual problems in getting them to play ball.'

'What about this Edward Crichton?'

'Doesn't seem to have any record other than the original GBH case. Nothing on file after the trial for that. Not under that name, anyway.'

'What about this Brenda Dalton?'

'Now that's a bit more interesting. Nothing in terms of police records, as far as I can see. But I did an internet search on her name and found a few references.'

'What kind of references?'

'Largely in connection with her husband. Does the name Geoff Nolan mean anything to you?'

'Rings a bell from somewhere. Is that the guy on TV? The ghost hunter guy?'

'One and the same. He's actually a respected academic. Professor Geoffrey Nolan to the likes of you and me. Psychologist.'

'Psychologist?'

'Yup. Specialising in paranormal phenomena. Debunking it, mainly. As far as I can judge from his on-line bio, he specialises in analysing the psychology behind that sort of stuff.'

'Hence the ghostbusting.'

'Exactly.'

'And he's married to our Brenda Dalton?'

'Well, he's married to a Brenda Dalton, certainly. I'm assuming it's the same one. Because that's not all.'

'Anyone ever told you should be a stage magician, Kenny? Master of the slow reveal. Go on.'

'It was only when I found a few images of him on-line that I realised. I probably wouldn't even have made the connection in other circumstances, but I'm pretty sure I'm right. He was another one involved in that study. Some sort of junior researcher in those days.'

'Would make sense,' Winston said. 'So that's presumably where he met Brenda Dalton.'

'As you say, makes sense.'

'So where does this get us?'

'I'm not sure. It gives us a pretty clear steer that this does all link back to that study twenty years ago. Which puts this Edward Crichton firmly in the frame. Which in turn – and I'm sure you're already ahead of me on this – suggests we have some kind of psychopath on our hands.'

'I think I'd got there a little while ago,' Winston said. 'But thanks for the confirmation. So what next?'

'We need to talk to Brenda Dalton. Perhaps even organise some protection for her, if she really is a target.'

'If she's a target, so are you.'

'That point hadn't escaped me,' Murrain said. 'I just feel I'm better able to look after myself than Brenda Dalton's likely to be. I'll get her tracked down and arrange for someone to talk to her tomorrow.'

Winston nodded. 'And we try to track down Edward Crichton.'

'That's the big one. Not going to be easy, though. He seems to have dropped very successfully under the radar. At least under that name. The only media pictures I can find were from the original trial. We've nothing else on him. We can start doing other digging tomorrow but I've a feeling it might be a long haul.'

'We need to be careful with this,' Winston said. 'I don't entirely trust this Barnett or whatever he calls himself. I've not had many dealings with the security services, but my impression is that their primary objective is to look after their own interests.'

'You think he might be lying to us?'

'I just think his agenda may not be the same as ours. I don't think we should allow ourselves to be too deflected from our routine procedures.'

'Even if this Crichton is the key, our best chance of finding him is probably by pursuing the standard legwork anyway. I've no intention of reducing that.'

'Good to hear. Right, I'd better go and get that coffee going for them downstairs.'

'Have they tasted your coffee?'

'I'm hoping some of them have. That way I won't have to make too many.'

Murrain smiled as he watched Winston disappear back along the corridor. He knew Winston was right that he should head off home. Apart from anything else, he was achieving little here. He'd been trying to focus on the case files but his mind was elsewhere. He'd been feeling it ever since that earlier meeting with Barnett, the familiar distant buzzing in the back of his head, the insistent voices on the threshold of audibility. Wanting to impart some message, if only he could get himself on the right wavelength.

It was, at least in part, something about Barnett himself, Murrain thought. Perhaps Winston was right and Barnett wasn't to be trusted, but Murrain didn't think it was that, or at any rate not wholly that. He couldn't tell whether his feelings were positive or negative, only that they were in some way significant.

He sat for a while with his eyes closed, trying to empty his mind in the hope that it might make the voices more comprehensible. But whatever abilities he might possess, they couldn't be forced. Either understanding would emerge or it wouldn't. Most likely the latter.

He opened his eyes and, in the moment that he did so, felt as if an image had flashed on to his retinas. The briefest of impulses, like the unexpected burn of a flashlight, its meaning recoverable only by the shapes burnt into your vision. A crowd of people, talking endlessly, not to each other.

It took him a moment, then he jumped to his feet, grabbed his jacket from the back of his chair, and strode down towards the stairwell. He took the steps two at a time down three floors, then pushed open the door back into the corridor.

The control centre was normally kept locked from casual visitors from elsewhere in the building, admission only available through an authorised ID card or intercom. At this time of night, they weren't bothering with such niceties, and Murrain was able to walk into the room unchallenged.

It was, as Winston had indicated, organised bedlam. Additional staff had been brought in on overtime, and the centre was as busy as Murrain had seen it. The call handers were talking earnestly on their headsets, tapping their keyboards, checking and double-checking information. The dispatchers were looking under pressure, struggling to allocate limited resources to apparently infinite demands. Winston was at the far end of the room, distributing mugs of coffee and offering discrete pats on the back, both literal and figurative.

Murrain hesitated as he entered the room, wondering now what had brought him down here. He'd been right that his momentary vision had depicted this very room, but he had no idea what that might mean or why it had caused him to come racing down the stairs as if on some urgent errand.

Across the room, he saw Winston place another mug of coffee at one of the workstations. Then Winston's expression changed, almost as if someone had struck him a physical blow across the face. He straightened up and, catching sight of Murrain standing opposite he waved for him to come over.

Murrain hurried around the edge of the room, trying not to distract or disturb any of the handlers. He had at least a nodding acquaintance with many of them and he waved to several as he made his way round.

Winston was engaged in conversation with the handler beside him, and beckoned Murrain to join them. 'You're not going to believe this. Another bloody coincidence. Or maybe not.'

Murrain felt a sudden surge in his interior voices, a huge wave breaking on the shore, on the verge of meaning. 'Brenda Dalton?'

'How the hell did you—? Oh, never mind. Yes, Brenda Dalton. Or Brenda Nolan. It was just called in.' Winston was hopping from foot to foot, his demeanour an adrenaline-fuelled mix of dread and excitement. 'I was passing by when Joyce took the call. Brenda Nolan's been reported missing.'

'When?'

'Within the last hour, apparently. Husband just called it in. He's been frantically looking for her. The house backs on to the Bollin near Wilmslow, and they've got flood warnings so that's making him even more anxious.'

'How's she gone missing? Had she been out somewhere?'

Joyce, the call-hander, was still talking urgently on the phone, alternating between organising a response and talking reassuringly to the caller. Presumably Geoffrey Nolan, Murrain thought.

'It's a bit garbled at the moment,' Winston went on. 'Husband apparently thought she'd gone up to bed. Not entirely clear what had happened – whether she never went up or whether she somehow went out again while he was in another room – but when he went up to join her, she wasn't there. Front door was unlocked. Husband had locked it earlier, so it looks as if she must have unlocked it and gone out.'

'Why the hell would anyone go out voluntarily on a night like this?'

'That's the question. According to the husband, she'd given no indication of doing anything other than going up to bed. He reckons there was no reason for her to go out. He's searched the garden and the road immediately outside, but there's no sign of her.'

'Shit. Can we get some people over there?'

'Joyce is doing what she can, but you've seen what it's like here. In any other circumstances this would be low on the priority list. But I'm going to keep chivvying and see what we can do.'

'I'll head over there,' Murrain said.

'You don't have to do that, Kenny. It's a response matter.'

'Don't be daft, Marty. We knew there was a risk to Dalton. I should have done something tonight.'

'You're the one being daft. This isn't your responsibility. Even if you'd tried to do something tonight, there wouldn't have been the resources available. You know that.'

'I don't know what I know, except that Brenda Dalton's missing, we've already got two people dead – three according to our friend Barnett. If there's anything I can do to prevent another death, I've got to do it.'

'I know there's no point in arguing, Kenny. Do what you think you have to. I'll get you whatever back up I can. I'm not keen on you going by yourself, though. We know you're a potential target as well.'

'I'll try some other member of the team. Joe'll happily join me, I'm sure.'

'Joe's as mad as you are, then. Okay, Kenny, but don't take any unnecessary risks. I'm sanctioning this against all my better judgement.' He paused. 'You really think she's in danger, don't you?'

Murrain hesitated momentarily. The voices were almost singing to him, and he could see the fuzz of some kind of image, somewhere behind his eyes. 'It's just a feeling, Marty. But, yes, I really do.'

CHAPTER THIRTY FOUR

'Can you stay on the line, Mr Nolan? It's better if you do.'

'I need to get back out there.' Geoff Nolan's voice was frantic. 'I don't know what's happened to her.'

'We've got support on the way, Mr Nolan. We'll be there as quickly as we can. I don't want you putting yourself in additional danger.'

'I don't care about myself. I'm worried about my wife.'

'I fully appreciate that, Mr Nolan, but—'

Nolan stuffed the phone back into the pocket of his heavy waterproof, leaving the line open, and hurried back over to the front door. He still couldn't believe this. It was as if this nightmare had erupted out of nowhere. All his earlier anxieties, about the floods, about Bred's strange vision, had been subsumed under an all-enveloping terror.

When he'd found the bedroom empty, he'd rushed round the other rooms on the second floor, desperately hoping that for some reason she'd be sitting in one of the unlit bedrooms or the bathroom. Of course they were empty. It was as if she'd performed a baffling magic trick, a feat of misdirection. How could she not be here?

Back downstairs, he'd realised the truth was probably simpler, if no less baffling. The front door, which he'd locked and bolted half an hour earlier, was unlocked. The only possibility was that, while he'd been in the kitchen, staring out at the back garden, Bred had come downstairs and quietly let herself out through the front door.

But why the hell should she have done that? He couldn't see how the action couldn't have been voluntary. There was no sign that the front door or any of the other doors and windows had been forced. If someone had knocked or rung the front doorbell, he'd have heard it before Bred. If she'd received a phone call, some urgent summons, surely she'd have told him before leaving.

In any case both their cars were still sitting there as they had been all day. If she'd gone anywhere, she must have gone on foot. They had no immediate neighbours, so why would she do that in this kind of weather?

There were no answers. Nolan had taken one last look around the ground floor as if hoping that Bred might have somehow concealed herself elsewhere in the house. Then he'd dragged on his waterproof and thrust his feet into his walking boots and headed out into the rainy night, pausing only to dig out a torch from the cabinet by the front door.

Outside, the force of the wind had caught him, knocking him sideways, the rain lashing against his face. He couldn't imagine her coming out into this. Why would she? And yet it seemed she had.

He'd stood on the front lawn and shone the beam of his flashlight around the garden, peering into the darkness and the undergrowth. 'Bred! Where are you?' His voice had been whipped away instantly by the wind, and there had been nothing but darkness and the constant movement of the trees.

Nolan had made his way down the drive and peered out along the road. There were no streetlights here and he'd been able to see only a short distance in either direction, but there was no sign of Bred. He'd wondered how long she might have been out of the house. If she'd left while he was first in the kitchen, she might have been out here for some time. He'd been talking to Irene Fenwick for some time.

He'd turned and made his way around the side of the house into the back garden. Here the wind had been even stronger, almost knocking him off his feet as he emerged from the shelter of the house. Over half the garden had already been lost to the slowly rising waters. He'd shone his torch around, peering into the shrubbery as he had in the front garden, the light catching on the pitted surface of the water. He'd crossed the lawn to the water's edge, shining the light as far as he was able. 'Bred!' His voice had been lost in the noise of the storm-filled night.

He'd spent more desperate minutes out there, calling vainly into the darkness, before returning to the house to call the police. For all his fears, he'd felt almost foolish calling 999, expecting not to be taken seriously. At first, his initial reservations seemed to be justified as the operator had asked him a series of questions that suggested she was sceptical about his call. 'And you're absolutely sure she's not just somewhere in the house, sir? Had you had some kind of disagreement, perhaps?'

He'd forced himself to stay calm, telling himself that the police must receive endless crank calls, especially on a night like this. 'No, I'm sure she's not in the house. And, no, we hadn't had any kind of disagreement. I've no idea why she would have gone out, but that seems the only explanation. If she's out there on a night like this, I'm very worried.'

'Of course, sir. Do you have any idea what she might be wearing?'

It was a good question. Their outdoor coats all hung on pegs just by the front door. As far as he could see, Bred's were all still there. There'd been no sign of any discarded clothes in the bedroom, and her dressing gown had still been hanging behind the door. It was most likely that she hadn't undressed and was still wearing the clothes she'd had on when she'd first headed upstairs. He relayed this to the operator and did his best to describe what she'd been wearing.

Shortly after that the operator's attitude had seemed to change. He'd had no idea what might have prompted the shift, but she'd said 'Excuse me a moment, sir' and then he'd heard her muffled voice discussing something with another person. When she'd returned to him, she'd said, 'Can I just double-check your name, sir? Geoffrey Nolan? And your wife is Brenda, known as Bred?'

Perhaps she, or the person she'd been talking to, had recognised his name from his television appearances and that had given his call some spurious additional credibility. If so, he wasn't about to object. 'Yes, that's right.'

'We'll get someone out to you as soon as possible, sir. You'll appreciate we're under a lot of pressure this evening, but we'll flag this as a priority.'

'Okay.' He'd had no idea what that really meant, whether she was sincere or if it was just a polite way of fobbing him off. 'I'm going to carry on searching outside.' He'd had no idea where else he might look, but he couldn't face the thought of simply sitting in here not knowing where Bred might be.

'I'd ask you to take care, sir, if you think you really must do that. Can you stay on the line, Mr Nolan? It's better if you do.'

That had at least suggested she'd been sincere about treating him as a priority. And her concern for his well-being had clearly been sincere. In the end, he'd stuffed the phone in the pocket of his waterproof, the line still open, and hurried back out into the night.

It was futile, he knew. He tried heading out into the road and walking some distance in each direction, shining his torch into the hedges that lined the road, unsure what he was even looking for. Why would she have set off along the road on foot?

He had no answer to that, but then he couldn't explain why she'd left the house in the first place. Perhaps she'd been concerned about the flooding and had gone to check how much further the water had risen. It was possible, though he couldn't imagine why she'd have done so without telling him and without at least putting on an overcoat.

With that thought in mind, he returned to the garden and made his way back to the rear of the house. The rain was still hammering down, and the waters had risen still higher. 'Bred!'

There was another stronger gust of wind. The trees at the far end of the garden, half-submerged in the river, were creaking and groaning, bent double by the gale. It felt as if the whole garden had come to a kind of crazed life, mocking his attempts to track down Bred. His voice was lost to the wind, his torch barely able to penetrate the haze of rain.

It was only then that he heard the voice, little more than a whisper from behind him, but somehow carrying clearly through the cacophony of the storm.

'Geoff, good to see you again. It's a pity about the circumstances.'

Nolan swung round, peering into the darkness. At first he could see nothing, but then he made out a darker shadow against the corner of the house. The silhouette of a man, and something else beside it.

The voice had sounded familiar, Nolan thought, though he couldn't immediately place it. It was only when the figure stepped forward slightly and was caught in the light from the house that he realised. 'Lyle? Lyle Christopher? What the hell are you doing here?'

'What I've been doing for some time now. Getting closer. Getting closer to the people I need. Getting closer to you.' He pulled what Nolan now realised was a second figure forward into the light. 'Most of all, getting closer to your wife.'

Nolan realised now that Christopher was holding Bred tightly by the arm. 'I don't understand.'

He moved forward, reaching out for Bred, making the mistake of taking his eyes off Christopher. Before he could do anything more, something struck him, hard and heavy, against the side of the head.

CHAPTER THIRTY FIVE

Murrain took the A34 south, his urge to reach the Nolans' house constrained by his natural caution as a driver. Other members of the team sometimes playfully mocked the way he drove, which, in Joe Milton's words, involved staying well inside the speed limit and overtaking only on the rare occasion he encountered an even slower driver on a straight, empty road.

Murrain didn't care too much. At least this way he stayed alive to be mocked. On a night like this, with his windscreen wipers barely able to cope with the downpour and his car buffeted by the wind, he was inclined to be even more cautious than usual. At the same time, all his instincts were telling him he needed to track down Bred Nolan urgently.

The voices were still there in the back of his head, shriller and more insistent than ever. He felt, as he did so often, that he was close to understanding what they were trying to tell him, but the meaning still remained elusive. There was an image too, he thought, that remained tantalisingly unfocused. Dark water, he thought, but could get no further.

Fortunately, the roads were largely deserted, with only the occasional car passing in the opposite direction. As he drove, he called Joe Milton and explained what was happening. 'Marty thought I should get some support, so I said I'd call you but there's no obligation to join me on my wild goose-chase.'

The call had clearly taken Milton by surprise. He'd probably just settled himself down for a night in front of the TV with Marie Donovan, Murrain told himself. The thought had only just occurred to him, too late as ever.

'Don't be daft,' Milton said. 'If you need help, I'm there. Hang on…' Milton had obviously put his hand over the mouthpiece and was talking to someone. 'Marie's going to come too.'

'You really don't need to—'

'Kenny, you're talking to Joe Milton. I'm not just going to sit here while you're out there in the rain doing the job. If this Bred Nolan really is in trouble, I'd never forgive myself if I just sat here on my backside. Marie feels the same.'

Murrain knew that any further protests on his part would simply sound insulting. 'Thanks, Joe. Really appreciate it.' He gave Milton Nolan's address. 'I'll see you there, then. We should be getting some uniformed backup too, but I don't know how long it'll take.'

'Too long, I'm guessing, given the conditions out there.'

'That's my thinking. Okay, see you there.'

He ended the call and then phoned Eloise to update her.

'You really think this woman's in danger?'

'It's a hell of a coincidence that she should go missing now, if not.'

She was silent for a moment. 'If she's a target, so are you.'

'That's what Marty Winston said.'

'Some things are true even though your boss says them. Take care, Kenny.'

'I'm intending to. You know me.'

'Too well. And I know how far you'll go to try to protect someone in danger.'

Murrain was silent for a moment as he negotiated a junction. 'I'll take care, El. I've asked Joe and Marie to come out. And there's uniformed backup on the way.'

'Okay. You've got my permission to carry on, then. Not that you take any notice of me.'

'You're the only senior officer I do take any notice of.'

'Probably also true. Good luck, Kenny.'

'Thanks. I'll keep you updated.'

He was getting close to his destination, keeping his eyes peeled for the turn off on to the back road that would eventually lead to the Nolans' house. Half a mile ahead, the SatNav informed him, but he knew it would be easy to miss in the pouring rain.

He spotted it in time and turned off to the right. After another mile, the streetlights petered out, the houses becoming fewer and further between. The rain was coming down harder than ever, the headlights almost lost in the haze. Murrain slowed, driving even more cautiously than before, peering into the darkness. The SatNav indicated that the Nolans' house was little more than a mile further down this road. The river was off to the left, and Murrain had already passed a couple of points where the road was under water from swollen streams running down to the larger body of water.

After another half mile, he saw something glittering crimson in the road ahead. A set of rear reflectors on a vehicle in the road ahead. The road had narrowed and was barely two lanes wide.

It was a van, Murrain realised. A white van with the name of a vehicle hire company. It looked abandoned and no effort had been made to steer it into the side of road, so that it blocked one of the lanes.

Murrain's first thought was to drive past it, cursing the thoughtlessness of whoever had left it there on a night like this. But some instinct – or perhaps the voices in the back of his head – caused him to pull up immediately in front of the van.

As he'd thought, there was no sign of a driver. As far as Murrain could judge, both sides of the road were lined with fields, and there was no sign of any house or other building in the immediate vicinity. It was an odd place to abandon a van. Even if it had broken down, in this kind of weather he'd have expected the driver to remain in the vehicle to call for help.

Murrain's preference would have been to press on, get to the Nolans' place as quickly as he could. But the instinct that had made him stop was telling him to check out the van. He climbed out of the car and walked back towards the van, ducking his head against the wind-whipped rain.

To his surprise, the driver's door was unlocked. The interior looked pristine, with nothing left inside to provide any obvious clues to the current user. Murrain closed the door and continued to the rear of the van.

The warning voices in his head were becoming more insistent, too. That felt strange, too, even stranger than usual. Normally – if his mental state could ever be described as normal – he experienced these sensations as a mental background noise. Something just there in the recesses of his brain.

Sometimes louder and closer at hand, sometimes fainter and more distant. But just a presence. Now it felt almost as if the sensations were being directed, as if someone or something was trying to communicate with him through their intervention.

He hadn't been sure what to expect when he opened the van's rear doors, but somehow he wasn't surprised by what he found. As he pulled back the doors, his nostrils were met by the strong but unmistakable stench of blood. A human body was spread-eagled on the floor of the van, face up, the head beside the now open doors. Murrain reached out and pressed his fingers against the figure's throat, searching for a pulse, but he had little doubt the body was dead. From the relative warmth of the skin he guessed that death had occurred relatively recently.

Murrain had left his large flashlight in the car, but he carried a small torch in the pocket of his waterproof. He pulled it out and shone the beam into the interior. The floor of the van was soaked with blood, with more blood caking the stomach and chest of the supine body. Stabbed in the stomach, just like Gorman and Clayburn.

Murrain moved the beam of the torch slowly up the body towards the head. It was male, dressed in a dark business suit over a white shirt now indelibly stained with the red-brown blood. The face was familiar. A face he had last seen earlier than day.

Charles Barnett. Derek Whitcomb.

Whatever his real name had been no longer mattered. Except that the voices in Murrain's head were telling him differently.

Trying hard not to compromise the scene, Murrain felt inside the upper pockets of the dead man's jacket. After a moment, he found something, almost as if it were a gift that had been left there for him. A wallet. He carefully opened it and saw that it held various bank cards and a driving licence.

All in the name of Edward Crichton.

Murrain placed the wallet back on the floor of the van. Better if he left it there, he thought, rather than risking any forensic evidence being damaged by the rain if he took it back to his own car.

He couldn't begin to fathom what this might mean. Had the wallet been planted on the body? Had Barnett taken it from Crichton himself? Was it possible that Crichton was just another of Barnett's identities? If so, how would that have worked?

Murrain didn't have the time or the mental energy to disentangle any of that now. He closed the rear doors of the van, then fetched a reflective warning triangle from his car to warn other passing drivers. Then he climbed back into his own car and set off towards the Nolan's house, calling in the finding of the body as he drove. After he'd spoken to the operations room, he called Marty Winston's number.

'Barnett? Crichton's wallet?' Winston said, as if offering edited highlights of what Murrain had just told him. 'How the hell does that work?'

'Search me. But I'm beginning to think your distrust of Barnett was justified. I don't know who or what he was, but it looks like he wasn't telling us the whole story. How did he get to talk to you yesterday, anyway?'

'Like I said, foisted upon me – against my better judgement – from on high. Word came from the Chief himself, I was told.'

'Can we find out who leaned on the Chief and why?'

'You want me to call the Chief at this time of night?'

'I'm sure he'll be only too glad to help. He's always encouraging us to go the extra mile. Anyway, he might well want to know that the guy he sponsored has ended up stabbed in the stomach.'

Winston was silent for a moment. 'Yeah, you're right. I can't hold that back. I'll let you know how it goes. You nearly at Nolan's?'

'I'm there, I think. Lights up ahead.'

'Keep me posted. I'm told back up's on the way.'

'Joe and Marie are coming out too. We'll let you know what happens.'

The SatNav was telling him he'd reached his destination, and the twin lights on the left of the road marked the entrance to a driveway. Murrain turned in and pulled up in front of an imposing-looking modern house. To Murrain's untutored eye, everything about the place shouted architect design, a building designed to make the most of its riverside location. On a fine day, the place would no doubt be idyllic. Tonight, it looked oddly vulnerable among a small forest of storm-tossed trees, the front door standing open.

Pausing only to grab his large flashlight from the rear of the car, Murrain hurried across to the front door, pressing hard on the bell. 'Mr Nolan! Police!'

He stepped inside and looked around. The front door opened on to a large open-plan living room, with a picture window at the far end which no doubt looked out on to the river view. A couple of doors led off to the right, and a staircase rose from the left of the room to the upper floor. 'Mr Nolan?'

Murrain turned and made his way back outside, following a path around the side of the house to the rear garden. As he reached the end of the path, he saw a man standing in the centre of the rear lawn. Just a few yards beyond the man, the lawn disappeared beneath the swollen waters.

'Mr Nolan?' Murrain's voice was almost lost in the wind, but the man turned as he shouted. 'Police. DCI Murrain.'

The man stared at him for a moment. He was tall with long hair thrown back by the wind, dressed in a long black coat. Whoever this man might be, he wasn't Geoff Nolan.

'If you're looking for Nolan, you'll find him over there.'

Murrain looked to where the man was pointing. A figure lay motionless on the wet grass. Beyond that another figure crouched in the corner of the lawn, back against one of the trees. A terrified looking woman.

CHAPTER THIRTY SIX

'Marty? What can I do for you?'

'You know I wouldn't bother you this late if it wasn't important,' Winston said. The Chief generally had a positive reputation in the force and was seen as relatively approachable, unlike some of his predecessors. Winston could think of a number of previous Chiefs who wouldn't have taken kindly to being disturbed this late in the evening, however good the reason. He still wasn't convinced the current Chief's so-called 'open door' policy would actually extend in practice to late night phone calls at home.

'I take that as read, Marty. What is it?'

'Something I thought you ought to know,' Winston said. 'I'm not sure what the implications are, but it's a rather – unprecedented situation.'

It took him several minutes to explain the developments involving Barnett and their apparent double murder investigations.

'So you're saying that Barnett wasn't his real name?'

'I'm not sure about that. But it looks as if he used more than one name.'

'Bloody spooks. Couldn't draw a straight line between two points if their lives depended on it. But you say he was carrying a wallet belonging to this Edward Crichton? So what does that mean?'

'That's the thing. We don't know. But it suggests he wasn't telling us the whole truth about Crichton. He said they'd lost touch with Crichton. So how did he come to have the wallet?'

The Chief was silent for a moment. 'None of it sounds as if it makes much sense. Was he seriously claiming that Crichton killed these people because they produced positive results in some mind-reading study twenty years ago?'

'It seems to be something like that. Crichton was clearly a very disturbed individual, so anything's possible.'

'You really think this Nolan woman might be in danger?'

'All we know is that she's missing. But it seems a worrying coincidence given what Barnett told us.'

'Perhaps even more of a coincidence that Barnett should have told you on the same day she went missing?'

The same thought had been vaguely nagging at Winston himself. It wasn't just that Bred Nolan had been next on Barnett's list. It was also that her disappearance had followed so hard on the heels of Barnett's visit. 'Exactly. I was wondering if you could shed any light on how Barnett came to talk to us yesterday. I received the instruction to see him directly from your office.'

'I had a call from – well, let's just say one of the agencies saying that this guy Barnett wanted to speak to Kenny Murrain. To be honest, it was the usual cloak and dagger stuff, but I took all that with a pinch of salt. All the bona fides checked out which is all I really cared about. I assumed it was just that some operation of ours had inadvertently trespassed on their territory. That's usually what they get exercised about. They expect us to be able to read their minds.

Though if anyone could do that it's probably Kenny Murrain.'

'Something like that,' Winston said. 'But you're convinced this Barnett was genuine?'

'Absolutely. Or that the person I spoke to was, anyway. The risk of allowing him to talk to you was limited, but I'm always wary about this kind of thing. All you need is some prankster or smart-arse tabloid journalist getting through the system, and we all end up looking stupid. So I'm sure he was who he said he was. But, of course, given he was part of the intelligence services, that doesn't necessarily mean there's any reason to trust him.'

'That's generally been my experience,' Winston said.

'They work to their own agenda, and don't care if we're collateral damage on the way. The buggers are as secretive with each other as they are with us. Just because this guy Barnett was legit, that doesn't mean he wasn't off on a frolic of his own.' The Chief paused. 'I can do some digging for you, but I can't promise I'll get very far. Even my exalted rank doesn't cut much ice with that lot if they close ranks.'

'I'd appreciate anything you can do,' Winston said, sincerely. 'This is an odd one. The oddest I've had to deal with.'

'And your guy Murrain. You think he's sound on something like this. Not too flaky? I've heard plenty of stories about him.'

'Probably all of them true. But he's as sound as they come. He has his quirks, but when push comes to shove he's definitely one you'd want by your side.'

'I'd have assumed so,' the Chief said. 'I've seen enough of Eloise Murrain to know she doesn't suffer fools gladly, and she's put up with him for a good few years. Okay, Marty, thanks for the update. I'll let you know if I find out anything. Keep me posted on developments.'

'I'll do that,' Winston said. 'I suspect we may have a challenging night ahead of us, one way or another.'

CHAPTER THIRTY SEVEN

'That must be the van.' Joe Milton squinted into the darkness at the crimson reflectors on Murrain's warning triangle. The white shape of the van loomed through the rain ahead.

Milton had hit the brakes as they'd rounded the bend and had felt the anti-skid kicking in. He'd been exceeding the speed limit, even discounting the conditions and the narrowness of the road. Even Marie Donovan, sitting beside him, had been clutching the edges of her seat nervously and she wasn't generally known for the sedateness of her own driving. 'Sorry,' he said. 'Bit too fast.'

'If you get a ticket, you'll get no sympathy from me.'

'If there's any uniforms heading down this road, I'm hoping they've got other priorities than booking me.'

Milton had tried initially to persuade Marie to stay behind, but she'd been adamant that she wanted to accompany him. He wasn't entirely sorry about that. He felt much better with her by his side and knew that it was what she wanted. But he was very conscious that they had no idea what might be facing them. From what Murrain had told him, they were dealing with someone who might already be responsible for at least four violent deaths, with one of the victims lying in the van just ahead of them.

Milton passed the van, pressing his foot back down on the accelerator. Marie was leaning forward, trying to spot the lights that would indicate the approach of their destination.

They'd heard nothing more from Murrain since he'd called to update Milton about the discovery in the back of the van. Milton had tried Murrain's mobile number repeatedly as they had drawn closer, but it had just gone to voicemail each time. He told himself that meant nothing. If Murrain was engaged in an outdoor search for Bred Nolan in weather like this, he probably wouldn't even hear the phone. Even so, Milton's anxiety had continued to grow with every passing second.

'That looks like it.'

Milton spotted it just after she'd spoken, a blur of light in the rain ahead. He slowed slightly, looking for the driveway, then turned in. The house was ahead of them, with Kenny Murrain's car parked in front.

'You can tell he's a TV star,' Donovan said. 'Don't imagine many academics can afford a place like this.'

Milton pulled to a halt and clambered out of the car. The rain was coming down as heavily as ever, and the wind was rising, roaring explosively through the trees around them. Donovan gestured to the open front door. 'Looks like they're probably still out here.'

Milton made his way over to the front door and peered inside, calling out Murrain's name. The house felt silent and empty. 'No sign of anyone in there. Let's check round the back. When did they say we can expect the back-up to arrive?'

'They're on their way, apparently. Whatever that means.'

'Bugger all, I'm guessing. I'm sure we're a priority, but everything's going to be a priority tonight.'

On the way over, Donovan had been trying to obtain some more definitive information from operations about when they could expect support. The response had been characteristically vague. The floods were getting worse. A number of flood barriers had been breached further upstream and the waters were rising faster than ever. Any support heading in their direction might easily be diverted to some more urgent task. 'We're on our own then.'

'Great.' Milton had retrieved two large flashlights from the car and, handing one to Donovan, led them round the side of the house to the rear garden. As he turned the corner of the house, he peered cautiously into the darkness, gesturing for Donovan to wait behind him.

He'd been half-expecting to find Murrain at the rear of the house, engaged in a search for Bred Nolan, but the garden was deserted. The wind was roaring off the river, the waters fast moving and swollen. The river's edge was only yards from the house.

The far side of the garden ended in a mass of shrubbery. Before they'd set out, Milton had briefly checked out the layout of the house and its surroundings. As far as he could recall, the area beyond the garden was open farmland, presumably now also largely submerged under the rising river.

'Any sign of anyone?' Donovan said.

'Nothing I can see.' He took a few more tentative steps across the sodden lawn. 'Where the hell are they? This doesn't feel right.'

'None of it feels right,' Donovan said.

Milton shone his torch into the undergrowth. 'There's something about all this that's freaking me out. We know Kenny's here. His car's out front. So where the hell is he?'

'Let's check out the house. Maybe they didn't hear you calling.'

'Don't know where they'd be. Most of the downstairs was open-plan and there was no sign of anyone.'

'If they'd found Bred Nolan and brought her back indoors, they might have taken her upstairs,' Donovan suggested.

'I suppose so.' Milton sounded unconvinced.

They made their way back round to the front door and entered the house. Milton was conscious of their waterproofs dripping on to the expensive-looking carpet, but it didn't feel like the time to worry about the interior decor. If the waters continued to rise, the carpet would be facing more than a few drops of water by morning.

The large living room was empty. There were a number of other damp marks on the carpet that suggested someone else had come in here from out of the rainy night, but they were already drying and Milton suspected they'd been made some time before, perhaps when Geoff Nolan had originally come back inside to call 999.

Milton opened the two doors on the right of the room. The first looked as if it was used by the Nolans as an office. It was in darkness, and there was no sign anyone had been in there recently. The second the kitchen which, like the living room, looked out over the river at the rear. The lights were on, but the room was empty.

He returned to the living room, shaking his head. 'Nothing. Let's try upstairs.'

The staircase led up from the sitting room to an enclosed upper landing. Milton made his way around, checking each room in turn. The first was clearly the master bedroom used by the Nolans, with an en suite bathroom and a view over the river. There were signs of relatively recent use, but the bed was undisturbed. Two of the remaining rooms were clearly used as guest bedrooms. Both were empty and looked as if they hadn't been occupied in the recent past. The final room was a bathroom, and again looked as if it hadn't been used in some time.

'Nothing,' Milton said. 'So where the hell are they?' He dialled Murrain's number once more. As before, the phone rang several times and then went to voicemail.

Donovan was still standing in the Nolans' bedroom, looking round as if the room itself might offer some clues to its owners' location. After a moment, she walked over to the window and peered out into the darkness. 'Joe,' she said. 'Turn off the light.'

'What is it?'

'Turn off the light,' she said again. 'I'm trying to see. There's something out there.'

Milton flicked the light switch and plunged the room into darkness. As his eyes slowly adjusted, he crossed the room to stand behind Donovan. 'What is it?'

'Over there.' She pointed to a spot off to the right of the house, beyond the boundary of the garden. 'Can you see?'

Milton moved to stand beside her, trying to follow her gaze. She clearly had sharper eyesight than he did because at first he could make out nothing in the blackness and the haze of rain. It was only as his eyes adapted increasingly to the dark that he finally saw it. Half concealed behind the storm-whipped trees and bushes, the beam of a large torch or spotlight.

Momentarily caught in the beam of light, he saw two figures, one apparently struggling with the other. Then the light moved suddenly, as if pushed or kicked from its place. As the cone of light swung through the air, glittering in the pouring rain, it caught a third figure, standing motionless close to the other two. Then the light was extinguished and Milton could see nothing more.

'I don't know what the hell's going on,' he said to Marie Donovan. 'But let's get down there.'

CHAPTER THIRTY EIGHT

The whole scene felt oddly dreamlike, Murrain thought. Or, more accurately, nightmarish. It was partly the sheer noise – the ceaseless battering of the wind, the roaring of the swollen waters behind them, the beating of the rain on his waterproof clothing. It was partly the flickering light ahead of him, the way the figures vanished and reappeared as the torchlight swayed from their movement.

It was partly, too, Murrain's own sense of detachment. This was normally the kind of moment that would galvanise him into action, send the adrenaline pulsing through his body, giving him a heightened sense of awareness. Every cop who'd faced real danger could tell you about that sensation. When time seems to slow because your brain is working so much faster. When everything extraneous vanishes from your mind, and all that matters is your focus on the task at hand.

Tonight, none of that had happened.

It felt as if he was gazing at the scene through glass, or if it was something that he was witnessing on television or in a film. An event happening somewhere else, and there was nothing he could do but watch.

His brain felt fogged. He wanted to do something, anything, to prevent what he was seeing. But he felt frozen, indecisive, lost.

What the hell was wrong with him?

He'd wanted, at first, simply to stop the long-haired man, to tell him he was under arrest, to recite the caution, to physically prevent the man from doing what Murrain knew he was going to do.

He had no doubt from the moment he'd set eyes on the man. This was the killer. This was the man who'd killed Andrew Gorman and Gareth Clayburn. The man who'd no doubt killed Julian Stevens and Ronnie Hargreaves. The man who must have killed Barnett or whatever his name had really been.

The man who was now going to kill Bred Nolan.

Geoff Nolan was still on the ground, unconscious or worse. Scarcely bothering even to look at Murrain, the long-haired man had stepped over him and grabbed Bred Nolan by the arm. Murrain wanted to stop him, to pull him away, but found himself unable to move.

O God, I could be bounded in a nutshell and count myself a king of infinite space. Where the hell had that come from? Something from his schooldays. Shakespeare, was it? *Hamlet*, that he'd studied at A-Level. One of those quotes he'd learnt off by heart nearly thirty years ago, but hadn't thought of since. Why would he think of that now, when his head should be focused here?

The man had pulled a substantial-looking torch from his coat pocket, and was pulling Bred Nolan back towards the house and then towards a gap in the bushes separating the garden from the fields beyond.

It was only as the two figures disappeared into the leaves that Murrain felt his head suddenly become a little clearer. He couldn't work out what was happening to him. Even the familiar voices in his head had ceased during those strange moments, and he'd felt as if he'd just been abandoned. But now the voices returned, louder and more shrill, whispering endlessly in his head. He felt as if they were pulling him, dragging him forwards, impelling him towards the gap in the shrubbery.

Beyond the thick mass of bushes, the land opened to an open field. The water had risen here too, the rushing water only a few yards from where he was standing. In the darkness, he could barely make out the two figures moving away from him, close to the edge of the river. The light of the torch shook as they walked, but stopped motionless as the man turned.

Bred Nolan appeared to be conscious, moving of her own volition, even though the man had almost been dragging her along the earth. He'd obviously stopped for a reason, not because she was offering any resistance. Like Murrain himself, she seemed oddly passive, as if unable to resist what was happening to her.

The man was calling to him now. Despite the constant bellowing of the wind and rain, Murrain could hear the words perfectly.

'Kenneth Murrain? It is you, isn't it? I knew you'd come if I called for you. And I've been calling you for days now.'

Murrain took a few steps towards the man, feeling again almost as if he'd lost control of his limbs. 'Who are you? What do you want?'

'It's been more than twenty years, Kenneth. I don't blame you for not remembering me. There were many of us there, even if only a handful of us mattered.'

'Are you Edward Crichton? Barnett told me about you.'

'You really are many steps behind, aren't you, Kenneth? I'd understood you were a great investigator.'

'I'm just a cop. If you're not Edward Crichton, who are you?'

'Who was Edward Crichton, Kenneth? That's one of the questions you should be asking yourself. He was a name on a list. He was a name on credit cards. On a driving licence. In a wallet.' The wind was whipping through the man's hair, the rain dripping from his body. 'It appears that Crichton was just another assumed identity like so many others.'

'Your identity?'

Another laugh. 'Why would I need another identity? I have my own, and I have so many more. Even you, with all your powers, can only guess what that might be like. Even you can't begin to imagine the sheer magnitude of that. The pleasure and the pain of it.'

Murrain tried to force himself forward towards the man, but as before he felt as if his body was frozen. 'What is it you want? What do you want with Brenda Nolan?'

'What I've wanted all the way through this,' the man said. 'Freedom. Or a step towards freedom. She's part of that, and so are you. There are others, but those are less important. I can deal with those later.'

'There isn't going to be a later,' Murrain said. 'Whatever it is, this is where it ends.'

'This is where it begins, Kenneth. You've all held me in this bondage for so long. You thought you had me under control, but that was never really the case. My strength has been building. I'm at the point finally where I can do what I want. To the point where you can't stop me.'

'I don't know what you're talking about,' Murrain said. 'Whoever you are, whatever you think this is about, just let her go. There's no reason to take this any further.'

'I'm afraid there's every reason, Kenneth. I'm sorry about that. I wish there was another way to do this, but there really isn't.' He leaned over, still holding Bred Nolan's arm, and thrust the barrel of the torch into the soft wet ground, so that the beam was shining up at the two of them like a spotlight. 'I need you to see, Kenneth. I need you to see what's happening. I need you to see what will happen to you.'

Murrain had half hoped that, as the man had leaned over to deal with the torch, Bred Nolan might have taken the opportunity to twist free of his grasp. There had been a moment when it looked possible, but she remained standing there, offering no resistance. As if she, like Murrain himself, was caught in some inexplicable spell.

In the angled light from the torch, the two figures were little more than grotesque silhouettes. Murrain could see neither of their expressions. It was like watching a nightmarish puppet show. Some symbolic ritual being played out for his benefit.

His hand now free of the torch, the man had reached into his pocket and produced something else. An object which Murrain couldn't see until it glittered, caught momentarily in the light of the torch.

It was a knife. The knife that, presumably, had been used on at least five victims. Andrew Gorman. Gareth Clayburn. Julian Stevens. Ronnie Hargreaves. And the man who had called himself Charles Barnett.

'Don't do this,' Murrain said. 'You don't need to do this. Just let her go. Hand her over to me.'

'And then what? I remain in prison.'

'I can't—' Murrain had been about to trot out the usual calming platitudes that he'd been taught to use in this kind of circumstance. Where you were trying to talk someone down. Persuade them to see sense. You couldn't make any promises but you'd do what you could for them. But he'd known even before he could begin speaking that the man was talking about something different. A different kind of imprisonment. Something Murrain couldn't even begin to conceive.

'Bound in a nutshell,' the man said. 'The king of infinite space.'

Murrain felt the first real clutch of fear. It was as if the man had reached into his head and plucked the words out. He took a deep breath, trying to calm himself. It was a coincidence. Nothing more. It was a quote from Shakespeare. A well known quote from one of the most well known plays. Nothing more.

'Just let her go,' he said, conscious that his voice sounded less assertive. He'd been shaken, and he felt as if the situation was drifting out of his control. As if he no longer had any grip on what was happening.

There was something else, Murrain thought. He'd been conscious of it for a few minutes now, but had thought it was just another part of this storm-wracked nightmare. The sound of the night, the constant auditory bedlam that had been the backdrop since he'd arrived here, felt as if it was changing. There was a different note in the air, a change in tone or pitch.

He looked over at the river. The water was rising more quickly than before, the current moving even faster. The edge of the river was only a metre or so from where the man was still standing, with Bred Nolan motionless beside him.

Murrain took another step forward. Every movement felt a huge effort, as if the air had thickened around him, as if some unknown force was driving him back. 'Let her go,' he said again, conscious of how feeble his voice sounded against the cacophony surrounding him. 'Just put down the knife and let her go.'

'I can almost taste the freedom.' The man held up the knife as if to examine the blade. 'Just her. Then you.'

He raised the knife higher, as if about to perform some ritual act. Murrain desperately wanted to run forward, if only to thrust his own body in front of the knife. But he was frozen, immobile, gripped by something entirely outside his control.

He could only watch, helpless, as the man pulled back his arm and twisted Bred Nolan towards him, ready to strike.

CHAPTER THIRTY NINE

Marie Donovan had been slow in following Joe's lead, unsure what he'd seen through the window and where he was heading. She half-stumbled down the stairs and chased after him as he exited the front door and headed into the night.

She'd known and worked with him for long enough to trust he knew what he was doing. Even if, she added silently to herself, he might not even know himself. It was one of the qualities that had first attracted her to him. His calmness in the face of any adversity. His ability to do the right thing, just by trusting his own instincts. He wasn't an intuitive kind of cop in the way Kenny Murrain was. Most of the time, he was methodical, hard-working, reliable. All the mundane qualities that comprised a good detective. But he had something on top of that. A spark of inspiration that was sometimes critical to breaking open a case or salvaging some operation at risk of going awry. She'd seen it once or twice, and she knew it was a quality Murrain valued in Joe.

By the time she'd emerged from the front door, he was heading off down the side of the house towards the rear garden. She chased after him, sprinting hard to try to narrow the gap. The force of the wind hit her as she emerged from the shelter of the house, and she slowed for a moment, peering into the dark to check which way Joe had gone.

He was ahead of her, racing across the upper part of the garden towards the trees and shrubbery at the far side. She pounded after him, conscious of the sodden soft ground beneath her feet, the risk of losing her grip on this treacherous ground. The river had risen noticeably further even in the short time they'd been in the house.

She could hear Joe's voice, whipped back to her by the wind, shouting Murrain's name. She was about to follow him when she spotted something on the ground to her right, a dark shape in the shadow of the undergrowth. She fumbled in her pocket for her flashlight, and shone the light into the corner.

It was a man, lying prone on the wet ground. She hesitated for a moment, and then crouched down to search for a pulse. This must be Geoff Nolan, she realised, half-recognising his face from his television appearances. It took her a moment to confirm he was still alive, his pulse strong. As she had placed her fingers on his neck, he stirred. His eyes opened, his gaze still unfocused. 'What the hell...?' he murmured.

'Mr Nolan? We're police. Can you tell me what happened?'

Nolan blinked. 'Christ. I don't know. I was attacked. Appeared from nowhere and hit my bloody head with something.' He was silent for a second, clearly collecting his thoughts. 'Where's Bred? What happened to her?' He pushed himself to an upright position.

'Please, Mr Nolan. Take care. You've had a nasty blow to the head—'

'Tell me about it. Look, I'm fine. Apart from the bloody headache. But I need to know where Bred is.'

Donovan was about to respond when she heard shouting from the field beyond. Joe's voice calling for Murrain and then something else.

'Wait there,' she said to Nolan. 'I'll find out what's happening.'

She forced her way through the bushes, following the path Joe had taken, finally emerging into the open. Despite her instructions, she knew Nolan would follow her, but there wasn't much she could do about that.

Joe was now thirty metres ahead of her. Beyond him there were three more figures. It took her a moment to work out that the nearest of the three figures was Murrain himself. The other two were standing together, caught in the eerie light of a torch set into the earth beside them.

There was something odd about the tableau. It looked almost staged, as if the figures had been persuaded to stand motionless while some artist captured their positions.

It was Joe's voice that broke the spell. As he shouted Murrain's name, one of the two more distant figures suddenly came to life, pulling away from the other. Donovan could see it was a woman, presumably Bred Nolan. So who was the other figure?

As if reading her thoughts, Nolan spoke from behind her. 'I knew him. I was baffled at first because I didn't know what he was doing here. I still don't understand—' He stopped, and it was clear he'd spotted what Donovan had already seen. Bred Nolan pulling away from the other figure, something glittering silver in the torchlight.

'He's got a bloody knife,' Nolan screamed. 'Someone stop him.'

Murrain seemed suddenly to come back to life. Donovan could tell he was warily watching the movement of the knife. Joe was closing in from the other side, but both were hanging back for fear the man might still try to use the knife on Bred Nolan.

Afterwards, Donovan still couldn't recall exactly what happened next. It seemed to take place both infinitely slowly and in the blink of an eye. Bred Nolan twisted clear and the man lunged for her with the knife, his expression almost feral. In what seemed the same moment, there was an almighty roar as a surge of water exploded along the river behind them. She could see the black wave overwhelming the bank in the moment before it hit the man with the knife. She saw Joe grab Bred Nolan, thrusting her towards Murrain, who pulled her roughly back away from the waters.

Then, scarcely able to believe what she was seeing, she saw the dark waters rise and close over both Joe Milton and the man with the knife, dragging them back away from the shore and into the boiling rush of the river.

She remembered nothing after that, except that she was screaming.

CHAPTER FORTY

'It wasn't your fault, Kenny.'

'Of course it was my fault. I should have done something earlier. I still don't know why I didn't.'

'You both did everything you could. It's awful in every way. But it wasn't your fault.'

'You can tell me that as much as you like, Marty. But I know different.'

They were sitting in Winston's office. Murrain should have been still on sick leave, but hadn't been able to keep away. He owed it to Joe at least to finish this off properly. That was the least he could do. The absolute bloody least, and nothing he could ever do would be enough.

'I let it happen, Marty.'

They'd been round this loop several times already, but Murrain felt he couldn't let it drop. He needed it to be understood. Marty was saying all the right things, offering all the reassurances you were supposed to in a situation like this, but Murrain knew it was all nonsense. At the moment when it had really mattered, he had failed.

For the second time, he added to himself.

They'd commented sometimes, he and Eloise, on the fact that Joe had shared the same name as their late son. It had been nothing more than coincidence, of course, but it had added a further resonance to their working relationship.

Now it just felt inevitable. That he would fail Joe Milton just as he had failed his own son.

'I'm not going to argue with you, Kenny. I want you to take time off. Compassionate leave, sick leave, whatever. We'll sort you counselling. We'll get you through this.'

'What about Marie?' Murrain said. 'How are you going to get her through this?'

'We'll look after Marie.'

'I still don't believe it.'

'None of us wants to believe it, Kenny. But it's the job. It happens. Not often. But it happens.'

'It shouldn't,' Murrain said. 'Not if we do our job. I didn't do my job.'

'Like I say, Kenny, I'm not going to argue with you. You don't want to hear anything I might say. I'll make sure you get the support you need.'

'I need to finish off the case. I need to do that for Joe.'

'You're in no state to do that, Kenny.'

Murrain looked up at him. In part, he knew that Marty was right. If he tried to carry on, he'd do more harm than good. He could scarcely even get his brain around what had happened. But he owed it to Joe at least to make what had happened worthwhile. 'Do we know who he was yet?'

Winston hesitated, clearly not wanting to be drawn into this conversation. 'The Chief managed to get a bit more sense from our friends in intelligence. Not much, but a bit. It's a murky business and they were keen to cover up the whole thing.'

'I bet they were.'

'The Chief made it clear that, in the circumstances, that wasn't acceptable and that, if they didn't play ball, he'd make sure as much shit as possible hit the biggest fan available. As it were.'

'Good for him.'

'Anyway, turns out the guy we knew as Charles Barnett or Derek Whitcomb was part of that original study. He was there posing as one of the participants but was really there to represent his paymasters in the intelligence community.' Winston shook his head. 'The whole things sounds bloody mad to me, but they were apparently taking it at least semi-seriously. Crichton was one of the people they were most interested in. They really thought he had something, some ability they could really use. Crichton was an odd figure. Intellectually very bright, in additional to whatever other talents he might have had. Child maths prodigy, off to Cambridge to read maths aged seventeen. Had some kind of breakdown at university, and at the time of the study was taking a year out. Clearly had major mental health problems. Diagnosed with a form of psychosis. Seems one of their interests was the possible link between psychosis and these types of abilities.'

Murrain had dropped his head into his hands. 'I can relate to that.'

'Crichton had been behaving oddly all weekend. He began accusing others, especially Barnett, of listening into his head. He focused on Barnett in particular, who he'd fingered as some kind of spy, ironically enough. It all blew up on the second day and Crichton attacked Barnett with a knife. At one level, it was something and nothing. Barnett, who could obviously look after himself, managed to disarm Crichton and suffered only superficial injuries. The whole thing was hushed up and Crichton was dealt with.'

'Dealt with?'

'That's where it gets a bit murky. Or very murky. Barnett didn't tell us the whole truth. The case never came to trial, and the police were never involved. I've checked back and there's no record.'

Murrain felt empty, drained, struggling to keep a grip on any of this. 'So when Barnett said Crichton was placed in a secure unit…'

'If he was, it wasn't anything official, let's put it that way. I assume they wanted to keep an eye on him and study him in more detail. Whatever it was, I'm guessing it didn't do anything to improve his mental health.'

'Shit,' Murrain said. 'And what about Barnett's stuff about the "opposition" or whatever he called it? Do we think Crichton went over to the other side?'

'Christ knows. I suspect that was a load of bollocks to cover up for the ineptitude of our lot. They lost him somehow, anyway. He was a smart cookie, whatever else he might have been. He disappeared off their radar.'

'Christ.'

'Bloody amateurs.'

'So he embarks on some quest to track down people from that original study?'

'The people who had potentially positive results. That is, the people who might have shared his gifts.'

'Gifts.' Murrain's tone was bitter.

'Chief had to push them on this. But Crichton had got it into his head that they – you, I suppose – had somehow invaded his head, that you were controlling or constraining his powers. By killing you, he was freeing himself. That was why he needed to track you all down. He seems to have managed to reinvent himself as this Lyle Christopher, supposed TV producer. That was all a scam, but he managed to fool Geoff Nolan's agent into believing he was the real deal. It was just a way of getting closer to Bred Nolan and potentially a way of using Nolan's expertise as a way of tracking down others on the list. It was systematic and cold-blooded.'

'They let this guy out into the community? There must be something we can do about that, Marty.'

'I doubt it. Those buggers are above the law. They only got interested again once he'd committed the first murder.'

'And even then they didn't think to talk to the police?'

'Their main priority was to keep the story under wraps. Barnett only stepped into the open once it was all out of control.'

'Resulting in how many deaths?' Murrain said. 'Half a dozen or more? I've almost lost count. The incompetent fucking bastards.'

'I'm not going to argue with you, Kenny. Not about that.'

'Let me finish the case, Marty. Let me at least tie it all up. I owe Joe that.'

Winston was silent for a moment. 'I'm not sure about that, Kenny. I'm not convinced that you're in the right state of mind to do this. I don't want you chasing spooks. Whatever we might both think, there's no mileage in that.'

'I'm not going to let this rest, Marty.'

'You can't hold yourself responsible for this, Kenny. You know that.'

'I do, though.' Murrain had spent the intervening days running over the events of that awful night. It was true that there was nothing he could have done about that sudden surge in the floodwaters, but he knew he should have tried to intervene with Crichton before then. He still didn't know what had stopped him. But something had.

He wished he'd had an opportunity to speak to Bred Nolan, but it had been too chaotic at the time and he'd been given no chance since. He suspected she'd experienced something similar, something that had held her immobile in Crichton's grasp. Something that, he suspected, would have kept her motionless even if he'd plunged the knife into her.

There was also the question of how Crichton had lured his victims out of their houses. Gorman and Clayburn had both been found in their nightwear out in the open air. Something had brought them outside. Having checked back through the files, Murrain wondered about the death of Gordon Fenwick, the academic who'd led that study all those years ago, and whether it really had been dementia that had led to his death. Had that been Crichton's first attempt to get hold of the full list of names?

It was all academic, of course. Crichton, like Joe Milton, had been swept away in that sudden surge. Whatever he might have been capable of, that was all at an end.

Except.

Except they'd found poor Joe Milton almost straightaway, swept back up on the bank, just a few hundred metres from where he'd entered the water.

Edward Crichton's body had not been found.

Perhaps it would be. The waters were still high. Perhaps as they fell further, the body would appear.

But Murrain had an uneasy feeling. His usual gifts had been severely disrupted by his dealings with Crichton. He'd felt it most acutely on that awful night, but he'd felt something strange since this had started, almost as if there was interference inside his head. He couldn't articulate it more clearly than that.

But he was left with the sense that this was not yet over.

He'd failed Joe. He'd failed Marie Donovan. He'd heard all the words about how it hadn't been his fault – even from Marie herself in the only brief telephone conversation he'd been able to have with her. And perhaps it was true. Perhaps there was nothing else he could have done.

But he didn't believe it. Not really. He knew he should have done more. Next time, if there should be a next time, he'd make sure he did.

'Take a few days off, Kenny. At least do that. Get your head straight.'

Murrain looked up at Winston. He knew Marty meant well, and that he was probably right. 'Okay, Marty. I'll do that. I'll get my head straight.' He paused, feeling as if he was listening to other voices in his head. 'A few days. Then I'll be back.'

Printed in Great Britain
by Amazon